Embrace the
HIGHLAND
WARRIOR

ANITA CLENNEY

Jefferson Madison
Regional Library
Charlottesville, Virginia

sourcebooks
casablanca

Sourcebooks and the colophon are registered trademarks of Source-books, Inc.

Published by Sourcebooks Casablanca, an imprint of Sourcebooks, Inc.
P.O. Box 4410, Naperville, Illinois 60567-4410
(630) 961-3900
FAX: (630) 961-2168
www.sourcebooks.com

Printed and bound in Canada
WC 10 9 8 7 6 5 4 3 2 1

This book is dedicated to my hero, my husband, Austin, for believing in me and running alongside as I chased my dream.

Prologue

IT WASN'T THAT TWENTY-SEVEN WAS TOO YOUNG TO die; she just had too many loose ends in her life, things she needed to fix. Shay huddled in the darkness, heart thudding, as she listened to the floor's ominous creak. Images flickered out of sequence in her head, Aunt Nina in the kitchen. Cody and his brothers playing hide-and-seek in the yard. Shadows lurking in the dark, statues, and empty graves. A hayloft and a dark-haired boy—almost a man—looking at her with passion and bewilderment on his face, the one face she'd never been able to forget.

She shut her eyes and tried to quiet her breathing as the footsteps crept closer to her hiding place. She heard an evil chuckle, the sound thick with anticipation, as a broken table leg skidded across the floor next to her hiding place. Was that what Mr. Calhoun had heard just before his heart attack? The first of her clients to die. And Mrs. Lindsey, now with a gaping hole where her throat should have been. They'd been vandalized too.

Shay forced her eyes open, terrified she would find his face inches away, but only his boot was there, the square toe so close she could have touched it. She clamped her lips together and listened to him breathe while her own lungs screamed, until nothing mattered but the next breath of air.

Chapter 1

SHE WASN'T IN SCOTLAND. THAT WAS THE FIRST THING Shay registered when she smashed her foot against the wall. She sat up, disoriented. This bedroom hadn't been hers for nine years. Rubbing her toe, she tilted her head, trying to pinpoint the sound that had woken her. Was it the strange dream? This one was always the same, a place that glowed, a man she couldn't see, speaking a language she couldn't understand. It was better than the one where she was buried alive in a casket, listening as dirt fell on the lid. The only twist in her dreams these past weeks was that *Cody* haunted them. Shay hoped this impromptu trip would exorcise at least one ghost from her life.

The scuttling noise came again. Probably just mice. Aunt Nina said they'd become a problem with the house empty. Another guilt trip to get Shay to move back. Seemed everyone she knew was trying to get her to Virginia. She turned on the dim lamp next to her bed and saw the silver candlestick, exactly where she had forgotten it. She hadn't been brave enough to come back for it. She turned it over and stared at the picture taped underneath. Sighing, she put it back and climbed out of bed. It was already 9:00 p.m. She'd slept for hours. Sheer exhaustion and fear had a way of doing that.

Her stomach rumbled, reminding her that the last thing she ate was a pack of tasteless crackers on the airplane. She needed food, if the mice had left anything. Naked, she walked to the bathroom and checked her clothes, but they were still wet from the deluge of rain that welcomed her the moment she arrived, which wouldn't have been a problem if the airline hadn't lost her luggage. She'd been so glad to see a bed, she hadn't worried about putting her clothes in the dryer.

She picked the driest thing, a damp T-shirt, and slipped it over her head, wrinkling her nose at the smell. Bourbon, courtesy of the drunk on the airplane. Oh well, the mice wouldn't care if she went commando and smelled like a brewery.

She cracked a window to air out the room and saw the two-story brick manor next door. The MacBain house. Her eyes sought out the dark window on the top floor. Her heart gave a little kick.

Another soft noise from downstairs sent a chill up her as she remembered huddling in the darkness, afraid to breathe. Shay grabbed the silver candlestick and moved to the door. She felt safer with something heavy in her hand, even against mice. Her bare feet padded across the hall toward the stairs. She flipped the light switch, but nothing happened. That bulb was always burning out. It didn't matter. She'd spent most of her life in this house. She could walk it blindfolded. Stepping lightly, she avoided the squeaky fourth step and heard the noise again, so soft she wasn't sure if she imagined it. Her hand brushed the banister at the bottom as she stepped into the foyer. Another sound registered in her head. Not tiny claws, but the creak of a footstep. Something cold and hard pressed against the back of her head.

"Don't move," a low voice growled.

Blood rushed from her head to her feet. How could he be here if he was in jail? *Don't panic. If you lose your head, your attacker will win*. She'd practiced this a thousand times, playing soldiers and spies. In the seconds that stretched like droplets of frozen time, Shay forced her body to move, spinning quickly to clear his weapon. She struck with the candlestick, and something clattered to the floor. The gun?

A hard hand grabbed her wrist, and the candlestick fell. She lifted her knee and heard a grunt. Lunging, she tried to get past him. His foot shot out, and she crashed to the floor. What little breath she had left exploded from her lungs as a muscular body landed on top of her. A startled exclamation hissed next to her ear. She shoved against broad shoulders, but the weight didn't budge. Lifting her head, she took a bite of T-shirt and flesh.

He leaned back, swearing as he grabbed both wrists. He held them over her head with one hand, crushing her knuckles against the hardwood floor. His other hand clamped over her mouth. She twisted and jerked her wrists, freeing one, but he moved his hand from her mouth and recaptured the arm. She tried to use her teeth again, but he countered every attempt she made to free herself, as if he were inside her head. She went limp. If she didn't struggle, maybe she could reason with him.

His face was so close she could feel his breath, warm against her ear. They spoke at the same time.

"What do you want?"

"Who are you?" His voice was soft, deadly.

Shay drew in a sharp breath that echoed close to her ear.

"Shay?"

"Cody?"

She lay on the floor, pinned under him, as her mind spun back to a time of warmth and laughter, betrayal and pain, and above it all, the agony of love. She opened her mouth but couldn't speak. In spite of the darkness she closed her eyes and tried to pull in his scent. She'd always loved how he smelled, like mountains and air, but all she could smell now was bourbon.

"Shay?" His voice was strained with disbelief. He leaned back, and his weight shifted, pressing his lower body against hers. A finger touched her hair and then brushed her face, like a blind man searching for proof. "What are you doing here?"

"I was going to ask you the same thing." He was supposed to be out of the country, as usual, trying to save the world from deranged dictators and terrorists.

"I thought someone had broken in. I didn't know you were coming."

Stillness settled around them again. The only movement, breaths mingling, chests moving in unison, and was that a stirring of another sort, lower? The memories started a fresh assault. She shoved against his shoulders. "Get off me."

"Sorry." The weight lifted, and he helped her to her feet. She yanked free, using the five steps it took to reach the light switch to compose her face. She'd always wondered what she would do if she saw him again, what she would say. What he would say. She'd never pictured it happening like this. Her hand hovered over the switch. Drawing in a steadying breath, she flipped on the light, squinting at the brightness, and turned. Her mouth dropped open.

The essence of him was still there; the boy next door who'd kept her secrets, bandaged her scrapes, and comforted her against his scrawny chest, but there was nothing scrawny about him now. He was tall, with broad shoulders and lean muscles undisguised by his soft gray T-shirt and worn jeans. Dark hair brushed his collar, giving him a rugged, dangerous look. His face was still stunning. Strong jaw, straight nose, and those intense hazel eyes that even at nineteen had tempted married women to watch as he walked past. Her gaze caught on the scar above his eyebrow, a trophy from the motorcycle wreck when he was sixteen, and she remembered the terror of finding him sprawled on the rocky hill, so still she thought he was dead.

He appeared dumbstruck as well, staring as if she were the ghost. He swallowed hard, eyes moving down her body and back up.

Shay remembered what she wasn't wearing. She grabbed the edge of her damp T-shirt and stretched it down as far as she could, which further outlined her breasts. "Could you hand me that sweater on the coatrack?" It was a long, belted cardigan, probably dusty, but she didn't care.

He blinked and nodded, reaching for the sweater. A tattoo covered the side of his neck. A series of swirls. Maybe it was something to do with Special Forces. She accepted the long sweater and slipped her arms inside, watching as he picked up his gun and holstered it.

"Sorry about that. You don't smell like you." He

sniffed, nostrils flaring inappreciatively. "Smells like a party." His gaze locked on her left hand. "Are you alone?"

"Yes. A guy on the airplane spilled bourbon on my shirt."

"What are you doing here?"

Her first reaction was to say it was her home, she could come whenever she wanted, but it hadn't been her home for nine years, so some explanation was due. "I was supposed to meet Renee in Leesburg, but she wasn't answering her phone. Since I had to drive this way, so I thought I'd stop here first." And face old ghosts. "I was surprised the gate wasn't locked." It stayed locked when she was here.

"Marcas has been working on it," Cody said, darting another glance at her left hand.

"How long are you staying here?" she asked, fiddling with the belt.

He frowned, his hazel eyes so familiar, yet different, as if something fierce lurked in the depths. "I live here," he said. "Next door, I mean. I've been here for months. Nina didn't tell you?"

"No." Shay bent and picked up the candlestick to hide her shock. He *lived* here. Her reports on Cody were always the same, off fighting battles in some godforsaken place, putting himself in death's way so other people could live free. And now, here he was standing in front of her, larger than life, and all the accusations she thought would come shooting off her tongue if she ever saw him again had dried up and blown away. All she could think about was twining her fingers in his hair and kissing him, finding out if his lips felt as familiar as his body had, pressed against hers. *Get a grip, Shay.* "Are you still Special Forces?"

"No. I'm a PI now. I have an office in town. I'm surprised Nina didn't tell you."

Why hadn't she? If Shay had given in to Nina's pleas and moved back here, it would have been one heck of a shock. She licked her lips. "I need a drink."

Cody nodded, watching her. "Nina has wine, but you don't…" he cleared his throat. "Do you drink wine now?"

She'd tried it once, when she was sixteen. They'd sneaked one of Nina's bottles out to the lake. Half a bottle later, Shay threw up in the bushes while Cody held her hair. "No." But it might be a good time to start. "I'll see what's in the fridge. I fell asleep as soon as I got here." She hadn't even brushed her teeth or washed her face. She probably had mascara smeared under her eyes.

"Should be something here. We try to keep a few things on hand in case Nina pops in."

Shay set the candlestick by the stairs, and Cody followed her into the big kitchen where she'd eaten most of her childhood meals, more often than not, with a MacBain boy or two, sometimes all three, joining them at the table. *The Four Musketeers*, Nina had called them.

Shay found two cans of soda in the fridge and turned to find Cody leaning against the counter studying her, something working hard behind his eyes.

"Still like Pepsi?" she asked.

He nodded. Shay glanced at him again, wondering if she could just light into him and demand answers after nine years, or if there was some kind of etiquette regarding the first face-to-face with a best friend who had betrayed you. "Sorry I bit you."

Cody rubbed his shoulder and a smile played at his lips, sending a tingle blasting through Shay's chest. "You've still got wicked teeth. Knee's not bad either." He started to cup his groin, but caught himself. "You didn't forget everything we taught you." His smile faded. "You're sure I didn't hurt you?"

"I'm fine." Where was this concern years ago, when it mattered? She eyed the Glock holstered at his side. "Do you always carry a gun?"

"When I'm working. Do you always carry a candlestick?"

"I heard a noise. Aunt Nina said there were mice."

"You were going to throw the candlestick at a mouse? Well, you always did have good aim."

Thanks to the endless hours of practice they'd bullied her into.

"She wants us to get a cat for the barn—" he met her eyes and looked quickly away. "I've been meaning to call an exterminator." His gaze narrowed. "What's wrong? You seem jumpy."

Of course she was jumpy. She'd intended to confront memories, not Casper in the flesh. "I had a break-in," she blurted out, not wanting him to know it was his presence that had upset her. "I guess I'm still a little shaken." She handed him the Pepsi, keeping her lashes at half mast in case he could still see through her lies.

"Your house?"

"My shop. The police arrested the guy after I left."

"Was anything taken?"

"Not that I could tell." She hadn't stayed long enough to check. "The guy claimed it was all a mistake."

"Nina said you sell antiques."

"I do. I'm opening another shop in Leesburg with Renee." Shay wished she had gone straight there. Renee was bound to show up sooner or later. Cody's eyes flared at the mention of Renee. Shay knew why Renee didn't like Cody, but what did Cody have against Renee? They'd always gotten along before Renee moved. "What made you decide to move back home?" Shay asked.

The overhead light reflected in his eyes, highlighting flecks of gold. "It was just time." He set the drink down and ran his finger over a gouge that had been in the pine table for as long as Shay could remember. "Lots of memories here. Shame for the place to sit empty. Nina's crazy to choose Matilda over this."

The place was beautiful, a quaint house smack in the middle of rolling hills, surrounded by woods. At one time this had been the carriage house. When the MacBains bought the estate, they sold Nina the smaller home.

"You know Nina. She's like some kind of fairy godmother, always trying to fix everyone's life. Even a crazy cousin who dreams of traveling the world before she croaks."

"If Matilda croaks, it'll be from one of the tour guides pushing her off a pyramid." Cody popped the top on his Pepsi. "Nina's threatening to call off the trip to Egypt in the spring and stick Matilda in a retirement home, if she doesn't stop being such a pest."

It irritated Shay that he knew more about the woman who had raised her than she did, but it had been her choice to stay away. "Aunt Nina said Marcas and Lachlan would be back in a couple of days."

"Aye. Tomorrow, I expect."

The sound of his voice made her ache inside. She'd forgotten the hint of accent she'd found so enchanting. "You've spent nearly all your life in America, and still you have a touch of brogue."

He shrugged. "Guess you can take the boy out of Scotland, but you can't take Scotland out of the boy." Ewan and Laura MacBain had moved here when Cody and his brothers were little more than babies, but they were Scots through and through.

"Remember when we were kids, you and Marcas tried to teach me some words in Gaelic to use as our secret code?" Shay smiled.

Cody's gaze dropped to her left hand again. "I'm surprised you're not married by now, with a couple of kids of your own." His voice was soft; his eyes weren't. "You always loved kids. Are you waiting for a real knight in shining armor to show up?"

Shay gripped the counter until the edge bit into her hands. "Knights aren't all they're cracked up to be. Armor tends to get rusty after a while. What about you? Are you married?" Nina hadn't mentioned it, but she also hadn't said he'd moved back here.

He shook his head, focusing on his soda for so long the silence grew awkward. "Why did you do it, Shay?" He looked up at her, his eyes burning with emotion. "Why'd you leave without telling me, without even saying good-bye? Now you show up, nine years later, after refusing to speak to me." He plunked down the can and pushed away from the table. "I need to get some sleep. I'll get an exterminator out here."

With one brief glance over his shoulder, he walked

out the door, leaving Shay feeling as if she'd been hit by a tornado.

Refusing to speak to him? What about the blasted letters he hadn't bothered to answer?

—⁓—

Cody walked until he reached the gate. He turned, looked at Nina's house, and blew out a hard breath. Shay was safe. She was here. He didn't know whether to run like hell or get on his knees and thank God for another chance. He pulled his phone from his pocket to call off the bodyguard. No answer. He left a message, shoved the phone in his pocket, reminded himself to charge the battery, and then detoured into the woods. He needed to cool off. He'd call Scotland tomorrow and see what this burglar business was about. She might not have been home in years, but he knew her well enough to know she was hiding something. He jogged along the old trail, blaming the prickly feeling in his spine on the fact that his world had just exploded at his feet.

—⁓—

Shay tried eating, but her encounter with Cody left her with no appetite. If he hadn't gotten her letters, then she'd spent nine years blaming him for something he hadn't done. Hoping a walk would clear her head, Shay ambled along the old trail behind the house, leaves crunching beneath her feet, the earlier rain having already soaked into the thirsty earth. The moon was bright, eliminating the need for a flashlight, but the trees were taller and thicker now, making the woods feel more isolated. She shivered and glanced over her shoulder, then chided herself for foolishness. All she had to worry about here were wild animals and painful memories.

The small lake came into sight. She'd spent hundreds of hours there with Cody and his brothers, fishing, swimming, racing to the pier... skinny-dipping. She passed the old boathouse she and Cody had used as a castle, spy headquarters, and army base. How ironic that her real father had actually been a spy, or something top secret, and Cody's job was about as secretive. So was Jamie's, for that matter. Maybe that was part of the reason she couldn't commit to him. Secrets had nearly ruined her life.

Shay sank down on the white sand Ewan had brought in, making the shore kinder to tender feet. The sun and wind had dried the sand while she slept, but her jeans still chaffed with dampness.

The scenery made up for the discomfort. The moon hung like an amber globe over the glistening lake as the water gently lapped the shore. She took off her shoes, wriggled her toes in the cool, gritty texture, and leaned back, cushioning her head on her arms as she studied the stars. They were all still there, winking and twinkling, as if welcoming an old friend, or the prodigal daughter returning home. She felt the familiar prick of guilt for abandoning the place, abandoning the people she loved. Nina, Matilda, and Cody's brothers had occasionally visited Shay in New York or Scotland, but she had never come home, not once. She closed her eyes, letting the smells and sounds of the place settle in, cedar and sand, water and dying leaves, bringing voices from another time.

"Get out, or I'm going home," Shay said, wishing she had a rock to throw at Lachlan's butt.

"Come on, Lachlan," Marcas said impatiently. "Stop being a jackass."

"What's the big deal?" Lachlan grumbled, trudging back out of the water he'd just entered without a stitch of clothing. "She's seen it before." He joined his brothers, who were facing the woods with their backs turned.

"You said she could get in first," Cody said.

"Okay, Miss Hoity-toity-now-that-you've-turned-fourteen," Lachlan fussed. "Go ahead."

Shay was too old for skinny-dipping, but mice had made a nest out of the swimsuit she had left in the boat-house, and she wasn't going to turn down a challenge. If she lost, or forfeited the race, she had to clean all three boys' rooms that night. She could almost smell the dirty socks already. If she won, they would have to do it themselves, which meant they wouldn't be at the dance, hovering like bodyguards. The cute new guy in her science class hadn't heard about the MacBains yet. He might ask her to dance.

When she was sure she was safe, she stripped to her panties and bra and darted into the water, not stopping until it lapped at her neck. "You can turn around," she called. Within seconds, a splash covered her head, and Cody emerged, laughing beside her. She swatted him away and got ready for the race.

Shay opened her eyes and smiled. She won the race, but she suspected Cody had followed her to the dance anyway. That was the last time she went skinny-dipping. She wished she had a swimsuit now. After that encounter with Cody, her skin felt scorched. A brisk swim might cool her off. Compared to Scotland, this weather was balmy.

Why not? It was dark. No one could see her. Not many people would venture out for a swim in the middle of an October night, Indian summer or not. Cody was the only person around, and while she'd rather kiss a rattlesnake than see him there, she doubted he even came here anymore. Besides, he'd looked exhausted.

She started shedding her clothes before she could change her mind. She stepped into the lake, letting the water seep between her toes. It was chillier than she expected, reminding her of the ice swimming they'd braved every January. When the water reached her thighs, Shay dove in, gasping at the cold. With her head underwater, she swam until her muscles ached, feeling her fear and stress grow fainter with each stroke. Lungs burning, she swam toward the shore so she could rest before starting back. She stood up and saw Cody ten feet away, staring at her.

Shay squealed and dove back into the water, emerging when it was chest high. "What are you doing here?" she asked, struggling for a steady breath. Was he following her?

The water barely covered his hips. He stepped back so he was decent. "Same thing as you, I'd say. We always did think alike." They stared at each other in silence, his expression shadowed.

"That was a long time ago." And he didn't have all those rippling muscles back then.

"Yeah," he said, looking at the waves nudging the top of her breasts.

In the dark, his tattoos were a blur across his chest. He got them a year or so before she left, but didn't like talking about them. He still wore the same necklace, a rectangular piece of metal suspended on a leather cord. Jamie wore a similar one. His chest was tattooed as well. It seemed as if every man she knew had tattoos, but the others hadn't filled her with this strange longing.

"What you said back at the house, about no word from me. How can you say that? I sent letters."

"What letters?" Cody asked.

"I wrote you two letters after I left. I sent them to the address your mom gave me."

"I never got them." His eyes narrowed. "Doesn't make sense. I got mail from everyone else."

"I don't understand." If he hadn't gotten them, where were they? Her stomach twisted into sick knots. She needed to go somewhere quiet and think. "I should go. I didn't expect anyone to be here."

"You don't have to leave." He moved a few steps closer and touched her shoulder.

She jerked away, and her foot slipped off a rock, plunging her underwater. She flipped, trying to regain her balance. Strong hands grabbed her, setting her on her feet. She spat out a mouthful of water as Cody's hands gripped her waist. His hand moved lower to her hip, gently steadying her. The front of his body brushed her back. His skin was warm and hard. Something touched her shoulder. Hair? Lips?

When she was eighteen, she had fantasies of this: him and her in the lake with no clothes. She wasn't eighteen anymore, and she couldn't risk another heartbreak. She pulled away, putting some distance between them, but her ankle gave out when she turned.

He steadied her. "You okay?" His voice sounded strained.

"I twisted my ankle. It's no big deal."

"I'd better carry you out."

"No. It'll be okay in a minute." Up close, he was even more intimidating. Broad shoulders, well-used muscles, and tattoos that made her want to run her fingers over them, caress them with her lips.

His gaze moved from the water skimming her breasts to her mouth. His eyes darkened as a low rumble rolled from his throat. She was trying to decide if her head was spinning or his was lowering, when a stunned voice came from the shore.

"Hell's bells… Shay? I thought you were in Scotland."

Cody turned, shielding Shay behind him. "What are they doing here?"

Marcas and Lachlan stared, mouths open. Marcas found his voice first. "Uh… should we leave?"

"Leave?" Lachlan pulled off his shirt, and his necklace caught the moonlight. "We just got here," he said, unsnapping his jeans.

"No," Cody barked. "We're getting out. I was helping Shay."

Lachlan raised an eyebrow. "Helping her do what?"

"She twisted her ankle. What are you doing here?" Cody's voice was curt.

"That's a dumb question. You're the one who asked us for help," Lachlan said. "We had to come home and pack—"

"I mean at the lake?"

Marcas hooked his thumbs in his pockets, quietly surveying the scene. "Lach thought he heard someone in the woods when we got out of the car. Figured it might be a bow hunter scouting out a place to hunt. Probably heard you two."

"Somebody run around to the other side of the lake and get Shay's clothes," Cody ordered.

Marcas nodded and trotted off.

Lachlan snapped his jeans and snatched up his discarded shirt. "What brings you all the way from Scotland, Shay?"

Lachlan was the daredevil with the mischievous twinkle in his eyes—and his foot in his mouth, although his laid-back attitude was partly an act. Marcas was the sensitive one, serious. He usually knew what people were thinking before they did, one of the reasons Shay had avoided him nine years ago, and one of the reasons she hadn't come back. Marcas was twenty-nine, one year older than Cody. God, she'd missed them all.

"I was on my way to see Renee," she said, shivering with cold. "I thought I'd stop by for a visit."

Lachlan asked about Renee and Scotland as they waited for Marcas to return. "About time you came home. Hope you're planning to stay awhile."

"It d-d-depends."

Cody's arms were covered in chill bumps as well. He took a step back and stopped. He'd put his arm around her hundreds of times over the years to keep her warm, but they weren't grown up and naked then.

"Why don't you go help Marcas?" Cody said to Lachlan. "Never mind. Here he comes."

Marcas trotted up, not even winded. All the brothers were fast, although she could almost keep up. Marcas dropped Shay's clothes next to Cody's. "Better get out of there before you end up with pneumonia."

"How about some privacy?" Cody grumbled.

"Want us to leave?" Marcas asked.

"No," Shay said, quickly. "You don't have to leave." The last thing she needed was to be alone and naked with Cody.

Marcas and Lachlan turned around, but Shay could hear them whispering. Cody scooped her up. She squealed and grabbed his neck, to keep from falling. She saw Lachlan start to turn, until Marcas kicked him. "What are you doing?" she whispered furiously, trying to cover all her pertinent parts.

"Getting us out of the lake before we freeze our asses off." He trudged through the water, keeping his gaze straight ahead. "Stop squirming. You're slippery as a bloody eel."

At the water's edge, he set her gently on her feet. He helped her into her sweater, and she was so cold she let him. She didn't bother with her bra.

"Here," he said, handing over her panties.

She snatched them from his hand, afraid he would offer to help with them as well. She wiggled into them, trying not to look at his bare backside as he dragged his underwear over damp skin.

"You decent yet?" Marcas asked.

"No!" Cody said, after glancing back to see Shay tugging on her jeans. He was already snapping his.

After Cody and Shay dressed, the brothers discussed the best way to get Shay back to the house. "We could haul her out on the four-wheeler," Lachlan offered.

Great, she thought. *Like a deer carcass.*

"Battery's dead," Marcas said. "We can carry her back to our house. It's closer."

"Thanks, but it's really not that bad." Shay pasted a blank look on her face as she slid her throbbing foot inside her shoe. "See?" She moved around a few steps, gritting her teeth so she wouldn't wince. "You go on. I want to sit here awhile and enjoy the night." She needed to be alone so she could think. Her homecoming was turning into a nightmare.

"I'd rather you came back with us," Cody said. "You don't have a flashlight, and your ankle—"

"I'll be fine," Shay insisted.

He glanced at the sky. "Don't be long; a storm's blowing in."

"You want to tell us what that was about?" Lachlan's voice carried on the rising breeze.

Shay sat down on the pier and shook her head. What was she doing here, besides leaping from the frying pan into the fire? She couldn't trust her emotions where Cody was concerned. Had she not learned this lesson before?

She sat for several minutes, trying to decide if she had the guts to stick with her plan and make peace with her past—especially given the fact that her past wasn't what she had believed—or just cut and run. She stood up, turned to go back, and found herself face-to-face with a tall, white-haired man.

—◆◆◆—

"It was nothing," Cody said.

Lach snorted. "Didn't look like nothing to me, both of you stark naked in the lake."

"She fell." Cody gave them the nonchalant look he'd practiced while dressing, but his face felt like dried cement.

"I guess the water dissolved her clothes," Lach said.

Cody thumped Lach on the shoulder. "I was taking a swim and didn't know she was there. Mind your own business. I don't ask about every girl I see you with. That'd take the rest of my life."

"They're not Shay," Lach said, crossing his arms over his chest. "You two looked pretty cozy."

"He's got you there," Marcas agreed. "This isn't just any girl. Shay's family."

Family. If only they knew, but they didn't, and he wasn't about to explain it now. "It was nothing," he said again, though it felt like a whole lot more than nothing. "But just for the record, hands off, Romeo." He gave Lach a hard glare.

"Hey." Lach threw his hands up. "I wasn't the one plastered all over her at the lake."

A moment's panic turned to recognition, though Shay hadn't seen him in years. Old Elmer was tall, with the kind of face that looked ancient but never seemed to age. When Shay was a toddler, she thought Old Elmer was Santa Claus, and when she got older, she decided he was Merlin. He'd lived in these woods for as long as she could remember, though he was rarely seen. What was he doing here now?

"Elmer, you startled me."

"Haven't seen you around for years," he said.

"I live in Scotland now. I just came for a visit."

"Scotland." His green eyes were steady, penetrating. "Your home's here."

Shay glanced in the direction Cody, Marcas, and Lachlan had gone. She wasn't feeling good about either place at the moment.

"You ought not come in these woods alone. Bring one of them boys with you. There's dangerous creatures out here." He stared at the woods in front of her, as if he could see through the curtain of darkness. "There's a storm coming. You best hurry home."

She followed his gaze, and when she turned back, he was gone. Shivering, she wished she'd gone with the boys. Her ankle was throbbing. She limped along the path, occasionally reaching out to caress a clump of pine needles or the bark of a favorite tree. She loved the rugged landscape of Scotland, but she'd spent most of her life in these Virginia woods. The memories here were part of her soul. She heard a whisper. Old Elmer? Cody? Had he come back for her?

"Cody?" She stood still and listened, but there was only silence. It must have been a dead tree creaking. There it was again. "Cody, is that you?"

A tree limb snapped close by, and she jumped. *An animal out for a midnight snack*, she thought, limping faster. She didn't want to be that snack.

Shay peeked behind her and saw a shadow dart across the path. It stood upright. Human. "Lach, if that's you, knock it off." Another whisper sent her scampering behind an oak. She flattened her back against the rough bark. *Calm down, Shay. You're in the woods. Animals live in the woods, and a lot of them are nocturnal.*

But animals didn't whisper.

She scurried from her hiding place at a fast hobble as leaves swirled angrily around her ankles and trees twisted in the wind. She heard another sound, like breathing. Or was it her? The moon had vanished, leaving the night black as she moved off the trail, taking a shortcut back to the house. She felt something closing in behind her, but was too frightened to turn. She ran faster, sweat beading her brow, drying in the wind that whipped at her like claws. A white owl swooped down, and a sharp pain shot through her arm as she dove to the ground. Screeching noises echoed around her in the darkness, like birds of prey fighting. Tearing at the dirt, she scrambled to her feet and ran. Branches clawed at her face and arms. A figure stepped onto the path in front of her, and she screamed as strong arms grabbed her.

Chapter 2

"SHAY?"

She gripped Cody's waist, trying to catch her breath. "You scared the daylights out of me. What are you doing here?" *And where were you ten minutes ago?*

"I came to make sure you got home before the storm hit. You okay?"

"I heard something and got spooked." She should have stepped away, but she stayed a few seconds more, comforted by the solid feel of his body, his steady grip on her arms.

"You? Spooked?"

"This big white owl almost took my head off."

"I've spotted one around here, but they usually avoid people. Let's hurry; it's going to rain." His hand dropped to her back, but after all the running, all she could manage was something between a drag and a hop. He turned the flashlight toward her feet. "Damn it, Shay. You're still as hardheaded as a bloody ram. Why didn't you tell me it hurt that much?"

"It wasn't that bad then." Before her mad sprint through the woods. For the second time in one night, Cody scooped her up in his arms.

"Put me down." She hoped the request didn't sound as halfhearted to his ears as it did to hers.

"No," he said, stepping over a fallen tree. "I do believe my lady lies about her ankle."

He was one to be accusing her of lies. She wanted to be irritated, but he was so darned warm, and she was cold and tired. "*My lady?*"

"What? You thought I'd forgotten Lady Shay?" The lights from the airstrip behind Cody's house came into view. Nina's wasn't much farther. "I didn't forget. You made us play knights at least once a week."

"I got sick of always playing soldiers and spies. At least knights dressed fancy."

"You were never a proper damsel, anyway. You were too good at fighting and throwing knives."

It hadn't helped her handle a real-life threat.

Cody kept the conversation flowing as they continued toward the gate leading to Nina's house. He carried Shay across the yard and inside the house, closing the door with one foot before mounting the stairs.

"Thanks for checking on me. I'm just going to take a bath and snuggle up in bed."

He pushed her bedroom door open with his shoulder. "You got a man hiding in the closet?"

"What?" She gave him a startled glance.

"Last time I checked, it takes two to snuggle," he said, gently depositing her in the adjoining bathroom.

When had he last checked, she wondered, feeling a stabbing sensation in her chest. "A pillow works just as well." *And it doesn't tell lies*. Her stomach rumbled.

"Hungry?"

"A little."

"We have plenty of food at the house, unless Lach's gone on a feeding frenzy."

"He still does that?"

"Unfortunately."

"Thank you, but I'm sure there's soup in the pantry."

He touched his shirt, damp from carrying her. "Don't you have anything dry to wear?"

"Just Nina's sweater. I'll throw my stuff in the dryer after I take a bath."

"I've probably got some old sweats at the house. And you'll need something orange. Don't want you getting shot. Bow season's in."

Shay doubted she would be here long enough to get shot by a poacher. A poacher. Was that what she'd heard? Had she surprised someone looking for a place to hunt? Or had she just disturbed the owl?

"Sit down. Let me see your foot." Cody guided her to the toilet, took her swollen ankle in his hands, and eased her shoe off. For the first time, she noticed his boots, square-toed. A ribbon of fear curled around her spine.

"You should have told me how badly you were hurt," Cody said, breaking the spell. "I would've carried you back."

Precisely the reason why she hadn't mentioned her ankle.

"I should take you and get it X-rayed."

"It'll be fine in the morning." She had always healed quickly, physically. Emotionally was a different story.

"Take a bath, then I'll wrap it. You'll need to stay off it for a day, at least." He crossed to the large bathtub and turned on the water. "Want a bubble bath? You used to love that stuff."

Shay sighed. He wasn't going to leave until she was settled. "Check under the sink. Nina may have left some." Shay sat quietly, watching as he dug in the cabinet, muttering to himself.

"Here we go." He sniffed a bottle and then poured in half.

He stood, watching the bubbles rise faster than the water. "Think I put in too much?"

"A tad. Are you going to leave?" The bathroom wasn't small, but it felt like a closet with Cody standing so close to the tub large enough for two.

"Do you need help?" He cleared his throat. "Getting in, I mean."

"I think I'll manage."

A spark of mischief lit his eyes. "I don't know. For someone so agile, you don't do so well with water. I'd hate to call Nina and tell her you drowned in the bathtub."

"Get out of here!" Without thinking, she swatted him playfully, as she would have in the past.

"I'll be outside. Yell if you need anything."

After he left, Shay removed her damp, dirty clothes and slowly lowered her body into the water. Her right arm stung. There was a long scratch at the top. Had the owl done that, or a branch? She leaned back and closed her eyes, letting the warmth seep into her bones. Her head slipped lower and lower into the water as she listened to the rain pattering at the window, the rhythmic sound reminding her of whispers and the brush of wings.

Her throat tightened as she approached the three graves. What did she hope to find? Reconciliation? Closure? To make sense of the lies? A whisper brushed her ear, a fluttering sound, and she tilted her head, listening. Skin prickling, she turned. A statue stood in the corner, an angel watching over the dead? She didn't remember seeing it the last time she was here, but it had been years before, and her head had been blurred with pain. A soft breeze ruffled her hair and stirred the dying October leaves. Just leaves rustling, not whispers. After the last few weeks, she jumped at every sound.

She studied the names engraved on the larger head-stones, then knelt before the tiny one cradled between them. Her finger traced the worn name—Dana Michelle Rodgers—under the angel's outstretched wing, thinking she should have some sense of recognition.

After all, it was her grave.

Something flashed in her mind, a memory, a dream— fire and pain. Shay shook her head and frowned. Some guardian angel. The clouds shifted, and a shadow crossed the angel's face, as if he didn't appreciate her disrespect. She heard the whisper again. It came from near the statue. Was someone hiding there? What if it was him? She squinted, trying to focus, and then watched in horror as the statue turned and looked at her.

A pounding noise yanked her from the dream. Shay sat up quickly, bumping her ankle on the edge of the tub. She gasped in pain.

"Shay, you'd better answer, or I'm coming in."

"I'm fine. Just give me a minute."

Still trembling from the dream, she grabbed the side of the tub and the built-in soap dish for support and eased up on her good foot. She was in mid crouch when the soap dish broke. She fell back into the water with a screech.

The door banged against the wall, and Cody rushed in. He stopped, sucked in a breath, and stared at her naked body, limbs askew. "Shi—"

"Get out!"

"I thought… sorry." He turned and smashed into the

door casing. "You and water," he said, holding his fore-head as he shut the door.

A blush warmed her entire body. She hadn't laid eyes on him in nine years, and now he'd seen her naked twice in one night. She quickly dried off and put on Nina's sweater, belting it tight. Shay pulled her wet hair into a ponytail, brushed her teeth, and then gathered her damp clothes. Blowing out a breath, she opened the door.

Cody had turned her bed down. He gave her an awkward glance. There was a red mark on his head where he hit the doorjamb. "Are you okay?"

"Yes."

"You screamed."

"I did?"

"Bloody murder."

"I must have been dreaming."

"Sounded more like a nightmare. I found soup and some Tylenol." He pointed to the tray next to the bed.

"I need to wash my clothes first."

"I'll stick them in the washer on the way out. You heal fast, but you need to get off that ankle. It's probably sprained."

She sighed, dropped her dirty clothes in the doorway, and crawled into bed still wrapped in Nina's sweater.

"You're gonna sleep in that?" he asked, one brow cocked.

She knew what he and his brothers slept in. Same thing they swam in. "I'm cold," she said defiantly.

He shook his head and pulled the covers up. He brushed her arm, and she winced. "What's wrong?"

"It's just a scratch."

"Let me see." He eased the sweater aside. Shay clutched the sheet to her chest to keep from exposing a breast. "You need a bandage. I think Nina's got a first aid kit downstairs."

She rolled her eyes and picked up the bowl of chicken noodle soup. There was no swaying Cody when his mind was set. She'd finished most of her soup by the time he returned.

The mattress gave as he sat on the edge. He bandaged her arm first, his fingers gentle but sure. She had always loved his hands. She'd seen him snap a board in half and minutes later, splint a robin's leg.

"I guess you have to treat a lot of field injuries in your job," she said.

He looked startled.

"Special Forces… I imagine there are times you can't just go to the local hospital."

"Aye," he said, uncovering her swollen ankle. "Good thing I got lots of practice bandaging you." He gave her a crooked grin.

"I bandaged you more than you bandaged me. Remember when we were kids, sneaking out to save the world, signaling from our bedrooms with flash-lights?" They spent half their childhoods saving the world from evil, be it fire-breathing dragons, evil monsters, or top-secret enemy spies. With Cody at her side, she had felt invincible.

"Nina would've had both our hides if she'd caught you bypassing the alarm, shimmying down that old oak to meet me." His hand touched hers, his finger finding the scar on her palm that she got during one of those escapades. "What the hell happened to us, pip-squeak?

I know I was irresponsible, but I tried to make it right. Why did you shut me out? Did you hate me that much?"

Shay glanced away, feeling tears prick her eyes. At one time, she had been closer to Cody than anyone in the world... before *that summer*, when everything fell apart. "I didn't hate you. I was confused and angry. You lied to me."

"Some things are more important than the truth."

"We were best friends. We never kept secrets."

"I'm sorry, Shay. We did what we thought was best."

"Did you ever think what it was like for us? Losing someone who'd been there all our lives? Having you wash your hands of us and walk away?"

He dropped her hand. "For weeks after you left, your aunt begged my father to go after you, to make you come home."

"I didn't know. No one came after me."

"My dad said it was your choice. You were eighteen, an adult, and we'd hurt you enough, though it wasn't intentional. We needed to give you room to think and make your own decisions."

She had decided to stay away, to avoid them all. Until the letters Cody hadn't gotten.

"We can't change the past, might as well forget it and enjoy your visit."

"I guess that's why I came. To see if I can forget." Or had she come because this was where she felt safe?

"If you can't do it for yourself, do it for Nina. Your leaving nearly killed her." He stood. "I'm going to turn in. I haven't slept much lately." He looked like he hadn't slept for a week. "Yell if you need something. I'll be down the hall."

"You're staying here?"

"I'm afraid your ankle might be fractured. I'm not having you go up and down those stairs if you need something to eat or drink. You got a spare toothbrush?"

"There should be some in the guest bathroom."

His eyes narrowed. "You're sweating."

She was roasting, but she wasn't certain if it was from the sweater or Cody's hands.

"Sure you don't want to take off the sweater?"

"I don't have anything else to wear."

He eased her wrapped ankle under the covers and then disappeared into the bathroom. A moment later, he returned shirtless, buttoning his jeans. He tossed his T-shirt and underwear on the bed. "They're clean. I showered and changed after the lake." He picked up her wet clothes. "Sleep tight," he said, and with a shuttered look, he left.

Shay stared at the T-shirt and boxer briefs, still half-molded in his form. She slowly picked them up. A rush of heat surged from her head to her bandaged ankle. She'd worn Cody's underwear before, when she was in a jam, but that was when they were kids, not with him all… filled out. Swallowing, she got out of bed, took off the sweater, and put on his things. They smelled like him, clean but male. Sensations she didn't want to describe zinged through her body.

She climbed back in bed, but was too wound up to sleep, thinking about how close Cody's T-shirt and underwear had been to his body. She needed a distraction. Renee. She would have a conniption when she found out who had just left Shay's bedroom. Renee would douse Shay's fire. Shay dialed from the phone by her bed, but still no answer. Where was Renee? She was prone to spontaneous trips, but it wasn't like her to disappear when she knew Shay was coming.

Shay glanced at her watch. Nina and Matilda never went to bed before midnight. Better check in with Nina before she and Matilda showed up pounding on the door. Matilda answered the phone before it finished the first ring. "Frank Simpson, go jump in the lake, or go find that floozy, Ethel Mae. She's probably strutting her stuff over at the Moose Lodge right now, since she got rid of those big ol' varicose veins."

"Matilda," Shay shouted, but the phone went dead. She sighed and redialed.

"You oversexed pervert—"

"Aunt Matilda, it's Shay." Matilda wasn't her aunt; she was Nina's cousin, but Matilda didn't have kids, and she liked it when Shay called her aunt.

"Shay?" Matilda's voice dropped from deafening to almost deafening. "I thought you were Frank Simpson."

"I'm sorry I called so late. I hope you weren't asleep."

"How could anyone sleep with Frank Simpson roaming the earth?"

"What's he up to now, Aunt Matilda?" Matilda and Frank were always fighting over something.

"He's writing a review for some old folks' magazine. Keeps pestering me to check out some bed and breakfasts with him. Old folks? Well! You know as well as I do that I just turned fifty-nine." Matilda had been fifty-nine since Shay finished middle school. "Says he needs a female perspective. Last year he asked Janice Childress to check out ski lodges with him. The stories I heard would've made a sailor blush. It wasn't her *perspective* he was after. Had to get her to repeat the tale twice, just to make sure I heard right. Thought I'd have to go to confession, just from listening to it, or do penance or something. Do they still do that?"

"I—"

"Anyway, the man just won't take no for an answer. It's my red hair, you know. It's like waving a red flag in front of a bull. I'll bet Frank's over at the pharmacy right now picking up Viagra. Pervert. It took me five years to find this color, and now I'm going to have to change it. I'd rather have my heart ripped out than tell Eduardo. He customized this color for me. Razzing Red, he calls it. Nobody else has it. I just don't know what he'll do. You remember, Eduardo. He's so temperamental. All those artists are. I think he's a *Homo sapien*."

"You mean homosex—never mind."

"All the good ones are. They just understand hair. I think it's genetic."

"I just—"

"You really think that Viagra works? I've heard that some men go around... you know, stuck like that for hours. Must be uncomfortable, not to mention embarrassing. Why, you couldn't even leave the house. And what if you had to tinkle? Oh, listen to me blabbering on when you must want to talk to Nina. She's been going on and on about you coming home. I'm so glad you're there. You belong in Virginia. It's a good, safe place. No one would break into your shop here. I'll call Nina for you."

Shay yanked the phone away from her ear, but not fast enough.

"Nina! It's Shay!" Matilda yelled. "Now you take

care of yourself, Shay, and kiss those boys for me. If you were smart, you'd marry one of them."

Marry? Shay looked down at Cody's T-shirt draping her body and his underwear caressing her intimate parts.

"Shay, how are you?" Nina's voice was a hair lower than Matilda's. Neither of them could hear squat. In the background, Matilda continued to rant about Frank.

"I'm okay, Nina."

"How nice to hear a sane voice. Did you talk to the police?"

"They arrested the guy. It's fine."

"Did you happen to get his name, this intruder?" Nina asked, her voice stilted.

All Nina knew was that someone had broken into Shay's shop. Shay wouldn't have told her that much, but Nina had known something was wrong. "It was some strange name. Franklin or something."

"Oh, well, that's good."

It was?

"Tell me, how is it to be home? The boys should be back soon."

"The boys came home early. I didn't know Cody was back."

Nina paused. "I didn't mention it? Are you sure?"

"I'm certain—"

"I must have forgotten. You know how distracted I get around Matilda. I'm telling you, she's driving me insane, dragging me to all these bingo games. Now she wants to take me to Atlantic City to meet some of her friends. I swear, I think she has a gambling problem. I might have to do an intervention. I saw this program on TV where they had to do that. I shudder to think of it, but a woman her age ought to have more control. But enough about Matilda. Isn't it just like old times with all the boys there?"

"It does bring back memories." Some that would shock Nina's socks off her dainty feet.

"You should've come home once in a while. I do hope you'll forgive us and move back now. The place needs someone living in it, and I just couldn't leave Matilda alone. God knows what kind of trouble she'd get into."

"I'm still considering it, Nina." Of course that was before she found out Cody was back.

"Well, I'd better go calm Matilda down before she has a stroke. It's her own fault. Imagine, a woman her age showing cleavage. It's ridiculous. Last month I talked her out of breast implants. Say hello to the boys for me. Hasn't Cody turned out handsome? Joan, you remember my friend Joan? She's the one who moved to Scotland a year ago. She tried to set him up with her daughter when he was in Scotland last month, but I wasn't having any of that. The girl wasn't right for him at all."

"He was in Scotland?"

"Yes. She had a necklace stolen. He went to help her find it."

"When?"

"Oh, three or four weeks ago. Turned out her neighbor's son had stolen the necklace for his girlfriend. Cody's the best PI around. You can ask anybody. I'm surprised he didn't stop by to see you. He was asking about you. Remember how close you two were? Two peas in a pod."

Shay hung up, dazed. Cody *had* been in Scotland recently, just about the time she acquired a stalker.

Malek stared at the empty drawer where the book had been hidden. He could still feel the texture of the yellowed pages, see the faded ink. It had taken him centuries to learn of the book's existence and even longer to find it. It had fallen in his hands like manna from hell and disappeared just as fast. He was sure the girl had stolen it. Shay Logan's friend. He'd hired her so he could spy on Shay, and all the while, they had been spying on him, plotting to steal the book. A surge of anger thickened his bones and made his skin stretch. He had to find the book, and he had to find Shay. If she was the one, the mother of his enemy, she must be destroyed before she could breed. The doorbell jingled, startling him. He shifted back to human form, checking his appearance in the antique mirror on his office wall: auburn hair, silver streak, immaculate as always, suit, perfect. Shaping his lips into a smile, he opened the door with a manicured hand and stepped into the front room of his antique shop. His human heart stilled.

The man in the doorway had long, raven hair, and a face so beautiful queens had thrown themselves at his feet, but Malek knew what lurked inside was far from beautiful. Tristol's eyes turned red as blood. "Where is my book?" he hissed.

The scent of fear drifted to Tristol, making his mouth water. He watched Malek's face tighten, his shoulders tense as he tried to control the shift. It was too late. Malek's human clothes and skin fell away, leaving a thick, gray hide, long arms and fingers tipped with lethal claws. Tristol sneered. Nearly a thousand years in this dimension, and still Malek couldn't control the veneer of sophistication he wore as his disguise.

"What book?" Malek asked, trembling.

Tristol moved toward him, feet barely touching the floor. "The one you stole from my lieutenant as soon as my back was turned."

"I don't know what book you're talking about." Without the human shell, Malek's voice was guttural, harsh. "Maybe Druan took it."

Blame the dead demon, Tristol thought, but he remained silent. He had his methods of obtaining information. "I'll be watching." Tristol withdrew from Malek's office, rang the shop doorbell, but didn't leave. He shifted to mist and rose, slithering along the ceiling, then hovered outside Malek's office.

Malek pulled out his cell phone. "Have you found Shay Logan? She's left Scotland? Then find her. And find the book, or I'll have you destroyed."

Malek had stolen the book and lost it. Rage stirred inside Tristol, but he reined it in. He hadn't lived this long to be undone by anger or one pathetic demon. Certainly not a human female. He had time, enough to make Malek wish he had never lived, and he had the name of the thief. Shay Logan.

Chapter 3

AFTER AN HOUR OF TOSSING, CODY CLIMBED OUT OF the guest bed and put on his jeans. He moved quietly down the hall and slipped through the open door of Shay's bedroom. She lay curled on her side, her breasts rising and falling in an even rhythm. How many times over the years would he have given his sword arm to be this close to her? He touched the lock of hair spread across her pillow and brought his fingers to his lips. The sight of her braless in his T-shirt made him long to crawl into bed with her. He cursed himself as soon as the thought crossed his groin. It would be wise to leave before he did something he would regret. He noticed a lump under the covers beside her. He lifted the edge and saw the candlestick in her hand. A weapon? What did she expect him to do? Molest her? Then he saw the black and white picture carefully taped underneath. He studied it for a minute, then rubbed his hands through his hair. His chest felt hollow. What had they done to her? He reached down and tucked in her covers, letting his thumb stray across her cheek. Sighing, he walked to the sofa, sat down, and watched her sleep.

The light was so bright the man seemed to glow. She tried to look at his face, but it made her eyes hurt, so she concentrated on his deep, melodic voice, attempting to understand his words. He was speaking to someone, another man, she thought, but she couldn't see him clearly either. A baby began to wail, and then she heard the glowing man say, "Take her back. It's not time."

Shay woke with a gasp, heart hammering against her ribs, arm stinging. She looked around the room, half expecting to see the glowing man. Cody sat on the sofa, head slumped to one side, asleep. His hair was messy, as if he'd been running his hands through it, the way he did when he was thinking. In the hours since she arrived, she hadn't had an opportunity to really look at him. She eased out of bed and moved closer. There were shadows under his eyes, but his face was relaxed. A hint of beard darkened his jaw. She watched the subtle movements of his body as he drew and released each breath, making his tattoos move. The grip on her heart tightened. For months after she left, she dreamed of him every night and woke crying with his scent still in her head, as if he were in the room with her. She'd spent the last nine years thinking he betrayed her. He'd spent them thinking she had done the same to him. Granted, he lied about her past, but he believed he was protecting her, as they all had. She forgave Nina and Cody's brothers, but not him, not her best friend.

She stretched out her hand to touch his arm, but stopped. He was a stranger now. At one time they'd shared everything, thoughts, fears, and dreams. They kept no secrets—or so she thought—but she had no idea who this Cody was, what he liked, what he didn't, what made him smile, or what made him sad. What were his mornings like? His evenings? Did he go to bed content at night? Did he go to bed alone? Had he loved? Been loved?

The feeling hit her in a sickening wave, like waking up and finding her legs were gone. She backed away. She needed to get some air, refocus. She was a grown woman, successful. She had built a life. *One that didn't include Cody,* an empty voice whispered.

Shay quietly brushed her teeth, trying not to wake him. He'd looked exhausted last night. Grabbing a small throw from the bottom of the bed, she wrapped it around her shoulders and tiptoed from the room. She went to put her clothes in the dryer and found that Cody had already done that too. He'd even gotten the bourbon stain out of her shirt. It made her want to run upstairs and wake him, tell him she was sorry for ruining their friendship, but she didn't.

She changed her clothes and looked outside. The sun was peeking above the trees. If she hurried, she could make it to the tree house in time. Throwing the blanket around her, she stepped outside and breathed in the crisp, morning air. She crossed the back yard and headed for the woods. Her ankle was still tender, so she moved gingerly over branches littering the woods from last night's storm. Shay remembered Old Elmer's warning, but it was daylight. What danger could there be? All the predators would be asleep.

She climbed the small hill, heading for the pink blotch showing through the red and gold leaves. The color had faded with time, but Shay still smiled, remembering her victory. It took them weeks to build the tree house. They threw darts to see who chose the color. She won... that time, her victory recorded for posterity in Nina's photo albums, Shay smiling triumphantly while the boys looked like martyrs being burnt alive.

Shay tested the ladder. The boards were still strong. Her ankle ached, but she wasn't going to stop. She climbed inside, gently stretched out her leg, and felt an irrational sense of joy watching the pink ribbon in the sky turn to gold as it slid over the trees.

She was home. She was safe.

"What the hell are you doing?"

She peered over the edge. Cody stood with his hands folded across his bare chest, jeans low on his hips, glaring at her.

"Watching the sunrise."

"Are you crazy? You sprained your ankle. Not to mention there could be poachers around."

"No, I'm not crazy. My ankle's okay." Or it had been, before she walked up the hill.

"Then why are you holding it?"

"Go away or shut up. You're ruining my sunrise." She settled back in her blanket. The leaves around her shook, and Cody's head appeared. He climbed inside and plopped down beside her. He had chill bumps on his arms. "Here," she said, opening the blanket. After all, he'd given her his T-shirt.

He moved closer, pulling it around his shoulders. The feel of his bare arm against hers was more intimate than some full-body encounters she'd had. The beauty of the sunrise distracted her from the warmth melting into her skin. Shay sighed and leaned back. How had his arm gotten around her? Her head found the curve of his shoulder. "It's beautiful, isn't it?"

"Aye."

She felt his breath on her face and turned to look at him. He was staring at her like he had at the lake. She tried to look away, but she couldn't. His eyes spoke of things she only imagined in her dreams. He turned, facing her, and a hand crept up her arm, slowly winding in her hair. He tilted her head and lowered his, letting his mouth hover over hers, taking in her breath as she took in his. Every cell inside her vibrated with longing. She could feel him, smell him, almost taste him. He licked his lips, put both hands in her hair, and brought their mouths together.

Little shocks zinged through her body like a pinball machine. Her mouth opened, welcoming his tongue. Her hands gripped his shoulders, fingers digging into his skin. The kiss grew desperate, harder, faster, bodies pressing, and then she was lying with him on top of her, bodies aligned, hips nudging. She was distantly aware of her ankle creeping up his leg, when she bumped it on his thigh. She gasped, and Cody jerked his head back. He stared at her, gave a disgusted grunt, and rose. "I'm sorry." He helped her sit up and blew out a breath. "Are you okay to walk back?"

"Yes," she lied, pulling the blanket around her.

Jaw tight, he started down the ladder, and then stopped. His eyes burned into hers. "No. I'm not."

"Not what?"

"Sorry."

She caught one glimpse of his broad shoulders before he vanished like a ghost.

What the hell was wrong with him? Cody yanked off his belt as he walked into the house. He stripped off the rest of his clothes, dropping them as he went. He cranked the shower on cold and stepped inside. Even the freezing water didn't stop the burn. He ran his hands through his hair. If he didn't slow down, he would scare her off. What then? He'd waited nine years for this. Would he blow it now because his body longed for what he knew was his? He let his hand slide down his stomach, closed his eyes, and imagined Shay as he tried to ease the ache so he wouldn't destroy his last chance.

―⁓―

Shay waited until Cody was out of sight before she left the tree house. For one thing, she didn't want him to see how much her ankle hurt; for another, she needed another plan. This one wasn't working. How could she even consider, or reconsider, marrying Jamie, when all she could think about was Cody? Instead of heading back to the house, Shay detoured off on another trail. The bushes were thicker, taking over in the absence of a human presence. The tiny cemetery was surrounded by a split-rail fence the boys built. All their pets were buried here, dogs, hamsters, and birds. There weren't many weeds. The area was covered in pine needles and moss. She stepped inside and brushed her hand over a stone with the name Neo and a date scratched into the surface. The boys had held a funeral for the black lab. Afterwards, Shay had run away to the boathouse. Cody was the one who found her and held her while she sobbed.

How could she have walked away from this place, the people and the memories it held? With a sense of sadness, she went back to the house. A cat sat on the back porch watching her. It was huge, its fur white as snow, with eyes green as an emerald.

"Where did you come from?" It didn't look like a stray. It was big enough to attack a grown man. "Go home, cat. I can't even sort out my own life." As if it understood her, the cat darted off the porch and into the woods.

Shay went inside and climbed back into bed, jeans and all. She dreamed of French toast. When she woke, Cody was stepping into the room carrying a tray.

"You made French toast," she said, staring at the plate. "I thought I was dreaming."

"Figured you were hungry after climbing that hill. Brunch might be a better welcome than..." his eyes flashed once, hard and dark, "than the one at the tree house." He set the tray on the bed. "I'm sorry for... for whatever that was."

Shay let him flounder for a minute, wondering if he hadn't realized she'd had her tongue in his mouth too, but men let their chivalry run amok sometimes. "I guess we can chalk it up to old memories."

He looked relieved. "I know you like French toast." His brow flattened. "Do you still?"

"I love it," she said, accepting the tray. "I didn't think there was any bread in the kitchen."

"I made it at the house."

"I'm surprised you got past Lachlan."

"He's gone. He and Marcas had to get back to their assignments... uh, work." Cody looked at the bed, but moved to the sofa. He leaned back, tapping his fingers on his thighs.

"Did you eat?"

"No. I wasn't hungry." He was watching the plate closely now.

"Changed your mind?"

His eyes lit. "If you feel like sharing."

They used to share everything. Cody had thought nothing of snatching something from her plate, and vice versa, unless it was a brownie. Brownies were sacred. "I might be persuaded," she said.

There was the flash in his eyes again, reminding her that they were a long way from kids. "I suppose I should share, since you made it." She took a bite and moaned. "Maple syrup. Nina used to make French toast for me every Sunday morning."

Cody gently moved her ankle aside so he could sit. "Not bad, eh?"

"You did good." The breakfast tasted almost as good as Cody looked. What was wrong with her?

She cut a bite, but he reached out and grabbed the fork. He put the bite in his mouth, nodding as he chewed. "If the PI thing doesn't work out, think I could become a cook?"

Women would pay Cody MacBain to deliver burnt toast. "I think I'll need another meal before I decide."

Between them, they finished six slices of French toast. Shay reached for the orange juice, but Cody had already raised it to his mouth. How easily they were slipping into old routines. Her gaze raked over him, mussed hair to booted feet, and every inch in between. These weren't old times, the tree house proved that. Things were moving too fast. Going from hating him to... to what? Whatever it was, it scared the heck out of her. She felt her control slipping, felt the urge to sit back and let him take over. Shay had been taking care of herself far too long to let anyone take over.

"Let me check your ankle." Cody lifted the covers and took her foot in his hand. He unwrapped the elastic bandage, his touch sending tingles through her leg. She'd had more tingles in her body the last twelve hours than she had in the last twelve months.

"Swelling is mostly down. You still need to take it easy for a day or so," he said.

"I have to get groceries and some clothes. I'll rest after that."

"Maybe you can find some clothes in the attic. Nina never throws anything away. You look about the same size you were before." He looked her over, his gaze slowing at her breasts.

"I think I took everything with me, but I'll check. It's hard to tell where my luggage will end up." Shay moved the tray and slid out of bed.

"You shouldn't be climbing those stairs. Your ankle will never heal."

"It's fine. Thank you for the French toast and for washing my clothes and loaning me your T-shirt and… stuff. I'll wash them and give them back."

"Maybe I'd rather you didn't," Cody said, brushing against her. "I like how you smell." His voice was low, laced with something so hot it sent a jolt through her nether regions.

She took a step back. "What are you doing?"

"Damn it, I don't know. I'll be downstairs." He picked up the tray and left without looking at her.

She had to get out of here. Maybe she could go to Leesburg and wait for Renee. A couple of days with her might take the edge off whatever this thing was with Cody. It was ridiculous. He was gorgeous, but she had been around plenty of gorgeous men. They never affected her this way.

After Shay made the bed, she called Mr. Ellis and left a message, giving him the bad news about his table, and then she called Lucy to see if everything was okay with the house. Lucy Bell was ninety, the closest thing Shay had to family in Scotland. The old woman had lost her husband a few years before. She and Shay looked out for each other. Shay had just gotten to the attic, when Cody appeared.

"Thought I'd find you up here," he muttered. "You don't listen very well."

"Then stop giving orders." She dug through a stack of boxes. "I don't think I'll find anything. Oh, remember this?" She pulled out her Tinker Bell costume. Nina had made it for her in first grade.

"I remember. You drove me crazy trying to get me to help you practice for the play."

"I don't know what you had against Peter Pan," Shay said, putting the outfit back.

"He wore tights."

"So did Robin Hood. I don't hear you complaining about him."

"His bow made up for the girly clothes. You used to be good with a bow."

"I haven't shot one in years," Shay said. "I probably couldn't hit the barn." Underneath the Tinker Bell outfit was Shay's graduation gown. She brushed her finger over the red material. That was the worst year of her life.

"I have a friend who could help, but I'm afraid he'd give you more than just tips." Cody helped her check the rest of the attic, but there weren't any clothes.

Her cell phone rang. It was the airline informing her that her luggage had been delivered.

She hung up. "I guess I'm going to Leesburg. The airline delivered my luggage there."

"Leesburg?"

"I thought that's where I would be staying."

"Can't you buy new stuff? I thought women looked for any excuse to shop."

"I have plenty of clothes in my suitcase. No need to waste money."

"I'd rather you didn't go."

"Why not?"

"You might feel fine now, but Leesburg is a two-hour drive. That's four hours working the accelerator and brake on a sprained ankle. Not one of your better ideas."

"I'll manage."

"No, you won't."

"I'm going," Shay said.

He sighed. "Come on, then."

"I didn't ask you to come."

"You don't have a choice."

"You're bossier than I remember."

"Too bad. Let's get this over with."

"I'm going to shower first. Do I need your permission to do that?"

"Not unless you need my help."

Shay shoved past him and tromped down the stairs. She stumbled only once, and he grabbed her before she could fall.

"Stubborn," he muttered.

"Tyrant."

Shay showered and dressed in the same clothes. Cody

pulled the truck around so she wouldn't have to walk across to his house.

"You look like you're going to your execution," Shay said.

"If Renee sees me, it might be."

"You two used to get along."

"It's a long story."

"Care to explain?"

"No."

He didn't explain about Renee, but they talked as they rode, catching up on things from the past nine years, avoiding the touchy topics like fake parents and lies and letters and other things that couldn't be mentioned, which was like tiptoeing around the Grand Canyon. They grabbed a late lunch from a drive-through and arrived at the shop late afternoon.

"Her car isn't here," Shay said. "This is odd. She was expecting me." She pulled the key from her purse. "Are you coming in?"

He grimaced and got out.

Shay's luggage was sitting outside the back door, where she had instructed the airline to leave it. "Let's try the apartment first."

"She hasn't been here for a few days," Cody said, after they looked around the apartment.

"How do you know, Sherlock?"

Cody opened the refrigerator. "Observe, Watson. The milk's almost full, but past its expiration date. We passed a neighbor pulling his trash can off the street. Trash must have been picked up yesterday." He sniffed. "Hers hasn't been put out. I noticed mail sticking out of the mailbox outside too."

"It looks like she just walked off. Why would she do that when she knew I was coming?"

"Did she have business that could have called her away?"

"She travels a lot, and she's always meeting up with some new hot guy and taking off."

"How about you?" Cody asked quietly. "Do you ever run off with some new hot guy?"

"No. That's Renee's thing, not mine." Shay couldn't even commit to a decent, honest, hot guy who wanted to marry her. What would she do with a new one? "She kept complaining about a new client who's kept her busy. She didn't like him."

Cody stopped to look at a coat hanging on a rack by the door. He frowned. "You got a phone number for him?"

"No, the client database is separate for the shop in Scotland and this one."

"What about her parents? Where are they?"

"Florida. They left right before I moved in with Renee. I'll try them."

"Let's check her workroom, and then we can check the store. I'd like to see her files."

"It isn't locked," Shay said as she opened the door.

Cody looked at pieces lying haphazardly around Renee's workroom, mostly chairs and cans of varnish, brushes, and paint. "Looks like the place was trashed."

"It always looks like this. The store's neat, but this place is a mess. What are you doing?"

Cody had bent and was touching something on the floor. "Nothing."

As she turned away, she saw him sniff his finger.

What was he looking for? He moved about the room, padding lightly from spot to spot, stopping occasionally to examine something. His expression was intent, fully focused. There was something about the way he moved, a gracefulness that surrounded all those muscles, that left her in awe. He'd always had it, even when he was young. She'd tried to emulate it, but never got it right. "On to the shop?" she asked.

Cody nodded. Shay opened the back door, and they stepped inside.

"Nice," Cody said, admiring an old sword on a shelf.

"We carry everything from furniture and tapestries to weapons and jewelry. If it's old, we're interested," Shay said, closing a table drawer.

"I've got a friend you should meet," he muttered.

They stepped farther into the shop, and the hair on Shay's neck rose.

"Wait. Let me go first." Cody put a hand over his chest and eased inside, not touching anything. He moved like a predator, eyes narrowed, scanning the shadows.

"The guy who broke in my shop smashed a table too."

"You didn't tell me that. Was anything else damaged?"

"Not that I know. The police didn't mention anything. I wonder if it's the same guy."

"Who was he? A local guy?"

"I don't know him. He had a strange name. Franklin or something. He claims it's a mistake."

"They all do." Cody eased past the broken furniture. "We'll call the police in Scotland. There must be some connection if the only things he messed with are the tables."

"Maybe someone's trying to hurt my business."

He put a hand on her shoulder. "This does feel personal, but I think it's something else. Look at that table over there." He pointed to a small end table. "It's a simple design, one drawer, and it's opened, just like the one near the back door. He's looking for something."

"What could he be looking for in both Leesburg and Scotland? We need to call the cops."

"Quiet." Cody tilted his head, listening. "Stay here. I want to look around outside."

"No. I want to come."

"I'll just be a minute."

He left, and the shadows crept into Shay's mind, the footsteps, and evil whispers. Statues that moved. She started toward the sword, when a noise sounded in the back. She scurried toward the door Cody had left cracked. She slipped outside and saw him crouched near the side of the shop. Had he spotted someone? She crept up behind him and touched his back. He whirled, and she leapt back as the tip of his dagger pointed at her throat.

"Damn it!" he whispered harshly. Four ravens shot up from the trees.

"Ravens. Just birds," she said, touching her neck. That blade had almost cut her throat.

"Do you ever listen? What are you doing out here?"

"I heard something. Those ravens, I guess."

Cody watched the birds soar away before turning back to the trees. "Let's go. I don't like the feel of this place."

"Where did you get that dagger?" He didn't have his Glock.

"I always carry it."

She looked him over. "Where?"

"In my boot." He always wore boots. "Don't ever sneak up on me. I could've cut your throat."

He ushered her to the truck, then made a quick search for Renee's laptop, which held all her files, and locked up.

"Did you find her laptop?" Shay asked.

"No. Did she have any enemies?" he asked, after he loaded Shay's luggage.

"Not that I know of, but there's something I haven't told you. The burglar in Scotland wasn't exactly a burglar or a vandal. Well, he might have been those too, but he's really more of a stalker."

Cody's face went slack with surprise and then tightened in anger. "A stalker? You've had a stalker this whole time, and you didn't tell me? What were you thinking? I'm a war... a PI, for God's sake."

"Stop yelling at me! The police arrested him. I thought it was over. I didn't see any point in mentioning it. But he must have trashed this place first."

Cody drummed his fingers on the wheel. "No wonder you freaked out at the lake. How long has this been going on?"

"About three weeks. I felt like someone was watching me, saw shadows, then the night I left Scotland, I'd gone to my shop, when I saw him coming after me. I ran inside, and there was a table I'd just gotten for an American client, all smashed up on the floor. I called the police, but before I could get out of the shop, I heard footsteps. I hid behind an armoire. He was so close I could've touched him. Another few seconds, and he would've had me. Something scared him off. I talked to the police between flights, and they told me they arrested him."

"Was there anything special about your table?" Cody asked.

"It wasn't valuable. My client wanted something unusual. Renee had just gotten these two matching tables, at an auction, I think. They sounded perfect, but Mr. Ellis wanted only one. Renee shipped it from Leesburg. Another client took the other one. Renee was fixing some scratches on it. I didn't see it in her workroom. Maybe it's been delivered."

"We need to find out where she got those tables," Cody said.

"I don't even know where she is."

"We'll find her." He put his hand on her leg. At first it just laid there, then he started rubbing slowly. She knew he did it without thinking, distracted by the new puzzle. She wondered if she should say something or just enjoy the warmth until he realized what he was doing. His hand slid inside her thigh, and she saw a mark on his inner wrist. She tried to see what it was—another tattoo?—but the rubbing was starting to heat more than her legs.

"What's that mark on your wrist?" she asked.

Cody jerked his hand back, frowning. "Nothing."

It looked like a sword. He was still hiding things from her, but wasn't she doing the same? "What do you have against Renee?"

He stared straight ahead, and she thought he was going to ignore the question, but then he spoke. "I tried to see you."

"After I left?" she asked. What did this have to do with Renee?

"Aye. You weren't home."

"When?"

He glanced at her once, and Shay could see the memories replaying in his eyes. "April third, a few months after you left."

Shay felt the air freeze, too sharp to pull into her lungs. She swallowed. "I was at a funeral."

"I'm sorry," Cody said. "I guess it was bad timing on my part."

Shay bit the inside of her cheek to keep from crying and nodded. When the tension in her throat eased, she said, "I'm surprised Renee wasn't at the house." She had gotten ill and couldn't attend.

"She was." Cody's voice was flat. "She tried to throw me out."

Shay swung around to look at him. "Renee?"

"She planted herself in the doorway and said you weren't there." Cody's hands clenched the steering wheel. "I didn't believe her, so I picked her up, set her aside, and went in anyway."

Shay gaped at him.

"She was right. You weren't there. She said you'd moved on with your life. You didn't want anything to do with me. That you were seeing someone."

"Why would she say that? I didn't even go on a date for two years after that." Shay clamped her lips together.

Cody glanced across at her, his eyes pinning her to the seat. "Why?"

Because the only one she ever wanted, didn't want her. Shay turned and looked at the scenery flashing soundlessly by. "I was distracted with other things. Renee must have thought she was trying to protect me."

"From what? What the hell did you tell her about me?"

"I didn't tell her anything." Not intentionally. Why hadn't Renee told her Cody had come to see her? Shay would have given her right hand to have known. She let the spark of anger toward Renee die. She was just trying to help, but God, Shay wished she had known. Her phone rang, a puzzling call that distracted Shay from considering the damage Renee's actions had done to Cody and Shay's friendship.

"What was that about?" Cody asked.

"This just gets stranger. That was Julie, who ordered the mate to the table in my shop. A man called two days ago asking if she'd gotten the table, but she had already canceled the order with Renee. We don't have any male employees."

"He didn't give a name?"

"No, and she said another of Renee's clients was burglarized. Nothing taken, but a table destroyed."

"What the hell was this guy looking for? We'll call the police in the morning and see what the guy says."

Shay yawned. "I don't know why I'm so tired. I slept well last night." The best night's sleep she had in weeks. She touched her arm. The scratch was burning.

"Here." Cody reached behind the seat and pulled out a pillow. "When I'm hunting, I have to sleep wherever I can."

Shay put her head on the pillow. "Hunting?"

"Uh, criminals."

As she drifted off to sleep, she felt his hand cover hers.

"Your husband's going to kill us both. You know that,"

Ronan told Bree as she dug through a bag of junk food she bought at the airport.

"I'll send you in first, let you talk some sense into him."

"Not me, darlin'. Faelan's already gonna think this is all my fault."

"I'm supposed to be on my honeymoon, not bailing my husband out of jail."

"You're the reason he had to play bodyguard. You and your bloody visions."

"I had to warn Cody. The woman I saw in the vision with him was going to die."

"You did the right thing," Ronan said, scrubbing his knuckles over Bree's head. He grinned. "I could take you on the honeymoon."

"Sorry, stud. You need to age at least another century."

"Don't know what you're missing."

"From what I hear, I'm the only one."

Ronan's grin turned to a grimace. "You shouldn't listen to gossip. There's more smoke than fire." The reputation was probably his own fault, but if he didn't flirt once in a while to lighten the load, he would explode from the guilt hanging around his neck. The clan still didn't know his part in things. He would tell them, after he figured out where the vampires were and what they wanted. "So what's the story between Cody and this woman?"

"I don't know, but you'd best keep your hands to yourself if you don't want to lose them."

"Like that, huh? Well, I have no plans to put my hands anywhere except on this steering wheel. If I was going to go messing with some man's woman, not that I would, I wouldn't choose the only warrior besides Faelan who's battled an ancient demon and lived to tell about it. Give me a little credit, darlin'. That'd be suicide."

"You don't fool me. You're not afraid of anybody. Including my fierce husband."

Bree was wrong. He was afraid... of himself. "What'd you do with Cody's address?"

Bree pulled a piece of paper from her purse. "I just hope Faelan's there. I'm worried about him."

"The Mighty Faelan can take care of himself."

"I know." Bree twisted her ring, frowning.

"Can't you just call and check on him?"

"He's not answering his phone. He keeps losing it, but no, I need to see him."

Something was bothering her. Ronan had some kind of connection with Bree that he couldn't explain, a need to protect her that confused him and drove Faelan insane.

Ronan eyed the box of Milk Duds she was munching. "You shouldn't be eating that crap."

"I can't help it. Pregnant women have cravings." Bree clamped her hand over her mouth, her eyes round.

"You're pregnant? I'm going to be an uncle?" He gave her a hug and kissed her cheek. "And he left you alone, knowing—" he narrowed his eyes. "He doesn't know, does he? Is that why I'm risking my neck bringing you to Virginia? So you can tell him?"

"No, he can't know."

"Why not? He's the father." Ronan lifted a horrified brow. "Isn't he?"

"Of course he is, but he can't be distracted now. You know how he is, even with me hale and hearty. Can you imagine how he'll act if he knows I'm carrying his baby?"

"Blimey. You sure I can't talk you into going home? You can rest, stay healthy, and I can stay alive."

"I have to see him, but don't you dare breathe a word. Promise me."

Ronan sighed. "Scout's honor."

"Shake on it."

Ronan extended his hand, and Bree clasped it. She looked taken aback for a moment and stared at their clasped hands.

"You scare the hell out of me when you get that look."

"It's probably the pregnancy."

"Give me that." He grabbed the box of Milk Duds from her lap and flung it into the backseat.

"What are you doing?"

"Faelan's going to blame this whole fiasco on me. I'll be damned if I'll let him blame your poor eating habits on me too."

"But I'm craving them. I'll eat broccoli tomorrow."

"We'll probably both be dead tomorrow," Ronan said as he pulled away from the airport and headed toward Charlottesville.

"Shay, we're home."

Shay sat up, blinking her eyes as Cody pulled into his driveway. It was already dark. "I can't believe I slept the whole way. Did I snore?"

"Either that or there's a kitten purring under the seat." His lips thinned, and he looked away.

Shay didn't want to think about Cody and kittens; that's where the trouble started. "I'm going to go straight to bed."

Cody pulled his truck up beside a blue car. "Wait, I'll come with you."

Shay raised her eyebrows.

"I'll walk you over. I need to get some things from the house first." He looked at the blue car and frowned. "Why don't you wait out here?"

"You're staying at the house again? Why?"

"I'm not taking any chances."

"My ankle's okay."

"What? Yeah, your ankle. Stay here. I'll be back."

"I don't want to sit here and wait. I'm going on. You can come when you're ready."

"I think you were a mule in a previous life. Go on, then. I'll be over in a few minutes."

She got out of the car, wondering why he was so distracted that he'd let her walk home alone. In fact, she was fairly sure he was trying to keep her out of his house. What was he hiding?

She turned around and walked to Cody's house. She eased in the back door as she had a thousand times before. He wasn't in the kitchen. She crept into the living room and down the hall. Her fingers skimmed the banister she and Cody had slid down while his mother, Laura, hid a grin and pretended to scold. Voices were coming from upstairs. A woman's. Was Laura home? Shay eased up the steps to what had been Cody's room. His door was cracked. Shay froze, her eyes locked on the long dark hair spread across his pillow. A woman was in his bed.

A girlfriend? Cody had a girlfriend? Shay eased back into the hall, trying to breathe.

"You're right about the candy," the woman said. "I

don't think it did me any good. I wish I could just lie in bed all day." There was a thump, like a pillow hitting flesh, and a low male chuckle.

"Serves you right," Cody said.

Shay backed away and slipped down the steps, her brain and legs numb. Marcas and Lachlan were in the living room, their voices coming closer. She couldn't face anyone. She turned and went down the hall, opening the nearest door. When she was a child, the door stayed locked. Ewan MacBain had forbidden them to go down there. Shay adored Ewan, sometimes even pretended he was her father, but she wouldn't have dared defy a direct edict from him. She closed the door and waited for the voices to pass. Someone had left a light on. Curious, she looked down the stairs, expecting rickety steps, cobwebs, and spiders, dangerous things for kids, not a Bat Cave with rows of computers and weapons lining the walls, guns, swords, and battle-axes, a blend of high tech and medieval. Was Ewan a collector?

She moved down the steps in a daze. The weapons were amazing, authentic, from what she could tell. There was a sitting area with worn leather sofas and chairs. Another room had weights and workout machines. Beyond that, she could see a large, empty space with what looked like wrestling mats covering the floor.

A tall cabinet caught her eye. It was an old piece, probably eighteenth century, in great condition. It held several old books, a few small knives, and a long, wooden box. The grain of wood was unusual. Shay couldn't resist peeking inside. She saw a thick, round necklace, similar to the one Cody and his brothers wore, but this one had three swirls in the center, etched with some kind of symbols. There were other things, too, gadgets she'd never seen before. Off to the side, a small door stood ajar. She nudged it open and peeked inside, gaping at the wall of monitors. Good heavens. It was Nina's house. They were recording Nina's house, from every angle; front, sides, and back, even views of the woods.

She rethought her childhood, wondering if she had missed the signs of insanity in her next door neighbors, but then she saw that their house was monitored as well, again, from all sides. The entire perimeter was covered on both houses. Did this have something to do with her father's top secret job? Ewan was involved. He'd admitted that much when he and Laura called to apologize a few weeks after she left. But video surveillance?

How could she have spent so much time in this house and not known about this basement? She and Cody had sneaked into plenty of places they weren't supposed to. Thinking of Cody brought Shay's attention back to the woman in his bed. Who was she? Did he love her? Want to spend the rest of his live with her? Grow old with her? How many had there been before this one? It shouldn't matter; it was his life, but she couldn't stay and watch. Why would he kiss Shay if he had a girlfriend? Was he just trying to exorcise old ghosts so he could move on? As Shay was? The thought left her feeling as hollow as a straw.

If she hurried, maybe she could leave before he noticed. She could go back to Leesburg, call and apologize, say Renee had called. Shay slipped up the basement stairs. Faint voices came from the kitchen. She hurried into Lachlan's bedroom, passed his unmade bed, and slipped out the back door onto his cobblestone patio. She ran toward Nina's, stopping once when she thought she would throw up. After a few steady breaths, she continued to the house.

The white cat was waiting at the front door. It stood, tail swishing, as Shay approached. "Move over, cat. I'm in a hurry." The cat didn't move, so Shay stepped around it. Her hands were still shaking as she opened the door. A soft thud came from the sitting room. She walked to the doorway and stepped on something. Stooping, she picked it up. A book? Her foot struck another one. She flipped on the light switch. A man stood in the center of the room. He had long, blond hair and icy blue eyes.

One second he was by the fireplace; the next he was in front of her, eyes as clear as glass. "You can make this easy… or hard," he said with a tight smile.

Shay screamed and hurled the book at him, hitting him in the face. She turned to run, but tripped over the cat who had wandered inside. It hissed and darted into the room. Shay scrambled off the floor and sprinted outside. She looked back to make sure the man wasn't following her and ran headlong into a wall. Someone grabbed her arms. "Cody, there's—" She looked up and saw it wasn't Cody, but the man who broke into her shop in Scotland. There were two stalkers? Shay punched him in the nose.

"Damnation, woman. What the hell's wrong with you?"

"Stay away from me." She wasn't sure which way to run. One was in the house, one was outside. She would have to fight. She attacked the man, punching and kicking, when a pair of arms like steel bands encircled her from behind.

"Are all the women in this century bloody deranged?" the man said.

"What're you doing here? I almost shot you." That was Cody's voice, and Shay could smell his scent. He was the one restraining her.

"Shoot him," Shay yelled.

"You need a new cell phone," the man said. "I've been trying to call you."

"I haven't been home much, and I left my cell phone on the charger. I've been distracted," Cody said.

The man looked at Shay and rubbed his nose. "I can see. I didn't have your home number, only your address."

"You know this stalker?" Shay demanded.

"I'm not a stalker," the stranger said.

"Then why are you stalking me?"

"He's a friend," Cody said.

"A friend?" Why had Cody sent a *friend* to spy on her? "I guess I need to apologize to the other guy for hitting him," Shay said.

Cody frowned. "What other guy?"

"The one inside the house."

Cody tensed. "Who's with you?" he asked the stranger.

"No one."

Cody released Shay so fast she staggered to catch her balance, and both men rushed past her into the house. Shay hurried after them.

"What in blazes?" Cody looked at the bookshelf knocked over and books strewn across the floor. "Did you see anyone?" he asked the stranger.

"No. I just got here when I heard a scream and ran to help. She came at me like a madwoman."

"The last time I saw you in Scotland, I thought you

were going to attack me," she said. "You shouldn't creep around spying on people."

The stranger gave her an exasperated look, similar to the one Cody wore. "I was trying to protect you."

"Well, you should have introduced yourself and said, 'Hey, I'm here to protect you,' instead of scaring the daylights out me."

Marcas rushed in the front door, with Lachlan right behind him, hopping as he shoved one foot into his boot. "What's going on?"

"Someone just broke in here," Cody said.

"I thought I heard something tearing through the woods," Lachlan said. His sense of hearing was unmatched.

"Shay, lock the doors. We'll search the woods," Cody said. "Let's go, before the tracks get cold."

The night was dark, the moon hidden behind clouds. Cody tuned in his vision and saw something dart between the trees. He sprinted toward it, but nothing was there. He stood still and listened, sniffing the air. There was a strange smell, almost sweet, and everything was quiet.

Too quiet, he realized, a second before something slammed him into a tree. Cody caught a glimpse of pale hair and lunged, tackling the man low. The guy felt like he was made of metal. Cody heard a grunt and tree limbs breaking as they fell. The moon emerged. There was a whooshing sound, and the man disappeared. Cody spun around, but his opponent was gone. Alarm prickled up his spine. A stalker, and now this? Had the clan been wrong about Shay? He wouldn't let anything harm her, not after he'd just gotten her back. He turned around and bumped into Shay.

"What are you doing out here?"

"I'm not staying inside. Let's go after him, before he gets away," she said.

"I didn't see which way he went," Cody said.

"He ran that way." She pointed north.

"You saw him?" How was that possible, when he hadn't? "You need to get inside."

"No. I want to help."

Cody took her arm and escorted her back to the house. They met Faelan coming around back.

"Nothing in the barn or behind it," Faelan said.

"I saw him, but he got away. Shay said he went north."

"Shay?" Faelan said, looking surprised.

<center>~~~</center>

"If the stalker was here, then who's in jail?" Shay asked. Cody had a tight grip on her arm as he pulled her into the house.

"That would have been me. Faelan Connor, ma'am."

Faelan was tall and muscular, with long, dark hair pulled back in a ribbon, exceptionally good-looking. Shay was used to being surrounded by tall, exceptionally good-looking men, but most of them weren't in kilts, even when she lived in Scotland.

Cody turned to Faelan. "You were in jail?"

"Afraid so. Bad timing, and she definitely has a stalker. I'm not sure which variety, if you understand what I mean."

"Did you get a look at him?" Cody asked.

"No. Police arrested me before I could go after him."

"You didn't smell him?" Cody asked.

Shay glanced from Faelan to Cody. Smell him?

"No," Faelan said. "But there was definitely something in the shop with her. It ran out the back when I came in, and I glimpsed a shadow watching her earlier, but not enough to make out if it was a man or..." he trailed off, giving Cody a furtive look.

"It wasn't a woman," Shay said. "It was a man. He had big feet." She glanced at Cody's square-toed boots.

Cody turned to Faelan. "You tailed her wearing that?"

"Didn't have time to change," Faelan said.

"Keep an eye on Shay. I'm going to track him."

"I'm not staying with him," she said, looking at Faelan's dagger.

Cody shook his head. "Then come with me." He led her into her bedroom.

"What are we doing here? We need to help them." Where had this bravery come from? Was it because Cody was with her?

"You can't leave the room," he said.

"We're just going to wait here while they search? No. I'm going to help." She turned to leave the room, but Cody stopped her.

"Damn it." He touched his necklace. "Look out the window."

Shay turned and opened the curtain. "What?" There was a whirring noise. Cody grabbed her wrist and slapped it to the headboard. Shay heard a click. He'd cuffed her hand to the bed. "What are you doing? Let me go!" She struggled, rattling the bed.

"Sorry, but I need you to stay put."

"You bastard!" She tried to hit him, but Cody pulled her close, trapping her free arm.

"I'm sorry," he whispered, pressing his cheek to hers, "but I have to protect you." He kissed her and left.

Shay yanked at the handcuffs as he locked the door and closed it behind him, but she hurt her arm, and she was afraid she would damage the bed. She could dismantle the headboard, but she wasn't going to ruin an antique just to get free. She sat down, fuming, cursing, calling Cody every name she could conjure. She examined the handcuffs. She'd never seen any like them. They were etched with symbols and made of a strange metal she couldn't identify, not quite silver or gold. They must be antique. After the adrenaline rush left and there was still no sign of Cody or the stalker, she grew tired. Her arm was burning again. She lay down, thinking of ways to kill Cody, and fell asleep.

—◈—

Cody listened at the door. It was quiet inside. He had a moment of panic until he saw the door was still locked, and then another when he remembered how good she used to be at climbing out her window. He'd been gone for an hour. If she had escaped, he would probably never see her again. His fingers fumbled as he picked the lock. He eased the door open. She lay on the bed, asleep, one arm dangling from the headboard. His gut tightened. He walked over to her, torn between dread and relief that she hadn't left. She was going to be furious. He was angry at himself for not putting the clues together—her panic after the lake and the scream in the bathroom—and angry at her for not telling him. Didn't she know by now that he would move heaven and earth to protect her?

He looked at the shackles holding her to the bed and realized he had come close to doing that. He hadn't thought twice about it. He'd let concern for her make him forget the rules. Again. He rubbed the brand on his wrist, imagining the Council's outrage if they found out. Michael wouldn't be happy about it, either. Well, the Council and Michael didn't have the troublesome task of protecting Shay.

Cody debated whether to leave her shackled while he explained why he locked her up. Either way, there would be hell to pay. What really worried him was what she would do when she found out he hadn't told her the whole truth. And he would have to tell her soon.

A voice came from the doorway. "Hey, we're heading back to the house—hell's bells, you didn't." Lach gaped at the shackles on Shay's wrist. "Are you out of your bloody mind?"

"I had to do something fast. She was trying to get outside and track down her stalker. It was either use the shackles or sit on her." He knew they wouldn't hurt her, he'd used them once on a minion.

"You'd better hope the Council doesn't find out. I don't care if you have suspended an ancient demon, they'd rip you apart for this."

"I couldn't let her go running around with a stalker on the loose. There isn't a chance in hell that he's human. He was too strong and too fast. I have to protect her."

"You'd better think about protecting yourself. When she wakes up, she's going to be loaded for bear. I just saw her finger twitch. I'm out of here." Lach gave him a nasty grin. "Have fun."

Cody sighed. Might as well get it over with. He

removed the shackles, returned them, and bent over her. "Shay, wake up."

Her eyes flew open. She planted both hands against his chest and shoved, knocking him on his back, then sprang on top of him. "How dare you handcuff me to a bed?" she yelled, punctuating each word with a shake that rattled his brain. He didn't fight back. She had to get it out of her system, and he didn't blame her. He'd be more than pissed if someone shackled him.

She landed a fist into his stomach, and the breath rushed out of him. Okay, enough was enough. He captured her hands and rolled, trapping her under him.

"Get off me, you oaf."

"I'll get off when you stop beating the snot out of me."

She let out a war cry and lunged for his throat, teeth bared. Intrigued, he hesitated a second too long, and she sank her teeth into his neck. A jolt of desire shot straight to his groin. He'd never been one for the rough stuff, but damn! He pulled back before she could do more than leave a bruise. He trapped her legs with his and held her hands above her head, letting his full weight press her into the soft mattress. She still struggled but could move only enough to get him excited.

"I'm sorry, Shay. I had to do it. It was too dangerous to let you go traipsing through the woods. I had to keep you safe."

"What if he was hiding in one of the other bedrooms and sneaked in here while I was handcuffed to the bed? You left me so I couldn't even protect myself."

"Lach heard him out in the woods, but that's why I locked the door, just in case. If this guy had broken it down to get to you, you would've screamed, and I would've come running. I was never far from the house. I heard every name you called me."

Her eyes still flashed fire, but her breath was steadier, and she kept glancing at his mouth. He thought that was a good thing. He wondered if she'd calmed enough not to hit him, because he should move. She had to notice the effect all the wiggling around was having on him. He felt her hips push against his, and he groaned. He relaxed his grip and lowered his head, letting his lips touch her chin. He kissed his way to her mouth, and she head-butted him in the nose.

While the stars exploded in his head, she shoved him aside and bolted out the door. He jumped up and went after her as she pounded down the stairs. He caught up with her outside. She was swinging her purse like a whip, headed for the car.

"Where are you going?" he demanded.

"Get away from me."

"You can't leave."

"Watch me." She opened the door. "I'm tired of people hiding things from me. I thought you were going to stop. Now you're handcuffing me to the bed."

"I explained it to you."

"Don't touch me," she said, jerking away when he grabbed her arm.

"You're not leaving."

Shay straightened her shoulders. "You can't stop me."

He grabbed her, tossed her over his shoulder, kicked the car door shut, and stomped up the steps.

"Put me down!" Shay kicked and twisted, cursing at him. He dumped her on her feet inside the door.

She blew her hair out of her face, and as soon as she could see, she threw a punch at his chin. He deflected it and grabbed her arm. "Stop hitting me."

"How dare you throw me over your shoulder like some kind of caveman," she spat, trying to wrench her arm free. It didn't work, so she used her knee.

"Ah, not there." Cody trapped her knee. "I made the mistake of letting you leave here nine years ago without listening to me. By God, I won't do it again. You'll listen if I have to sit on you," he growled.

She drew back her other arm, and before she could throw the punch, he had her on the floor and was sitting astride her, pinning her wrists to the floor. She bucked and twisted, but he held her down. "We can do this all night if you want, but you're going to listen to me this time."

"Listen to more lies? You're still hiding things from me. Like the fact that you have Nina's entire house under surveillance. Like the fact that you've got a Bat Cave in your basement. Like the fact that you were in Scotland when the stalking started."

"You think I'm your stalker?" he yelled. "Me! I'm trying to keep you alive. We're all trying to keep you alive. That's what the clan's been doing your whole damned life, trying to keep you alive! And just like always, you're making it hard as hell. Your father wasn't a bloody spy, and that thing in your living room wasn't a man. Damn!"

Chapter 4

SHAY SAGGED AGAINST THE FLOOR. "WHAT DO YOU mean, my father wasn't a spy? And that man... if he wasn't a man, what was he?"

Cody cursed. He sat up, letting go of her wrists, still astride her. "He was a demon."

"A demon?" A cackle escaped her lips. "Is this a joke? Another lie?"

"Do I look like I'm joking?"

He looked angry. "Like a hell-and-brimstone demon?"

"Aye, but they spend a lot of time here."

"I don't understand."

"Why do you think we had to keep your identity hidden?"

"Because my father was with the CIA or some top-secret organization, and I was in danger. That's what you said."

"No. That's what you *thought* I said. I just didn't tell you any different, but you got the top-secret organization part right. Your father was a warrior."

"What kind of warrior?"

"The kind that fights demons. The kind of warrior who keeps humans alive." Cody blew out a breath and stood. He ran his hands through his hair. "Why do I let you do this to me? This is going to blow up in my face, just like last time."

Shay stood and faced him. "This is insane. You've already lied to me once. How do I know—"

"I didn't lie. I just withheld information that wasn't my place to give. After you walked away, I couldn't tell you the whole story. The clan wouldn't allow it."

"Who is this... clan that's making decisions for me?"

"Your mother and father's clan. Your clan. When you were a baby, someone killed your mother and left you for dead. That's how you got the scar on your shoulder."

"Nina said the scar was from a bicycle wreck."

"She had to tell you something. It was a car wreck, but it wasn't an accident. You were meant to die, but an old man pulled you from the burning vehicle."

Speechless, Shay shook her head. "They didn't catch the killer?"

"No. He was probably a demon."

"I'm sorry... this is just insane. Assuming you're correct—"

"I am."

"Assuming you are, then why did this demon want me dead?"

"The clan didn't know if you were the target or if it was revenge, but you were marked, so they had to hide you. That's why the house is monitored. That's why we're here. To keep you safe."

"I'm marked?"

"Your scar is probably a demon's mark."

Shay touched the pale, jagged line beside her collarbone. "Does Nina know about this?"

"She does. Matilda doesn't."

"Why would a demon target a baby?"

She'd known Cody long enough to recognize the fear

that slipped past his eyes before he put on his blank face. "Probably revenge."

"My mother died?"

"Aye, and your father died not long after. The clan hid you, buried the empty casket, and gave you a new name, a new family. They had to make it look like you'd really died."

The empty grave had been to hide her from a demon, not a mobster or a terrorist?

"Is Nina really my aunt?"

Cody lowered his gaze. "No. She's mine. My mother's half sister. My father was friends with Nina's husband, who died just before my father was sent from Scotland to watch over you. Nina was grieving. She needed someone. You needed someone. So they gave her you."

"Ewan was a warrior?"

Cody nodded. "The whole family came here, with the understanding that when my brothers and I grew up, it would be our mission too."

She'd known Ewan was involved, which was part of the reason she left. She didn't want to be anyone's job. She hadn't known Cody, her best friend, the boy she'd trusted with her heart and soul, had protected her because it was his *job*?

"The clan planned to tell you the truth after you graduated from high school, but you left before they met to see who would break the news. It probably would've been my father."

"And they let me walk away, with a demon after me?"

"The demon your father had been hunting when all this happened had disappeared. Just before you left, the

Watchers found out he was dead, so they thought you were safe."

"Watchers? Demons? This sounds like something out of a movie," Shay said, rubbing her throbbing temples. "They should have told me."

"They couldn't. You wanted nothing to do with us, and there was too much at stake. Outsiders can't know about the clan. They had no choice but to let you go. Besides, you'd just turned eighteen. Nina couldn't force you to come back here."

"Did the clan know why I left?" she asked, braving a quick look at his face.

He rubbed the tattoo on his neck. "Not all of it."

"You and your brothers are warriors too?"

"I'm retired. We're active from age eighteen to twenty-eight. Marcas chose to stay active. Lachlan has another year and a half."

What about the hayloft? Where did that fit into his mission? "You were never in Special Forces?"

"No."

"And Marcas and Lachlan's expeditions are a cover?"

He nodded.

"How long have you known about... me?"

His mouth twitched with indecision. "Since I was seventeen."

Two years before *it* happened. "And you didn't tell me? We never kept secrets from each other."

Cody looked away, and when his eyes met hers again, they were sad. "I was afraid if I told you, you'd start looking into your past and on the off chance that this demon wasn't dead, he would find you. I didn't want you hurt. I wish I'd done a better job explaining

it then; maybe things would have turned out different."
He hesitantly reached for her arm. "I don't want to
fight, Shay. Come on. I'll help you clean up the mess."

So much for leaving Virginia.

He followed her into the sitting room. She was still
furious that he handcuffed her to the bed, but her anger
was overshadowed by shock. Nothing about her world
was what she thought. Her stalker had followed her
here. Someone had broken into Nina's house. Cody had
a girlfriend. She didn't have the surplus of emotion to
ask him about her.

"So these demons, what do they want?"

Cody righted the bookshelf "They want to get rid of
humans. They want the earth for themselves."

"My God. I'm living in *Lord of the Rings*." People
usually told lies to make something seem believable.
This was too bizarre to be a lie.

"This makes *Lord of the Rings* look like a lullaby."

She picked up a photo album and put it on the bookshelf. "You'd think even a demon would have the de-
cency to leave a person's family photos alone."

"Demons don't care about anything but evil."

She picked up a book and saw something white lying
beside it.

"What's that?" Cody asked.

"Looks like a piece of ivory," she said, laying it on
the shelf.

The cat appeared in the doorway, still as a statue,
other than its swishing tail.

Cody frowned. "You brought a cat?"

"It's not mine. It showed up this morning. I thought
it might have been yours."

"No. Maybe the Peterson's."

Shay gave a sarcastic laugh. "Maybe it belongs to the demon. It came inside the house and ran toward him. I tripped over it."

Cody handed Shay a stack of books. "Not likely. Demons hate animals. That's why they rarely take on an animal form."

"Demons can take other forms?"

"Aye. Their natural forms aren't a pretty sight. They stink, and they're ugly. The problem is they can shift into disguises. They might be your neighbor, the little old lady down the street. The older they get, the more powerful they become. The ancient ones are particularly deadly."

Shay put the last book on the shelf. "Ancient ones?"

"They can live around a thousand years."

"Good grief! What are they doing all that time?"

Cody shrugged. "Trying to come up with ways to destroy us."

"Do they all live that long?"

"No. There are three orders. The first is eternal. Humans don't see them. The second, they're the ones who cause the most trouble, full demons. The third, the halflings, they live a couple hundred years."

"Halflings? Like in half human?"

Cody nodded.

"Can only warriors kill demons?"

"For the most part," he said. "And even then, the powerful ones have to be assigned to match the warrior's strength or the warrior could die. A demon can kill a human in a heartbeat."

"Good thing I didn't have gun or a knife."

"You scare me sometimes," Cody said.

After the room was straight, the two started back to his house. The cat trailed along behind them. "You sure this cat's just a cat?" Shay asked. "He has white fur, and that intruder was blond."

Cody turned to look at it. "It showed up long before the demon did. Probably belongs to the Petersons." Shay heard yelling even before Cody opened his front door. "Damn! I forgot to tell him," he said, rushing in.

Faelan had a man pinned to the kitchen wall, while Lachlan, Marcas, and a beautiful woman Shay assumed was Cody's girlfriend tried to drag Faelan away. Cody grabbed Faelan's arm, and the group finally restrained him.

"I swear, if you weren't my ancestor," the new guy said, giving Faelan a hard shove, "I'd lock you in a time vault myself."

"How could you drag her off on one of your adventures?" Faelan shouted, looking as fierce as an ancient Highland warrior with his kilt and angry face. "You were supposed to make sure she got safely from Scotland to New York."

"*My* adventures? Have you lost your bloody mind? I came to protect her. Damned woman tried to sneak off and come to Virginia alone. You're lucky I figured out what she was up to."

The woman scowled. "Hey."

"Are ye trying to drive me to madness?" Faelan said to the woman, his face hot with anger. "If you don't start listening to me—"

The woman grabbed a loaf of bread off the counter and swung it at his head. Faelan ducked, and the loaf caught Cody on the ear. The woman planted her hands on

her hips, glaring at Faelan. "You jackass! Sorry, Cody."
She glared at Faelan. "This isn't the nineteenth century.
You think I'm supposed to sit home bored, while you're
out having all the adventures? I don't think so."

"Told you," the new guy said.

So she was with Faelan. Every muscle in Shay's
body sagged with relief. But why had the woman slept
in Cody's bed?

"I forgot to tell you they were here," Cody said, flick-
ing a slice of bread off his shoulder. "Shay and I had just
gotten back from Leesburg."

"What am I supposed to think?" Faelan asked the
woman. "You're supposed to be safe in New York, and
I walk in and find you here. With *him*." He pointed at
Ronan. "I haven't slept, and I need food."

The woman rolled her eyes. "God help us."

"There's some food left over," Lachlan said. "It's
probably cold."

The woman turned and saw Shay near the door. Her
eyes widened. She blinked several times and smiled.
"I'm Bree Connor, this Neanderthal's wife." She nodded toward Faelan, who was lifting pot lids, still scowling. "You must be Shay. Sorry to stare, but you look
just like you did in my vision." The others in the room
stopped talking and were watching her. "I get these...
premonitions sometimes."

Cody touched Shay's back. "Bree had a vision that
you were in danger. That's why Faelan came to keep an
eye on you."

Now she had perfect strangers trying to protect her.
"But you don't even know me," Shay said.

"I know. My premonitions aren't normal. Usually

they're about family or friends, but lately I've been having them about strangers."

The good-looking man chuckled and ruffled Bree's hair. He seemed unfazed by Faelan's attack. "Darlin', there's nothing normal about you."

"This is Ronan," Cody said. He surprised Shay by placing his arm around her shoulders, pulling her to his side. Marcas watched the gesture, and Shay thought she saw a glimmer of a smile.

"Sorry about the scuffle." Ronan grinned, and Shay's heart skipped two beats. She could almost understand Faelan's frustration. What man would want his wife going anywhere with someone who looked like that?

Ronan bumped Faelan with his shoulder and stepped up to shake Shay's hand. "Glad you're okay. We were worried."

"Are you all part of this clan?" Shay asked.

"You told her?" Lachlan said. "Are you crazy? The Council's gonna hang you this time."

"I'll deal with the Council," Cody said, but his jaw tightened as he said it.

"We're all from the same clan," Ronan explained, "but we're from Scotland, not far from where you live, I understand. I'm surprised we didn't run into you over the years."

She would have remembered if she had run into Ronan. "Guess that explains Faelan's kilt," Shay said. "It looks authentic."

"It is authentic. Nineteenth century, him and the kilt. He's my great-great-great-uncle, the Mighty Faelan. Bree found him in a time vault while she was searching for treasure. I think sometimes she wishes she hadn't. I know I do."

Faelan looked like he wanted to hit Ronan again. "If you don't stop calling me that I'm going to stick you in a time vault," he said, pulling off another slice of ham.

"Time vault? Are you saying he was born in the nineteenth century?" He couldn't be.

"Aye," Cody said, rubbing his neck. "He was born in 1833."

"That's impossible."

"There are a lot of impossible things in this clan," Bree said.

"More than demons and... what was it, a time vault?" Shay asked.

"You can't imagine," Bree said. "These time vaults imprison demons until Judgment. Time stops inside."

Cody hadn't told her that part. What else wasn't he telling her?

"What happened to your neck?" Marcas asked Cody.

Cody touched a red mark just over his jugular vein. "Shay bit me."

Everyone stared at her, cocked eyebrows leading to grins.

Shay's face heated. "That's what you get for handcuffing me to the bed."

The grins grew wider, and Shay's face hotter.

"Sorry," Cody said looking at her lips. "Do you want something to eat?"

"Careful," Ronan said. "She might take a chunk out of the other side."

"No, thanks," Shay said, spearing all the men with a glare.

"Good," Lachlan said. "'Cause Faelan just took the rest of the food."

"You wouldn't believe how much that man can eat after being suspended in time for a hundred and fifty-one years," Bree said. "Come on, let's get away from all this testosterone before we choke."

"Who brought the cat?" Lachlan asked, looking at the cat, who'd pushed through the cracked door.

"It showed up at Nina's," Cody said. "Probably belongs to the Petersons."

Bree and Shay left the room. "Now," Bree said, lifting one dark brow. "Why exactly did Cody handcuff you to the bed?"

Tristol hovered outside the window, watching Malek pace the floor, his ear to the phone. "When I get back from Scotland, you'd better have Shay and the book," Malek hissed. He stopped, his face convulsing, but he controlled the shift. "She's with Cody MacBain! He's the one. Get her away from him. If she's Edward Rodgers's daughter, she and the warrior can't be allowed to breed."

Edward Rodgers? The shock of that name jerked Tristol upright from his hiding place. The woman who stole the book could be Edward's daughter? Was this the real reason Malek wanted her? Did he know about the powerful emerald Edward Rodgers was supposed to possess? This shed new light on things, but he didn't have time to investigate. The Dark One had summoned him again. It was getting tedious, continuing this thousand-year-old charade, when he needed to monitor his prisoner. Tristol found his lieutenant and issued new instructions. If this Shay woman was Edward's daughter, she was more valuable than any stolen book.

Chapter 5

SHAY WOKE TO THE SMELL OF CODY AND BACON. THE bacon part she understood. The Cody part didn't make sense. A suspicious dent was in the pillow next to hers. Had Cody slept there? She didn't remember anything after that cup of tea he gave her. She sat up, and her head swam as if she had been drugged, or was it the dream of the glowing man again? No, this felt like drugs. Cody must have put something in her tea. She threw on her clothes, brushed her teeth, and stormed out of the room. He had put her in Ewan and Laura's old bedroom, insisting she stay at his house where they could protect her. She found him in the kitchen with Faelan and Bree.

"You bastard! So you've gone from handcuffing me to the bed to drugging me?"

"You drugged her?" Bree asked.

Faelan's eyebrows rose. "You handcuffed her to the bed? Damnation. I wish I'd thought of that."

Bree pointed her finger at him. "Don't even try it."

Cody scowled. "It was just valerian root. You needed rest."

"Rest? I was practically unconscious."

"Maybe Cody was afraid you would bite him again," Faelan said to Shay. Bree elbowed him. "Sorry," he said, grinning.

Cody scooted past Shay. "We're going out to check

the woods again. I want to warn Old Elmer to be on the lookout."

Faelan gave Bree a lingering kiss. Cody looked at Shay's mouth, licked his lips, but kept his distance. "Be back before long. Stay here."

Shay followed him to the door, itching to hit him... or something. "Why don't you just tattoo that on your hand? *Stay here*."

"You look like you want to bite him again." Bree grinned. "Or maybe you want to handcuff him to the bed."

Shay's cell phone rang. She grabbed it, hoping it was Renee. It was Jamie. She hadn't talked to him since he moved from Scotland to Virginia.

"So what's up with the table? Is it a consolation prize, or have you changed your mind?"

"Table?"

"I've got a table here with my name on it. It came from your shop in Leesburg."

"I didn't send it." Why would Renee send Jamie a table? "What kind of table?"

"It has four legs, a top... it's a table."

"Funny. Pretend you're describing your knife collection."

"Hmmm, it's round, dark wood, has these little drawers in the middle and doors on the sides. Funny designs on the edges."

The mate to the one in Scotland. The one Julie had canceled. Why would Renee send it to Jamie?

"Keep it there. I'm coming to get it." Jamie's place in Luray wasn't that far away.

"You're taking it back?" Jamie asked.

"It might be a clue."

"To what?"

"Someone broke into my shop in Scotland and destroyed the mate to that table. The shop in Leesburg was vandalized too, and last night someone broke in here."

"Your house?" Jamie asked, alarmed.

"No. I'm in Virginia, at Aunt Nina's."

"I'm coming to get you."

"No. I need to get away from the house for a while anyway. I'm bringing a friend with me."

"Who?" he demanded.

"A woman."

"You trust her?"

"I do." She did. It was one of those instant connections, like with Lucy Bell and Renee. And Cody. They didn't happen often, but when they did, it was strong.

"If you're not here in two hours, I'm coming after you."

"Cody's going to kill you, you know," Bree said, when Shay told her where she was headed. He and Faelan were out in the woods, trying to track whoever broke in.

"I'm not sitting around like a prisoner. Anyway, it's probably safer away from the scene of the crime."

Bree grabbed her purse. "I like the way you think. Let's go get the table. Some fresh air and excitement will do me good. We'll be back before the men know we're gone. What about the cat?" It sat in the doorway, ears raised like antennae, eyes so green they seemed to glow.

"I'll put it outside. Maybe it'll get bored and go home."

"Why are men so overbearing?" Shay asked as they drove.

"They can't help it," Bree said. "I think they're all born that way. My father would hardly let me out of his sight."

"Why?" Shay asked.

"I think he got paranoid after my Aunt Layla died. She was only twenty-five. As if my father weren't protective enough, I go and find Faelan buried in the family graveyard, and he's even worse. When he gets too chivalrous, I remind him how many times I've rescued him."

"I bet that goes over well," Shay said, thinking how fierce Faelan looked.

"Like a ton of bricks. We fight as hard as we love. How can you not argue with a man who believes women should sit at home while men protect them? You should've seen his face when he found out Sorcha was a warrior. You haven't met her yet. Picture Xena the warrior princess with red hair. And Anna. Actually Anna has the black hair and turquoise eyes. Drop dead gorgeous and tough as nails. Faelan doesn't have a clue what to do with them. They didn't have female warriors in his day."

"There are female warriors?"

"I keep forgetting, all this is new to you. I'm sorry," Bree said, catching Shay's frown. "I know it bothers you that they hid your identity from you. That's a bummer, growing up thinking you're someone else, not knowing your real family. I'd be angry too, but if there's one thing I've learned in the short time I've known these warriors, it's that they're as protective as grizzlies when it comes to family. It's instilled in them in the womb, this need to protect, to guard, even strangers." She rubbed her stomach again. "Did they tell you anything about your real parents?"

"Only their names. Edward and Elizabeth Rodgers. I know everyone thought they were doing the right thing, but I can't help feeling betrayed."

"Betrayal sucks," Bree said, a shadow of pain clouding her eyes. "Don't be too hard on Cody for hiding your identity. He was only doing his job. Did you know he was punished by the Council of Elders for telling you that your past was faked? Even though he didn't tell you about the clan, he told you your real name, and that opened Pandora's box."

"Punished? What did they do to him?"

"I don't know. I just overheard part of a conversation. The Council of Elders isn't to be taken lightly. They're like the supreme court of the clan."

"I had no idea." Had he suffered because of her?

"Will they punish him for telling me this time?"

"I don't know enough about the Council. Only acknowledged warriors can get near them. I hope Cody's reputation will weigh in his favor. Since the seventeenth century, he and Faelan are the only warriors who've been assigned one of the demons of old. Everyone in the clan looks up to them."

Cody, her Cody, had done this?

"I hope you realize how lucky you are. Most women would kill to have a man look at them like Cody looks at you. He's in love with you, you know?"

Shay swallowed, feeling panic rising in her throat. In love?

"I'd hate for Old Elmer to get caught in this mess," Cody said to Faelan as the truck bumped along the

dirt road leading to the old man's cabin. There was
an easy silence between the warriors. Faelan was the
only one who understood the pressures of being assigned an ancient demon. Other than his own clan,
most warriors treated him with awe or envy, neither
of which he wanted. All he wanted was to do his job
so he could keep his mind off Shay. That would never
happen; he knew it now. No matter if she was in another country or in the next room, nothing would get
her off his mind.

Cody parked his truck, and he and Faelan got out.
Old Elmer's front porch ran the length of the cabin
with a railing waist high. A solitary rocker sat by an
old table that held a cup and a book. Old Elmer liked to
read. He had no TV or electricity. The cabin had only
rough plumbing and a woodstove for heat. The interior
was little more than three rooms. Cody had only been
inside once, a long time ago. He couldn't remember
what it looked like. Both the MacBains and Nina had
offered Elmer a job, and when that didn't work, they
tried to install electricity, but he liked things the way
they were. He did allow them to give him books or
a batch of cookies. In turn, they noticed little repairs
miraculously done. A squeaky door greased or loose
barn plank nailed, and he had an eerie way of showing
up when someone was in trouble, like some kind of
guardian angel.

"Looks quiet," Faelan said as they climbed the
steps. A walking stick stood by the door, but Old Elmer
had several.

"He's probably hunting. He takes what he needs to
survive with an old bow. If he's not here, I'll leave a

note on the door." Cody knocked. No answer. A prickle settled between his shoulder blades. He saw Faelan's nose to the wind, eyes alert. "We're being watched," Cody said quietly.

"Aye," Faelan said. "I hope it's an animal."

Cody searched the trees, sniffing the air. No demon, not in natural form, anyway, but they didn't know for sure that Shay's intruder was a demon. "Let's get out of here." He felt uneasy being away from Shay. How had he survived nine years without her, when he couldn't go ten minutes without needing to see her face, even knowing she was angry enough to stab him. Cody left a note on Elmer's door and started for his truck.

Something white streaked through the trees. Cody and Faelan both whirled, pulling daggers from their boots. They both hit the catches, extending the blades into full swords. The sound of clanging metal echoed off the trees. Something moved off to the left. "I think it was just an owl," Faelan said.

"There's one around here."

"A big white one?"

Cody nodded and retracted his sword blade.

"We have one in New York like that," Faelan said. His cell phone rang. "It's Ronan." Faelan stuck his sword in the ground, leaning on it as he listened. "Bree and Shay? They're at Cody's, why? Damnation." Faelan retracted his blade and motioned Cody toward the truck. "I remember what she did to Conall... you don't have to remind me."

"What have they done?" Cody asked, shutting the door.

"Ronan said they aren't answering the phone." Faelan hung up and dialed another number. "Where are you?

Luray? Where the hell's Luray?" He scowled. "Text me the address. Aye, I can text. Ronan showed me how. Are you doing this because we missed our honeymoon? I told you I was sorry you had to bail me out of jail, but if you don't stop disobeying me, I'm going to start carrying handcuffs."

"Disobeying?" Bree was yelling so loud Cody didn't need a warrior's ears to hear. "I can't believe you said that to me. I'm hanging up."

"Don't—" Faelan glared at the phone. "Bloody woman. They're on their way to someplace called Luray. Shay's boyfriend has a table Renee sent him, just like the one that was destroyed in her shop. She thinks it could be a clue."

"Boyfriend? She said she didn't have a boyfriend."

"Don't growl at me. I'm just repeating what I heard. You're paying for my bloody honeymoon when this is over."

Jamie's house was a brick Victorian on several acres just outside town. It used to belong to his grandfather. Jamie spent a lot of time there. That's where he'd met Marcas and Lachlan, on a camping trip nearby. They'd been friends ever since. He'd put a lot of work into the place. It was the picture of domestic tranquility. Shay touched the white porch swing and felt a twinge of regret.

"The door's open," Bree said.

"Jamie, we're coming in." The first thing they noticed was the overturned table. "Jamie?"

"Oh no." Bree hurried toward the living room, and Shay followed. Jamie lay face down on the floor.

Shay knelt and checked his pulse. "He's breathing. Jamie? Can you hear me? Help me turn him over." He groaned as they rolled him. "There's a phone in the kitchen. Call 911." Shay cradled his head. He had a knot on his forehead and a large gash on his arm.

"No hospital," he said, voice uneven.

"You need a doctor."

"No," Jamie mumbled. "No doctor."

"He sounds like Faelan," Bree said.

"Where does it hurt?" Shay asked Jamie, but he closed his eyes again. She checked him over, hands prodding body parts she once touched in other ways. "I think his head and arms took the worst of it. Let's get him to the couch. You get his feet."

Bree eyed Jamie's six-foot, two-inch muscular frame and touched her stomach. "He looks heavy."

"He is," Shay said, remembering exactly how heavy he was.

Bree grabbed his feet while Shay put her hands under his shoulders and pulled. "Lord, what's he made of?" Bree grunted.

"I think we're doing more damage than good," Shay said. They were both panting, smeared with blood, and still hadn't lifted him onto the couch.

"I'll get a washcloth," Bree said.

"There's some in the hall closet, and get some ice from the kitchen."

Before Bree could leave, Jamie opened his eyes and groaned.

"What happened?" Shay asked.

He touched her face. "You're safe. I was afraid you'd get here before they left. Who's she?"

"My friend, Bree. What happened to you?" Shay asked.

"There were four of them." He groaned and sat up. "Felt like twice that. Didn't even hear them come in."

"Sit still," Shay said. "You could have other injuries."

"I'm fine," he said, flexing his arms. "Just banged up."

Shay looked at his wound. "Your cut doesn't look nearly as bad as it did a minute ago."

"Uh… I need a bandage," he said, grimacing as he quickly stood.

"I'll get it," Bree offered.

"No. You two check out the table," Jamie said, holding his hand over the cut. "They seemed more interested in it than me."

"The table? Are you serious? You could've been killed," Shay said.

"I'll be back as soon as I wash off this blood." He walked toward the bathroom. Shay and Bree examined the table while they waited for him.

"What is it with these tables?" Shay asked.

"It's pretty," Bree said, touching the top.

"But not that valuable. It's only 1890s… Bree, are you okay?"

"That's better," Jamie said, entering the room. He had washed off the blood, put on a clean shirt, and bandaged his arm.

"You scared the heck out of me." Shay wrapped her arms around his waist, and he pulled her close, dropping a kiss on her head.

"What the hell?" said a voice from the doorway.

Shay and Jamie turned. Cody stood just inside the door, his face drained of color. A flush of anger crept up his neck. "Jamie Waters? He's your boyfriend?"

Shay stepped away from Jamie. "He's not my boyfriend."

Cody stormed across the room. "You know the rules. Does the clan know about this?"

"The clan?" Shay asked. "Jamie knows about your clan?"

"You didn't tell her, did you? You bastard!" Cody threw the first punch. It hit Jamie's chin, and he staggered.

"Stop it! He's hurt," Shay yelled.

Jamie returned the swing, catching Cody in the jaw.

Shay jumped between them, and they both drew up short, glaring at each other over her head. "What's going on?"

"Ask your boyfriend about his talisman."

"Talisman?" She looked at Jamie. Guilt was written on his face. Her gaze fell to the necklace he never took off, not even in bed. He'd said it was a family heirloom. It resembled Cody's. And Marcas's. And Lachlan's. "No," she whispered.

"I'm sorry, Shay," Jamie said. "I didn't intend—"

"You're one of them?" She backed away until she hit something solid. Strong hands gripped her shoulders. Shay turned, her eyes level with Faelan's necklace—talisman—outlined beneath his shirt.

"You're bleeding. Where's Bree?" He followed Shay's gaze to where Bree stood by the overturned table, bloody hands extended over it, a blank look in her eyes, while Cody and Jamie hurled insults like knives.

"Be quiet," Faelan told them. He hurried to her side. "She's having a vision."

Bree ran her hands down the front of the table,

reached underneath, and a drawer popped out. A piece of paper lay inside.

"I didn't know it did that," Shay said.

Bree snapped out of her vision as Faelan reached for the paper. "The *Book of Battles*." His voice was grainy, like it was made of sand. "It's the last page from the *Book of Battles*."

"What's a *Book of Battles*?" Shay asked, alarmed at the stricken looks on the faces around her, even Jamie's. She was the outsider again.

"You think the book was in there?" Jamie asked.

"You're the one with the table. Why don't you tell us?" Cody said.

"Go to hell, MacBain."

"You were sent to protect her," Cody growled. "Not sleep with her."

"You were sent to protect me?" Shay shook her head in disbelief.

"I'm sorry, Shay. Marcas and Lachlan asked me to keep an eye on you. I didn't mean to—"

Cody stepped in front of Jamie. Shay slipped from the room while they circled each other like predators.

Shay dug for her keys as she hurried to her car, but they weren't in her pocket. She must have dropped them when she and Bree moved Jamie. She wasn't going back in there. She looked inside Cody's truck. His keys were in the ignition. He could drive her car or stay with Jamie. As far as she was concerned, Cody and Jamie could both rot in hell.

Bree ran out as Shay opened Cody's truck door. "Where are you going?"

"I need to get away from here."

"You can't go alone. It's too dangerous." A roar erupted from inside the house. "Heck. I'm coming with you." Bree opened the passenger door and slid in. "Let them fight it out."

———

The servant parked down the street, watching the house through binoculars. It was the ex-boyfriend's house. What was she doing there? Reconciling? A truck pulled into the driveway, and two men got out. The warrior who was always with her, the one the master said she had to stay away from, and the man in the kilt. He was tired of all these men hovering. It was impossible to get near her. Her house was like a damned hotel. Was she sleeping with one—or all—of them?

The rage built inside him, growing until he thought it might burn him alive. He pulled out his knife, put it to his arm, and stopped. He'd cut something, all right. The master said it was crucial that they not have children. He couldn't kill her yet, even if the master wanted him too, but he could get rid of the warrior. The master would like that.

After the men entered the house, he pulled closer and parked his car behind a thick maple covered with red leaves. He glanced at the house. All clear. He approached the man's truck and lay down beside the wheel, holding his knife and an empty 7-11 coffee cup. It didn't take long.

Hurrying back to his car, he moved out of sight and wiped the fluid from his knife blade with a dirty handkerchief. He heard an engine start, and the warrior's truck backed out of the driveway. It wouldn't be long.

As the truck sped by his hiding place, he saw Shay in the driver's seat.

"No!" he screamed.

———◊◊◊———

"Get your hands off me—" Jamie said, bristling.

"Shut up! Both of you," Faelan shouted, pulling Jamie and Cody apart. "Where's Bree and Shay?"

An engine roared to life. "That's my truck," Cody said. "Damn it, that's my truck!" They sprinted outside in time to see the Toyota pull away with Shay and Bree inside. "Stop!"

The truck kept going, spitting dirt and gravel. Cody ran to Shay's rental car and yanked open the door. "No keys."

"We can take my truck." Jamie ran into the house and returned with keys to his grandfather's faded green Chevy. Faelan shoved Cody in the middle and climbed in beside him. The old engine thundered and grumbled. Jamie threw it in drive and pulled onto the road. The men bounced along, jammed shoulder to shoulder, as the truck whined and climbed the winding mountain road.

"If you two weren't fighting, they wouldn't have run off," Faelan said.

Cody didn't know Jamie as well as his brothers did, but he always considered him a friend. A few weeks ago, Marcas told Cody they'd had Jamie keeping an eye on Shay for the past several months, since he lived in Scotland, not far from Shay. They hadn't bothered to tell him Jamie was her bloody boyfriend. Cody had gone to Scotland to find her as soon as his duty was over. He'd felt as nervous and excited as a teenager... until he saw the ring on her hand.

"Why didn't you tell me you were engaged to her when I saw you in Scotland?" Cody asked Jamie. He'd sat next to Jamie at the castle, never dreaming it was his ring Cody had seen on Shay's finger.

"Marcas told me to keep my mouth shut. And Shay and I weren't together then anyway," Jamie said, his voice tight.

They reached the top of the mountain, nearing the entrance to Skyline Drive. "Any idea which road they took?" Faelan asked.

"Call them," Jamie said.

Cody and Faelan looked at each other. "My phone's in the truck," Cody said.

"Mine too. Use yours," Faelan said to Jamie.

Jamie grimaced. "It's in the house."

"Shay'll take Skyline Drive," Cody said. "She likes the scenery."

"I know that," Jamie said.

"I see them. Won't this thing go faster?" Faelan grumbled as they turned onto the scenic mountaintop road. He shifted, knocking Cody in the ribs, and peered out the window. "Nandor was quicker than this."

"This truck's probably just as old," Cody muttered.

"I should have connected the dots," Shay said as the truck moved along the scenic drive. "Those blasted necklaces—talismans. But I grew up around men who wore necklaces... wait, are the tattoos part of all this?"

"Yes. All warriors have them."

Shay thumped her palm on the steering wheel. "Is there anyone who hasn't lied to me?"

"I don't blame you for being angry, but keep in mind that warriors are sworn to secrecy," Bree said. "They can't reveal clan secrets without permission from the Council."

"But the man asked me to marry him and never bothered to mention he was a warrior sent to baby-sit me!"

"Men can be jackasses sometimes, but don't forget how much they've all sacrificed to protect you. Especially Cody."

There was something in Bree's voice that made Shay look at her. "What's wrong?"

"I don't know. Just this feeling. There's something about this whole thing. I don't think it's just about you. I think Cody is involved too."

"You think the stalker is after Cody?" Shay glanced in the rearview mirror, frowning, and the truck swerved toward the low wall that lined the road.

"It's somehow connected to both of you. Do you want me to drive?" Bree asked.

Shay frowned. "No. Sorry, I thought I recognized the car behind us."

"They'll be following us, no doubt about that."

"Not the men. It looks like Renee's car." The truck veered again, moving close to the wall that blocked the drop to the valley far below. Shay tapped the brakes, but the truck picked up speed.

"Could we slow down a tad? My stomach's feeling queasy." The tires squealed as Shay rounded the curve. The truck scraped the wall, throwing Bree into the door.

Shay gripped the steering wheel and pumped the

brakes. "The brakes aren't working!" She pulled the truck back onto the road, and it continued picking up speed. She tried to calm her panic and listen for Cody's voice. *Keep a clear head. Think. You've been equipped with what you need.* She pictured his face as the next curve loomed ahead. "Hang on, I'm going to try to slow the truck down."

"Hurry!" Bree's panicked voice sounded far away. The engine whined as Shay lowered it to third, then second gear. The truck slowed, but they were still approaching the next curve too fast. She dropped it to first, and the truck jerked.

"Hold on," Shay yelled.

"Oh my God! We're going over!" Bree covered her stomach with both hands as they hurtled toward the edge of the mountain.

—⁓—

"I see something red," Faelan said, craning his neck. "No, that's a car. It's the same color as Cody's truck."

Cody squinted. "There they are. A few curves ahead."

"I see them," Jamie said, speeding up. "What the— she almost hit the wall!"

"What's she doing?" Faelan scooted forward.

Cody moved to avoid getting his ribs cracked and bumped Jamie's arm, causing the truck to jerk. "Something's wrong," he said, as they lost sight of Cody's truck.

Faelan had his knees against the dashboard, head moving like a bobblehead doll, trying to spot Cody's truck. "Where'd they go?"

Cody shoved Faelan's hand off his leg and tried to scoot forward. "There it is. She's going too fast." The truck righted itself, only to veer toward the next over-look. It lurched several times, slowing, but not enough.

"Damnation—"

"She's headed for the drop-off!" Cody's throat went dry. They watched as the truck careened toward the edge and disappeared. Jamie jammed the accelerator to the floor.

As soon as they reached the accident site, Faelan opened the door and jumped out before the truck came to a complete stop. Cody was on his heels. He could see the red car speeding around the next bend. Bastard hadn't even stopped. The front of Cody's truck was wedged against a cedar, the only thing keeping it from plunging down the mountain. The passenger door was open, and Bree lay on her side a few feet away.

"*Mo ghaol.*" Faelan's voice was choked as he dropped beside Bree.

"Shay!" Cody rushed to the driver's side, skidding to a halt as the ground dropped away. He ran around to the other side, where Faelan was trying to wake Bree. Blood trickled from Bree's head, and three tiny drops were on the back of her neck, peeking out from under her hair. Or was it a mark? There was something odd about it.

Cody edged around them and peered in the open passenger door. A flip-flop lay on the floor and another on the seat, but Shay wasn't there. His heart thudded. Had she been thrown out? The pine creaked and the truck shifted. God, don't let her be under there. Cody knelt to check, but the space beneath the truck was covered with rocks and trees that could hide a body.

Jamie rushed up, carrying a wench line. "Attach this to the frame. If that tree snaps, the truck's gone."

"Shay's not in the truck," Cody said.

"Then where…" Jamie paled. Both men looked down the mountainside, covered in trees and jagged rocks that could shatter bones and tear flesh. Even if she was alive, if she was in the path of the truck, it would crush her.

"Hurry." Cody put the hook in place while Jamie rushed back to his Chevy and tightened the line, steadying the truck. "I'll check down there," Cody said. "You check the top."

"Shay!" Cody yelled, scrambling down the hill, holding onto trees. He wedged his feet against outcroppings of rocks to keep from falling.

"She's here!" Jamie called a minute later.

Blood rushed past Cody's ears like a cracked dam. She was upset when she left. She must have forgotten to fasten the seat belt and been thrown. He pulled himself back up, one tree at a time. Faelan still held Bree, but she was conscious, struggling to get up.

"Where's Shay?" she asked.

"Here," Jamie called. He was bent down close to the road. A pair of bare feet stuck out from behind a rock.

Cody ran, every muscle and bone in his body screaming with fear. He couldn't lose her. He couldn't. Shay's eyes were closed. Cody dropped beside her. "Is she—?"

Shay's eyes fluttered, and she touched her stomach. "Baby."

He was so glad she was alive that it took a minute for the words to sink in. Baby? Cody stared at her stomach as his turned. Was Shay pregnant?

Chapter 6

DUNCAN CONNOR TAPPED HIS BOOT IMPATIENTLY against the tire as Sorcha dug through one of her bags, giving him an unwanted glimpse of too much sleek, toned leg under her black skirt.

"I hope there's a horde of demons waiting," she said. "I've got all this pent-up energy since the battle with Druan. I need some hard, physical activity before I go insane."

Kill me now. "Can whatever you're doing wait? We'll be there in an hour. What'd you do, bring your whole closet?"

"Stuff it, cousin. I've got a lot on my mind. There." Sorcha pulled out her small dagger, a *sgian dubh*, and tucked it inside her boot, giving Duncan another unwelcome glimpse.

"Sorcha, your turn to baby-sit," Anna said, opening the front passenger side of the SUV. "You know how I feel about kids."

Brodie crossed his muscular arms over his chest. "Blimey. A guy tries to have a little fun, and that's cause to treat him like a kid? What's wrong, Anna, you got PMS? You've been in a foul mood for days."

Sorcha opened the back door and glared at Brodie. "No practical jokes. If I see a snake anywhere in this vehicle, I'll tie your legs around your neck and strangle you."

Duncan grinned. She could do it. He started the engine and pulled away from the rest area.

"So Cody MacBain and the Mighty Faelan, two of the most powerful warriors in clan history, need our help," Brodie said. "I'm not sure whether to be honored or petrified."

"If you and Ronan don't stop calling Faelan that," Duncan said, "you're gonna wish you were in a time vault. So what's Shay's story, and why is Cody so worked up about her?"

Anna flipped open her notebook. "Her real name is Dana Michelle Rodgers. Her father was a warrior, Edward Rodgers, a warrior from the Connor clan. When Shay was a baby, she was almost killed in a car accident in Scotland. The mother died, but Shay survived. An old man rescued her. The clan thought she had been marked by a demon. They didn't know if she was the target or if it was just revenge, so they faked her death, changed her identity, and moved her to America in the middle of the night, sending Cody's father, Ewan MacBain and his whole family to protect her."

"Ewan MacBain?" Brodie said. "I've heard of him."

"And the woman who raised her?" Sorcha asked.

"Ewan's wife's half sister, Nina. Her husband was a friend of Ewan's."

"So Shay never knew her father was a warrior?" Sorcha asked.

Anna shook her head. "They decided it was more important to hide her than to reveal her past. They figured if she survived her childhood, they'd tell her. This is where it gets confusing. Just as they were ready to tell her, Shay moved to Lake Placid with her best friend, Renee, and refused to have anything to do with the clan. It's not common knowledge, but I've heard rumors that Cody almost walked away from his duty."

"I can't imagine a warrior as powerful as Cody refusing his duty. Must be a story there," Sorcha said.

Anna closed her notebook. "A few years after college, she went to live in Scotland."

"They let her go?" Duncan asked.

"The demon her father had been hunting at the time disappeared. Right before Cody was about to tell Shay who she was, they found out the demon was dead. The clan thought she was safe," Anna said.

"And out of the blue, she's in danger again," Brodie said.

"And her friend in Leesburg somehow gets her hands on *our* book and sends it to Shay's ex-boyfriend. Is anyone else disturbed by this?" Sorcha added.

"I've been disturbed for the past month," Brodie said. "Vampires and demons, and now we've got to ask who in his right mind would go up against the Mighty Faelan and Cody MacBain."

Malek reached through the shattered window and felt for the baby's pulse. None. A smile crept over his lips. Her face was plump, cherubic, eyes closed as if asleep. The fire hadn't reached her yet, but it would soon. Perhaps it was the frustration that had been building for the better part of two centuries that caused him to run one long claw down the tiny shoulder, bared by a flowered sundress.

A large owl swooped down, landing in the crooked branches of a pine, as Malek watched the letter fill with blood. Destroying her would eliminate his enemy before he was even born. He stepped back from the flames so his human skin wouldn't sear, while the owl watched with round, unblinking eyes. Malek let out a roar of triumph. The job was done. All he needed now was the book.

The ping of shovel on metal brought Malek back to the present.

The halfling in the grave raised his head and grinned, showing long, yellow teeth. "We found it, Master."

Malek kicked dirt off his shoe and ran his finger over the name etched under the angel's wing as the men positioned the ropes. Had he been tricked? Had he spent the past twenty-six years deceived by mere humans? If he was right about the contents of the grave, Shay Logan and Cody MacBain must be killed without delay. The night breeze ruffled his hair, irritating him. "Hurry."

The men stood on each side and slowly raised the tiny casket. Moonlight glinted off the white lid.

"Move!" He shoved them aside, grabbed the shovel, and wedged in under the lid, prying it open. He looked at the satin trim and tiny pillow. No body. His claws extended, bones stretched, and skin thickened. "No," he roared, as the others ran for cover. "No!"

Cody brushed a strand of hair from Shay's forehead. His neck tingled, like it always did when she was near. He touched her lips, remembering the agony of those few moments he feared she was dead. He couldn't live without her. He was deceiving himself if he believed otherwise, yet he couldn't force her to love him.

There was also Jamie to worry about, and what Shay had said after the accident. Maybe he misheard. Jamie hadn't mentioned it, and Cody hadn't had the guts to ask. If Jamie had gotten Shay pregnant and abandoned her, Cody would kill him. Or was that why Jamie was here? Had he just found out Shay carried his child? That might give him cause to stalk her.

"She needs rest," the sullen nurse said, refilling Shay's pitcher of water.

Shay and Bree had been checked out at the hospital and released, both suffering from concussions. Cody had gotten Marcas to find the closest clan nurse to make sure the women followed orders, but looking at her dour face, he regretted it. The woman had the bedside manner of a goat.

"Ba…" Shay turned her head, her fingers gripping the sheet over her stomach. "Baby."

Cody's ham sandwich started climbing up his throat. He tried convincing himself again that she was just saying something that sounded like baby.

The nurse moved closer, staring at Shay. "Is she pregnant?"

"I don't know."

She looked at him as if he were a worm. "You don't know?"

"She's not married."

"I thought you were her husband."

He shook his head.

"Who are you?"

"A friend."

"Humph," she said, as if he'd tricked her. "Well, go on, now, and let her rest. You can come back later. You should get some dinner." She touched her nose. "And take a shower."

She was right. He could smell his own sweat. He'd

spent every spare moment near her, trying to outlast Jamie, who was doing the same. Both of them bounced back and forth between sitting with Shay and standing guard. What would he do if Shay was carrying Jamie's child? His stomach knotted up just thinking about it. Cody pulled two Rolaids out of the packet he kept in his pocket since Shay was back. His phone rang. It was his FBI contact.

"Someone's opened the grave."

Cody walked down the hall to his room. "Shay's grave?"

"And they opened the casket. The body's gone. Want to tell me why someone would open a twenty-five-year-old grave?" Sam asked.

To see if a body was inside? "You're better off not knowing. When did it happen?"

"Probably dug it up during the past thirty-six hours. Police are blaming vandals."

Cody kicked off his boots. "We both know it's not."

"You might. I don't know what the heck it is. This stuff's getting old. I could lose my job."

"I know. I appreciate all you've done for us." Sam wasn't even a buffer, one of the humans who knew about the warriors and helped hide their secrets so warriors could fight evil without fear of being arrested by the ones they fought to protect. They had buffers at all levels, local, state, and international. In this day of information and technology, the warriors needed help covering their tracks. Usually an entire generation served as buffers, which helped keep the knowledge contained. Sam was more effective than most of them. Cody should make it official.

"Enough to tell me what it's about? I've covered up stuff I can't even explain. Like that *drug bust* in Albany. Those men in that hotel weren't... normal. I feel like I'm the freakin' *X-Files*."

"I know. If you want me to, I'll explain after all this is over, but you might wish I hadn't." The clan wouldn't like it either, but Sam deserved some answers.

"Nothing would shock me concerning you. I'll try to keep the grave robbing away from the press, but I can't promise anything. This stuff stirs up public interest, and it's getting close to Halloween."

Cody hung up, took a quick shower, and headed back toward Shay's room before Jamie got back and monopolized her time. All the while, Cody thought about Shay's fake grave and how close she'd come to having a real one today. He had just replaced the brake pads and rotors on his truck the week before. Had he screwed something up? If this was his fault— His train of thought was interrupted when he ran into Lachlan, Marcas, and Ronan on their way out.

"Heard from the mechanic yet?" Lachlan asked.

"No. He towed the truck. He's checking it out now."

The nurse appeared at the top of the stairs, carrying a tray. She glared down at Cody, who had one foot on the bottom step. "Where do you think you're going?"

The woman acted like it was her bloody house. "To check on Shay." He glared back, daring her to stop him.

"You can't. She has someone with her. He requested a few minutes of privacy."

Cody bounded up the stairs, head exploding with visions of the blond intruder. He heard his brothers and Ronan behind him.

The nurse planted herself in the way, and Cody stopped, rather than plow her down, which is what he would have preferred to do. The door was cracked. Cody saw Jamie lean over and press his lips to Shay's forehead.

"What the hell is he still doing here?" Cody asked. "I thought he left."

"*He's* her boyfriend," the nurse said, as if Cody had misled her into believing he was Shay's husband.

"Boyfriend, my ass." He started toward the door, but Marcas grabbed his arm.

"Give him a break," Lachlan muttered. "Jamie's a good guy."

"If he's a good guy, why did he take advantage of her? He was sent to protect her, not—"

Marcas lifted one brow, the way he always did when he knew more than he let on, which was most of the time. "Sure you want to go there, little Brother?"

Cody had sometimes wondered if Marcas knew the truth about him and Shay.

"Yeah," Lach agreed. "Who went and told Shay her whole life was a lie, before the clan even had time to prepare her?"

Cody looked at Jamie, feeling the knife twist inside. Shay had spent months with Jamie, talking with him, sharing her life with him. He gritted his teeth. Sleeping with him. Maybe getting pregnant by him. "I'm going in," he said, brushing the nurse's hand aside. "Time's up, Waters."

Marcas and Lachlan followed. Ronan put his hand on the nurse's back. "We'll just be a minute," Ronan said, winking at her. "What can it hurt? She's sleeping."

The nurse flushed, looking at all five men dwarfing

the room. She rolled her eyes. "Five minutes, then I'll toss all of you out. I don't care how big or how good-looking you are."

———✦———

"Come on, Cody, we don't have all night." Shay glanced over her shoulder as she ran toward the barn. The weather was warm for October, and the smell of fall reminded her of pumpkins and the haunted trail they used to make every Halloween. They had grown too old for monsters and demons and fake swords. She missed it. Missed the closeness. They were all growing up, and it scared her. She was afraid she would wake up one morning and they'd all be gone. How would she live? They were her family, her whole life.

"I thought Nina already checked the barn," Cody grumbled behind her. He was home from college for a few days. He seemed different, older, as if he knew things she didn't, and it bothered her. They'd always shared everything. He looked different, too, taller, his shoulders broader, and muscles popping out everywhere. He was also grouchy as a bear. He had barely spoken two words since he arrived. If she didn't know better, she would have thought he was avoiding her. It made her sad, since he was all she had thought about for months.

"She didn't check the hayloft. The cat might have gone there to have her kittens."

Cody held the narrow ladder for her and then followed. "You check this side; I'll check over there," he said when they reached the top. He turned away, but not fast enough. Shay didn't miss his quick glance at her breasts.

That was strange. The last thing Cody MacBain

*would be interested in was her breasts. She was the one
with the obsession eating her alive.*

*They spent several minutes searching. "There's no
cat here," Cody said, leaning over a stack of hay bales,
stretching his faded Levi's across his rear.*

*She was so preoccupied with his butt, she caught her
foot on a piece of twine and fell flat on her face.*

"You okay?" Cody asked.

*"Just winded." She rolled to her back, trying to catch
her breath. She realized how stupid she must look and
glanced up at Cody, expecting to see him laughing at
her. He wasn't.*

*The muscles in his jaw tensed as he leaned down and
stretched his hand out to help her up. She slipped her
hand in his, gave a nervous laugh, and tugged, hoping
if he fell too, it would wipe that somber look off his face.
Caught off balance, he tumbled forward, landing on top
of her. Once again, her breath whooshed out. His eyes
were dark, and she could see a muscle ticking in his jaw.
His gaze dropped to her mouth and he licked his lips a
moment before lowering his head.*

Shay woke to voices, one of them Cody's. At first she
thought it was the dream, and then she saw the men ar-
guing near the bed. Cody and Jamie were in the middle
of the fray.

"Stop it," Shay said softly.

Cody whirled at her voice, and both he and Jamie
rushed to her side. Lachlan, Ronan, and Marcas were
behind them.

Shay's eyes sought Cody's, mentally comparing this
version with the Cody in her dream. It was like comparing a tiger to a house cat.

"How are you feeling?" Cody asked, stepping in front of Jamie.

"I'm fine." It took a few seconds to shake the heaviness of the dream. In the hours since the accident, every time she closed her eyes, she had jumbled dreams; the accident, the past, Renee, and the glowing man she couldn't see, who wanted her to do something she couldn't understand. She couldn't do anything about the accident or the past, and she couldn't make sense of the glowing man, but she could do something about Renee.

Jamie stepped closer, edging Cody aside. "Do you want something to eat?"

"Thanks, but not now." Shay threw back her covers and stood.

The scar above Cody's eyebrow deepened with his frown. "What do you think you're doing?"

"I'm getting up."

"You need rest," Cody said, glancing at her stomach.

"You hit your head," Jamie added, also looking at her stomach. "You have a concussion."

If she had a concussion, why were they looking at her stomach? She touched it, and Cody and Jamie clenched their jaws in an alarmingly similar fashion. "It's not the first concussion I've had. I doubt it will be the last. Did someone call Renee's parents?"

"They're not answering," Marcus said.

"You still think you saw Renee's car?" Ronan asked.

Shay knew they didn't believe her. "I know it was. She has a little rainbow sticker on the bumper."

"Did you see her before or after you hit your head?" Lachlan asked.

Shay scowled at him.

"If it was Renee, she would have stopped," Cody said gently.

Jamie nodded. "Renee wouldn't have left you there."

At least they were agreeing on something, but Shay knew what she had seen. She picked up her clothes. "She would have if she didn't have a choice."

Marcas frowned. "You didn't actually see her?"

"No. Her side windows are tinted."

"Whoever it was drove off after seeing them crash," Cody said.

"Who would drive past an accident with someone trying to wave them down for help?" Jamie asked.

Ronan rested a thumb in the pocket of his jeans. "Someone who didn't want to be seen."

"I think she's in trouble and couldn't stop. Where's my cell phone?" Shay asked.

"It's probably still in the truck," Cody said. "Get back in bed. We're trying to track Renee down."

"It was only a bump on the head." She ruined the declaration by swaying. Cody and Jamie both leapt at her, as if she teetered on the edge of a ten-story building. "What's wrong with you two?" One or the other, sometimes both, had been there every time she woke up. "Am I dying?"

"No," Cody said.

"Then get out. I'm getting dressed. I'm going to check on Bree, and then I'm going to find Renee. You can help me or not."

"We brought your rental car back from Jamie's, but surely to God you don't think we're just going to let you walk out of here with a stalker after you," Cody said, glaring at her.

The warriors moved in closer, creating a wall of muscle.

"What are you going to do? Handcuff me to the bed again?"

"What?" Jamie's eyes narrowed.

"He was just trying to restrain her," Marcas said.

"With demon shackles," Lachlan muttered.

"Demon shackles!" Shay said, gawking at Cody.

Jamie's eyes widened. "You used demon shackles?"

"I needed something fast. It was either that or knock her out. I didn't think she'd appreciate that," Cody muttered. "She doesn't realize how dangerous this is."

Shay would have to find out later what demon shackles were. Right now, she wanted out of this room.

Lachlan nodded. "Cody's right, Shay. It's not safe. You can't be alone."

"You can come home with me," Jamie said.

"She's staying here," Cody said.

"Okay, boys, you're not dogs, and she's not a bone. Everyone can stay here. We have plenty of room." Marcas put a hand on Jamie's shoulder. "You're involved in this. There was a reason Renee sent that table to you."

Shay reached for her jeans. "If all of you don't get out now, you're going to see more of me than you want."

"I doubt that, darlin'." Ronan grinned, earning frowns from both Cody and Jamie.

"Don't you all need to go hunt demons or something?" Shay asked. After a minute, she gave up and headed to the bathroom. When she came out, Cody was the only one waiting. "Where's Jamie?" she asked.

"Don't worry. I didn't kill him. He went to check Renee's shop again for her laptop."

"I'm going to see Bree."

"I really think you should—"

"Are you sure there's not something wrong that you're not telling me?"

"I was going to ask you the same thing."

"I'm fine."

They ran into Ronan outside Bree's room. She stood by the bed, glowering at Faelan, who was planted in front of her and appeared to be blocking the door.

Bree's eyes lit up when she saw Shay. "Thank God, a female."

"I'm just trying to keep you safe," Faelan grumbled. "Which you're making damned hard. Are all the women in this century like this?"

"I just hit my head," Bree said. "You hit your head plenty of times. Instead of protecting us, maybe someone would be kind enough to offer us food while Shay and I talk. Girl talk."

The men looked uncomfortable and quickly turned to leave. "What do you want to eat?" Faelan asked from the doorway. "You had dinner not an hour ago."

Bree considered. "Olives… and… Cody, do you have chocolate ice cream?"

"I think so," Cody said. "Uh, you sure about the olives?"

"That sounds bloody awful," Faelan said. "Are you feeling all right?"

"Just hungry," Bree said.

"How about a salad and a glass of milk instead?" Ronan suggested.

"Good idea," Cody said. "I'll bring Shay the same."

Since when had she liked salad and milk? She was beginning to think the men were the ones who hit their heads.

"He's killing me," Bree said, after the men left.

"He loves you." Shay couldn't bear thinking about the anguish Faelan would have suffered if something had happened to Bree, after everything he had already lost.

"Don't." Bree squeezed Shay's hand. "I see that look. It wasn't your fault."

"It was. I shouldn't have rushed out like that."

"The men deserved it, the way they were carrying on. Stop blaming yourself. Something went wrong with the brakes. It happens. Besides…" Bree's eyes clouded. "If it hadn't been you and me, it would've happened to Cody and Faelan. It could've been worse. You know how men drive."

The two women stared at each other as the weight of Bree's words sank in. The thought seemed to deflate Bree as much as it did Shay. "Do you think that's what you sensed about Cody?"

"I don't know, but for now, I'm fine, you're fine, and the men are safe. If we only knew where the book was."

"I heard Cody and his brothers talking about it," Shay said. "What's so important about the book?"

"It belongs to Faelan's clan. The book has a list of battles fought between warriors and demons. It went missing from Scotland in the mid-1800s, around the time Faelan was locked in the time vault. I found it in my attic a few weeks ago."

"You found Faelan and the book? I guess the clan was happy to see you."

"They suspected Faelan had the book with him in the time vault."

"They thought he stole it?"

"They weren't sure what to think, but most of them believed if he did steal it, he must have had a good reason. He was highly revered in the clan, even back then."

"If he didn't take it, how did it get to America?"

"We think the Keeper brought the book when he traveled with Faelan's father and brothers to help him battle Druan. Faelan said there were threats against the book then. The Keeper may have been moving it to protect it."

"How could it have gotten inside that table?" Shay asked.

"I don't know. My ex-fiancé, Russell, stole it from my house. He was helping Druan."

Shay had thought she had it tough. At least the people who lied to her thought they were helping. Maybe that was why she felt such a bond with Bree. She understood the heartache of betrayal.

"What are you going to do about Cody and Jamie?" Bree asked.

"I don't know, but I have to sort it out before they kill each other."

"Are you in love with one of them? Or both?" she added quietly.

She did love them both, but not in the same way. "I don't know what I feel, beyond wanting to wring both their necks."

"I know that feeling well," Bree said, smiling. "Living with a man from the nineteenth century, I guess I got my piece of history. I swear he's driving me crazy with all this hovering. I'd climb out the window and run away, if it weren't for the baby—"

"Baby?"

Bree pressed her lips together, staring at the door. She leaned closer and whispered, "I'm pregnant."

"Pregnant?" Shay grabbed Bree's hand. "The baby, it's all right?"

"It's fine."

"You're sure?"

"Yes. Stop worrying."

"How far along are you?"

"Not far. I wasn't even sure until a couple days ago. You can't say anything to Faelan. He doesn't know."

"Why?"

"If I tell him, he'll worry about me and the baby and won't focus on this battle. I can't take that chance."

"Ronan knows, doesn't he? That's the reason for all the secret looks between you, why he's trying to make you rest and eat healthy."

Bree nodded.

"That's a relief. I was afraid you were having an affair with him."

Bree laughed. "Ronan? I do adore him, but as a friend. I hope Faelan hasn't noticed. He'd kill Ronan if he thought... Maybe I'd better tell him... No. I can't risk it."

They heard Faelan's raised voice out in the hall, fussing at Ronan. "You wouldn't know it to listen to them fight, but he and Ronan are like brothers. I think he reminds Faelan of the ones he lost. He had two, Tavis and Ian, and a sister. She was only thirteen." Bree sighed. "Here I am going on about betrayal, when he lost everything the second that time vault was locked. His family, his world, his time. He would never have been captured if he hadn't been trying to save the warriors who were with him... and his brothers. He didn't want them around when he destroyed Druan. If one of them had accidentally aimed his talisman at Druan while trying to destroy one of Druan's lesser demons, the warrior would've been killed."

"No wonder they call him the Mighty Faelan," Shay said.

Bree started sorting through things on the nightstand. "Cody's a lot like him. He would do anything to protect someone he cares about. Have you seen how he looks at you?"

Shay had, but she didn't know what to do about it.

Bree lifted a pillow and looked underneath.

"What are you looking for?"

"I can't find my necklace. I hope I didn't leave it in the emergency room. It belonged to my father."

"Maybe Faelan has it. Did you tell the doctor you're pregnant?"

"Yes, but I asked him not to tell Faelan."

"He'll be excited that he's going to be a father."

"He will." Bree touched her stomach. "This baby will give Faelan something of his own flesh and blood, after all he's lost. That's why I can't risk distracting him."

Cody came in, glancing from Shay to Bree. His gaze dropped to Bree's stomach. Had he overheard about the baby? "We have trouble," he said, but he wore a pleased expression.

"What's wrong?"

"Nina and Matilda are coming up the driveway."

—◁◁◁—

"Pretend everything is normal," Shay said as she and
Cody hurried across to Nina's house. Lachlan and
Marcas had gone ahead to run interference while Shay
exchanged her large bandage for a less noticeable one.

"Normal?" Cody pulled Shay into the shadow of
the back porch. "Is it normal that all I can think about
is kissing you?" His head lowered. "And more than
kissing. Do you know how often I think about more
than kissing?"

There was a hiss from the back porch. Marcas appeared above them, frowning. Shay's face burned.
"Do that later," Marcas said. "Nina's ready to mount a
search party. If she finds out you have a stalker, they'll
never leave. And God forbid Matilda sees Faelan in
his kilt."

Shay let Cody pull her up the steps. They had to get
Nina and Matilda away from there. Shay might be willing to take her chances with a stalker, but she wasn't
willing to risk her aunt and Matilda.

Both ladies were sitting at the table drinking iced tea.
Lachlan sat next to them, looking like a caged bear.

"Nina. Matilda. What are you doing here?" Her aunt
was slim, with short, gray hair, the kind that looked like
it came from an expensive salon, but didn't. Matilda's
hair was a shocking color, something between orange
and red, resembling a baboon's nose, a jarring contrast
with her purple jogging suit.

"We're on our way to meet some of Matilda's friends
in Washington. We thought we would tour some muse-
ums," Nina said.

"Maybe we'll run into the president," Matilda added. "I have a thing or two I'd like to get off my chest."

"You could start with that push-up bra," Nina said.

"Then we might go to Atlantic City. We're taking a road trip from here," Matilda said. "Like Thelma and Louise."

"Not if I can talk her out of it," Nina whispered as she gave Shay a hug.

"Why didn't you tell me you were coming?"

"We wanted to surprise you. We flew into Richmond and rented a car. I just had to stop by and see all of you together. It's been so long." She moved to hug Cody. "Look at them, Matilda. All grown up. Aren't they just beautiful?" Nina clutched her hands to her chest. "I think I'm going to cry—Shay, why do you have a bandage on your head?"

"I uh… tripped over the cat," she said, looking at the creature perched at Lachlan's feet.

"Maybe we should stay a few days, Matilda. Shay might have a concussion."

"No," Cody and his brothers chorused the word abruptly, startling both women.

"My head's fine. We wouldn't want to interrupt your trip," Shay said. "It'll be an adventure."

"I could use an adventure," Matilda said, nodding. "Speaking of adventure—"

There was a scraping of chair legs, and Lachlan called out, "I just remembered something," as the back door slammed.

"If I didn't know better, I'd think that boy was avoiding me," Matilda said, her eyes—was that blue eye shadow?—narrowed thoughtfully. "You talk to him,

Cody. He promised me a camping trip, and I'm not getting any younger."

"Then stop dressing like a teenager," Nina said. "Have a cookie, Shay, boys. There's oatmeal raisin and peanut butter."

"There's nothing wrong with my clothes," Matilda said.

"Oh, this is just like old times," Nina gushed. "Does my heart good, I tell you. I even saw Old Elmer peeking out of the woods when we pulled up. I worry about him. If Shay won't move back, maybe I'll give the house to him. All he has is that old cabin out there in the middle of nowhere."

Cody gave Shay a puzzled look. "Give Shay the house?"

"I've been trying to get her to move back here for a year now. I don't want to wait until I'm dead and gone and can't see this place filled with love... and grandchildren. Maybe you boys can help me persuade her."

Shay had to admit, coming home, while alarming in some aspects, had made her realize how much she missed everyone. Everyone she cared about was here, other than Lucy Bell. Perhaps it was time to come home.

"That's a great idea," Marcas said. "She's been gone too long."

"Why didn't you tell me?" Cody whispered, giving Shay a sullen look. "Now who's keeping secrets?"

"It's not the same thing," she whispered back.

"Says who?"

"She's over there in Scotland all alone," Nina continued. "This break-in at her shop proves it's not safe. The world's become a dangerous place. Hasn't it, Matilda?"

"Very dangerous." Matilda broke off a piece of her

oatmeal cookie. "Muggers, thieves, rapists. You should move back home. Here, kitty." She handed the cat a morsel. It gave her an arrogant look, turned its head, and flicked its tail. "There are perverts out there too," Matilda added, inspecting the cookie tray. "And psychos. Scotland's full of them. I saw it on the news." She chose another cookie. She handed the cat a nibble, again. It stared at her and its chest heaved once, as if sighing. "Does anyone besides me think this cat acts odd?"

Nina nodded, either in response to Matilda's perverted psycho assessment, or the question about the cat. "This is a nice, safe place."

"My break-in was probably just a… secret admirer."

Nina and Matilda shared a startled glance, followed by twitching eyebrows and widening eyes obviously meant to convey a private message. What were the two of them up to? Matilda fluffed her hair, a sure sign she was flustered. Usually she sprayed it stiff and dared anyone to touch it. "You have to watch those secret admirers. They could be dangerous. I had one in high school. His name was Willy. He stuck notes in my books for the longest time."

"If he was a *secret* admirer, how do you know it was Willy?" Nina asked. She seemed a little on edge.

"Well, I didn't know it was him at first, because he was so shy. I finally caught him sneaking a note into my math book. I think it was because of his ears being so big."

"What does the size of his ears have to do with being a secret admirer?" Nina asked.

"I mean that's why he was shy. The kids called him Dumbo. He was afraid to approach me. I was so popular all the boys wanted to court me. That's when my hair was naturally red, of course. The color of love, you know; that's what Willy said in his note. Poor boy. Kids are so mean sometimes. Teasing someone just because of the size of his ears. Nowadays, he would just put one of those big metal rings in it. The bagger down at Kroger had holes so big I could've stuck a poker through them. His ears *were* big, come to think of it. That's why I didn't go out with him."

"The bag boy asked you out?" Nina asked, in astonishment.

"No. Willy. He turned out to be a wife beater. Secret admirers can be dangerous. How about you, Cody? Are you seeing anyone?"

"Uh…" Cody shook his head.

"Hmmm," Matilda said, looking at Shay.

Cody leaned closer to Shay, his voice low at her ear. "Think I should tell her exactly how much I've seen of you?"

Shay stomped his foot, missed, and hit the cat's tail. It hissed and clawed its way out from under the table, using Matilda's purple pants as a ladder. Matilda let out a screech and flew backwards in the chair, feet sticking in the air. Everyone jumped up and rushed to see if she was okay.

"Oh my Lord," she said, as Marcas and Cody hauled her to her feet. "I think that cat's possessed. Did it mess up my hair? Where's my water bottle? I'm feeling dehydrated."

Cody's cell phone rang. He pulled it out of his pocket and looked at the number. "I have to take care of some business with Sam. You sure you're okay, Matilda?"

When she nodded, he excused himself. "I'll see you ladies in the morning."

Who's Sam?" Matilda asked, giving Nina a worried look.

"His FBI contact," Marcas said.

"Well, that's all right then," Matilda said, frowning at her push-up bra, which had shifted off center during the fall.

After half an hour, Marcas left, and Nina and Matilda insisted on getting to bed early, since they planned to leave at dawn. Shay suspected Nina's trip was to make sure Shay was all right. The cat went out too, and Shay headed to her room, still thinking about Renee. The others doubted the car was Renee's, but what if someone had stolen her car? *Oh, come on, Shay.* What were the chances that her best friend's car would show up on Skyline Drive behind her and not stop when Shay tried to wave her down? Maybe the men were right. She was probably addled from the wreck or it was another red car with a rainbow bumper sticker. After all, she had been thinking about Renee a lot. And she couldn't be the only person in the world with a rainbow bumper sticker.

Shay opened her door, and the first thing she saw was a red rose on her pillow. Who had put it there? Aunt Nina didn't like roses. Shay picked it up and sniffed. Did Cody feel responsible because his brakes failed? Or was he trying to make up for the past? Shay put the rose on her dresser and tried Renee's number again, and then Renee's parents. Still no answer. They were probably at their cabin. There was no cell phone service there.

Shay had just gotten out of the shower when she heard the tap at the window. She peeked around the bathroom door. Cody was sitting in the tree, motioning for her to open the window. Her head reeled as if she'd gone through a time warp, traveling back nine years. Cody had perched in the tree, forehead pressed to the glass, waiting for her to let him in. She didn't. She hid in the closet, her eyes swollen with tears, until he finally dropped his head in anguish and left.

Shay dried off, quickly dressing in yoga pants and a soft T-shirt, then opened the window. "What are you doing?"

"You didn't think I was going to let you sleep here with Nina and Matilda as guards? Might as well invite the stalker in for tea. Take this." He handed her his Dopp kit, then stuck his head and one arm through the window. "This is tight." He tried to pull himself through. "I think I'm stuck."

"You can't be stuck," Shay said, leaning over him.

"My shirt's hung on something."

Shay lifted the window higher. "It's a nail." She freed his shirt, and he twisted sideways, wiggling his body until he landed on the floor with a thud.

"Quiet. All we need is for Nina and Matilda to see you."

"They're both half deaf." He rubbed his shoulder. "That wasn't as easy as it used to be."

"You're twice the size you were the last time you climbed in here."

Cody glanced at her face. "You look terrible."

"Pardon me while I swoon from flattery." Wasn't this the man who just tried to make out with her beside the back porch?

"As long as you fall on the bed. You have a concussion."

She gave him a hard stare. "You'd better not have handcuffs on you." She hadn't forgiven him for that.

"Want to search me and make sure?" His leer died as he turned to close the window. His body tensed. "Turn the light off."

"What?"

"Turn the lamp off. Now!"

Shay hit the switch. Cody opened the curtain a sliver and stood still, watching.

"What's wrong?"

"Not sure. I saw a streak of... something." He let the curtain drop. "You can turn the light on." He pulled out his cell phone and punched in a number. "Lach, you on guard duty? Check the woods again, and keep a close watch on Nina's house until the others get here." He hung up and turned to face her. He saw the rose and frowned. "Where do I sleep?"

"Nina's in her room, and Matilda's in the one next to it. Both beds on the other side of the house are made up, and there's the one downstairs."

"Too far away." He took the blanket from the bottom of her bed and draped it over the small sofa, then unzipped his jeans.

"What are you doing?"

"Getting undressed."

"Why?"

"I'll do a lot of things. I won't sleep in jeans again."

"You're going to sleep here?"

"I am." He shucked his jeans, stretched, and grimaced at the small sofa.

"Why didn't you bring something to sleep in?"

"I'm wearing underwear."

"Don't you ever wear pajamas?"

"Not if I can help it." He picked up his Dopp kit and padded toward the bathroom, giving her a long look at his backside in boxer briefs. "I'm going to brush my teeth."

"Geez." She took a blanket from the bed and put it on the sofa, accidentally knocking a photo album off the table. It fell open to a picture of the MacBain boys in full knight garb, scowling. Shay had paid them from her allowance to pose in the costumes. She was the damsel, of course, draped in yards of calico fabric Laura MacBain had found in her attic.

The bathroom door closed, and Shay's skin tingled as Cody moved behind her, looking over her shoulder. He reached around her and turned the page to a picture of a young Shay and Cody, the same day she chipped his tooth. He flipped another page, and a loose photo fluttered out, falling to the floor. Shay picked it up and looked into the smiling faces of the people she grew up believing were her parents, Bob and Nancy Logan, who died in a plane crash and were buried in a cemetery in Vermont. Who were they? Distant relatives? Actors? Picture frame models? She lost not one, but two sets of parents, neither of whom she knew. Or were they both a lie? The only proof would be to dig them up and check DNA. She felt the old frustration raising its head as she closed the photo album and put it away.

"I'm sorry, Shay." Cody closed a warm hand over her shoulder and then pulled her into his arms. "We were trying to help."

She closed her eyes, standing stiff-armed in his embrace. The warmth of his body took the edge off her irritation, and she relaxed against him, letting her softness melt into his harder planes. What was it about him? She couldn't even think straight when he was near. Her face was pressed against his shoulder, and she could see the bruise her teeth had made on his neck. "I shouldn't have bitten you, even if you did deserve it." She touched her lips to the mark.

He pulled in a harsh breath and his hands slid down, resting at the top of her hips. He dropped a kiss on her hair, before moving lower. He nipped her ear with his teeth, and she went boneless, sagging against him. His legs bumped the sofa, and they both sat down hard, Cody first, Shay sprawled across his lap. She licked the bite on his neck, and he groaned.

There was a knock at the door. "Shay?"

Shay scrambled up, patting her hair and clothes, then swiped a hand across her lips, as Cody slipped into the bathroom. She opened the door. "Yes, Nina."

"Just wanted to say good night."

"Good night, Nina. It's good to see you."

"I'm so glad you're home. I worry about you, with all the terrible things happening in the world. You look tired, dear. If you're not sleeping well, Matilda has some pills that'll knock you out cold." She turned and looked up the hall. "Matilda! What are you doing? I swear... I have to go." Nina hurried off, muttering to herself.

Shay closed the door. Cody stood just inside the bathroom watching her. "My turn," she said, walking toward him. With each step, she prayed, first that he would move; then that he wouldn't, so they could pick up where they left off.

He moved, and Shay sighed with relief as she entered the bathroom. When she returned, he was settled in. If you could call it settled, with his feet hanging off the end of the sofa. "You don't look comfortable."

"I'd be more comfortable in a bed," he muttered, looking longingly at hers. He glanced at the rose again.

Was he waiting for her to thank him? "Did you leave the rose?"

"No."

Probably Jamie or Marcas. If Marcas ever gave up being a warrior, he would make a damn fine husband, thoughtful, sensitive, and all male. Shay pulled back the covers and climbed into bed.

Cody lay on his back, arms behind his head, watching her. The tiny rows of symbols on his chest fascinated her. They reminded her of an ancient scroll she once saw in a museum. "Now I know why you wouldn't talk about your tattoos."

"They're called battle marks."

"Yours are different from Marcas's and Lachlan's." And Jamie's.

"No two are the same, just like our talismans. They're sacred, like a written prayer of protection and blessing. We get them when we accept our duty as a warrior."

"You have a choice whether to accept?"

"A warrior can choose to walk away."

"Were you ever tempted?"

"Only once." He didn't elaborate, and she didn't ask. No one could get answers out of Cody MacBain if he didn't want to give them.

"I'm sorry about your truck."

"I don't care about the truck, I'm just glad you and

Bree are okay. I don't want you hurt. That's why I hand-cuffed you to the bed. You still mad at me?"

"Yes."

He folded his arms across his chest. "Well, get over it. I'm not going to let anything hurt you, and that includes you. You're smart, and you're the toughest girl I know, but you can be too brave for your own good. You can't go up against a demon. He'll rip you to shreds."

"I'm not going to sit back and do nothing. This threatens everything I love."

"Let us handle the demons."

"Are there female demons?"

"There are, and you don't want to tangle with them either. They're as bad as the males. Sometimes worse."

"You didn't tell me you'd destroyed an ancient demon."

He yawned. "We take our assignments as they come."

She'd brought him nothing but trouble. He got in trouble once already with the Council. What would they do if they found out he told her the whole truth? "What did the Council do to you for telling me about my past?"

"You've been talking to Bree. They just… reminded me of my priorities."

"Thank you for helping me."

He pulled the covers up to his chest. "That's what we're here for."

"Your duty, right?"

"It's not duty when it's someone you care about." Cody looked at the rose again. "Get some sleep, pip-squeak." He closed his eyes and curled his long legs on the sofa.

He had to be exhausted, and it was her fault. He was too busy chasing stalkers and trying to protect her to sleep. "Cody, if you want to sleep on the bed, you can."

His eyes stayed shut. "If I get in that bed, I'll do more than sleep."

———ᴖᴖᴖ———

The servant parked his car across the road and crept through the dark woods, trying to shake the feeling of being watched. He caught a flash of something off to the side of the house, but it disappeared. He wasn't scared of the dark. It soothed him, quieted the gnawing in his head. The gnawing was strong now. Nothing was going according to plan. The warrior should be dead; instead, Shay almost died, and the warrior got to play the hero by rescuing her. If the warrior hadn't followed her, she would already belong to the servant. She did anyway. She just didn't know it yet. Neither did his master. Malek didn't know everything about his servant. He didn't know about *them*. His treasures.

He climbed a sturdy maple and propped himself against a thick branch, settling in to wait. He had to get that book, or the master was going to get rid of him. He searched the house while she was at the hospital, no great feat for a security-systems expert, but the book wasn't there. She must have hidden it somewhere else.

He swung his binoculars toward Shay's house. A light went off downstairs. She was going to bed. He would wait until she fell asleep, then sneak in and grab her. He let the anticipation build, planning all the things he would do to her. Three lights appeared upstairs. He sat up so fast he almost lost his perch. Did she have company? He couldn't see her driveway. It was probably *him*. He should have died today, like that piece of scum in Scotland had, after the servant had caught him spying on Shay, messing with his plans.

The anger started a slow burn, growing stronger, until it gnashed at his insides. He had to release it, or it would eat him alive. Bloodletting was the only way to control the fury. He took off his jacket and pulled the knife from his pocket. It clicked softly as the blade released, glimmering in the moonlight. He set the sharp edge against his skin, the metal cold, hard, biting. He pressed until soft flesh gave against the greater strength of the blade. He gave the knife a slow pull, welcoming the sting. He closed his eyes in ecstasy, imagining it was another arm, another throat.

Chapter 7

A SCREAM SENT SHAY SHOOTING OFF THE BED. SHE collided with Cody.

"Lock the door. Don't leave." He pulled a gun from somewhere and was gone before Shay could blink.

She took off after him to Matilda's room. Matilda was clutching the edges of her fuchsia robe, red hair stiff as a ball of wax. Nina rushed in behind them. "He was peeking in the window," Matilda said, "his eyes filled with lust. Hurry, before he gets away."

Neither of the older women seemed concerned or surprised to see Cody in the house, wearing only underwear and carrying a gun.

"Don't leave this room," Cody said, running out the door. "Please."

Matilda grabbed the phone and called to alert Marcas and Lachlan. Nina and Shay watched from the window as Cody made his way across the backyard, moving like a whisper. "Oh. There's someone beside the barn." She screamed for Cody to watch out, forgetting he couldn't hear through the glass. Cody lunged, and the two figures went down in a tangle of shadows. They moved out of sight, and Shay raced from the bedroom, followed by Nina and Matilda.

Seconds later, the back door crashed open. Cody stomped in, followed by another man, voices raised.

Jamie.

"I wasn't looking in the windows. I was guarding the house. What the hell are *you* doing here?" His eyes narrowed, taking in Cody's underwear. Jamie moved closer to Shay.

"Why is he guarding the house? Is something wrong? Is Shay in trouble?" Nina asked.

"Oh no," Shay said. "This is my friend, Jamie Waters."

"Jamie? This is *your* Jamie? Oh dear." Nina glanced at Matilda, who was putting on her bifocals.

"Look at him, Nina. He's a dish. Much better looking than the one we — Holy Mother of — you stepped on my bunion."

Nina made some gestures with her eyebrows.

Matilda frowned, trying to interpret, and then settled into a look of dawning comprehension. "Oh... Cody's a dish too. In fact, they look like they could be brothers. Cody has a nice job. He's a PI. What do you do, Jeremy?"

"His name is Jamie," Nina said. "Shay, you're pale. Is it your head?"

"Just tired." Shay looked at the two men standing side by side, both well over six feet, longish dark hair, both handsome. Until that moment, she hadn't noticed how much Jamie resembled Cody, in fact how much all the men she dated resembled Cody.

"It's lovely to meet you, Jamie," Nina said. "We wanted to before, but we were traveling. You'll excuse us if we get back to bed. I think this has been too much excitement for Matilda. Shay, you should get some rest."

"Too much excitement? It's just getting good," Matilda huffed, still peering at Jamie and Cody as if inspecting turkeys for Thanksgiving.

"Matilda, we have things to *discuss*."

Matilda's eyes widened. "Of course, well good night, everyone. Nice meeting you, Jeremy." They left in a flurry of whispers, much louder to everyone else, since both had terrible hearing. Shay caught the word *plan*.

Lach appeared from the hallway. "What happened?"

Where had he come from? Shay hadn't even heard the front door open.

"Your brother can't tell the difference between a prowler and a guard," Jamie said, scowling.

"What was I supposed to think? Matilda said she saw someone looking in her window," Cody said.

"I asked him to guard the house," Lachlan said, rubbing his eyes. "I'm going home. I'd just fallen asleep when Matilda called and said a rapist was coming in the window. Marcas is right behind me. He can take the next guard. You coming, Jamie?"

Jamie looked from Cody to Shay. "I'm staying here, if that's okay," he said to Shay.

"There's a bedroom across the hall," she said, which didn't make Cody happy. She shrugged at him. "You did say I needed protection."

Lachlan started back down the hall.

"Lach."

"Yeah?"

Cody nodded toward the back door.

"Ah." Lachlan gave Shay a kiss on the cheek and went out the back. "Don't let them kill each other."

Shay settled Jamie in the bedroom near the sitting room. He helped her put fresh sheets on the bed. "I miss you," he whispered, catching her fingers as she brushed by. He pulled her into a hug, lips brushing the soft hair at her forehead.

Standing close to him brought back a flood of intimate memories. She'd spent almost a year with Jamie, even considered marrying him. Turning him down might be the biggest mistake of her life, but it was clear she had too many unresolved feelings for Cody. Jamie deserved a woman who loved him for himself, not because he subconsciously reminded her of someone else. She needed to settle things between Jamie and Cody before someone got distracted and died.

"We have to talk, Jamie," she said, pulling out of his hug. He left one arm around her shoulder, keeping contact.

"Talk?" he said, the question hopeful, until he saw her face. "I'm sorry I didn't tell you I'm a warrior, but I couldn't."

Why did everyone keep saying that? They could have told her, but that wasn't the point.

He dropped his hand, capturing hers. "I didn't mean to fall in love with you, if that makes any difference. By the time I realized it, it was too late. You were in my blood. I would have told you before we married, but I kept it a secret so long I wasn't sure how to say it. I was trying to work up the nerve when you broke things off."

"There's more to it than you not telling me you're a warrior. You're one of the best men I know, and I thought coming back here might help me see things more clearly, but... it's no good... I love you, Jamie, I do." She touched his face. "But not... not like that. Not like you should be loved."

His eyes looked flat. He glanced over her shoulder. "It's him isn't it? It's always been him."

Shay turned and saw Cody in the hallway, body stiff, face shadowed. His gaze met hers before looking away. He disappeared toward the stairs. She wanted to run to him and apologize.

"I… it's not that… I don't know—" her voice broke. She couldn't deny it. "I'm sorry." She had betrayed him every bit as much as he betrayed her. At least he did it because he loved her, wanted to protect her. She had used Jamie to replace a ghost.

"I know, babe. I know," he said, pulling her close again. They stayed that way for several moments, grieving over the hopelessness of love.

"Friends?" she asked, her voice soft against his chest.

"Always." He kissed her hair, his lips lingering several seconds.

She left him and headed back to her bedroom, her head and stomach churning over what Jamie had forced her to admit. She wasn't over Cody. She never had been, and she feared she never would be. Should she let this thing play out between them and see where it stood? How could she ever move on and not second-guess her feelings if she didn't know for sure?

"That took long enough," Cody said, without looking up as she walked in. "What'd you do? Tuck him in like a bloody baby?"

She started to say something rude, but he glanced up, and she saw the hurt in his eyes, quickly disguised. She pushed the door closed so Jamie, Nina, and Matilda wouldn't find out Cody was in her room. "You shouldn't be so hard on him." Shay settled in awkwardly and stared at the ceiling, wondering how she would ever sleep. She felt guilty over Jamie, confused over Cody, and angry at herself.

"Do you love him?" Cody asked softly.

"I thought I did."

"What's that mean?"

"He's a good guy. I cared for him. I still do, but something wasn't... there."

Cody started to say something, hesitated, then started again. "He took advantage of you."

"You did worse. You stole something from me."

He looked confused for a moment. "Your father, you mean?"

"My father, my mother, my life. I never even saw a picture of the woman who gave birth to me until I Googled her name and read her obituary. I believed some stranger named Nancy was my mother. Do you have any idea how it feels to find out the people you thought loved you were imposters sent to do a job?"

She heard the sofa creak as Cody rose and moved to the bed. "It was more than a job," he said, sitting next to her. "We did it because we loved you. We still do. How do you think we felt—how *I* felt—losing you? You wouldn't see me or talk to me, and I had to go off and fight demons, when all I could think about was you. When I found out you'd left home, I dropped the demon I was hunting and rushed back. Caused a bloody uproar. My mentor had to kill the demon. My dad was ready to kill me. I almost walked away from being a warrior. My mentor grabbed me by the ears and told me I was a fool. Not only would I betray my family and my clan, but it would endanger you."

His voice sounded hollow, and Shay remembered a younger Cody pleading with her to understand, to stop and listen. Like the starved fool she was, she leaned against him, seeking comfort, as she had so many times before. He put his arms around her. Shay's cheek tingled where it pressed against his chest. That sensation had never happened when she was with Jamie. "I didn't mean to hurt you. I was just confused. I didn't know how to face you."

"What was in those letters that made you so angry when I didn't answer?"

"That I was sorry for shutting you out." ... *I'm sorry for leaving angry, for not talking to you, but I need you now. Please call me. Please. It's important...*

In the second letter she begged. Her heart had broken, and it hurt to breathe. She had needed him more than she needed air, but she couldn't tell him that now. If he got distracted and didn't focus on this threat, he could die. Oh God. She was doing exactly what the clan had done to her, hiding things to protect him.

"I wasn't at college. I was training in Scotland. I could see one letter getting lost, but two? It doesn't make sense. Coira made sure we got our mail."

"I called too, before I sent the letters. A woman answered."

"One of the female warriors probably. I didn't get your message."

"I didn't leave one. I thought..."

Cody leaned back and stared at her. "So all these years you thought I ignored you because I had a girlfriend?"

"What else could I think, after what happened? I didn't know you tried to see me."

"A lot more than that. You know me. You were my lif... my best friend." He put an arm around her, pulling her close again. She leaned against his shoulder, her cheek next to his battle marks. She heard a whisper; the sound ancient, familiar, as if the marks called to her. In a matter of hours her life had become as intertwined with his as it had been before. Whether she craved him or wanted to kill him, her very soul seemed connected to his. He covered her hand with his, holding it tight against his heart as sleep slipped over her like a soft blanket.

Cody tried to distract himself from Shay's scent by thinking about the letters—what she could have written that would have made her so angry when he didn't answer—and he thought about the rose on her dresser. It was a sad indication of how rattled he was, that at the moment the rose concerned him more. Who sent it? Jamie? Shay didn't belong with Jamie. He couldn't know her the way Cody did, know that underneath the tough-girl exterior she was sensitive, that she cried when she laughed too hard. That she loved bubble baths, but was clumsy around water. How she felt wrapped around... he ground his teeth and moved his arm so he could slip back to the safety of the sofa, but she murmured something—he hoped it wasn't Jamie's name—and her hand dropped, curling around the waistband of his underwear. He talked himself out of nudging her hand lower. He managed to scoot both of them down in bed, so they didn't get cricks in their necks, but he couldn't sleep with that damned rose taunting him and Shay's hand on his underwear.

He tried counting sheep. He was at 123 when her ankle slid over his. He caught his breath, torn between leaping from the bed and hoping she was awake. A sleepy sigh killed that thought. He counted at least two hundred more sheep, naming several of them, when her calf eased over his, then her thigh. He groaned, and the hand clutching the band of his underwear tensed, and she quickly removed her thigh from his lap.

"Sorry," she said, sleepily. "I thought you…"

Thought what? That he was Jamie. Did she think it was Jamie's bloody underwear she was holding? Well, hell!

He rolled over, half on top of her, and she let out a startled gasp. With no finesse at all, he kissed her neck. He wanted to bite her, like she'd bitten him, leave his mark on her, so she would know it was Cody MacBain she was in bed with and not Jamie Waters. At first she stiffened at the onslaught, and then her body melted under his. Her pulse pounded like a drum against his lips. He licked the pulsating skin, and she moaned. Her skin was softer than he remembered. Warmer. Fuller. He trailed kisses over every inch of flesh above her neck, and then moved lower to her breasts, stomach, and thighs. All that mattered was making sure Jamie Waters had no place in Shay's heart or her head.

She wrapped her arms around his neck, locking her hands in his hair. Don't let this be a damned dream like the others, he thought. Her hands moved down his back, caressing his skin, tugging at his underwear, the fabric catching on the part of him screaming for attention. He yanked off his boxer briefs, throwing them to the floor. In seconds, her clothes had joined them. He settled between her thighs, rubbed against her, then slipped inside. He tried to slow things down, but his hips wouldn't stop moving. He was halfway to paradise when she froze. She pushed against his shoulders.

"What is it?" he asked, dazed. Was he doing something wrong? He was out of practice but—

Her green eyes were wide, panicked. "Condom."

"I don't have one." He hadn't needed one. He couldn't remember the last time he had sex.

"We have to stop."

"Stop?" Stop. He gritted his teeth, surged once more, so hard he was afraid it was all over anyway. He pulled out and rolled over, chest heaving. He was so close that the touch of the sheet would probably set him off.

"I'm sorry, Cody."

"It's not your fault. I'm to blame." He wondered if she would be offended if he finished the job himself.

Shay rolled toward him. "You look like you're in pain."

He gave one affirmative grunt, afraid to move. "Just give me a minute."

Before he could drudge up some grisly distraction, her fingers brushed his navel. The muscles of his stomach quivered. Cody sucked in a hard breath when her hand closed around him. He groaned and rolled toward her. She adjusted her grip, his lips locked on hers, and his hips rocked against her hand.

"Don't stop," he begged against her mouth. "Please don't stop." His breathing was ragged, chest ready to explode. His groin tightened, and the release came. He buried his face in her hair as his body emptied onto her stomach.

He rolled to his side and leaned his head against hers, unsure what to say. *Thank you. Stay with me forever. I love you.* After his breathing slowed, he grabbed a handful of tissues from the nightstand and cleaned them both off. She still hadn't said anything, but he felt the thrumming in her body. He tossed the tissues in the trash and leaned over her. He kissed her shoulder, moving his lips to her breast. She gripped his hair, and he slid lower. It didn't take her any longer than it had him. She moaned and her body tensed before going limp. Cody moved beside her, gathering her close against him.

He knew he was holding her too tight, but he was afraid if he relaxed, she would slip away again. "We could take a shower," he said, but neither of them moved.

They lay locked in each other's arms for minutes... hours, maybe it was eternity, not speaking, just feeling, until he heard her even breathing and knew she'd fallen asleep. He felt a sense of peace he hadn't had in too many years. But peace was an illusion, until he got rid of whoever was after her. Then, he would convince her to give him another chance and hope to God she didn't hate him when she found out what else he'd hidden.

Shay woke in the night. She heard a thumping sound downstairs. The noise didn't concern her as much as the fact that she was draped over Cody and they were both naked. She lay for a minute, reliving what they had done, wondering how different things might have been if she had known he hadn't ignored the letters. Would she have forgiven him for hiding her identity and moved on? Maybe to this? His life? His bed?

Cody nudged her shoulder. "Don't follow me this time," he said, untangling his limbs from hers and slipping out of bed.

She watched him pull on his boxers and pick up a gun from under a pillow on the sofa before easing out the door. Shay scrambled quietly for her clothes. She crept down the stairs, not far behind him. She couldn't see his face, but she felt his glare. The front door was cracked. The chill of night air brushed her skin. As they slipped outside, busy little whispers met her ears, a grunt, and then another thump. Cody turned on a bright flashlight. She didn't know where he got it. Shay saw a flash of red and heard a squeal as Matilda's hands flew up in the air. The wheelbarrow dumped over, and Jamie rolled out like a sack of flour.

"We panicked," Matilda said, between gulps from her water bottle. "So I thought if I gave him a little of my sleeping medicine—"

"A little?" Shay said, her voice shrill. "He's out cold."

Cody had carried Jamie back to bed and was with him, making sure Jamie was only drugged, not dying.

"Well, I may have given him too much. We didn't want him to wake up in the car. He's big, and he looks strong. That's a nice, sturdy wheelbarrow. I need one of those to move rocks in my garden," Matilda said.

"Where were you taking him?" Shay asked.

"Somewhere safe," Nina said. "We didn't want to hurt him. He seems like a nice boy. We just wanted him out of the way."

"Out of the way of what?" Shay asked, exasperated.

"You and Cody," Nina said.

"Cody and me?"

Nina clutched her robe tighter. "Here you are, after

all these years, and we're thinking you finally came to your senses, and this Adonis shows up to ruin it all."

"He wants to marry you," Matilda said. "We couldn't have that."

Oh heavens. "You think Cody and I are…?"

"But of course, dear," Nina said. "We've always known. We were just waiting for you two to realize it."

Matilda clutched her water bottle. "For a smart girl, you can be slow sometimes."

"Jiminy Christmas." She had lived in fear that someone would find out how she felt about Cody and think she was a pervert or had committed incest, and the whole time they were listening for wedding bells.

She assured Nina and Matilda that she had no plans for marriage to anyone and then went back to bed. Her head ached too much to worry that Cody might put a pillow over Jamie's face and smother him.

The next time she woke, it was to whispers at the door. "That's a good sign, don't you think?" Matilda asked.

"Yes, but they really should be married first," Nina answered.

Shay cracked one eye and saw fuzzy images of red and gray in the doorway. A snore erupted beside her. Shay turned her head and saw Cody sprawled next to her, one muscular arm flung across her stomach.

"Sorry to wake you, but we're getting an early start," Nina said. "We'll call you from the road."

"Tell Jeremy we're sorry. It's nothing against him, but he can't marry you," Matilda said. They waved and disappeared.

~~~

Shay had one toe on the floor when the door opened. "Nina and Matilda—" Lachlan stopped. "Uh... sorry. Guess I should've knocked. The door wasn't closed."

Shay jumped up, accidentally pulling the covers off Cody. Why couldn't the man sleep in underwear? She threw the sheet back over him and stood, her face on fire. "I'm sorry, what did you say?"

Lachlan's eyebrows settled back into place. "Nina and Matilda are gone."

"What?" Cody asked, sitting up.

"Nina and Matilda are gone," Lachlan repeated.

"They left early this morning," Shay said.

"I came to tell you breakfast is ready. The others arrived last night. We've got meat, eggs, and more meat. I'll tell Jamie."

"Don't think he'll want to eat," Cody said, looking under the blanket. "Matilda drugged him last night." He explained what happened.

"I'd better check on him," Lachlan said. "I swear that woman's a freak of nature."

"I expect he'll have a headache and a half." Cody lifted a pillow and then peered at the floor.

Lachlan bent and picked something up. "Looking for these?" He tossed Cody's underwear at his chest and left.

Shay gave Cody an awkward glance. He dropped the sheet and stood. Shay turned away until she heard the brush of fabric over skin. What had she done? What on earth had she done? He hadn't gotten the letters, and he hadn't abandoned her; still, there were a lot of unresolved issues.

Cody grabbed his jeans from the floor and slipped

them on. He paused, hand on his zipper. "Do you need to… uh take a shower or something before we go eat?" His gaze dropped to the rumpled bed.

She nodded.

"I'm…" Several emotions stirred in his eyes. Some she recognized, some she didn't. "I'll shower in the bathroom down the hall. I'll wait for you."

"You don't have to. I can walk over when I'm ready."

"No." He picked up his shirt, looking like he wanted to say something else, but he left the room.

Shay took a long shower, hoping he would give up and go home without her. Things were moving too fast. She had gone from hating him to having sex with him. Or nearly sex. Same thing. She went downstairs and found him staring out the window, waiting.

"Ready?" he asked.

She nodded. "We should check on Jamie."

"I did. He's still sleeping."

Cody's house smelled as delicious as it was loud. They followed the sounds and smells to the dining room. Most of the chairs were occupied with people talking and laughing as plates were loaded with food. It reminded her of all the holiday meals shared here.

"You can't walk into a hospital with your weapon in plain sight," a red-haired woman was saying. "Any idiot knows that."

"Are you calling me an idiot?" the man beside her said. He had reddish hair himself, tied back in a leather strap. "Like you've never made a mistake."

"Would you two shut up? You're giving me a head-ache." The dark-haired man who spoke looked as if he could be Faelan's brother, but considering how old

Faelan was, Shay didn't think it possible, unless there were two time vaults.

"Whatever, Coz," the red-haired woman said, passing a plate of biscuits to another woman who had long, dark hair and a face so beautiful Shay wished she had taken time to put on makeup.

Cody made introductions. The redhead and the beauty were Sorcha and Anna, the female warriors Bree had told Shay about. Duncan was the one who resembled Faelan, and was in fact his descendent, as they all were.

"We thought you were still at the hospital," Duncan told Shay. "Brodie forgot to leave his knife in the car, and we got chased by a security guard."

"We ended up in the maternity wing and had to drag Brodie away," Sorcha said. "He wanted to see the babies."

"I like babies. What's wrong with that?" Brodie grumbled.

Bree and Shay exchanged a knowing glance.

Sorcha pulled out a chair next to her. "No one's sitting here, Cody."

Shay wasn't sure if the look Cody gave her was a plea for help or understanding.

"Better get food while there's some left," Bree said. Her plate was loaded with enough for two men. "We have bacon, sausage, eggs, biscuits, pancakes, doughnuts, and orange juice. Ronan went grocery shopping this morning."

"A man's gotta have meat," Ronan said, holding a heaping plate.

"You'll make some woman a good husband," Shay said, taking a seat between him and Lachlan, which didn't seem to please Cody.

"You proposing?" Ronan asked, grinning, "I hope you like long engagements. I have two more years of duty."

"So?" Shay asked.

"Warriors can't marry until they've finished their duty, according to clan law," he said.

"There are clan laws about marriage?" Shay asked.

"Who a warrior marries is important to the clan," Lachlan said, unusually sober. "I'm surprised Cody didn't tell you that too. He told you everything else. Our mates are destined long before we're born."

Chapter 8

SHAY'S STOMACH FELT LIKE A BAG OF ROCKS. "YOUR mates are destined?"

"You gonna talk all day or pass the food?" Cody asked.

Ronan grinned. "Hey, I may be getting a proposal here."

"Won't that put a kink in your *sleeping* habits?" Cody asked, pouring a glass of orange juice.

Ronan threw a biscuit at Cody. He snagged it and added it to his plate.

"Destined mates?" Shay repeated.

"Kind of like love at first sight," Bree said, her green eyes softening as she gazed at Faelan. "But usually it happens after a warrior retires."

Like Cody.

"Sometimes it happens before, but it doesn't make the Council happy," Lachlan said.

Brodie grabbed a piece of sausage as the plate passed him. "Does anything make the Council happy?"

"The mates have to be from one of the clans. They get a mate mark, something like Faelan's." Bree touched a round, jagged circle behind his ear, visible with his hair pulled back.

Shay glanced at Cody's tattoo peeking out from under his hair. It was different from Faelan's, larger, but were they all the same? Did it mean that somewhere out there was a woman destined to share Cody's heart and his bed? Shay's gaze swung to Sorcha, who was staring at Cody's tattoo as well. She wasn't married, and she was part of this clan. So was Anna. Did one of them bear a mate mark that Shay didn't have?

"That's an interesting place for a tattoo," Sorcha said, running one red-tipped fingernail over Cody's neck. Shay wanted to throw a biscuit at her, or maybe a fork. "I noticed it when you were in Scotland. Nice. Duncan has one there too."

Duncan lowered his head and kept eating.

"Thanks. It's just a tattoo," Cody said. "We need to bring everyone up to date and figure out sleeping arrangements, now that we're all here."

Shay knew him well enough to recognize an evasion tactic. It was probably wishful thinking on her part to hope he just wanted Sorcha to stop touching him.

"I'll sleep at Shay's," Ronan said.

"Over my dead body," Cody declared, drawing several curious looks. He scowled. "I'm not even sure I want you sleeping next door."

Ronan lifted an eyebrow. "What I meant was I'm sleeping wherever Faelan and Bree aren't. You try sleeping in the room next to the honeymooners."

Shay looked at Bree and Faelan, sharing passion-laced glances between bites of toast. Her own food was about as appealing as dirt. If Cody had a predestined mate, eventually he would find her, no matter what unresolved passion he and Shay shared. Jamie would find his mate too, and she would be alone, again.

"This is the only honeymoon I'll get for a while," Faelan said, digging into his breakfast.

"Well, have a little pity on the rest of us who're sleeping alone," Sorcha said, giving Cody a seductive glance. "Where's Jamie?"

Duncan gave Sorcha a dark look but didn't respond.

"Jamie's sleeping. Matilda drugged him," Lachlan said, forcing Cody to awkwardly explain that the women had been making a misguided matchmaking attempt and thought Jamie was in the way. He didn't mention that it was to clear the way for him, but every eye was on the two of them.

"Maybe we need to recruit Matilda, if she can neutralize a warrior like Jamie," Brodie said. "Have her slip the demons a sleeping pill."

"Isn't Jamie your boyfriend?" Sorcha asked.

"No," Cody blurted out before Shay could shake her head.

"He used to be," Lachlan said.

Cody frowned. "Anyone else think it's odd how he watches Shay?"

Lachlan snorted, while Faelan and Ronan grinned.

"I find it interesting that Jamie wormed his way in here, claiming this table was shipped to him, when it's obvious he's obsessed with her," Cody said.

"Are you saying Jamie could be her stalker?" Sorcha asked, slathering a blueberry muffin with butter. Shay doubted Sorcha worried about getting fat. Slaying demons probably melted off calories. "I thought the guy was blond."

"I'm not accusing him, but we've got a mess of trouble and no one to blame. We shouldn't rule out anyone."

"He was injured," Shay said. "You think he did that to himself?"

Cody shrugged. "Could have, if necessary."

Lachlan broke off a piece of bacon and slipped it under the table. There was a soft *meow*. "Bro, I think you need more sleep." He glanced at Shay. "Or something."

"Have you got that cat under there?" Cody asked.

Shay lifted the edge if the tablecloth. The cat was sitting at Lachlan's feet. "I thought you were going to call the Petersons."

"I did. It's not theirs," Lachlan said. "Ronan's going to take him to Montana if you don't want him."

"Go ahead," Shay said to Ronan. She couldn't take care of herself, much less a cat.

Sorcha raised an eyebrow at Ronan. "What are you going to do with a cat? You're never home."

"I'll put him in the barn. I have someone watching the place." He smiled at Shay. "Or we could share joint custody."

"You're not sharing anything with Shay," Cody said. "Cat or otherwise."

Ronan settled back in his chair, not bothering to hide his grin.

"You see what I have to put up with?" Faelan said to Cody.

"You live in Montana?" Shay asked Ronan.

Ronan nodded. "For now."

"That's where he goes when he gets sick of demons. And humans," Brodie said. "He owns a mountain. It's so isolated I doubt a demon could find it."

"Think we could train the cat to be a guard cat?" Lachlan asked and then grew serious. "Whoever broke in, and it wasn't Jamie, he knew how to avoid the cameras and get past the alarm." That led to a discussion of the recent events with Shay's stalker in Scotland and here.

"You think Jamie's and Shay's intruders are the same?" Duncan asked.

Lachlan swallowed his bite of egg and biscuit. "Shay's was blond, but we thought there might have been another one in the woods. Jamie said there were three of them at his house, but he saw only two clearly, both brown-haired, average height, slim. Said they moved fast, hit him before he could even reach for his dagger."

"Must have been some bad-ass demons," Marcas said. "Jamie's quick. He could take three humans blindfolded. Should've been able to take three demons."

"You think my stalker is a demon?" Shay asked, eyes wide with alarm.

Cody shrugged. "I don't know, but that intruder I fought seemed too strong and too fast for a human."

"This probably has something to do with your father," Anna said. "He believed someone was after him. Maybe that same someone wants you."

"He's definitely interested in your tables," Sorcha added.

"They had to be after the book," Cody said. "The only thing the intruder messed with at Nina's was a bookshelf. He must have called his buddies and headed to Jamie's after that."

"So how did they know the book was inside the table?" Lachlan asked.

Faelan gave Bree a worried glance. "We know Russell stole the book and took it to Druan's castle. Maybe we missed a demon who was working with Druan."

"How could Renee be involved in all this?" Shay asked.

"Did she know anyone named Russell?" Brodie asked.

"Not that I'm aware of."

"Since Renee's laptop has vanished, could you make a list of contacts? Boyfriends, friends, clients." Cody frowned. "I suspect someone isn't who he's pretending to be and doesn't want his name seen."

It was terrifying to think that her own clients, neighbors, banker, Realtor, or even the little old lady next door could be a demon in disguise. "Most of the Scotland and Leesburg clients are separate. I'm familiar with some of Renee's, but not all."

"There's something I haven't mentioned," Cody said. "Someone dug up your grave."

Brodie paused mid-chew. "Shay's grave? Oh, the empty one."

Lachlan raised an eyebrow. "Bloody hell."

"They removed the casket and opened it," Cody said. "I was going to tell you yesterday, Shay, but Nina and Matilda showed up."

He could've mentioned it last night. "Why would someone do that?"

He pushed back his plate. "To see if it had a body inside."

"So someone knows she's not dead," Duncan said. "When did this happen?"

"Sometime in the last day or two," Cody said.

"It could be teenage vandals gearing up for Halloween," Shay said, hopefully.

Cody shook his head. "I wish, but I suspect Anna's right, and it's something to do with your father."

"I thought the demon the Watchers thought was responsible died," Sorcha said.

"He did," Cody said. "But someone knows about the secret."

"Let's hope the clan wasn't wrong," Brodie said. "That wouldn't make the demon happy, finding out he's been fooled all this time."

Shay's stomach started crawling toward her throat. This wasn't normal stalker stuff, like on the news and TV, and Renee was in the middle of it.

"I think this is connected to the stuff with Druan," Duncan said. "We got all the demons on Angus's list, but even the Watchers suspected there was more happening than just Druan's attempt to destroy the world."

Sorcha studied her red nails, her gaze troubled. "What about Tristol and Malek and Voltar? Those dreams I had before. I couldn't make out all the details, but I saw five men. One was Faelan and one was Druan in human form, but we never figured out who the other three were."

"Don't even think it," Brodie said, crossing himself.

"Who are they?" Shay asked.

"Demons of old," Bree said. "Faelan saw those three riding with Druan back in 1860 when he was sent to stop the Civil War. They disappeared."

"Our Civil War?" Shay swung around to look at Faelan. Pain shadowed his face.

"I was sent to suspend Druan. He was stirring up strife and hatred that was turning this country toward war, trying to destroy it from the inside out. At least that's what we thought, but I found out the war was just Druan's distraction. He created a virus to destroy the world."

"Good grief. Is anything what it seems?"

"Not much," Faelan said. "Demons are involved in most everything bad. Human wars rarely start with humans."

"What happened to the virus?" Shay asked.

"Faelan destroyed it when he destroyed Druan," Bree said, her voice ringing with pride. "He saved the world."

Faelan smiled. "Not without help. If it hadn't been for Bree and Conall and the other warriors, there wouldn't be any world."

Shay looked at Cody, his handsome face set in a worried frown, and for the first time she understood why he tried so hard to protect her. "Could these three demons who were with Druan be dead?"

"Not likely. The ancient ones are hard to kill," Cody said. "They're quick and devious. If they'd been assigned to a warrior, we would have heard."

Sorcha pushed back her plate. "They've probably been roaming the earth, creating death and destruction, trying to become eternal. Supposedly they're behind some of our major diseases. Tristol supposedly created the HIV virus, although no one's seen him since Faelan did back in 1860. And Druan's father created the Plague. All this bad stuff humans think is just normal usually starts with a demon."

"I wish we had Angus's notes," Anna said. "He was onto something."

"Who's Angus?" Shay asked.

"The last warrior who was sent to find Faelan's time vault key," Anna said. "He figured out what Druan was up to, and Druan had him killed."

This stuff was life and death, not the thrilling games they played as kids, but in spite of its horror, it stirred something inside that Shay couldn't explain, like a supercharged rush of energy.

"I'll check Angus's things again when I get to New York," Anna said rubbing her eyes. "I should've gone straight there after the wedding."

The wedding. Faelan and Bree hadn't even finished their reception, let alone started a honeymoon, all because of Shay. Or had it started with Shay's father, a man she didn't even remember, who'd lost his wife and child. Well, she was alive, and if this was the same demon who killed her mother and father and stole her life, she wanted him dead, even if she had to do it herself.

"I can fly you to New York," Lachlan said to Anna.

Anna shook her head. "Thanks, but I'll drive. I have some things to sort out." She excused herself from the table.

"I hope she starts with that gloomy mood," Brodie said.

"Leave her alone," Sorcha said. "She's got a lot on her mind."

"Angus and Anna were researching the missing *Book of Battles* before he was killed," Bree told Shay. "Anna got busy with something else. When she went back, Angus seemed troubled, but wouldn't say what was going on. He mentioned something about secret societies and a league."

"And traitors." Brodie glanced at Sorcha.

"Are you accusing me of being a traitor?" Sorcha asked, rising to her feet, hands on hips.

Brodie crossed his arms over his chest. "Angus did look right at you when he said it. Now, I'm not saying I believe it. I'd slit your throat if I thought you were betraying our clan." Brodie's expression was grave, without his usual good-natured smile. Duncan tensed, eyes narrowed, as Brodie continued. "But I'd like to know why he looked at you when he said it."

Sorcha looked as if she might morph into a dragon and roast Brodie in his chair, but her shoulders dropped, and she sat down. "So would I," she said. "So would I."

"No one's accusing anybody of anything," Duncan said. "Who knows what was in Angus's head? He was always wrapped up in some mystery. Sometimes he saw clues that weren't there."

Anna came back in carrying her purse and a duffel bag. "Can someone give me a ride to the car rental?"

Lachlan dropped his fork. "I will." He wolfed down a piece of bacon, scraped and rinsed the plate he had just refilled, and loaded it in the dishwasher. "Ready?"

"I'll check on the time vault while I'm in New York," Anna said.

"Faelan's time vault is still there?" Shay asked. Talk about an antique! She'd love to see it.

"No. He sent his back, but he found another one in the cellar of my chapel," Bree said. "We thought Angus brought it, but it's not his, either. We can't send it back without the warrior's talisman."

"You don't know where it came from?" Shay asked.

"We have no idea," Sorcha said. "There weren't any other warriors in the area, that we know of."

"We don't even know how long it's been there," Brodie said.

"What about that warrior from Canada who was supposed to help Sorcha?" Ronan asked. "Did anyone ever locate him?"

"Yes. He had an accident on the way. Attacked by

two vam…" Anna paused and glanced at Shay. "He never got there, so he didn't bring the time vault."

"There's a key to the house hidden on the back porch," Bree said. "Feel free to stay there if you need some time alone."

Anna gave Bree a quick hug. "Thanks."

"Is she okay?" Shay asked, after Anna and Lachlan left.

Sorcha looked troubled. "She and Angus were close. If she hadn't been busy, she would've been with him. She blames herself for his death." Sorcha stood. "I'm going to work out my sword arm. I need a partner." She tugged Brodie's ear. "How about you?"

"I'd like nothing better than put you on your backside, but I've got some things to do," Brodie said, slapping her hand away.

"Maybe Sorcha could show me that trick where you guys flip through the air—" Bree started.

"No!" Faelan said. "You need to rest. You have a bloody concussion."

"I'll rest later. I want to practice with the dagger."

He sighed. "Ten minutes, then will you lie down?" He added softly, "Please?"

"Okay," she said, giving him a quick kiss.

"I'll take you on, Sorcha." Duncan rose to his feet, standing a full head taller than Sorcha. His gaze was shuttered, but whatever was behind it ran hot.

Shay saw a look of near panic cross Sorcha's pretty face. She tilted her head. "All right, big boy. After we clear the table, you can show me what you've got." She carried dirty dishes to the sink, her face flushed. She peered out the window. "Cody, there's a man with the kinkiest hair I've ever seen getting out of a truck in your driveway."

"Back in a second." Cody opened the door and jogged across the field.

<hr />

"Got her all done," Darrell said, rubbing his hands over the top of his head, making it look like he'd been electrocuted.

"What'd you find?" Cody asked, looking the truck over. There were scrapes in the paint and the hood was bent where the tree had caught. He'd have it fixed later.

"Brake line was cut."

Cody's stomach dropped. "You're sure?"

"Sure as my hair's naturally curly. You got any enemies? If you don't, you'd better start looking for one." A car rolled up behind them. "There's my ride. Gotta go." He patted Cody's truck on the hood. "She's good as new, except for that dent."

"Sorry I couldn't get over to pick it up. Things got a little hectic here."

"No problem. I'll deliver anytime. You guys always go to the top of the list. If it weren't for you, my sister Clarisse would be dead. I still don't know how you found the rat hole that scumbag boyfriend of hers was holding her in. Even the FBI couldn't find any sign of him."

The scumbag boyfriend wasn't hard to track. His human form couldn't hide his scent. Halflings couldn't shift, not like powerful demons, but some learned to project an illusion. The demon form was still there, as was the scent, usually. Humans weren't sensitive enough to detect it. "Luck," Cody told Darrell.

"Tell Lachlan that Clarisse said hi. She wanted to come, but she had to work."

Clarisse had been after Lach since she first laid eyes on him. Darrell left, and Cody crawled under the truck with a flashlight, not convinced until he saw with his own eyes that the line had been repaired. Shay and Bree could have died. This was the second time she almost died in an automobile crash, which made him wonder if the accident was meant for him or her.

He opened the truck door to look for Shay's cell phone and saw a glint of something shiny under the seat. It was a necklace. A cross. The chain had broken. Cody turned it over and saw the emblem on the back. Edward's family crest. The necklace wasn't a talisman. Edward's talisman was safe in the cellar, but this had belonged to him. How had Shay gotten it? The clan had agreed she wasn't to have anything that could be traced back to her father.

—◦◦◦—

"Nice setup," Duncan said, looking over the weapons, high-tech computer equipment, camera monitors, and gym in the Bat Cave. "Got a training room too. So this is how they kept their secrets."

Cody, who had rejoined the group, glanced at Shay and then looked away. It still bothered her that they lied, but she could understand why they thought it necessary.

"Are you okay?" Faelan asked Bree. She stood next to Shay, running her hands over the wooden box.

I'm fine," Bree said, frowning. She opened the box. A heavy piece of metal hung from a leather cord.

"That's a talisman, isn't it?" Shay asked.

"It was your father's," Cody said.

Her father's. A real flesh-and-blood man. Had he

loved her? Tried to protect her? Held her and tossed her into the air? Shay picked up the box, and a thought, a memory, something familiar, flashed in her head. She felt strong arms holding her, heard a deep laugh and a woman's gentler one and then softer arms reaching for her and the smell of perfume. Was it a real memory or a desperate attempt to connect with the man and woman who gave her life?

A door slammed at the top of the stairs. "Jamie," Sorcha purred, facing the door. "You're back."

Jamie stood at the top of the stairs, clothes rumpled, hair mussed, anger radiating off him like a fog. "What the hell did you do to me, MacBain?"

"Wasn't me," Cody said.

"You saying you didn't drug me?"

"No, Nina and Matilda did," Cody said. "Had you in a wheelbarrow trying to load you into the car."

Jamie's handsome face went slack. "What for?"

"They were matchmaking and wanted you out of the way." Cody didn't go into detail, but Jamie got the point. "Must have seen the rose you gave Shay."

"I didn't give her a rose," Jamie said.

Cody's puzzled look turned to alarm. "If you didn't give it to her, who did?"

"Her aunt, maybe," Duncan suggested.

Shay shook her head. "Nina never sends roses."

"You don't think…" Bree didn't finish her sentence.

"The stalker?" Shay asked.

"Where did you find the rose?" Jamie asked.

"On my pillow last night."

"That means he got in again," Cody said. "Damn it. Must have been while we were in Luray."

"How's he getting past the locks and security system?" Ronan asked.

"Guess they're not good enough," Cody said.

———✦———

The servant was on his way to Walmart for a clean change of clothes when he saw the woman leaving her car. At first he thought it was *her*, because of the blond hair, slim build, and long legs. She'd parked on the side of the store, away from the crowded lot. He watched her walk, a long-limbed sexy gait, and ached to touch, to tease, to cut. Her head was down, focused on something in her purse. He pulled around to the empty space on her driver's side, and eased his car in to wait.

Chapter 9

"DAMNATION. THE PLACE IS SURROUNDED WITH warriors and a state-of-the-art security system, and still the guy's getting in," Faelan said. "What the hell is he? A ghost?"

"But why would he come back here after the book was taken from Jamie's?" Duncan asked.

"Maybe there's more than one person looking for it," Cody said. "Might as well throw this bit in the mix. The mechanic said the brake line on the truck was cut. It wasn't an accident."

"You mean someone tried to kill you?" Shay's legs felt weak. She leaned against the cabinet for support. Maybe Bree was right about Cody being in danger too. Was it because of Shay?

"This doesn't make sense," Sorcha said. "First someone's after Shay, and now they try to kill Cody. Any bomb or death threats we don't know about?"

"I don't think this is about just Cody or Shay," Bree said. "It's about them both. Someone is trying to keep them apart, and he's willing to kill them to do it."

"Don't even look at me," Jamie said to Cody.

"I didn't say anything," Cody said.

Jamie gave him a surly look. "You were thinking it though. You know damn well I didn't have anything to do with this."

Cody scowled but didn't say anything.

"I don't know who the target was," Faelan said, his face so hard he looked as if he were made of stone, "but that bastard could've killed my wife. I'll hunt him to the ends of the earth."

"Get in line," Cody said. He plowed his hands through his hair. "I think we should move her to Scotland."

"What's in Scotland?" Shay asked.

Cody studied her face, his expression worried. "Connor Castle."

"You have a castle?"

"It's been the seat of our clan for generations," Duncan said. "You should be safe there. Its walls have never been breached."

"Not that we know," Sorcha added. "There's the nasty little problem that an identical castle exists in New York, and no one knows how it got there. And Druan had his demons follow Angus to Scotland. Let's hope they didn't get close enough to see where the castle is."

"Ronan thinks he killed them all," Faelan said.

"You have a castle in New York too?" Shay asked.

"It was Druan's," Bree said. "The clan is using it as a second base."

"She'll be protected in Scotland, and I can meet with the Council," Cody said. Thick silence filled the room.

The first to speak was Bree. "What do you think they'll do?"

"What can they do? I'm retired," Cody said.

"They can still make your life hell," Duncan added quietly.

"If they punish him," Ronan said, "they'll have to go through me."

The others nodded. Even Jamie looked troubled, and

he probably wanted Cody out of the picture at least as much as Cody wanted him gone.

Maybe the danger Bree sensed surrounding Cody was from his own clan. But it was still Shay's fault.

"We'll have to find out when the jet can get here," Cody said.

"You have a jet?" Shay asked.

"The clan does," he said.

Did they have a country tucked away somewhere?

"I'm going to Nina's to check the locks and cameras again, see if there's a malfunction in the equipment."

"I'll take a look," Ronan said. "Come on, Mighty Faelan. I'll teach you a thing or two about modern locks."

"Good. Then I can keep you away from my wife," Faelan said.

"You come too, Shay." Cody brushed his fingers along her lower back, sending a sizzle up her spine. "I want to know exactly what you saw."

Shay glanced back as she left the basement. The other warriors paired off and were filing into the area that had mats on the floor. Weapons appeared from pockets and boots, swords and daggers that looked like fancy pocket knives, until the blade was released by a small catch. They were the product of years of innovation, according to Bree, so warriors could move about without being arrested by the people they were trying to save. Shay wished she could get her hands on one.

The group crossed to Nina's house, and Shay recounted how she had interrupted the intruder. Then she went to get her luggage while the men studied the locks.

When she came downstairs, she heard muffled voices coming from the walls. She turned in a circle, trying to locate the sound, when the wall under the stairs opened, and Cody stepped out. Shay gaped as Faelan and Ronan followed. She could see stairs inside leading to a hole. Cody pushed something, and the panel slid closed.

"What's that?"

Cody's jaw ticked. "Uh… a tunnel."

"A tunnel? There's a tunnel under Nina's house?"

"It connects to our basement."

"How long has it been here?"

"A while," Cody said, not meeting her eyes.

"How long?" Shay ground out.

Ronan and Faelan glanced at each other and took a discreet step back.

"Come on now, Shay—"

"How long has there been a damned tunnel under my house?"

"Since you were a baby. We had to have quick access to and from the house," Cody said.

Shay backed away, standing stiff against the opposite wall. She remembered waking up to go to the bathroom one night when she was about six. She heard a noise and peered over the banister. Cody's father was standing near the stairs, and then he vanished. She thought it odd, but forgot about it in the morning. It shouldn't hurt, but they were *her* stairs. What else had they hidden from her? "Damn you, Cody MacBain!" Shay whirled and stalked out. Her suitcase caught the edge of the door and fell. Shay kicked it aside and kept walking.

She heard Cody curse behind her as she stormed across the porch.

"Shay, wait." He took her arm and stepped quickly in front of her, bringing her face-to-face with the outline of the talisman under his shirt. "We couldn't tell you. Any more than we could tell you the other stuff."

"You told them," she said, jerking her thumb toward Faelan and Ronan, standing in the doorway.

"I didn't think to tell you after you came back. I've been more worried about keeping you safe than telling you every secret this house has."

"That's the point. It's *my* house. I should've already known." She and Cody had gotten into all kinds of trouble together. Why hadn't he told her about this?

"Come on, I'll show you now." Cody took her hand and led her inside. He pushed what appeared to be a knot in the wood, and a panel slid back. She followed the narrow stairs down to a concrete tunnel roughly ten feet tall and ten feet wide with dim lights mounted on the walls.

"I can't believe you kept this from me," Shay said, her voice echoing in the confined space. "You know I love tunnels."

"He meant no harm, lass," Faelan said behind them. "You ought to trust him. The man pulled me from my wedding, at risk to his own life and limb—from my wife—to protect you." He passed them, kilt swirling around his knees, looking exactly like what he was, a warrior who stepped out of the nineteenth century, except for the Eddie Bauer suitcase in his hand.

Ronan moved past and brushed a knuckle under her chin. "It's hard to understand, but they did it for you." He jogged to catch up with Faelan.

"Maybe I don't want protecting," Shay yelled at Ronan's and Faelan's retreating backs, her voice sounding as if it came from a jar.

Ronan turned around, walking backward. "If you

knew what was out there, you'd appreciate what they've risked for you." His face was as grim as his voice.

She knew he was right. A demon like the one who may be after her had stolen Faelan's life, causing him to be yanked out of his own time and thrown into the future. He lost everything. Parents, brothers, his sister. This was bigger than just her hurt feelings.

Cody put one hand on her shoulder. "Can we get past this, Shay? Can you forgive me, forgive us? We had good intentions. Maybe we screwed up, but you and I can't keep hitting this issue every time we talk."

"I know you meant well, but stop protecting me."

He stepped closer, his body brushing hers. "I'll never stop protecting you. It's in my blood. I understand your frustration, but it's far more important to me to keep you safe than to worry if I've pointed out every little security detail that you might not be aware of."

"One more surprise, and I'm leaving," she said.

Even in the dim light she saw a flash of fear in his eyes.

When the door at the end of the passageway opened, the silence of the tunnel echoed with the clamor of fighting. Walking into the Bat Cave was like stepping into a gladiator ring. Sweat-slicked bodies, plus the clash of swords mingled with grunts, yells, and laughter. The men had removed their shirts, and even Sorcha had stripped down to a tank top. Off to the side, Shay saw the small room with monitors. "How long have the monitors been here?"

Cody's jaw clamped. "Longer than the tunnel. Let's go practice. You can take your anger out on me, aye? Let's see what you remember."

She nodded absently and followed Cody into the

practice area. While she emptied her pockets, Cody took a small sword from the wall.

Shay gave it an apprehensive stare. "It's been a while since I've used a sword."

He moved behind her, clasping his large hand over hers, demonstrating. "It'll come back to you. Remember, not too tight. Feel the weight, the balance, as if it's part of your arm."

What she felt was Cody's body so close she could smell the soap he used in the shower, and his skin, warm and masculine, made her think of what they'd done last night, what they hadn't done, and what she wanted to do. It took several minutes to focus on the sword she held. After a few practice swings, the weapon started to feel more comfortable in her hand.

"That's better," he said, nodding. "Feel the sword's power."

He backed away and slid a larger sword from the case on the wall. Facing her, he lifted the blade, body poised for attack. "What are you going to do?"

She gripped her sword, shifting slightly from foot to foot, watching his eyes. She lunged, but he stepped aside so quickly she almost fell. She caught herself and turned.

Several feet away, Sorcha sparred with Duncan, both faces intense, unreadable. Shay watched Sorcha execute a strike as powerful as a man's. Sorcha wouldn't have run away from a stalker, but Sorcha was a warrior, trained for battle, not a woman who'd learned some self-defense moves when she was a kid.

Cody's sword sliced through the air and stopped, the tip pointed over Shay's heart. She gasped.

"Pay attention," Cody barked. "Getting distracted is the fastest way to die. Be aware of your surroundings, but don't forget I'm in front of you holding a sword. Now, attack like I showed you. Remember when we were teenagers."

She'd thought it was just a cool game back then. No one had told her the fate of the world was at stake. She blocked out the yells and clashing metal and focused on Cody. His face, his hazel eyes, the set of his jaw, solid and strong. He stood so still she wondered how he could be breathing. She steadied her own breathing, stared into his eyes, and felt strength pouring over her like metal, clothing her in armor. She lunged. Her sword met his, a shriek of metal, the jolt jarring her shoulder, but she held on to her blade. She felt strong, powerful, the way she hadn't felt the past month. She jumped back, gripped the sword tighter, and lunged again. Cody whirled aside, moving quickly behind her, his blade at her throat before she even struck with her sword. She could feel the heat of his body, the cold metal at her neck. Her heart pounded so hard she was sure everyone could hear.

"What now?" His voice was soft at her ear. He wasn't even out of breath. Even though she was angry at him for keeping the tunnel a secret, she wanted to lean into him and feel his strength. What was wrong with her?

She saw Jamie stop and look at them, pausing long enough for Ronan to knock his sword from his hand, and she felt some of her training return. *Get clear of the weapon.* Shay brought her elbow back into Cody's ribs, and his blade relaxed enough for her to shove his arm aside and spin to face him.

He grinned, baring his nicked bottom tooth, and moved

like a streak of light. Shay's whole body rattled as he struck the sword from her hand. She stumbled backward, reaching out to grab hold of him. They both fell, but he twisted at the last second, and she landed on top of him.

"We seem destined to do this," he said, eyes darkening.

Shay's eyes locked on his, and she forgot about swords and warriors. She remembered his hands on her, hers on him—

"Feel like a real workout?" Jamie stood above them, his eyes boring through Cody.

Cody put Shay aside and stood. "If you think you're up to it."

"I am, but looks like you didn't get your beauty rest."

Cody gave Jamie an evil grin. "Hard to do with Shay talking in her sleep."

Jamie's eyes narrowed, and his hand clenched around his sword. "After a year, I got used to it."

"Shay, move back." Cody pulled his shirt over his head and flung it behind him.

"I don't think this is a good idea," Shay said.

"Move!" Cody and Jamie yelled at the same time. The men circled each other, faces fierce, bodies taut. Cody lunged, and Jamie met his sword. Shay's heart pounded sickeningly as their swords flashed and feet darted, the movements so quick she found herself as mesmerized as she was horrified. The power they exuded was overwhelming. She'd never seen anything like it, except in the movies.

Everyone else in the room stopped, swords hanging from their hands as they watched the two men. Cody's sword slashed across Jamie's stomach, leaving a streak of red.

"Someone stop them," Shay yelled.

"Enough," Faelan roared. He wedged himself between Cody and Jamie while Ronan and Duncan held them back. "Leave something for the enemy to fight."

Cody wiped sweat from his forehead with the back of his hand. He and Jamie were both panting, chests heaving.

Jamie held his hand over the cut on his stomach, his eyes furious.

"Come on, Jamie. You need a bandage." Shay picked up her cell phone and stuck it in her pocket, keeping it close in case Renee called. Shay led Jamie up the stairs to the bathroom on the first floor. She found the first aid kit and looked at the wound. It was low on his stomach, almost touching his belt. She reached for his buckle and started to undo it, but caught herself. She didn't have that right anymore. She felt his gaze burning into the top of her head. "Unbuckle your belt," she said. She backed up. "Maybe you should bandage it."

"You'll do a better job of it than me." Jamie unbuckled his belt and unzipped his jeans enough to push them clear of the cut. He leaned against the sink as she knelt and cleaned the wound.

"Sorry," she said, when he flinched.

"It's okay," he said, his voice strained.

"It doesn't look as bad as it was before."

"Warriors heal quickly."

He held his belt clear while she applied gauze and taped it in place. She was so close to him she could feel her breath on her fingers as she worked. She heard Jamie groan. Shay looked up and saw his eyes darkening with passion, and he was getting hard.

"All done," she said, jumping to her feet.

His hand touched her arm, sliding up to cradle her face. "Are you sure there's no chance for us?" he asked, searching her eyes. There was longing and sadness in his. "After this is over, maybe if we go away, take a vacation."

"I'm not right for you, Jamie. What about destiny and those mate marks?" He didn't have one, unless it was hidden underneath his tattoos. She'd seen every other part of him.

"It doesn't happen to everyone. My mother wasn't part of a clan, she was a buffer, so I've got mixed blood. I might never get a mate mark. I don't care, anyway. I know what I want."

"But you're a warrior, you must have a mate out there somewhere. She deserves you."

"I don't want her," he said, lowering his head. Before she could stop him, he touched his mouth to hers. His lips were warm, the taste of him comforting. He was everything a man should be. Decent, honorable, strong, and kind. And handsome to boot. Was she insane to pass him up? Another face came into focus, another body. She wouldn't use Jamie as a substitute.

Cody put the sword back on the wall and headed upstairs. He owed Jamie an apology, even though he started the fight. Cody had been an ass from the minute he saw Shay hugging Jamie at his house. It still pissed him off, thinking about Jamie's hands on her, but Jamie was trying to protect her now, and Cody respected that. He touched his neck. It was time to come clean with her. Tell her what he was holding back. How the hell would she take it? First, he'd take Jamie aside and explain to him, man to man. Cody reached the bathroom door, and the apology on his tongue fizzled and died. Shay was in Jamie's arms, locked in a kiss.

"What the hell?" He didn't even recognize his own voice, cold and rusted as steel.

The kissing couple broke apart. Shay turned, her face flushed. Jamie tensed. He still had one hand on Shay's arm, and his jeans were unzipped. Bloody hell. Was he going to take her right here with the door open?

Cody didn't think. All he saw was red. He stalked forward and took Shay by the arm. "I need to speak to you... alone," he ground out, pulling her toward the door. Jamie started after them, but Shay held up her hand. "It's okay. I'll talk to you in a few minutes."

The hell she would. Cody strode down the hall, opened his bedroom door, and pulled her inside. Slamming it shut, he faced her, his chest burning as if his heart were being ripped out, one chamber at a time. "You let him kiss you? After last night? Why?" His voice cracked. "How could you do this to me? Wasn't it enough that you destroyed me once?"

"Destroyed—" Cody cut off her words with his mouth. He would get Jamie Waters off her lips and out of her head one way or another. He kissed her, his mouth desperate, biting and licking and tasting until her body softened under his. He lifted his head, regretting his actions, but she clutched his shoulders, pulling him back. He could count on one hand the number of times he'd kissed her. How was it that her lips felt so familiar, like he'd been kissing them all his life? An explosion sounded behind Shay's head. Her teeth bumped his.

"Shay?" It was Jamie.

"I'll be out in a second," Shay called. She was breathless, her lips swollen.

"When we're finished," Cody added, his voice as ragged as Shay's.

"I'm leaving," Jamie said quietly.

Shay scooted past Cody and opened the door. "Jamie, wait." She smoothed down her hair and ran after him.

Cody's heart dropped. Was she choosing Jamie? Still? Over his dead body. He took off after them.

Jamie turned. "I'm outta here."

"Good idea," Cody said.

Jamie stepped closer, both men bristling like angry bulls. Shay inserted herself between them.

"Get back, Shay!" Cody roared, setting her aside.

"What's all the yelling about?" Marcas asked, walking toward them. The others were behind him.

"They're at it again," Lach said. "I haven't been back five minutes, and you two are fighting."

"I say we give them back their swords, and the last one standing gets the woman," Faelan said, scowling. Bree elbowed him in the ribs. "I'm jesting. I wouldn't actually let them kill each other."

"You're a damned hypocrite," Jamie said to Cody, eyeing Shay's swollen lips. "If I'm reading things right, I'd say you overstepped your boundaries a long time ago."

Frustration and anger rolled into a ball of fire inside Cody. "Hypocrite? I'm not a bloody hypocrite. I have a right to kiss her."

Jamie balled up his fists. "Says who?"

"Says this," Cody shouted, pointing at the tattoo on his neck. "It's a mate mark. For her. She's mine. She's always been mine."

Everyone froze, staring at him. Shay's mouth worked, but nothing came out. Jamie looked as if he'd been kicked in the stomach. Strangely enough, Duncan didn't look much better.

"Your mate?" Lach said. "Why didn't you say something?"

What had he done? Cody started toward Shay, but she took two steps back, bumping the wall. Her cell phone rang. She moved stiff as a zombie, prying it from her pocket. She looked at caller ID. "It's Renee," she said, her voice numb. She pushed the button. "Renee, where are you? I've been worried—" the blood drained from Shay's face.

Cody grabbed the phone and put it on speaker.

"Help..." the voice was scratchy, hard to understand.

Shay's hands trembled as she reached for the phone. "Renee?"

"Help me..." There was panting, as if she was running. "Help me. He's..."

Shay turned to Cody, her eyes wide with fear. "Renee, where are you?"

Everyone crowded in, listening, as heavy, rasping breaths filled the hallway. "He's coming. Oh God. Forgive me... the letters. I was wrong. I hid the... No!" she shrieked. "No!"

Shay's fingers dug into Cody's arm as they listened to the screams and sickening thuds. There was a loud noise, as if she dropped the phone, and then silence. After a few seconds, they heard even breathing, not Renee's panting.

Tears trickled down Shay's face. "Who are you?" she screamed, but the call disconnected.

Cody looked at the screen. "Try calling her back," he

said, handing the phone to Shay. He pulled out his own cell phone.

Shay swiped her eyes and redialed. "It's busy," she said, staring at the phone as if it were a bloody knife.

Cody punched in a number. "Sam, can you get a location on a cell phone? Shay's friend is in trouble. I'll owe you another one."

"I don't know what Shay's messed up in, but there's no end to this mess," Sam said. "There's been another murder, someone Shay knew."

Cody moved a few feet away so he could hear the details. He listened grimly. "The police in Scotland found another body," he told the others after he hung up.

Shay wobbled like she might collapse. Cody took a step closer, but Jamie was already there. Bree stood on her other side, holding Shay's hand.

"One of my clients?" Shay asked.

"No," Cody said. "A guy named Nick Deet."

"Nick? From the pub?" Jamie asked, still touching Shay's arm.

"You knew him?" Cody asked, not bothering to hide the suspicion in his voice.

"We stopped there in the evenings sometimes," Jamie said.

"How was he killed?" Shay asked.

"Stabbed," Cody said.

"Any suspects?" Marcas asked.

Cody nodded. "Yeah."

"Who?"

"Shay."

"Me? They think *I* killed Nick?" Shay asked.

"Your number was the last one he called," Cody said, staring at Jamie's hand on her arm. Cody had just told him Shay was his mate, and he still couldn't keep his hands off her.

"He called me? We weren't even friends. We chatted in the pub, but that was it," Shay said.

"Sam wanted to give us a heads up," Cody said. "The police in Scotland want to question you."

"There must have been more than just the one phone call," Marcas said.

"Try twenty-five over the past month," Cody said.

Shay's eyebrows rose. "Nick called my house twenty-five times? He must have been the person who kept calling and hanging up. The number was blocked."

"Could he be the one who broke into Shay's shop?" Lachlan asked.

Faelan shook his head. "I doubt it. When I was in Scotland keeping an eye on Shay, the bartender at the pub said Nick had missed work the day before without calling, so he was probably already dead when the intruder broke into Shay's shop."

"Maybe the intruder killed Nick," Shay said, "but why?"

"No idea, but we'll need to leave as soon as possible. You'll have to go to Scotland and talk to the police," Cody said. "Marcas, see how fast the jet can get here. You, Lach, and Jamie can stay here and look for Renee. You know the area, and you know Renee." He suspected Renee was past help. "The rest of you can escort us to Scotland."

Jamie shook his head. "I go with Shay. She still needs to be protected."

"I can't leave Renee," Shay argued.

"You have to." Cody's voice was soft, but firm.

"You can't stay. It's too dangerous here," Jamie said.

Bree looped her arm around Shay's back. "They're right, Shay."

"Another metal bird," Faelan groaned.

Ronan slapped him on the shoulder. "Don't worry. I'll knock you out, if it'll help."

"Not if you value that pretty face of yours," Faelan said. "I'll stay too. I can help look for Renee."

Cody rubbed the bridge of his nose. "Jamie and I will take Shay to Scotland. The rest of you stay here. There'll be plenty of warriors at the castle to protect her." If Renee was alive, she probably needed all the help she could get.

<center>~~~</center>

Shay sat in Cody's kitchen, only half listening to the Scottish police officer on the phone. She kept staring at the tattoo on Cody's neck, looking for the mark he claimed meant they were destined mates. Mates? What was she supposed to do with that? Nine years she spent hating him, and in a matter of hours she found out that he hadn't even gotten her letters, and he was her mate. Was that why she never got over him? Why hadn't he told her? Was he hiding more secrets? Her head was reeling so badly she had to keep asking the officer to repeat his question. She hung up, relieved that she wasn't a serious suspect, only a person of interest they wanted to see as soon as possible.

"We need to talk," Cody said.

"Not now," Shay said. She went upstairs, found her suitcase, and numbly gathered her clothes. Was Renee alive? Shay had spent the night snuggled with Cody, warm in bed, while Renee was probably bound and gagged, who knew where. Shay's cell phone buzzed in her pocket. She grabbed it, staring at the display. Her pulse pounded. "Renee? Are you okay? Where are you?"

There was silence, punctuated by heavy breathing. Shay's throat tightened.

"Renee?" she whispered.

"Listen, carefully," the raspy voice said. "Don't get help. Don't speak. If you want to see your friend alive, you'll come to me. Alone."

"Where is she?" Shay picked up a notepad and pen by the bed.

"Luray Caverns. Wait until dark. The door will be open. Come alone. If anyone follows you, she dies."

"I don't know if I can get away," she said as she scribbled on a pad beside the bed.

"Then she'll die." The phone went dead.

Chapter 10

"ANYONE SEEN RONAN?" FAELAN APPEARED, DRESSED in jeans for once.

Cody dropped the papers Sam had faxed and rubbed his eyes. "I thought you two were going back to Renee's shop." There had to be a clue somewhere to put them on the right trail.

"Ronan took off earlier," Lach said, selecting another knife. Some of the others were getting ready to search for Renee. "He said something about you staying here to watch Bree."

"Why's he so bloody worried about *my* wife?" Faelan looked over Cody's shoulder. "That's the dead guy?"

Cody nodded.

"He's just a kid. Damnation. If you need me to go to Scotland, I'll go," Faelan said.

Cody knew how much Faelan hated flying, but there was another reason he wanted Faelan to stay in Virginia, away from the danger following Shay. Faelan didn't know he was going to be a father, but Cody intended to make sure Faelan was around to raise his child. Maybe he and Bree could go on their honeymoon as soon as Renee was found, and Bree could share her news with him under more pleasant circumstances.

"Stay here and help look for Renee. There'll be more than enough warriors in Scotland to protect Shay. No one's infiltrated the castle since it was built. She'll

be safe there. We've kept it hidden for this long." Or
had they? They still didn't know who built the one in
New York.

"I've got a bad feeling about Renee," Faelan said.

"Me too." Cody saw the lid was ajar on the box
that held Edward's talisman. Cody opened the box and
frowned. "Did someone take Edward's talisman?"

"I saw Shay there earlier," Lach said.

She'd have to return the talisman. It was sacred, to be
worn only by the warrior it was made for, not to mention
it was dangerous.

"I'm going to try Ronan again," Faelan said.

"Is Shay packing?" Lach asked.

"Aye. And she was going to take a nap before we go."

"I still can't believe she's your mate and you never
even bothered to tell us. Your own brothers," Lach said.

Cody couldn't believe he told the whole bloody lot
of them.

Lach grinned. "Mom will be overjoyed. She loves
Shay. And Nina and Matilda—" His grin faded. "You
think the two of you could elope?"

"Who said anything about a wedding? I'll be lucky
if she even speaks to me after this." Cody gave Lach a
warning glance. "Keep your mouth shut. Shay already
feels pressured enough."

"I'm not the one who keeps blurting out secrets,"
Lach said. "We need to check Nina's house, make sure
it's locked."

"I'll check," Cody said. He walked through the tunnel, one of the hardest things for him to hide from her.
She always loved secret rooms and tunnels, but every
time he was tempted to tell her, he remembered that

sharing secrets could endanger her life. Cody checked the doors and windows and then noticed Shay's car was missing. His throat went dry. He ran back through the tunnel and upstairs to Shay's room. She wasn't there, or in the bathroom.

"What's going on?" Marcas asked from the doorway.

"Shay's not here. Her car's gone."

"Jamie's gone too. Maybe he took her someplace he thought was safer," Marcas said.

Someplace away from Cody and his mate mark. The guy was still in love with Shay, whether she was Cody's mate or not. Were her feelings for Jamie deeper than she realized? She almost married him. "Shay was upset with me. I probably scared her off."

"Blurting out that she's your mate in front of everyone wasn't the smartest thing you've done."

"I wasn't thinking straight. I saw her kissing him," Cody said, pulling out his phone.

"What kind of kiss?"

"A kiss kiss. His lips on hers, hers on his." Cody punched in Jamie's number, but he didn't answer.

"Maybe it was a sympathetic kiss or a good-bye kiss. Your head's usually screwed on tighter than anyone else's. That's why you were assigned an ancient demon. If you don't get your head on straight now, Shay's going to pay the price for your jealousy. You can't protect her if you're worried about keeping her away from Jamie."

"Why didn't you tell me he was dating her?"

"We didn't find out until just before they broke up, when Shay told Nina. Jamie didn't want us to know," Marcas said. "If I'd known about your mate mark, I'd have told you as soon as I found out. You should've told us Shay was your mate."

"Guess we've all been keeping secrets." Cody shoved the phone in his pocket. "I hope I haven't ruined my chances with Shay."

"She's upset, but she'll get over it. Let her make the decision on her own. No mate mark is strong enough to force a woman to marry a man if she doesn't want to." Marcas tapped Cody on the head. "Don't worry. It'll all work out."

What if it didn't? What if she walked away? Could he live with it? Again.

While everyone else searched the woods, the barn, and Nina's house again, Cody checked Shay's bedroom. Her suitcase lay on the bed, and he could see the top of her cell phone sticking out from underneath it. Why would she leave her cell phone? He picked it up and checked the calls. The most recent one had come from Renee's phone thirty minutes ago, and lasted twenty-three seconds. If Renee called and asked Shay to meet her, nothing would keep Shay from going. Had she asked Jamie to follow her, instead of Cody? He couldn't see her leaving without a note. She might be upset with him, but she wouldn't worry everyone else. He picked up the notepad by the bed. Nothing. He remembered her tendency to scribble while she talked on the phone. He held the paper to the light and saw the impression her pen had made. Two words: Luray Caverns.

He raced downstairs and across to Nina's house. The others were in the foyer. "She's gone to Luray Caverns."

"You found something?" Marcas asked.

Cody held up the notepad. "See the indention? No one but Shay has slept in that bedroom for a year—"

"And I just put that pad of paper there two months ago, when I was making a list of things Mom wanted shipped to her," Marcas said.

"Why Luray Caverns?" Lach asked.

"Maybe she went to meet Renee there. They used to go a lot, when they were kids. She'll probably take Skyline Drive. I'll go after her on the bike. I can get around the sightseers."

"We'll get the helicopter and meet you there," Marcas said. "The mechanic's making repairs, but it should be ready by the time we get there."

Cody's phone rang. It was Ronan.

"I just ran into four vampires behind Renee's shop," Ronan said.

Cody put the phone on speaker. "Vampires? What are they doing there?"

"I don't know, but they have our book."

"What the... did you get it?" Cody asked.

"No. There was a female with them. She disappeared with the book. And that blond from Druan's castle was there, but he won't be biting anyone anytime soon. I broke off one of his fangs. Someone else had already broken the other one. I can't come back," Ronan said, "just in case they're following me. I don't want to lead them there."

Fangs? Cody's stomach plunged. He picked up the piece of ivory from the bookshelf. "Too late. He's already been here. Shay's missing. We think she's headed to Luray Caverns."

"I'll meet you there," Ronan said.

Cody hung up. His skin felt cold with fear. A vampire had been in her house. She had wounded him, and now she was missing. He shouldn't have let her out of his sight. He prayed that Jamie was with her. At least he would keep her safe.

Lach's head tilted. He had the sharpest hearing of them all. "Here come the others now."

"We saw some footprints," Duncan said. "I think someone's been there, but no sign of him now."

Cody told them about Ronan's call and showed them the fang. "I hope she's with Jamie."

"I talked to Jamie about an hour ago," Duncan said. "He's alone."

Malek looked at the shrunken corpse of the woman. Strands of pale hair still draped a dark dress, moldy, probably expensive at one time. If this was Shay's mother, the body should have been burned. Malek turned his attention to the man. He was tall, had good bone structure, but there wasn't enough skin left to tell if it was him. A gold ring circled his finger, a thin gold band. He slid the ring over the knuckle and shriveled tissue. Something was engraved inside, a name, he hoped, though he wasn't sure he would trust a name after this trick. He pulled a handkerchief from the pocket of his suit and wiped off the ring. The inscription was in a language he didn't know. Unusual. He had lived in many places on this planet over the centuries and learned the human race and its languages well, but this he had never seen. The woman's ring was the same. Were they Shay's parents? He was almost certain Shay was really Dana, but he had to be sure. If he killed the wrong mother, all would be lost. If Shay was the one, she had to die, but not until she told him where the book was. In the meantime, he had to get her away from Cody MacBain. If they produced a child, it would ruin everything he had planned.

Malek pocketed the rings and ripped a chunk of hair from both rotted scalps. If all else failed, he could check the DNA.

Cody alternated between cursing and praying as he looked at the line of cars in front of him. There had been a head-on collision a few miles up the road. Someone had been thrown from the vehicle. Both sides of the road were blocked, with medevac on the way. Scenic Skyline Drive was quickly losing its appeal. He pulled his Texas Chopper motorcycle onto the side of the road. Ignoring the glares of frustrated drivers, he squeezed past the stopped cars. A few miles later, he spotted her, head out the window, chewing her lip as she stared at the traffic. She turned as he pulled up beside her. Her color drained. He killed the engine, got off the bike, and opened her door.

"No," she said, looking at him as if he held a gun. "You can't be here."

"Are you insane?" he asked, climbing in her car. The relief was so great his legs felt like twine. He grabbed her and crushed her to his chest, muffling her reply. "What were you thinking?" He pressed a fierce kiss on her head, until she shoved him away.

"You have to leave. If he sees you, he'll kill her."

"Who is he?"

"I don't know who he is, but he has Renee. He said if I want to see her alive, I have to come to Luray Caverns, alone."

"So he can get you too," Cody yelled.

"I won't let Renee die because of me. You have to leave. Please."

"I can't." He could no more walk away from her than he could harm a child.

Shay whimpered like a trapped animal. Cody reached across the seat and gathered her close again, needing to feel her warmth. "We'll get him. The others are on the way to Luray. They're some of the strongest warriors alive. I'd trust any one of them with my life." Even Jamie, if it came to that.

"But—"

"No. I'm taking you someplace safe." He looked at the line of traffic. Darkness was falling, which would make things worse. "If I can get around this traffic, we're going straight to the airport. If the jet isn't there, we'll take a commercial flight."

"I'm not leaving without Renee."

He knew she wouldn't budge. He'd have to knock her out to get her on a plane. It was tempting, but he wouldn't be able to protect her from inside a jail cell. He checked the halted traffic again. "We're not going anywhere in this mess anyway. Move your car off to that wide spot so cars can get past. We'll take the bike and find a place to stay. Without everyone there to guard the house, you're probably safer here."

Reluctantly, Shay left her car on the side of the road and climbed on the back of Cody's motorcycle. She hooked her fingers in his belt, the way she had when they were teenagers. They had ridden that way for hours, Shay holding on to him, laughing, as they climbed hills. Why the hell had he let her walk away?

He followed the shoulder of the road, Shay's hands burning at his waist, until he reached the cabin rentals.

The white-haired man ran a gnarled finger down the computer screen. "We're usually full this time of year, but a couple left today. Woman went into labor early. Good thing she left before the accident, or she might've given birth right here. Let's see... yep, here it is, cabin four, and it's off to itself, nice and quiet. Must be your lucky day, or night, that is."

Shay didn't feel very lucky. She should have already arrived at the caverns. What would Renee's kidnapper do?

"I talked to Lach, told him we'd stay here, at least until traffic clears. He'll call as soon as they get to the caverns. Renee might not be there, though. It could be a trap."

She heard in his voice what he didn't say. Renee might be dead. Shay remembered the screams and the sickening thuds. Her throat tightened. "I know."

Using Cody's flashlight, they found the trail that led to the cabin. It was growing dark, and the temperature was dropping quickly. It was colder on the mountain, reminding her of Scotland. She had blown their plans for leaving. Would the police in Scotland come looking for her?

The cabin was small, but she was glad to see two

beds, since she was still leery about the destined-mate stuff. If she was his mate, where was her mark? Did she have to take his word for it? He'd lied about a lot of things, or rather, withheld the truth. Could she trust him on something as important as this? What if he was wrong about the mark? What if he was saying it just because he wanted her to be his mate, like Jamie wanted too?

Cody came out of the bathroom zipping his jeans as she opened the front door. "Where are you going?"

"To sit on the porch. Is that allowed?" she snapped and blew out a frustrated sigh. "I'm sorry, Cody." Shay took two steps toward him, slid her arms around his waist, and tucked her thumbs under his belt. "I don't know why you put up with me." She laid her head on his chest.

He put his arms around her shoulders and rested his chin on her head. "Because you're family. You're my friend." He slid his hands down her back, making her skin melt. "And you're my mate," he whispered. He kissed her hair, trailing his lips down her cheek. "Not to mention you're reckless and don't take orders, and you bite. If I don't keep you out of trouble, who will?"

Shay pinched his waist. "I'm just stressed about Renee. I keep thinking, what if he sees the others coming and hurts her, because I didn't follow instructions?"

"They're trained to protect and to fight. If she's there, they'll find her."

Cody was right; the others would get there first anyway, and they were warriors, more capable of rescuing Renee than Shay. "Where's Bree?"

"At home, with Faelan threatening to tie her up. In

the meantime, Faelan's coordinating with Sam, trying to track down the names you gave us. It has to be someone you both know. Problem is, it'll be a disguise."

"I never met her creepy client. There's Mr. Ellis, my client whose table was destroyed. I just started working with him. He's American, a little eccentric, but most collectors are. I don't think he knows Renee."

"Did he order the table?"

"No. He never saw it."

"And this woman who canceled the order for the other table, did she seem... strange?"

"You mean like a demon hiding in a woman's body? No. She seemed normal."

"That's the problem," Cody said, his fingers trailing up and down her arm. "They all do. Sam's also trying to trace the call Julie got from the man asking about the table. Maybe a lead will turn up. Try to get some sleep. Traffic should clear up before long." He glanced at the beds, and she knew he was waiting for her to ask him to sleep with her. She wanted to, but she was afraid if she slept with him again, she would need to do it every night.

He took her silence for refusal and dropped a kiss on her head. "I'm going to shower," he said, sitting on the chair. He started removing his boots and socks. From this angle, his hair covered his mate mark. He tossed one sock at her. "Bathroom's small. If I get stuck, you can soap me up and slide me out."

Shay threw the sock back. "I'll call the lodge and let the old man take care of it."

Cody pulled off the other sock and wiggled his toes. He had incredibly sexy feet. He started unbuckling his pants as he walked to the bathroom.

"Cody."

He turned back at the door.

"I need you to know something. What I really want to do is get in the shower with you, rub that soap all over you, and make both of us forget that stalkers and demons even exist, but how can I do that, when Renee is in trouble?"

"I understand." He smiled. "Although I kind of wish you hadn't mentioned the part about putting soap all over me. Choose a bed. I'll be out in a few minutes."

While he showered, she checked her purse for sugarless gum in lieu of a toothbrush. She had just plopped down on the bed farthest from the bathroom, when Cody came out in his underwear. Shay jerked her gaze to her faded green quilt. She was buying him PJ's for Christmas. He climbed in his bed, propping himself on one elbow.

"You took your father's talisman."

Shay held it, her gaze steady on his. "Yes, and I'm not giving it back." She'd had nothing that belonged to her father until now.

He watched her for a moment, then nodded. "Take care of it, then. It's powerful."

"Can anyone use it?" She was intrigued by the new world of which she was suddenly a part, and conversation could distract them from their awkward confines. Although their confines had been awkward from the moment she arrived.

"Only the warrior it's given to. It's designed to destroy demons, but just like a bullet, if you get in its way, you're done."

"What happens to the demons when they're destroyed?"

"They just don't exist anymore. We try to suspend them so they're accountable for their evil, but sometimes we don't have a choice."

"What would happen if a warrior used his talisman against a powerful demon who wasn't assigned?"

"He would die. The strength of the talisman depends on the warrior's strength, and it's matched to the strength of the demon."

"I wonder if he—my father—killed a lot of demons with this." Shay felt the warmth of the talisman against her hand." She supposed the *Book of Battles* could tell her.

Cody looked a little uneasy to see her touching the talisman. "Aye, he did. Your father was a powerful warrior."

"Will you tell me about him?"

"If you'll stop playing with the talisman," he said. Shay dropped her hand, and Cody settled back against his pillows. "He was born in Scotland. So was your mother. They were childhood sweethearts—"

"Mates?"

"I don't know. The mate thing doesn't always work," he said quietly. "It's best if it does, but sometimes it just can't be."

"Where did they—we—live in Scotland?"

"Outside Beauly, not far from the clan castle."

She'd been all over that area, walked the grounds of Beauly Priory. Had she passed her own home?

"After we get rid of this problem, I'll take you to see where you were born. I know it's hard to understand why the clan did this, but they were afraid you'd be killed."

She reached for the talisman again, liking the way it felt in her hand, but stopped at Cody's frown.

"Careful. Talismans are not toys. Treat them with respect and a good dose of fear, because they'll destroy anything in their path. You can't even look at it if it's engaged."

"But you've seen it."

"It won't hurt the warrior it belongs to. Anyone else, even another warrior, has to close his eyes when the light is released."

"I'm glad you didn't have that thing in high school." She smiled. "All the guys were afraid of you and your brothers. None of them dared ask me out on a date. Only one had the nerve to ask me to dance."

"Who?"

"Zack Anderson. He was new."

"Where was I?" Cody asked.

"Home cleaning your room, unless you followed me. Remember the race I won?"

"Aye. I didn't realize we were such a pain. We were just trying to look out for you. There were a lot of guys interested in you, and we didn't want—"

"What guys? No one would come near me."

"That was because we…" Cody stopped.

Shay narrowed her eyes. "Because you what?"

"We made sure they didn't get close."

"Why?"

"We weren't sure if they were guys."

"You mean… you mean they could've been demons?" she squeaked. "*In high school?*"

"They don't come full grown," Cody said.

"I never considered… kids?"

"That's why Dad and Nina didn't want you going to public school. Dad had to do security checks on everyone around you. Teachers, principals, kids, even the lunchroom attendants."

"I just wanted to be like all the other girls. I was tired of tutors."

"The other girls didn't have a demon after them."

"I thought you were just being overprotective. Renee always said I expected too much from men because of you guys. She had a crush on you when she was younger."

"That changed," he said dryly. "What do you think she meant about the letters? Why would she say she was sorry?"

Shay had forgotten that part in all the chaos. "I don't know… oh, the missing letters, Renee was supposed to mail them."

"That explains why I didn't get them," Cody said. "She didn't want you talking to me."

Could Renee have done such an awful thing? She knew how upset Shay had been about everything. Was that why Renee asked for forgiveness?

"Let's try to get at least a few hours of sleep. We have a lot to do tomorrow."

Shay tossed and turned, drawing her legs closer to her body, but she was too cold to sleep.

"What're you doing over there? Wrestling?"

"I'm cold," Shay said.

"It's chillier up here on the mountain. Want my blanket?"

"You'll freeze," she said. What she wanted was him next to her. For warmth. For comfort. But how could she, when Renee could be hurting… or dead?

"I'll be fine." He spread his blanket over her and climbed back into bed, both of them staring at the dark space between them.

Shay rubbed her feet together, and a broken toenail made a scratching noise on the cheap sheets.

"What are you doing now?"

"My feet are still cold."

He sighed, climbed out of bed again, and walked over to her. He stood for a few seconds, lifted the covers, and slid in. She started to protest, and then his skin brushed hers, warm as a heater. She rolled over, and he moved behind her, tucking his body close. She wedged her feet between his calves.

He sucked in a breath. "You've got the coldest feet on the planet, pip-squeak."

"And you've got the warmest legs." She relaxed against him, the warmth making her forget the wisdom of the matter, and let his hips cradle hers.

"Your birthmark looks darker than it used to," he said, touching the spot at the top of her back. She felt a shiver, as she usually did when he touched her, but this one shook her. He wrapped his arms around her, obviously thinking she was still cold.

The odd-shaped mark on the back of her neck—Cody said it looked like a sliver of moon and three red stars; Lachlan said a toenail clipping and three warts—was hard to see unless she used a mirror. Even then, her hair usually covered the mark.

"I'm sorry I didn't tell you about the mate mark," he said softly, his breath warm against her ear.

"Why didn't you?"

"I'd planned to, that day I came to Lake Placid, and Renee stopped me. There were other times, when I couldn't go another day without seeing you, but every time I got there, I talked myself out of it. I couldn't be with you until I was finished with my duty, and I couldn't let you be part of my world. Fighting demons is dangerous, in case you haven't noticed."

"But you're twenty-eight. You're finished with your duty. Why didn't you come?"

"I did." He slid his hand down her arm and linked his hand in hers. "You weren't home. Some kid on the street told me he saw you walk down to the pub. I followed you. I got close enough to call out your name, when I saw the engagement ring. I was so stunned, I just left. I started to call Nina and ask who the guy was, but I was afraid if I found out I'd kill him for putting his ring on your finger when it should have been me. I didn't know it was Jamie."

Shay turned and faced him. "I'm sorry, Cody." She touched the tattoo on his neck. He pulled in a breath. "Where is the mark?" she asked, shocked that the words slipped out.

He reached for her hand. Taking one finger, he moved it to a spot behind his ear that was usually covered by his hair. There was just enough light from the bathroom to show a circle with notched edges in the design, but looking closer, she could see it was different. He hadn't tattooed over it, but all around it. A lump formed in her throat. She ran her finger over the mark and felt him shiver. Her hand tingled, then her arm, and her neck, until her whole body pulsed.

His eyes locked on hers, and Shay slid her hand around the back of his neck, pulling his mouth to hers. They were completely still, no sound except their breathing and the pulse pounding in Shay's ears. He moved, she moved—she didn't know which—but they kissed until Shay's lips and tongue felt numb. Cody lifted his head long enough to roll her to her back. He moved over her, and she could feel his hips pressing against hers, rocking gently, then harder. With a muffled exclamation, Cody reached for her shirt. She lifted her arms, helping him slide it over her head. His gaze dropped past her father's talisman to her breasts, softly touching them through her bra. His finger dipped underneath, then he shifted his weight off her and opened the clasp, groaning when her breasts were freed.

His hands and mouth were desperate, moving with such abandon that the two of them almost slid off the bed. He shifted to the side, and a second later, her jeans and panties, along with his underwear, landed on the floor. Shay stared at his body. He was perfect. Broad shoulders, flat stomach, and the sexiest hips and legs she'd ever seen on a man, not that she'd seen many. He settled between her thighs.

She grabbed his hips and pulled, nudging him inside. "Hurry. Please."

He didn't need any more encouragement. He buried himself inside her, his talisman clinking against hers as they moved. The pace was frenzied, cramming nine years of longing and need into every thrust, every grasp of fingers and touch of lips. Shay felt his teeth at her neck, and the feeling rushed at her, closer and closer, as breaths came faster. He locked his lips on hers as her body tightened, shattered into a billion pieces, and came back together again. He drove in hard, two more strokes, then stilled, his body pulsating inside hers. He collapsed, chest pounding against breasts. He dropped kisses along her forehead, her cheek, and her jaw.

"If I had any doubts that you're my mate, not that I

did, that just removed them." He pulled out and rolled over, taking her with him. "Are you all right?"

"I guess so." She'd never experienced anything like it, not even in her dreams, but already, doubts started creeping in. Renee, lying injured somewhere, maybe dead. The past. The mark. Cody getting distracted and dying. He'd never be able to focus on the battle now. "I should shower."

He released her slowly. "I'd offer to help, but there's barely enough room in there for a child."

A child. Shay's throat closed and her ears started to ring. *Blood. Stark walls. Nurses yelling.* She jumped up, scooped her clothes off the floor, and hurried to the bathroom without looking back. She locked the door, reached behind the shower curtain and turned on the water so he wouldn't hear. Her mouth opened but nothing came out, just gulps of air, then a keening sound. Her arms cradled her stomach and she rocked back and forth as tears streamed down her face. *The casket was so small she could have carried it in her arms. She stood at the edge of the hole, her heart numb, until a sharp edge of pain tore through. She dropped to the ground and sobbed, digging her fingers in the fresh dirt.* Holding her hands across her stomach, she rocked back and forth as tears streamed down her face.

There was a tap on the door. "Shay?"

She froze. Had he heard her crying? She remembered that he could hear things most men couldn't.

"Shay. Open the door."

"In a minute."

"Open the door, or I'm coming in."

A fresh bout of tears rolled down her cheeks. She hadn't had an episode like this in years, but when they hit, it was always unexpected, triggered by something simple, a tricycle on a sidewalk, a boy laughing and running with his dog.

She scrubbed at her face, and the door flew open. Cody stood, naked, his eyes worried, angry, afraid. "Care to explain what that was about?"

Shay grabbed a towel and held it against her stomach, covering herself. "I'm sorry. I just…"

"What? You just regretted it? You realized it was me in your bed and not Jamie?"

Shay gaped at him. "What does Jamie have to do with this?"

Cody reached over and shut off the shower. "Well, someone got between us in there. You almost married the guy. If it wasn't him, who was it?"

"It had nothing to do with Jamie."

His gaze was hard. "I don't believe you."

Her frustration, hurt, and anger spewed out like a volcano. "It wasn't Jamie. It was the baby," she yelled.

He looked like she'd slapped him. "Baby?" His gaze dropped to her stomach. He sat on the edge of the bathtub. "You're pregnant?"

What had she done? God, what had she done?

He rubbed his hands through his hair, shook his head, and she waited for the questions. They weren't what she expected.

"It doesn't matter, Shay. Even if it's Jamie's, it's still part of you." He held his hand over his heart, his beautiful, strong fingers trembling only slightly. "I love you. I can love it too."

Shay stared at Cody, her eyes filling with tears again. "I'm not pregnant, but I was, nine years ago."

Chapter 11

"NINE..." CODY'S EXPRESSION WENT THROUGH several levels of shock. "A baby," he whispered. "We made a baby? You and me?"

"Yes."

Raw emotion swept over his face. "But where is it?"

"Something went wrong. It was born too early."

"Why didn't you tell—*that's* what was in the letters?"

"I didn't mention the baby, I just said I needed you to come."

"And you thought I didn't care?" His voice strangled with hurt. "I would have done anything for you."

"I'm sorry. I should have known, but after everything that happened, after I wouldn't talk to you, I figured you were mad at me, or that you'd just moved on. I should have kept calling."

"A baby? We made a baby." Cody rubbed his hands over his face, his eyes lost.

Shay could still see the stark walls of the emergency room and the blood running down her legs, pooling on the white floor, so much blood for something so tiny and frail. The nurses rushing her to the delivery room as her uterus contracted, expelling the life it held before it could take its first breath. "I was five months pregnant. Five months and twenty-two days. No one knew, not even Renee, until I went to the hospital." Shay's voice dropped to a whisper and then cracked. "It was a boy.

He's buried in Lake Placid, in a small graveyard close to where I lived. That's where I was the day you came to the apartment. I was burying him. Renee was sick and couldn't come." Shay had named him Alexander. She would tell Cody that later.

"You buried him alone? Oh God, Shay." He dropped to his knees in front of her and pulled her close, his head pressed to her hair. A tear fell on her forehead and rolled down her cheek. They sat in the bathroom, her on the toilet, him kneeling before her, not speaking, just touching, grieving for a life they created and lost. She had carried her secret for so long it stripped her bare to finally share her grief, to acknowledge her son, Cody's son, after having to hide him from everyone. Hiding his existence had been almost as hard as carrying him inside her, feeling the little kicks and hiccups, and then having to bury him in the cold ground.

After the tears, she and Cody stood under the shower, holding each other as the water washed away the worst of their grief. As Cody wrapped her in a towel and dried her hair, they exchanged soft touches born of solace, not lust.

"Did you see that?" Shay asked as they stepped out of the bathroom.

"See what?" Cody asked.

"Something moved past the window."

Cody tensed, listening. "There's someone on the porch," he whispered. He quietly pulled on his jeans, grabbed the gun and his dagger. He handed her the gun. "Take this. Lock the door after I leave, and hide under the bed."

"Hide?"

"If anyone comes in, shoot for the heart." He held the dagger and pushed a button. There was a click as the blade extended into a sword.

Her pulse pounded. "Let me come with you," she said, quickly dressing.

"No. It's too dangerous."

"What if someone's out there, and this is exactly what he wants, for you to leave me alone?" She knew Cody was a skilled killer. At one time, that would have made her shiver. Now she found it comforting. She watched him struggle with his thoughts. "Please." She'd rather face a dragon with Cody at her side than wait alone for shadows to attack.

He sniffed the air. "No." His voice sounded like steel. "Don't leave this cabin. No matter what." Cody walked to the door, came back, cupped her head, and kissed her. "Don't leave," he said again, and then he was gone. She locked the door behind him and watched from the window as he melted into the night. Where did he go? Her eyes scanned the dark, trying to make out his form. At first she thought the shadows were clouds drifting over the moon, then she saw the shape of them, like men, but they didn't move like men. They glided. They were following Cody.

Cody gripped his sword and stepped lightly on the forest floor, ears tuned for any sound that didn't belong. He sniffed, eyes searching the shadows. Something was there; he could feel it. A soft laugh whispered through the trees. He whirled. A man materialized a few yards away, watching him with red eyes. He smiled, and sharp teeth flashed in the dark. Fangs. A vampire! What was it doing here? Before Cody could lift his sword, the man rushed at him like a streak, moving so fast Cody couldn't track it.

He learned in the battle at Druan's castle that the only sure way to kill a vampire was beheading or a direct stab through the heart. Talismans didn't work on them. He swung his sword as the thing zoomed past, but he missed. Whirling, it came back. Just as it slammed Cody to the ground, it went solid again, with fangs an inch long. He rolled to his feet, grabbed his fallen sword, and braced for the next attack. This time when it struck, he was ready. As he fell, he thrust his sword upward, into its heart. The creature turned to dust in mid-air, particles settling all around him.

Hisses filled the air as more creatures emerged from the trees. They stood out of sword's reach, their fangs bared. Cody searched out where each one stood, identifying the leader, who stood a little apart from the others, his stance cockier, more sure. When the next one attacked, Cody jumped aside and drove his sword into the leader's heart. The others hissed and looked at each other. They hadn't expected him to take the offensive when he was so outnumbered, but he was used to fighting against the odds.

They came at him like bullets, nothing but a blur, until they slowed. He swung left and drove his sword into what he hoped was the thing's heart, and dust rained down, covering his sword. Two of them hit him at once, flinging him in the air like a rag doll. His bones felt like they shattered, but he clung to his sword. They came at him again, and he rolled painfully to his feet, his blade catching another one in the neck. The swing wasn't strong enough. The vampire screeched and kept going. If he could just see the bloody things. Cody ducked as another one attacked and then swung harder, finishing off the one he missed. He was tiring, but he had to kill them all before they discovered Shay.

Two were left, but they kept attacking so close together that he couldn't strike them both. He waited for the first to attack. Using the side of a tree to spring clear, he flipped through the air, leveling his blade at what he thought was its neck. It disappeared, leaving only one.

"Come on, you bastard."

The vampire stood fifty feet away in human form. He turned his head, looking at the path leading to the cabin, and Cody followed his gaze. Shay stood there, her face pale, eyes wide with shock.

"We've found you at last," the vampire said.

Cody's blood felt like shards of ice.

"We?" Shay asked, her voice strong. "You're the only one left."

The vampire grinned. "Too bad I can't have a taste of you. The feisty ones are always better. I'll have to settle for him." Its fangs lengthened. "No one cares about him."

Shay's face darkened; her back straightened; her shoulders squared. "I care about him."

The vampire turned and streaked toward Cody. Shay ran after the vampire, moving just as fast. She tackled it, and they both rolled into the trees, a mix of swirling colors. Cody stood rooted in place, his mouth hanging open. What the hell?

The vampire looked as stunned as Cody. It attacked

again, catching Cody off guard, slamming his head against a tree. As he struggled to remain conscious, he registered several things at once. The vampire, who had retreated, now rushing at him again, and Shay, farther away, scooping up a stick and running after the vampire. No, what she did was faster than running. She streaked after the vampire, driving the stick into the blurred shadow. It turned solid, its fangs elongated, red eyes wide with shock. The vampire disintegrated, but Shay kept coming, moving too fast to stop. She hit the ground and rolled. Her stick drove deep into the earth, vibrating, inches from Cody's face, then everything went black.

———

"Cody! Wake up!" Shay shook his shoulder. Oh my God. Vampires! Nobody said anything about vampires! What about the demons? "Cody, you have to wake up!" Was he dead?

She heard a twig snap behind her. Her blood froze. She turned. "You." She was so shocked she didn't start fighting until the handkerchief covered her mouth and nose. By then, it was too late.

———

Have his eyes always been this sexy, Shay wondered as his head lowered. His body, warm and hard, with all those muscles pressed against her definitely wasn't the one she remembered skinny-dipping with. Something was different about him inside, not just the body. An edge. His lips touched hers, hesitantly, as if he weren't sure what he would find. A small sound of surprise, and pleasure, escaped. He tasted good. He lifted his

*mouth just a fraction. She expected him to apologize,
move away, laugh to ease the awkwardness—something.
Instead, he kissed her again, this time opening his mouth,
letting his tongue tease her lips. She had imagined this
in her dreams, but in her dreams, it hadn't felt this good.*

*Cody shifted, settling one thigh between hers. He
stroked her hair and face, whispering her name as
they kissed. He smelled good, like mountains. His
lips grew bolder, his tongue slipping curiously into
her mouth until she was on fire. The rational side of
her brain told her to run, but her hands gripped his
T-shirt and moved underneath to feel the bare skin of
his back, beginning to dampen with sweat.*

*Breathing hard, the two started shedding clothes. He
stared as her body was exposed, and she got her first
good look at his tattoos. He pushed his jeans and underwear down, and she forgot everything else.*

*Shay gasped as he nudged her legs apart and low-
ered his body to hers. His eyes, clouded with passion,
locked on hers as he joined their bodies together. Shay
felt a sharp pain and bit her lip to keep from crying
out. Cody went still for a moment and murmured, "I'm
sorry." The need to move was stronger than the sting.
She pushed toward him, and he pushed back, pressing
deeper. He stopped again, resting his forehead on hers.
She wrapped her ankles around his legs and her arms
around his waist to hold him tighter, and he groaned.
It was the most beautiful thing she ever experienced, in
spite of the discomfort. The confusion of the past year
vanished. Joined with Cody, she felt complete.*

*He kissed her again, and Shay clung to him, her nails
biting into his damp skin. Pressure started building*

inside her, gathering, searching for a way out. She felt like she was flying, her body tingling, and then she fell. She grabbed the feeling, holding tight as she plummeted. Cody tensed. The sensations washing over her in waves didn't drown out the soft "I love you" that brushed her ear as Cody's body pulsed inside hers.

"Shay? Where are you? I found the cat."

Nina!

Shay couldn't breathe.

Cody raised his head and looked at her in stunned silence, his body still throbbing inside hers. The passion that had clouded his eyes only moments before was replaced with confusion. "What have I done?" he whispered.

Shay opened her mouth but couldn't speak.

He pulled out and sat back on his heels, staring down at his body. "Condom…I didn't think about a condom," he said, his voice barely a whisper. He scrambled to his feet, pulling up his underwear and jeans, not bothering to zip them, while Shay reached for her panties.

"You're bleeding." Stooping, he grabbed his shirt from the hay and wiped away the blood. He helped her slip into her panties and jeans and pulled her to her feet.

"Shay? Are you there?" Nina called again.

"You'd better answer her," he whispered.

"Be right there," Shay called out hoarsely.

She pulled her bra down as Cody slipped her shirt over her head. She finished dressing and felt a touch on her shoulder. "Shay? Are you all right?" His face held a mixture of shame and tenderness.

"I don't know." She was torn, one part still lying on the floor beneath him, feeling passion and love like

she'd never known, the other part filled with humiliation. He was her best friend. He'd been like a brother to her. Everyone would find out. Their lives would be ruined.

She had to get down before Nina suspected something. Shay blinked back tears as Cody knelt and slipped shoes onto her feet. He stood, hand clasping the shirt smeared with her blood, his eyes searching her face.

He squeezed her arm, but quickly let go. "Go on, before she comes looking for you. Wait." He brushed a tear from her cheek. His hand lingered for a second and then dropped away. "I'll come by later tonight, then we can talk."

Shay moved to the ladder, her body numb. When she reached the bottom, she glanced up and saw him standing motionless, his jeans still unzipped, the blood-stained shirt in his hands, bewilderment and passion on his face.

The sound of a door closing pulled her from the dream. Shay opened her eyes, but her head throbbed. She started to touch it, but couldn't move. Her hands were tied to the headboard, and she was naked. What had he done while she was unconscious?

She tugged at the ropes, panic starting to build. They were too tight. Her chest hurt, her arm was on fire, and the gag was choking her. She tried to slow her breathing. She looked around the room. Where was she? A cabin. Not the one where she and Cody had stayed. Cody. Vampires. Had more come? Was he alive?

She heard a plank squeak and lightly closed her eyes, pretending she was asleep. Through the seam of her lashes, she saw Mr. Ellis enter the tiny bedroom wearing the neatly pressed dark slacks he usually wore. He was smiling at her, his face polite, cordial. He held a red rose in one hand, a scalpel in the other.

An owl's hoot woke Cody. He sat up, head spinning, covered in dust. He was in the woods, a stick buried in the earth beside him. The vampires! Shay. He jumped up, searching the trees. What the hell had she done? He'd never seen anything move so fast. Except vampires. Were there more? A sweet scent lingered in his nose, different from the vampire scent. He checked his watch. One a.m. He'd been out for an hour. Where was she? His talisman was warm against his chest. His battle marks tingled. She was in danger. He knew it in his heart. He had to find her.

Tracks covered the ground where he'd fought the vampires. Shay's footprints were there too, and another set, off to the side. Larger, a boot, square-toed, probably size eleven. Someone had followed her. She said the intruder in Scotland wore square-toed boots. Cody found his gun lying on the ground where Shay had dropped it before running after the vampire. He followed the sweet scent and saw the square-toed footprints leading away from the fight. The impression was deeper there. The man who followed Shay had gained more than a hundred pounds, or he was carrying something. Behind the tree where Cody had fallen, he found a white handkerchief. He picked it up and sniffed. Chloroform.

It took all Shay's willpower not to move or cry out. She let her eyes shut. She heard him move closer, heard something drop onto the table near her head. His hand brushed over her breast, and panic bubbled inside her. *Keep your head. Panic will get you killed.* Calm. Calm. Maybe he would think she was unconscious. An unconscious victim wouldn't be as much fun. She blanked her mind, focusing only on her heartbeat, hard and fast, like a drum. When it slowed, she let her mind go, let the smells of the cabin and Mr. Ellis's breath fade, released the brush of his hand on her body and the memory of the shiny scalpel in his hand. The lake shimmered before her. It was smooth. Tranquil. No wind today. She dug deeper into her mind. A boy and a girl stood on the shore, looking out across the water. They were skipping stones.

"Mine went farther than yours," Shay said, *planting her hands on her hips.*

"Did not." Cody grinned at her, tossing a flat, smooth rock into the air and catching it with the other hand.

"Did too." Shay chose another one and flicked her wrist, skipping it across the lake, sending out a wave with each plink. "There. Six skips. Top that."

He grinned again and tossed his rock. It made eight skips before the water swallowed it. He laughed and stuck out his tongue. Because he'd already turned thirteen, he thought he was better at everything.

"I quit." Shay flung the rest of her rocks at him, harder than she meant. She had been emotional lately. Nina said it had to do with becoming a woman. Puberty, she said. Shay didn't want anything to do with puberty. She didn't want to bleed and grow boobs. She wanted to ride her bike and play in the woods with Cody.

He covered his mouth, and when he removed his hand, blood trickled down his lips.

"I'm sorry, Cody. I didn't mean to hit you."

He wiped the blood on his shirt—his mom would clobber him for that—and the anger left his eyes. He brushed a tear from her cheek and gave her a bloody smile, revealing a chipped bottom tooth and split lip. "Aye. I know you didn't, pip-squeak." He dumped the rest of the rocks from his pocket and ran his knuckles over her head. "Come on, let's get home and clean it up before Mom and Nina get back. Maybe they won't notice it."

The other voice crept back in, and something sharp pricked her chest. It was all she could do not to scream. "Sleep now, my pretty," Ellis said above her lips, his breath reeking of onions and evil. "But not too long. I've waited too long for this game to begin."

She waited until the door closed and his steps faded, and then she waited a few seconds more. She opened one eye, then the other, letting out her breath in a soft sob. He wouldn't believe she was sleeping for much longer, and then he would come back and kill her. The cut on her chest was proof of that.

She pulled again, working at the ropes until her wrists burned. She'd always been good with ropes. The MacBains spent hours teaching her all about knots, how to tie them, how to get out of them. She felt one give. Turning her head, she saw the scalpel on the table. If she could reach it. She worked at the ropes again, her wrist raw, and gritted her teeth when blood trickled down her arm. The minutes passed like hours before she loosened one rope enough to get her arm free. She strained to reach the scalpel. Her fingers touched the tip. Not enough. A little farther. She stretched until her bones felt like they would pop. She had it.

She attacked the ropes on her other wrist, cutting herself in her haste, sat up, and freed her feet.

She removed the gag and stood. Her body ached, her head throbbed, and blood ran from both wrists. Stumbling with numbness, she grabbed her clothes from the chair, dressed, and picked up the scalpel. She eased to the window and peeked out. It was night, but the moon was brilliant. From its position in the sky, Shay thought it must be around midnight. She couldn't be more than a couple of hours from the cabin. Was she on Skyline Drive? Was Cody looking for her? Was he even alive? She turned the lock and tried to open the window. It was old, painted shut. Using the scalpel, she cut at the sealed joint and tried again. It creaked opened an inch. She laid the scalpel on the windowsill and pushed harder. It opened more, squeaking noisily. She heard footsteps in the next room and gave the window a final desperate shove. It opened, and she stuck her head out.

The door banged open. "What are you doing!" Ellis screamed.

Shay shimmied her upper body through. Ellis grabbed her feet, cursing, and tried to drag her back in. His nails dug into her ankles. She kicked and twisted. He grunted, and his grip slipped. She scraped through and dropped onto the ground. She grabbed the scalpel that had fallen and looked around. They were in the woods. A car was parked in front of the cabin. Shay ran toward the vehicle and she heard a door slam behind her. Ellis jumped off the cabin porch and charged, pointing a gun at her head.

Marcas's helicopter passed overhead as the warriors regrouped in the parking lot near the cabin. The tracks had led there, and the old man at the lodge remembered hearing a car speed away at about the same time Cody had been knocked out. It was unlikely that Shay was still in the area; the kidnapper had probably gotten as far away as possible, but there was a possibility that it wasn't a kidnapping. Cody swallowed. Whoever had her may have wanted her dead. They'd reported both Shay and Renee missing, so the cops were on the lookout as well. Sam's crew was concentrating on the area around Luray Caverns, where the warriors hadn't found any sign of Renee, but they'd been attacked by vampires. Sam didn't know that.

Buffers were helping out here and in Leesburg. Shay could be anywhere. No one had any idea where to look. If the vampires had her, she could be in another country by now.

"According to what that vampire said, we know they had been looking for her," Cody said, accepting the drink Bree handed him. Faelan had tried to keep her away, but she insisted on coming. "But I just don't see vampires driving and using chloroform. This feels human." He hadn't told them what he saw Shay do. He still wasn't sure what he had seen, but he hoped he hadn't been dreaming. It was of some comfort to know that she had skills to protect herself, although not enough to keep her from being kidnapped.

"Those things we fought at Luray Caverns didn't feel human. They felt like freight trains going at warp speed," Brodie said, rubbing his back.

"Shay was lured away from the house by a man

claiming to have Renee," Lach said. "If he was a vampire, then the vampires have Renee too. What the hell do they want? They already have our book."

Duncan slid a dirk into his boot. "Maybe one of them didn't get the message to call off the search."

Bree frowned. "How did they know where she was and where she was going?"

"If vampires use chloroform, maybe they use bugs too," Brodie said. "We know they were in Nina's house. Could've been eavesdropping on us the whole time. Or maybe they can read minds."

"I wish I'd known those SOBs who attacked me were vampires," Jamie said, his face drawn with worry. "We would've had a different battle plan."

"It's not your fault. I'm the one who didn't protect her," Cody said.

"The fault's mine," Ronan said. "The female vampire outside Renee's shop said something about watching *him*. They've probably been tracking me all this time. That blond vampire wasn't surprised to see me. He knew who I was."

"But he got here before you did," Lach said.

"Probably figured out where I was going. Who knows what they're capable of? From what little I've learned, I suspect they're not only strong, but well funded."

"That's comforting," Lach said. "A bunch of well-funded, invisible vampires."

"Who might be able to read minds," Brodie added. "Now we know how he got past the locks. Damn things can probably float right through keyholes."

"We don't even know how to fight them," Jamie said, "other than cutting off their heads or piercing their hearts. Do they come out only at night? Do they die in sunlight? We know demons, how they operate. How do we fight what we don't know?"

"I've been trying to find someone who knows about them," Ronan said. "All I'm getting are quacks and wannabes. We need to capture one of the vampires."

Sorcha pushed the button releasing her sword blade. "Lop off their heads. End of story."

"Good thing you're not in charge of gathering intel. You'd just kill everything in sight," Duncan said.

"It works," Sorcha said.

Bree handed out bottles of water as the warriors made one final weapons check. "I'm going to look into some old legends. If these things exist, there must be a record of them somewhere."

Lach's phone rang. Everyone stopped what they were doing. Any call this late must be related to the search. Cody felt hope rising. Someone had found her, or at least spotted something that would give them a location.

Cody was watching his brother and saw Lach's face pale. He met Cody's gaze and quickly looked away. "I see."

"Who's on the phone?" Cody demanded.

Lach nodded. "Okay. We're on the way."

"Who was that?" Cody's voice sounded like it came from a barrel.

Lach's jaw clenched. He met Cody's gaze, but his eyes were flat.

Denial balled up in Cody's throat, but he knew what was coming. "Spit it out."

"Two of the buffers just found a body."

Chapter 12

CODY'S CHEST ACHED; HE TRIED TO DRAG IN A BREATH. "Where?" His voice cracked.

"Just below one of the scenic overlooks," Lach said.

Cody walked a few paces before his legs gave out. The numbness faded, and he doubled over, unable to breathe. He leaned against a tree, staring at the path leading to the cabin, and remembered making love to Shay, holding her, learning about the baby. For nine years he had faced every sunrise not knowing that he'd lost a son, and now, before he could even wrap his head around it, he'd lost her too. He straightened with a wounded roar and punched the tree. The skin on his knuckles split, but the pain felt good, dulling the ache in his heart.

He felt a hand on his shoulder and turned.

Jamie stood there, his eyes as ravaged as Cody's fist. "We need to go."

Marcas drove them to the scene. "Let me do it," he said as they reached the site where the two men waited.

Cody opened the car door. "No, I have to. I'd rather you waited here." He didn't include Jamie. Mate mark or not, he understood Jamie's need to know.

Lach put his hand on Cody's arm and squeezed.

"She's just over there," one of the buffers said, flashing his light toward a low mound. "She was covered by leaves. We tried not to touch anything." Cody recognized him but didn't know his name. He turned on his flashlight and climbed down toward the spot. He heard Jamie's uneven breathing behind him.

Leaves had been piled over the body, but a foot was exposed. Cody jerked the light away, feeling the lump in his throat grow bigger. He remembered Shay sitting next to him at the lake, legs long and tanned, laughing as he buried her toes in the sand. Pink polish. She always wore pink. She wriggled them free before he finished, her eyes glistening with laughter, and he started all over again, while she tried to swat him away. Her eyes always glistened when she laughed. And when she cried. He made her cry too. Not that day, but later.

Jamie stood on the other side of the mound, his shoulders heavy with grief. He looked up and met Cody's eyes, and a bond was forged between the two men. He held the light just off the body, because it felt intrusive to let it hit her full in the face. Jamie's beam joined his. Steeling his jaw, Cody squatted and gently brushed aside the leaves, too numb to care that he was corrupting a crime scene. Blond hair. *God, he was going to be sick.* He brushed away a few more leaves, trying not to hit her face. Delicate forehead, with a gaping cut across the center, brows a shade darker than her hair, closed eyes. The lump in his throat was choking him. His phone rang, and he grabbed it so he could escape. "Hello?" The line crackled with static.

"Cody. Get me out of here."

The muscles in his legs felt like water. "Shay?" Cody's flashlight dropped, thudding softly in the leaves. The static on the phone grew louder. Cody looked at it, then the lump, vaguely aware of Jamie staring at him. Was this the mind's way of trying to cope?

"Cody? Can you hear me? I need you to get me out of here."

"Where are you?" he rasped.

Jamie knocked aside the leaves, shining his light on the woman's face. She could have been Shay's sister, they were so alike, but it wasn't Shay. Jamie dropped beside the mound, covering his face in his hands.

"Shay? Where are you?"

"I've been arrested. Renee's dead."

—◦◦◦—

Two hours earlier…

Shay froze as a shot fired over her head. A screech sounded above her, and a giant white owl, like the one she saw at the lake, swooped down, latching its claws into Ellis's shoulders. He screamed and threw up his hands to protect his head. Shay turned and ran. Ellis charged after her, bellowing her name, even as the owl clawed at his head. He fired off two more shots that went wild. Shay glanced up, and the owl's eyes—a startling shade of green—locked with hers and dug its claws deeper into Ellis's skin. Ellis screamed, eyes wide with pain, and came at her again. He had lost his gun. Shay watched her hand moving as if in slow motion, stretching, reaching, the scalpel dragging across his throat, slicing his jugular vein, blood spraying, spattering her face and clothes with gore. The scalpel dropped from her fingers. Ellis gurgled, his mouth and eyes wide with shock.

Shay backed away, turned, and ran, her breath coming in painful gasps. The car. She stopped hard. It was Renee's. Oh God. Was Renee in the cabin? Shay ran back, but it was empty. She hurried to the car, her legs starting to give. Open door. Get in. Keys. Please let there be keys. No. She gave a soft cry and looked back at Ellis lying on the ground. The owl was nowhere in sight, if it had even been there. Teeth clenched, she got out and ran to Ellis. She dropped beside the body, eyes avoiding the blood-stained ground and his gaping neck.

She dug in his pocket until her fingers touched metal. She pulled out the keys, ripping his pocket in the process, and stood. She looked down at the blood covering her feet, and her stomach heaved. She turned, spewing up the remnants of her last meal. Swiping at her mouth, she ran back to the car. She jumped in, started the engine, and threw the car in gear. She stomped on the gas and lurched onto the road, looking for something familiar. She came to a dead end. She was shaking and crying, and the smell of blood was making her ill. She turned the car around and backtracked, passing Ellis's body still lying in the grass. She glimpsed something white in the trees. She came to a sign. Front Royal, two miles. She was near Front Royal. She had to get to a phone and call Cody. Let him be okay, please, God. She couldn't lose him. How much time had passed? The clock said 1:00 a.m., but Renee's clock never worked.

She headed south. Her brain was full of questions, but she was going numb. Shock. She needed help. Should she flag down a car? She had Ellis's blood all over her. A phone. She dug through Renee's center console and found her *Best of the Eighties* CD, a fingernail file, and two packs of gum. No cell phone.

Lights flashed behind her. Thank God. The police. She pulled over to the side and waited for them to approach the car. She heaved once at the stench of Ellis's blood and rolled down the window.

"Ma'am," the officer said. His eyes widened at the blood on her shirt. He drew his gun. "Step out of the car. Slowly. Now."

Shay got out and opened her mouth to speak, when another officer joined them. "I need help. I've been—"

"You have ID?"

"No—"

"Whose blood is this?"

"I was kidnapped."

He sniffed and aimed his flashlight at the backseat of the car. "What's in the trunk?"

She moved slowly, pulling out the car keys.

"Stand back," the first officer said. The second one raised the lid. Shay saw him cover his nose.

"What is it?" She moved away from the first officer, ignoring his raised voice warning her to stop. She looked inside the trunk. Pink shirt, black pants, red hair. Blank, staring eyes.

Shay started falling and couldn't stop.

Malek slammed the phone down after the minion's report. "Imbecile." Ellis had nearly ruined everything. Malek shifted back to his human form and rubbed his aching head. Why couldn't the shifts come without the aches and pains? Halflings had it easier. They just created an illusion and hid behind it. They didn't have to fit into this damned skin, weaknesses and all.

He had to get Shay out of jail, but if he stormed in and took her by force, it would blow his disguise. He would have to go and fix things himself, before Tristol got the book and the girl. She had to die, and Cody would die with her.

"Apparently just after Shay called you, Ellis's boss came in with a letter he found in Ellis's things, confessing to everything, the murders in Scotland and the woman on Skyline Drive. And the prints from the scene where Ellis was holding Shay match the latent print found near one of the bodies in Scotland. All tied up, nice and tidy," Sam said.

Almost too tidy, Cody thought as the truck whizzed past morning traffic. "They told you all this?" He wondered if Sam could fix a speeding ticket.

"I pulled some strings that'll probably end up strangling me. I don't know what to tell you. It's like everyone around her is dropping dead. If what you say is true, she might be safer locked up."

The jail walls might as well be made of lace, with what was after her. "I need to get her to the castle in Scotland. I can keep her safe there." At least she was alive. He was still stuck on that fact. He could handle the rest, demons, vampires, police. She was alive.

"You have a castle?" Sam asked.

"Kind of."

"A kind-of castle? After this is over, you and I are going to sit down and have a heart-to-heart. I've taken too much heat for you to be kept in the dark."

"Fair enough," he said. "You can come to the castle, and I'll tell you what you want to know."

"So now it's a real castle," Sam said.

Lachlan rolled his eyes. "The Council is going to tear you apart."

———

"Where is she?" Cody asked, rushing into the house.

Bree looked up in surprise. "She walked to the barn. Don't panic. There are warriors patrolling the grounds, and Ronan's close by. He went to check the cameras at Nina's again. He's all worked up over this."

"She shouldn't be alone, not after what happened."

"She needed time to herself. She has a lot to work though." Bree put her hand on Cody's cheek and gave him a sympathetic look. Her eyes glazed over, and her knees buckled. Cody grabbed her to keep her from falling. "What's wrong? Is it Shay?"

Bree clutched Cody's arm, resting her head against his chest. He could feel her heart racing. She shook her head. "I don't know what that was."

"The baby?"

"How do you know... damn Ronan."

"Wasn't him. I overheard you telling Shay."

"Everyone's going to know before Faelan does."

"Damnation." They both looked up at Faelan standing in the door, glaring at them. "First Ronan, now you. Why's everyone touching my wife?"

"He's not touching me, you big oaf. I just felt weak."

Faelan bounded over to her, wrestling her from Cody's arms. "Blasted woman. It's the concussion. I told you to rest," he said, picking her up so fast that Cody figured if she wasn't dizzy before, she was now. He carried her to the sofa and sat down, cradling her in his lap.

Cody watched them for a moment, love pouring from them so thick a person could spread it on toast. "Can you keep everyone away from the barn? I need a few minutes alone with Shay."

Faelan nodded. "Aye."

Cody followed the path to the barn. The door was open, and the smell of hay was strong. The tattered remains of the rope still hung from the rafters. This is where everything changed. Shay had just turned sixteen, and Cody had found out about her hidden identity. It'd been hell having to keep a secret from her. He and Shay went to the barn to get a bucket for Nina. He climbed on the rope, swung off, and dropped into the hay. Not to be outdone, Shay followed, landing on top of him. She wrestled around with him for a minute, tickling him, like they often did, but Cody didn't laugh. It took him a few minutes before he could get out of the hay.

From that day on, he saw her as a girl, a soft feminine girl, with bumps and curves in all the right places. After that, he tried not to touch her and watched her only when she wasn't looking. He thought he had it under control, until the night they went looking for Nina's cat.

He started up the ladder. Up there his world had come to an end.

Each rung he climbed brought memories that would be part of him until he died. Her breasts, the feel of her legs opening for him. He hadn't thought about her being a virgin until he saw the blood, even though he was one too. He still didn't regret what happened, only what it had done. Five minutes in the hayloft ruined seventeen years of friendship. She refused to talk to him, wouldn't even look at him or let him explain, even when he climbed the tree outside her window, panicked because he was leaving to track a demon the next morning and would be gone for weeks. When he finally cornered her, late that night, he got so flustered that he told her about her father, her past, and the empty grave.

He would never forget that, either, the hurt and shock, no ranting and railing, just numbness slipping over her face. His third mistake was letting her believe her father was in the CIA, not that she would have listened to him at that point. He didn't sleep that night, but sat hunched by his window, staring across the field, long after her light went out. He woke up there, to a day as bleak as his future, not knowing that their spontaneous act of passion created a life inside Shay that would bring more loss and heartache.

Until a few days ago, that was the last time he saw her, except from a distance. Even though he'd known he couldn't marry her until his duty was finished, several times over the years he'd parked outside her house, first in New York, then Scotland, hoping to catch a glimpse of her, sometimes to make sure she was safe, sometimes to see if he'd gotten her out of his head—which he hadn't—and sometimes because he missed her so much he felt like he was suffocating. Occasionally, he saw her, laughing with her friends, hurrying in the rain; once or twice with a man. Cody had sat in the truck, his neck burning, wondering if she was happy, if she ever thought about him, if she remembered running in the woods, campouts, swimming in the lake. If she remembered the hayloft. Wondering if the bastard walking down the street with her, holding her hand, knew she belonged to him. Once, he got out, fists clenched, ready to throw her over his shoulder and take her home, but stopped, knowing if he told her about the mark and she accepted him, not only would he put her in danger, he would always question if it was for himself or out of duty.

Afterwards, he would go back to fighting demons, torturing himself for months, picturing her in some other man's arms, nails biting into his shoulders, legs wrapped around his waist, knowing she'd moved on, while he couldn't. What would he have done if he had known his baby was growing inside her?

When Cody's head cleared the loft floor, he saw Shay sitting on a bale of hay, her knees pulled to her chest. She looked lost. She turned, and he saw one tear roll down her cheek. He sat next to her and wiped it away with his thumb. "You okay, pip-squeak?"

Another tear escaped. He put his arm around her and held her tight. She didn't sob. She'd never been a noisy crier, but her shoulders shook, and he wished Ellis could die all over again. Shay sat up and sniffled, her face wet.

Cody pulled off his T-shirt and handed it to her. "It'll wash."

"Thanks." She wiped her face and nose.

Her wrists were scraped raw, but after seeing that body buried in the leaves, scrapes didn't have the same impact they might have had. She would heal quickly. She always had. That part of her ancestry came without a choice. Her heart would take longer. "I'm sorry about Renee," he said.

"Do her parents know?"

He nodded. "They're headed home. They were in Mexico."

"I keep thinking that if I'd gone straight to the caverns, maybe she would still be alive."

"It wouldn't have mattered," Cody said softly. "She was already dead when Ellis called you. It was a trap."

"If I'd known that, I would've killed Ellis slower."

"I know, but he'll face his judgment." Still, he wished he'd been the one to do it, so she didn't have to. Once the shock wore off, she would have a tough time. Taking a human life, even an evil one, was hard. Demons he had no problem with. He was born to destroy them; that was his job. If warriors didn't stand as a barrier between humanity and the underworld, humans would be annihilated. But killing anything with human blood left a stain on the soul.

"Was he a vampire?" she asked.

"No. Just a heartless human. I'm sorry I didn't protect you. I should've brought you home, instead of going to the cabin. I thought it would be safer away from the house."

"It's not your fault. I'm the one who ran off alone."

"But I should've—"

"What? What could you have done? Vampires were trying to kill you. Vampires! Everyone knows they don't even exist."

He shrugged and tried for a grin. "If it makes you feel better, we didn't know about them until a few weeks ago. Vampires were supposed to have been wiped out centuries ago."

"You knew there were vampires and didn't tell me?"

Would she ever trust him again? "We knew vampires existed, but we didn't know they were tracking you. Not until we saw the fang in Nina's house."

"Fang?"

"That piece of ivory you found was a broken fang. You hit a vampire in the mouth." It made him sweat just thinking about it. He thought about her moving like a streak of light, fighting those creatures with more prowess than he had, and that made him sweat too. What was she? "How did you kill that vampire?"

"I don't know. It's like I heard the word *stake* in my head, so I grabbed the stick."

"But how did you even see where to strike?"

"The movies say go for the heart," Shay said.

"That wasn't a bloody movie. How'd you know where its heart was? It was moving so fast, it was a blur."

"What blur?"

"You didn't see a blurred streak of light?"

"No. I just saw men... vampires. They looked blurry to you?"

"Aye, when they were running, and you ran just like them. How'd you do it?"

"I don't know. I just ran after it. How'd you do what you did? You looked like some kind of Ninja Terminator. You ran halfway up the side of a tree and then flipped through the air."

"All warriors can do that," he said, waving a dismissing hand. "You must have inherited something from Edward."

"It didn't do me any good with Ellis."

"Where was he?"

"After I killed that vampire, I turned around, and Ellis was there. He put a rag soaked in chloroform over my nose and mouth before I could move. I woke up in a cabin in Front Royal. I thought I was going to die. He had me tied to the bed, naked, and he had a scalpel."

Cody went hot and cold at her words. "I won't let anyone hurt you ever again."

"Thank you, but you can't do it all for me. I have to fight too. I'm tired of hiding behind locked doors and false names. Whatever this is, I'm going to confront it. Then I'm going to kill it."

He shuddered. If he didn't keep a close eye on her, she would do something dangerous. Even if she could move like one of them, she had no idea what lengths those creatures might go to. No one did.

"I heard about the note Ellis's boss found," Shay continued. "He came in right after I called you. All those people dead because of me. Renee, Mr. Calhoun, Mrs. Lindsey, and Nick. I still don't know why he was following me, but he didn't deserve to die. And that poor woman in the woods, he killed her just because she looked like me. Can you imagine how her kids felt, if she had any, knowing their mommy was dead, never coming home, because she looked like some woman they've never heard of? How can I live with that?"

"It wasn't your fault."

"But it happened because of me. Everyone who comes near me gets sucked into this nightmare. You could die. Your brothers and the other warriors could die." She leaned her head on Cody's chest, tracing the outline of his battle marks. "I can't lose you."

"You didn't lose me. I'll always be here."

"I guess I owe Ellis's boss lunch. What's his name?"

"Anson Masters." He captured her hands, trying to still them. He couldn't take much more or he would throw her down here in the hay, which wasn't what she needed.

"Sounds familiar."

Her hands somehow wiggled free, or was he not trying hard? They dipped lower, brushing his stomach, drawing circles around his navel, making his whole body ache. She raised her face to his, and he saw the hunger there, but he didn't want her coming to him because she needed to feel alive or because he had a mark on his neck that said she had to. She immediately regretted it when they made love at the cabin, thinking of the baby they lost. Did he dare make love to her now, *here*, where it all started?

"Shay, you need to stop touching me."

She looked up at him. "Why?"

"Because I've thought about you touching me like this every day for the past nine years. Especially since the night at the cabin, and I've spent the last several hours thinking you were dead. I'm so damned glad to see you alive, I don't trust myself."

She didn't stop. She continued trailing her fingers over his battle marks, stroking the quivering flesh covering his ribs and back, enjoying the differences in his body, the way the muscles attached to bone. There were far more muscles than he had at nineteen. She captured his wrist and kissed the mark there. Tattoo, scar, whatever. It was part of him.

"What is it you don't trust yourself not to do?" she asked, her heart knocking against her chest. She slipped her finger under the edge of his jeans.

He drew in a sharp breath. "This isn't smart," he said, leaning closer. His mouth touched hers, then moved away. She could feel his indecision.

"Kiss me," she said.

He dove in like a man starving for food. He alternated between yanking off their clothes and trying to talk her out of it. He stripped them to their underwear, stopping when he saw the small bandage between her breasts. "What?"

"He cut me."

Cody looked so fierce, she could believe he'd killed an ancient demon.

But warrior or not, he was Cody. Her Cody. She cradled his cheek. "Just make me forget, please? I need you."

A long moment passed between them. His eyes softened, and he pressed his lips beside the bandage. She ran her fingers through his hair, but it wasn't enough. When he raised his head, she let her hand drift over all of him, shoulders, neck, down to his thighs. "I can't stand it," she said, stripping off his underwear. Her panties and bra quickly followed, and he eased her back onto a bed made of their discarded clothes.

"You're beautiful," he said, slowing, running his hands over her as if she were a flake of snow. "So beautiful."

"Show me. Like you did at the cabin."

"I don't want to pressure you."

"You're not," she said, wrapping her hand around him.

"Don't do that. I want this time to be slower. Hang on." He reached for his jeans and removed a foil pack. He rolled the condom on and settled back between her thighs. His gaze was intense, his body warm. His jaw clenched as he slipped inside. "I think it's too late for slow."

She nodded and grabbed his butt. "I know."

His mouth found hers as his body started to move. "I'm trying to be gentle, but I don't know if I can," he said.

She locked her legs around his hips, holding on tight. "I don't want gentle. I want to feel." And she wanted to forget Ellis's touch.

The pace was frantic, as it had been at the cabin, and Shay suspected it might take a couple more times before they could relax. She didn't try to fight it, but let the feeling swallow her whole. Cody tensed, and his body shuddered. "I love you," he whispered, letting his weight settle against her. They lay that way for several moments, bodies and hearts joined. Did he realize what he'd said? Mate marks were one thing, beyond their control. Words were a choice. How could he know he loved her? He hadn't known her for the past nine years. Maybe he was confusing love with the sense of protection he'd always felt for her. Even if he wasn't... what if it was too late for them? She wouldn't survive another broken heart.

He sat up. "You hear that?"

At first she thought he meant those three little words, but then she heard the voices, one loud and panicked. Bree.

Cody and Shay scrambled up.

"Can't it wait, whatever it is?" That was Faelan. "You just passed out."

"No, it can't wait." Bree's voice wafted up through the rafters.

"What's all the ruckus about?" Brodie asked. "Looks like a barn party."

"Where's Shay?" Bree asked.

"Hurry," Shay whispered, struggling to get into her clothes. Cody rolled off the condom, looked around, then cursed under his breath and stuck it in his pocket.

"You up there, Cody?" Ronan called.

They heard a footstep on the ladder.

"For God's sake, man, don't come up." Cody stuffed his legs into his jeans and reached for his shirt.

"I blew my nose on it," Shay whispered.

"I've got a used condom in my pocket, I'm not worried about a little snot," he whispered, pulling the shirt over his head. He must have seen the question in her eyes. "Lach shoved it into my hand when we got out of the car."

"Well, hurry down," Ronan said. "Bree won't talk until you get here."

"It's complicated, and I don't want to have to explain it twice," Bree said, her voice shaky.

Cody and Shay scrambled into the rest of their clothes and climbed nonchalantly down the ladder.

The intensity of the moment was diffused, as everyone stared at them.

Shay discreetly checked her clothes, wondering if she'd put her bra on outside her shirt. "Is something wrong?"

Ronan's mouth twitched. He reached over and picked a couple of pieces of hay out of Shay's hair.

"Well, for one thing, Cody's shirt's on inside out, and you both look like scarecrows with leaky stuffing," Lachlan said, but he looked pleased.

"I don't care how my shirt's on," Cody said. "Why is everyone in the bloody barn?"

Jamie stuck his head in the door, saw everyone, and frowned. "Is Shay okay?"

"No," Bree said, her voice trembling. "He's coming for her. The demon, he knows she's alive."

Cody's eyes narrowed. "Which demon?"

"The one who marked her."

The fine hairs on Shay's arms lifted. Tension radiated from each warrior's body.

"Are you sure?" Cody asked. "You said sometimes the dreams get mixed up."

Bree twisted her ring. "No. He's the one who dug up the empty grave."

"So where do the vampires come in?" Brodie asked.

"They both want her," Bree said. "The vampires and the demons."

Cody put a protective arm around Shay. "Why?"

"I don't know," Bree said, "but it's connected to the *Book of Battles*."

"But the vampires have the book," Shay said.

"The demons probably don't know that," Cody said, grimly. "I don't know why the vampires still want you."

"It's a tug of war between the vampires and demons, and Shay's the rope," Brodie said.

"What did the demon look like?"

Bree closed her eyes. "I saw his human form. Neat, sophisticated. Auburn hair with a silver streak."

There was a chorus of hard-drawn breaths.

"What?" The word exploded out of Cody's mouth.

"That's... bloody hell," Jamie said.

Duncan took a step closer to Sorcha, and even Faelan looked stunned.

Cody pushed aside Shay's shirt collar and looked at the scar on her shoulder. "M," he whispered. "Malek."

Chapter 13

SHAY'S LEGS SHOOK. "ISN'T MALEK ONE OF THOSE demons Faelan saw?"

"Aye," Cody said.

Brodie crossed himself. "Why would an ancient demon be after Shay?"

Bree sank onto a bale of hay near the barn door. Faelan scooped her up in his arms. "Put me down," she said.

"I will not. You keep passing out. You won't listen to common sense. I'm taking matters into my own hands."

"Where are you taking me?"

"Bed, and by God, you'll stay there if I have to sit on you. I've lost everything in my life. I won't lose you."

"Marcas, find out how soon the jet can get here," Cody said.

Marcas made a quick call and reported that it would be morning.

"We leave at sunrise," Cody said. "All of us. If the jet isn't there, we'll take a commercial flight. Set up a barrier. I want the house surrounded. Not a mouse gets through."

Shay tried to sleep, but the dreams wouldn't stop. Ellis coming after her with the scalpel, his blood spraying from his throat, Renee's vacant eyes, and the vampires trying to kill Cody. Maybe if she saw him it would settle her nerves. He'd looked hurt when she insisted on sleeping alone. He was trying hard not to pressure her, even though she'd seen the hunger banked in his eyes, but she was afraid. The last thing she wanted was to have him distracted. She had already blown it and told him about the baby. While it was a huge relief to share her secret with him, now she worried for his safety more than ever. It had taken her years to deal with the loss. How could he focus on fighting demons and vampires, when something so traumatic had been thrown at him with no warning?

She eased of bed and crept outside.

Faelan sat in the hall, inspecting a dagger. "Are you all right, lass?"

Shay nodded, feeling her face flush. She considered and discarded the pretense of going for a glass of water and headed straight for Cody's room. He was stretched out in the middle of the bed, clothes folded on the floor. The sheet was crumpled around his waist, one leg sticking out from under the covers. His battle marks rose and fell with soothing steadiness. He stirred, and the sheet dropped lower. Shay was too tired to care whether or not he wore underwear. She hugged her arms around her body, shivering, as she moved closer to the bed. She should leave. She didn't want him distracted, but she needed to touch him. She started to turn, and his eyes flew open.

He sat up quickly. "Shay? What's wrong?"

"Nothing. I wanted to make sure you were here. I had a dream."

"I'm here. Are you okay?"

She nodded, but then shook her head. "No," she whispered.

"Come here," he said, pulling back the covers and scooting over to make room.

She didn't hesitate, but crawled in beside him, settling in the spot already warm from his body. He flipped the blanket over her and pulled her close, tucking his body around hers. She snuggled into his chest, letting his warmth and scent comfort her. He wore underwear, and it almost made her cry, because she knew he'd left them on in case he needed to go to her.

She was tired. She had to sleep. Just for a minute.

She woke several times during the night, once screaming, once shaking quietly, face soaked with tears. Cody was there each time, holding her close, trying to absorb her pain.

She woke to an empty bed. The sky was tinged with the pink of dawn. She heard noises downstairs and quickly dressed. The kitchen was like a train station. Some eating, some carrying luggage, some doing both.

"Did you sleep okay?" Bree asked.

"Finally." She glanced around the kitchen, but Cody wasn't there.

"He's at Nina's checking on something." Bree rubbed Shay's arm. "You'll be fine. Let him help you through it. He needs it as much as you do."

She didn't need to ask who *he* was.

"The men are loading the vehicles. We're waiting for Lachlan. He went to drag some poor veterinarian out of bed to give the cat its shots so he could take it to Scotland with us."

"He's taking the cat to Scotland?"

"Ronan's going to leave it there at the castle until things calm down." She closed the catch on her suitcase. "We're flying out of D.C. Marcas is going to take us there in the small plane to save driving time." Bree leaned closer. "My mother's here. She arrived last night. She was on the way home from the wedding and found out we'd been in an accident. She thinks we're going back to the castle so you and I can recover. She doesn't know about the warriors or this." Bree touched her stomach.

"Got it."

Bree picked up a suitcase, and Faelan appeared, like a growling genie, and removed it, complaining that it was too heavy for someone with a concussion. He patted Shay on the head as he went by. The gesture was oddly endearing. All these people, strangers, really, but they had dropped everything, weddings, honeymoons, battles, to come and help her.

A woman entered the kitchen. She looked elegant and graceful, even at this hour.

"Shay, this is my mother, Orla Kirkland." Orla was nothing like Bree, who was relaxed and laid back. This woman was as proper and refined as a queen.

"Good morning, Shay. I heard about your trouble. I'm so glad you're okay. Could I get you a cup of tea? Cody has some lovely Earl Grey."

"No, thank you." She had no appetite, not even for tea.

"Brodie, dear, do sit down and eat. Your food won't digest properly with you rushing around. What is that? Oh heavens. Cookies? At this hour?" Orla threw her hands in the air. "I give up," she said, and Brodie bolted out the door. "Are you sure you're both up to this? I can't imagine what your doctors are thinking, letting you travel after the accident and Shay's kidnapping." Orla moved about the kitchen as if she owned it. "Why don't you both come home with me? Let me take care of you."

"No, Mother. They're expecting us at the castle," Bree said.

Orla sighed. "Coira is a wonderful cook, and the castle was just lovely. Perhaps I should go with you."

"You know how you hate exploring. Shay and I were going to visit some ruins," Bree said.

Shay kept her eyebrows in place.

"Ruins?" Orla gave a delicate grimace. "You shouldn't be exploring while you're recuperating."

"They're close to the castle. Faelan and Cody won't let us get hurt. You go home and rest. You've been so busy with the wedding and helping Faelan restore the house. I'll bring him for a visit soon."

Orla brightened at that. "Ah, here he is now, my son-in-law," she announced as if introducing the president. "Faelan, would you carry my suitcase to the car?"

"It would be my pleasure."

"You'll take care of her for me, won't you?" Orla asked.

"Aye. I'll do my best." He raised his eyebrows at Bree in warning.

"And keep an eye on Shay," Orla added. "She looks pale."

"She'd put him in for knighthood if she knew about the baby," Bree whispered to Shay after Orla moved out of earshot.

"She remodeled your house?" Shay couldn't see Orla doing much remodeling.

"She provided the ideas. Faelan and the clan carpenters provided the brawn. It was my wedding gift from him. And the clan's way of showing their appreciation, since I brought him home to them."

"That's impressive. The clan has carpenters?"

"The clan has all kinds of people working behind the scenes. Not all of them are warriors."

Cody stepped inside, and his gaze locked on hers. "Did you pack your things?" he asked.

"Yes."

He frowned and reached in his pocket. "Here's one more thing. I just remembered it this morning. I'm not sure how you got it." He pulled out a necklace and handed it to Shay. At first she thought it was a gift. "I found it in the truck."

Shay examined the necklace, a silver cross. "It's not mine." Had there been another woman in his truck?

"You found my necklace," Bree said. "Thank God. I thought I'd lost it."

"This is yours?" Cody asked, his brows drawing into a frown.

"Yes, it was my father's."

"This belonged to Edward Rodgers," Cody said.

Orla gasped.

"There must be some mistake. My father was Robert Kirkland," Bree said, staring at the necklace.

Marcas entered the room, and he examined the necklace as well. "He's right. That's Edward's necklace. See that emblem on the back? That's his family crest."

Faelan joined the little circle. "I found the necklace under a floorboard in Bree's house. I thought the emblem looked familiar."

"Grandma told me it was my father's." Bree turned to Orla for an explanation. "Mother?"

Orla was slumped against the counter, feet splayed, face pale as her daughter's. She closed her eyes. "Oh God. Not like this."

"I don't understand," Bree said, clasping the necklace to her chest.

"He did it for you," Orla said.

"Did what?" Bree whispered.

Orla pressed her hands to her cheeks. "I knew it was going to come out, but not here. Not now."

"Were you married to someone else before Daddy?"

"No. There was no one before your father—before Robert."

Shay's head was swirling, knowing where the conversation was headed.

"Robert wasn't your father," Orla said.

"Not my father?" Bree slumped into a chair. "Was I adopted?" she asked, her green eyes wide with shock.

Orla's face crumbled. "He was your... uncle."

"Oh my God." Bree stared at Orla. "You're not my mother?"

Orla gave a little sob. "I *am* your mother. I raised you."

"Did you give birth to me?" Bree asked, her voice stiff.

"No. Technically, I'm your aunt, but we did it to protect you. He brought you to Robert and said you were in danger. He needed Robert to protect you, and he did." Orla dabbed at her cheeks and crossed to Bree. "He protected you his whole life. We loved you as much as if you'd been born to us."

"Who? Who brought me?"

"Edward Rodgers."

Shay's breath caught. If Edward was Bree's father, then that meant— She felt Cody move next to her. He reached for her hand.

"That explains the birthmarks," he muttered.

Bree shook her head. "My mother…"

"Layla is your mother. Edward Rodgers is your father."

Shay gripped Cody's fingers. "I have a sister?"

———ᨓ———

Connor Castle, Scotland

"You realize the awkward position this has put the Council in?" The chief elder folded his hands across his ceremonial robe. It was gold with a red border, and Cody idly wondered if the red represented the blood of warriors who broke the rules. "Not once, but twice, you've revealed information that wasn't yours to give. The clan decided it best to keep Shay's identity hidden from her, for her safety, as well as ours. We gave you only a warning the first time."

Only a warning, Cody thought. It had felt like more than a warning when the brand touched his wrist.

"But this time," the elder continued, "even though the Council recognizes your valor and your service, what you've done here has put us all at risk. For all intents and purposes, she was an outsider. Now you've revealed secrets that we've protected for thousands of years. Not only that, but you've brought her here, in our midst, to our clan seat. If you are correct, and there is a demon hunting her, if they follow, you've endangered the entire clan."

Cody felt the stirring behind him, the tension of the

other warriors summoned to the meeting. "What would you have me do, Elder? Leave her alone, unprotected?" His voice rose in anger. "She's part of the clan, and she's been targeted. I have to help her. We have to help her. That's what the clan is about, protecting humans. Now you tell me we are to turn our backs on one of our own?"

The elder frowned. "I understand it's a difficult decision, but the good of the clan must come first. If this clan fails, it won't be one woman who will suffer, but thousands could die. Hundreds of thousands. Do you want to weigh her against generations of humans that could be slaughtered, perhaps even the world, because the clan has been wiped out?"

"My apologies, Elder. I know the importance of our mission, but there must be a way to protect her and the clan as well." The muscles in Cody's face felt like rubber bands ready to pop. "I won't leave her unprotected... regardless of the consequences."

A quiet, collective gasp came from the Council members. Cody looked each one in the eye and then saw their gazes shift.

Faelan stood beside Cody, his arms stiff. "I stand with Cody MacBain."

Cody heard more chairs squeaking as warriors stood. "And I," Ronan said. All the voices rang out, one by one. His brothers', Duncan's, Sorcha's. Cody looked around and saw every warrior in the room standing.

The elder studied Cody for several uncomfortable moments. Cody kept his gaze steady as the elder's hooded eyes widened slightly and then narrowed. He glanced at the rest of the Council members behind him.

"We will convene and meet back here in one hour." The mood was somber as they left the room.

"If they do anything to you, I'll give up my duty," Brodie said, his face tight.

Duncan nodded. "They sit up there and enforce the rules but forget that not everything can be judged by law."

"Let's not panic just yet," Cody said, but his stomach was in knots. If they punished him, even took him away for an investigation, what would happen to Shay? "I'm going to check on something." He opened the heavy door and saw a movement behind the long drapes.

A dark head popped out. Bree peered both ways down the hall and then climbed out, watching the Council members disappear into a small meeting room several doors down. "What are they doing?"

"Convening." He rubbed his hand over his neck. "Does your husband know you're spying on the Council?" The woman had more in common with Shay than a father and green eyes. They both had guts. Too much, at times.

"No, but how else can I figure out what's going on? They won't let me in."

No one but warriors could attend a Council meeting, and they hadn't officially decided what Bree was, or Shay, and the Council stuck fast to its rules.

"Do you think I could hide inside the secret passage and leave the door cracked—"

"I think your husband would lock you in the tower. You'd better stick to listening at the door," Cody said, grinning. "I'll tell them I've suddenly grown hard of hearing and ask them to speak louder. I don't know why you bother. You know Faelan will tell you everything anyway."

"I want to know now."

"I should have known from the beginning that you and Shay were sisters. You have the same hard head."

"How is Shay?" The warriors weren't the only ones surprised that Shay and Bree were half sisters. The sisters were still reeling from the news themselves. It explained how Bree had sensed Shay was in danger.

"Still sleeping. She's been through a lot."

"I know but…" Two delicate lines crossed Bree's forehead.

He was getting worried too. He'd never known Shay to tire so easily. "Has Anna shown up yet?"

"No, but Sorcha says it's not unusual for her to disappear for days." Bree turned in the direction the elders had gone. "Darn, I want to know what they're doing." Her sweater scooped down in the back, exposing the mark he saw after the accident, the birthmark. He eased closer, pulling his vision into focus in the dim light. As he thought, it was similar to Shay's. A sliver of a moon and three stars. Damned odd.

"Are you sniffing my wife's neck?" The growl cut through Cody's concentration, jolting him back to where he stood, with his face inches from Bree's neck. Bree spun at Faelan's voice and bumped into Cody. He grabbed her, steadying them.

"If I wanted to sniff your wife's neck, I'd take her somewhere more private, not in the middle of the corridor."

Faelan scowled, and Cody said, "I'm going to check on Shay again. I'll be back."

Bree smiled and patted his arm before turning to her

husband. "I swear, your face is going to get stuck like that. Then we'll stick you on the roof with the gargoyles."

"What are you doing here… Bollocks! Tell me you haven't been eavesdropping on the Council."

Cody left them fussing and walked to the stairs. They had put Shay on the second floor, next to his room. Even though the castle was protected, surrounded by warriors, he didn't feel comfortable having her far from him, not with deranged humans, vampires, and ancient demons after her. Even if Bree was mistaken and it wasn't Malek after Shay, someone had dug up the grave, so someone needed to know if she was alive or dead. Cody kept coming back to that scar on Shay's shoulder. The letter was angled and crooked, but once he looked closely, it was definitely an *M*. If it was Malek who tried to kill her when she was a baby and put his mark on her, what was his purpose? Revenge against Edward, or to eliminate Shay?

There was another theory, but it was too horrifying to consider.

Cody opened Shay's door. She was still asleep, her brow furrowed, lips parted as if she were speaking to someone. Cody bent and kissed her forehead. He wanted to take her and run away from this mess, sort out the past. He could take her to Ronan's place in Montana. Maybe he should. The elder was right, this did bring some risk to the clan, but he had no choice. He lost her once before. He would not do it again, not for the safety of the whole world. He left her sleeping and walked outside to check on the guards.

"Any problems?" Cody asked, approaching the young warrior guarding the north side of the castle.

"Nothing's getting past me," Conall said, his grin wide. He was barely twenty, still reeling with excitement that he, along with Bree, had rescued the Mighty Faelan. Not many could say that, Cody admitted. He remembered his early warrior days, feeling like a hero. Countless battles later, and countless lonely nights later, knowing he couldn't go after Shay until his duty was fulfilled, it quickly lost its grandeur. There was no glory, only necessity, and necessity usually included sacrifice and harsh reality. After Conall had killed a few halflings that looked human—a teenager or a kid—that would take the edge off his good humor. And if he was lucky, he wouldn't meet his mate until his duty was finished, wouldn't know the anguish of years spent watching in silence, knowing if he revealed his heart, it could get her killed.

Cody walked the inner perimeter to make sure all the warriors were in position. There were two lines of defense: one just inside the wall that surrounded the castle, and this one, along the edge of the woods closer to the grounds. When he was sure everything was in order, he started back. After spending most of the month getting the castle in New York ready for use by the clan, it was shocking to see this place again. The two castles were so alike. Bree was looking into the history of both castles for clues. If there was a traitor in the clan, it would be devastating for them all.

Cody checked his watch. It was almost time for the meeting to reconvene. He was in enough trouble without showing up late. The fact that he was respected in the clan, a warrior who battled an ancient demon, should have some bearing on the outcome of the hearing, but if the elders tried to restrain him while Shay was in danger from an ancient demon and vampires, to hell with the clan. He'd go rogue.

———ww———

"Ellis was a serial killer?" Shane asked as they waited for the Council to return. He was a quiet one, like Marcas, but fast as lightning with a sword.

Cody rubbed at the knot of tension in his neck. He wished the Council would hurry so he could get this over with. "They've linked Ellis to seven bodies in four states. All female. Blond. Midtwenties. That's not counting Nick, Shay's clients in Scotland, or the woman in the woods."

"You think he's connected to the demons or vampires?" Declan asked. Clad in kilts, with their hair pulled back, it was hard to tell the twins apart.

"Probably demon. I think he was a minion," Cody said. "But he could be working with the vampires. He wanted to kill her, but I think the truck accident was an attempt to get me out of the way."

"You sure he wasn't a vampire?" Niall flexed his fingers, the muscles in his massive arms bulging. "All we need is for him to crawl out of his grave."

"He was human. I made sure. Before he was cremated, I cut his head off."

"Bloody hell," Brodie said.

Coira, walking by with a tray of cookies, thumped him on the shin with her foot. "Language, dear."

Brodie rubbed his leg and snatched a cookie before she got out of reach. "Who was his boss? I wonder if he knew he'd hired a serial killer."

"Anson Masters. Some reclusive rich guy. That's all I know," Cody said. He adjusted his kilt. He usually wore jeans or combat pants, but everyone dressed formally when meeting with the Council. Judging from Sorcha's raised eyebrows and pink cheeks, he was fairly sure he had just flashed her.

"I've heard that name somewhere," Jamie said.

"Sam's trying to find him," Cody said. "We want to see if he can tell us more about who Ellis associated with and where he spent his time so we can figure out how he was involved."

Faelan's brows gathered into a frown. "There are too many pieces to this puzzle. If Bree is right and Malek is the one who tried to kill Shay when she was a baby, we need to find out why. Revenge or something else?"

It was the *something else* that Cody didn't want to think about.

"If Malek believes Shay has the *Book of Battles.* Maybe he believes Edward had the book and gave it to his child," Declan said.

Sorcha studied the other warriors, eyes narrowed in thought. "Has anyone considered the fact that one of Edward's children *did* have the *Book of Battles*? Bree."

"True," Declan said. "Wonder if Malek knows about Bree."

God forbid," Ronan said, his tone grave, causing Faelan to frown.

"We've got to get rid of him," Faelan said. "One way or another."

They all knew Malek had to be assigned.

"Bree also believes Cody is in danger as well as Shay, that they pose some kind of threat together," Faelan said.

"But I heard the vampire say they didn't care about me," Cody said.

Declan's brows drew together. "So the demons are after you and Shay, but the vampires are just after Shay?"

"How'd they even find out about our book?" Shane asked.

Faelan drummed his fingers against his kilt. "It was missing for a long time before turning up in Bree's attic. It's possible other members of her family knew about it. Any one of them could've told someone else."

"Let's not forget Angus mentioned a traitor," Duncan said. "Maybe someone found out about it long ago."

"Don't even look at me," Sorcha said, glaring at him.

Cody didn't know what was up with them, but they'd been fussing at each other since they arrived.

"Nobody's lit the fire under you yet, Joan of Arc," Duncan said. "But every time you get defensive, it makes you look suspicious. I'd keep my mouth shut if I were you."

Sorcha stood, hands planted on her hips. "You think you're man enough to make me shut up? It's not your reputation on the line, Coz."

Duncan slowly rose and walked across the room. He grabbed Sorcha around the waist, bent his head, and kissed her until her body looked as boneless as a filet. Duncan raised his head. "That good enough?" He glared at her and then strode toward the door. "Tell the Council I had to leave," he said, without looking back.

Sorcha dropped onto a chair, mouth slack, speechless.

"Well, then," Brodie said.

No one had a chance to react. The quiet brush of

robes signaled the Council's return. Everyone quieted as the thirteen elders somberly filed into the room.

The chief elder took his place at the front of the room, his age-clouded eyes heavy. Cody felt the air thick with tension. He glanced at the faces of his brothers, his friends. Every expression was guarded but tight. If the Council decided to punish him, he would have to intervene, persuade the warriors to accept the verdict, or the entire Connor clan could crumble.

"I believe the Council was mistaken in believing the threat against Shay was removed, especially given the new information about Bree. The Watchers are disturbed."

Cody cleared his throat. "My apologies, Elder, but I believe we all made a mistake. She's in danger, whether it's from Malek or vampires."

The elder nodded, as if to himself, and glanced at the twelve robed men and women who sat behind him. They all gave a silent nod. "We've all shared the blame in this matter. We see no reason for further action. For the moment. It's more important to identify and wipe out this threat. Do you think the danger is only to Shay, or Bree as well, since she is also Edward's child?" The clan had been stunned to learn that the two women were sisters. They had protected Shay for most of her life, thinking her attack might be connected to Edward, when all along he had another child out there in the world. Two more. Bree said there had been a twin who died. It shouldn't have been much of a surprise. As the clan well knew, mates weren't the only destined things.

"We think the threat is against Shay, but we're keeping an eye on Bree as well," Faelan said. There was an increased air of respect from the elders when Faelan spoke.

"Shay has a right to know everything, to be trained so she can protect herself," Cody said. "With your permission, we'd like to begin immediately." He didn't tell them that Shay already wore her father's talisman. He should have taken it back, but he didn't have the heart to take away the only connection she had to the father they hid from her.

"I understand you started her training years ago."

"We did, but it wasn't completed."

"Go and train her."

Cody felt the tension in the room ease like a collective sigh.

"Bree as well," the elder said. His white brows bunched into a frown. "She's exhibited some... unusual qualities."

"That's an understatement," Ronan muttered.

The elder glanced at the other Council members behind him. "We need to determine how Bree has come by these unique abilities. We may need to take her for testing later."

Faelan's knuckled whitened against his thigh.

"But in the meantime, train the sisters as you see fit," the elder said. "It is the Watchers' and the Council's belief that we have a nightmare on our hands."

Chapter 14

MALEK WATCHED AS THE MAN VANISHED INTO THIN air. "It's cloaked, just like Druan's castle," Malek said to the hulking figure behind him. "But I doubt Druan cloaked it. That smacks of Tristol's handiwork."

Voltar stepped forward, dwarfing Malek, even in their human forms. He suspected Voltar stood too close on purpose, using his size as a threat. The members of the League hated each other, but they hid it well.

"You're certain that was Tristol's minion?" Voltar asked.

"I'm sure," Malek said.

"What's behind the cloak?"

"Take a look. You won't believe it."

Voltar moved to the spot where the man had disappeared. Half of Voltar's body vanished. When he turned, his eyes narrowed to slits. "How long has that been here?"

"I don't know," Malek said.

Voltar's fists clenched. "I've long suspected Tristol was up to something, but I didn't have proof."

"Is that why you've come?" Malek asked, keeping his voice steady.

"No. I have other business."

What business? Malek took a human breath, preparing to lay out his plan. "Tristol isn't what he appears. The Dark One's pet is hiding a secret." If Malek could convince Voltar what Tristol really was, Malek wouldn't have to worry about getting rid of Tristol himself. Voltar would do the job for him. He hated anything with mixed blood. Even halflings. There was no demon more prone to vengeance than Voltar.

"Tell me more," Voltar said, his body tensing under his leather pants and vest, ready for battle.

"You've lived how long?" Malek asked.

"One thousand years," Voltar said, his voice hard. If he and Malek didn't achieve immortality soon, they would both die.

"I'm nearly that old," Malek said. "Druan was eight hundred years old when he was destroyed." Malek leaned closer to Voltar and dropped his voice to a whisper. "How then has Tristol been here two thousand years?"

Voltar turned to Malek, his eyes dark. "Two thousand? Impossible."

"Is it? I stumbled on an ancient Celtic myth of a black-haired ruler who lived two thousand years ago. I found a sketch. The resemblance to Tristol is... remarkable."

"How could it be? We would have known if he'd been made immortal."

"I followed him last night," Malek said, "and watched him drink the blood of a human."

"He's a vampire?" Voltar hissed. "I thought they were dead."

"So does the Dark One. He won't be happy to discover his abandoned race still lives. We shouldn't tell him yet, not until we've gathered proof. It won't be easy to convince him that Tristol is one of them." Malek allowed a small smile, anticipating what the Dark One would do when he discovered that Voltar had killed his favorite pet. Malek would be the last of the League. With Dana Rodgers—or Shay Logan, as she was known now—and Cody MacBain dead, Malek would have the book and all of earth at his command.

<center>~~~</center>

The glowing man spoke to someone behind her. The strange language flowed like silk, so beautiful it saddened her that she couldn't understand the words. He turned to her, his eyes gentle and warm in a face beautiful and fierce, and she knew he wanted her to do something, needed her to do something. What? He opened his mouth to speak, and another voice intruded, this one smooth, but laced with darkness, luring her.

She rose from the bed and walked to the balcony. The breeze lifted her hair from her sweat-soaked skin as she searched the shadows.

Something brushed her legs, and Shay opened her eyes, startled to find herself on the balcony. How had she gotten there? She never sleepwalked. The sky roiled black over the trees, ominous clouds drowning the full moon, as leaves swirled furiously in the wind. Her nightgown brushed around her legs, sending a chill to her thighs. Her arm tingled, a feeling between pleasure and pain. She shivered, cold from the breeze, and heard something at her feet. The cat stood in front of her, hair bristling, tail swishing against her ankles. "Well, cat. You don't look any happier to be out here than I do. We should go inside." She hesitated, rubbing her arm as the night stilled, the tree limbs lifting like bony arms. Something moved at the edge of the woods. A man, several of them, lining the edge of the woods like sentries. They stared at the sky where the black clouds had cleared.

She stepped back into the room. That was the first she had seen it. She fell asleep on the way from the airport and had only a vague sensation of being carried. Someone had changed her into a nightgown. Cody? Had he slept there? No. The other pillow was undisturbed. The room was lit by a soft glow. A night-light? The walls were made of stone, the bed large and comfortable, covers tangled from her dreams. The room seemed to darken as she studied it. There was no night-light. The moon must have passed behind a cloud.

She relaxed a little. She was well protected there, from both demons and vampires. Ellis was dead. She still couldn't fathom that he had killed so many people because of her. Shay's eyes stung. How could she live with that?

The silver lining was finding out she had a half sister, though she hated the pain it caused Bree to learn that everything she took for granted—parentage, history, her name—had been a lie, just like with Shay. What a bizarre coincidence. Not just that both their pasts were shrouded in mystery, but that they were sisters, connected in different ways to the same clan. Shay was quickly learning that coincidence was commonplace within the clan. Destiny seemed to play a role in everything. Like mates.

It would take Bree some time to get over the pain. She said some harsh things to Orla before running out in tears. The devastation on Orla's face had hit Shay like a fist. Cody was right, she hadn't stopped to think how much she would hurt the MacBains and Nina by slamming the door in their faces. Their deception had been real, but so was their love.

Shay turned to close the balcony doors, and another figure caught her eye. He stood in the shadows, but she saw the jut of his shoulders, the familiar shape of his head. Cody. She opened her mouth to call out, but changed her mind. She needed to touch him. She brushed her teeth and dressed. The hallway was wide, lit by old iron sconces that would cost a collector a pretty penny, and thick rugs in rich colors that made her feel as if she had stepped back in time. Downstairs, she found the door and stepped into the cool night air. The cat darted past her, disappearing across the grounds. Even if she were blindfolded, she would have known she was in Scotland. The air smelled different there.

The guards stood tall and still, watching as she walked toward Cody. She saw the red-and-black flash of a kilt and thought she'd made a mistake, but he stepped from the shadows, moving close without touching her. The moonlight played on his striking face, making him look fierce. He had a sword strapped to his back, not the collapsible swords she'd seen, but a large broadsword. A gun was holstered on the belt of his kilt with a dagger sheathed on the other side. Ready for war.

"You okay?" he asked.

She saw flashes of blood, long claws, and white wings. Dead eyes, staring. She squared her shoulders. "I will be."

"That you will. You're a fighter." He pulled her into a hug, his kilt brushing her leg. "Did you finally get enough sleep?" His breath was warm, and she longed to grab his hand, run with him upstairs, and forget about stalkers, demons, and vampires, but she couldn't have him distracted.

"I suppose. I don't even remember arriving."

"You slept most of the way."

"Did you give me a sedative?" she asked, stepping back and crossing her arms.

"No. Your snoring was all natural."

"I don't snore... do I?"

He grinned, and the flash of teeth made her knees weak. "Not much. But you talked a lot."

"What did I say?"

"You said, 'Oh, Cody, come here and ravish me—'" His voice rose, imitating hers.

"I did not. You're lying." The words fell like water on a fire, drowning both their smiles. "I'm sorry. I didn't mean—"

"I know what you meant, pip-squeak."

"This is a beautiful castle."

"Aye, it is. This is where I trained. It's like a second home. Maybe a third. Guess I considered Nina's my second home."

"So there's a castle just like this in New York?" Shay asked.

"Unfortunately."

"You think Druan saw this place?"

"If Druan had seen this castle, even knew where it was, I think he would have at least made an attempt to slaughter the clan. There's a book in the library that gives the history. Bree's tracking down the names, but we'll probably find that they're just aliases Druan used. When the demons have been in one place too long, they move on, so no one realizes they aren't aging. Sometimes they pretend to come back decades later as their own relatives." Cody took Shay's arm, and they started back toward the castle. "You must be hungry. You haven't eaten in hours. Watch out, or Coira will have you round as a tub."

"Coira?"

"Sean's wife. You haven't met them. Sean's the Keeper of the book."

"The lost book?"

"That would be the one."

"Bree mentioned Sean. Where is Bree?"

"Last I saw, she was attempting to crash a restricted Council meeting."

Shay's hands clenched. "What did the Council say?"

"Well, they aren't going to flog me for spilling the beans... again. That's the good news."

"Can they flog you?" she asked, not sure whether he was joking.

"No." His fingers rubbed his wrist. "But they could've made things difficult. Still could, but they know they've made mistakes as well."

"I don't understand why demons and vampires think I have this book, or why they want it. What good would it do them to see a record of old battles? It's fascinating history, but useless."

"It doesn't just have the past. It has the future too."

"Future? Jiminy Christmas! You mean it lists battles that haven't happened yet?"

"Aye. A demon could get the names of warriors and kill them off as soon as they're born. That would destroy our clan."

No wonder they were so worried about the book. "I guess if the ancient demons are trying to earn immortality, that would certainly impress their master."

"Aye, it would. I'm meeting with some of the other

warriors in a few minutes to discuss how the book might tie in."

"I know the clan has issues, since it involves your book and demons and vampires, but on a personal level I need to know why Ellis did this, why Renee was involved, and how she got the book to begin with."

"We're trying to find out. Sam's looking for Ellis's boss. He may have some information."

"Was Ellis after the book?"

"I don't know, but they've matched his prints to several other unsolved murders."

"A serial killer? I was working for a serial killer?"

"Aye. He was a sick bastard."

"And I led him to Renee."

"It was nothing you did. For all we know, Ellis might have seen Renee first. She might have led him to you."

Shay yawned.

"Are you still tired?" Cody asked, frowning.

"I feel like I could sleep for a week."

"Let's get some food first, and then you can rest."

"I don't think I can eat. Maybe later." They entered the castle, and two men approached. "Who is that?" she asked. One man was big, with a shiny head and arms thick as tree trunks. The other was tall and slim with long, dark hair to his waist and eyes like a hawk. Both men wore kilts, leaving Shay with the feeling that she had stepped back in time.

"Shay, this is Niall, and that's Shane behind him."

"Shay." Niall shook her hand. His was so large it covered hers past the wrist. "We're glad you're here. Don't worry; we've got two dozen warriors surrounding this castle. We'll keep you safe."

Just like Sorcha, Duncan, Brodie, Anna, Ronan, Faelan, and Bree, these warriors were putting their lives on the line for her, when they didn't even know her. *But they would have known me, if I had been told who I really was*. These strangers would have been her family and friends.

"I'm off to raid the kitchen. Anyone want to join me?" Niall asked.

"And face Coira's wrath when she wakes up to an empty pantry and all these people to feed?" Shane shook his head. "Not me."

"Chicken," Niall said.

"You're on your own. I've got to get Shay to bed," Cody said.

Niall grinned, and Shane's eyes twinkled. "Aye? Well, have at it then," the burly warrior said. Shay heard them chuckling as she and Cody left.

"Sorry," Cody said as he walked her to her room. "That didn't come out right. Although..." he grinned.

"Don't you have work to do?"

"Aye, I reckon I do."

"You have more of a brogue. Is that what happens when you put on a kilt? I haven't seen you in one since you were thirteen."

"Want to see me out of it?" he asked.

"Aye, I reckon I do."

"I'll be back in a bit." He kissed her gently, with such feeling that she wondered how she could have ever hated the man, how she could have lived for nine years without him.

"Promise?" she asked, holding on to his kilt belt, reluctant to let him go.

"I promise. I'll never leave you."

—◦◦◦—

Lucy Bell climbed the steps to Shay's porch. She was glad to help Shay. Such a delightful girl, but with such deep-rooted pain behind her smile. She didn't talk about it, and Lucy didn't ask. Some things were too painful to relive. Lucy retrieved the hidden key and stepped inside. A tearing noise came from Shay's bedroom. Surely she hadn't come back and forgotten to call. Lucy tiptoed toward the bedroom and peeked inside. Furniture was upturned, and books lay scattered across the floor. A man leaned over the shredded mattress. He looked up at her and smiled, and she could see he wasn't a man at all. She didn't have time to register another thought before the thing flew across the bed at her.

—◦◦◦—

Someone tapped on Shay's door. It was her sister. *Her sister.* Shay rolled the words around in her head, amazed at the thrill.

"Hey," Bree said. "I wanted to see how you're feeling."

"Just tired. Come in. I wondered what you were doing, besides trying to eavesdrop on top-secret Council meetings."

Bree plopped down in a chair. "Cody told you?"

Shay grinned and sat in the chair beside hers. "If I'd been awake, I would have joined you."

"I couldn't hear a thing, but Faelan told me the Council is worried. They're not happy with Cody for telling you, but they aren't going to punish him. Not this

time. I found out what they did to him before. I made
Faelan tell me. They branded Cody's arm."

"They branded him for telling me the truth?"

"Calm down. It isn't really a punishment, but a reminder. They branded a small sword on the inside of his
wrist as a reminder of what's at stake."

The mark Cody had called a scar. "I think that's bar-
barous," Shay said, clenching her fists.

"So do I, but we have to remember that the entire
world is at stake here. They take this stuff seriously.
They could also remove his warrior status. Even though
he's retired, it would still be a big deal." Bree settled
back in the chair, resting her hands over her still-flat
stomach. "Faelan said if they had, every warrior there
would've told the Council where to stuff their robes.
They all stood up in support of Cody." Bree studied
Shay. "Seems like you two have worked things out."

"I guess so."

"Why do you seem so worried, then?"

"I did something stupid. I told Cody something I
shouldn't have, just like you're worried about distracting Faelan. There was another reason that I ran away all
those years ago. Right before Cody told me who I really
was, something else happened…" Shay licked her lips
and stared out the French doors. She had opened the
curtain so she could see the night. There was something
compelling, almost seductive about it lately. "I'd just
turned eighteen, and Cody was home for a few days. He
was hardly ever there, off fighting demons, I guess. We
were in the hayloft one night, looking for something, and
one thing led to another." Shay sighed. "Nina came into
the barn right after we'd finished. She didn't know what

we did, but it was just awful, scrambling to get dressed, afraid she would hear. Cody and I didn't even have a chance to talk about it. He tried, later that night, but I was so embarrassed, thinking we'd committed incest or something, that I wouldn't talk to him. He tried so hard, but I couldn't even look at him. He finally caught me out on the back porch when Nina was gone. That's when he told me about my past. He was frustrated, and I guess it slipped. When I left, it wasn't just because they lied to me, that my best friend had deceived me. I wanted to get away from Cody because of what happened in the hayloft." She had never confessed this much to anyone, not even Renee.

"A few weeks after I left, I realized I was wrong. What we did wasn't incest. He wasn't my brother, just the hot guy who happened to live next door. I tried to call him, but a woman answered. I thought it was a girl-friend. Then I found out I was pregnant."

"Oh, Shay." Bree took her hand and squeezed it.

Shay remembered staring at the pregnancy strip in disbelief. "I was scared, but I thought he had a right to know, so I wrote to him. Twice, asking him to call me. Begging. But he never called, never wrote back. I assumed he was still angry with me for running away, or that for him, what happened between us was just a moment of teenage lust." Shay swallowed with the memory. "I hated him after that, and I blamed him for what happened next."

"You lost the baby," Bree said softly.

Shay nodded. She didn't want to go into detail, since Bree was pregnant. "But it was all a mistake. I hated him for nothing. He never got the letters. Remember when

Renee called, she said something about letters? She was supposed to mail them."

"Oh no, she didn't—"

"I spent years hating him, but he never even got the letters. He had no idea. He even came after me, left in the middle of hunting an assigned demon to try to find me. Renee told him I didn't want to see him. I know she thought she was trying to help, but she ruined everything, and I can't be angry with her, because she's dead. And it's my fault she's dead. I didn't plan to tell him until this was over, but it slipped out."

"What did he do?"

"He was devastated. Heartbroken. Guilty. I think the kidnapping took his mind off it, but I'm still afraid for him."

"Then comfort him, don't hold anything back. If he already knows and he senses you're withdrawn, it'll make things worse." Bree patted Shay's hand. "He'll be okay. A lot of warriors are here to help. You know it's weird, we're both strangers here, but this is our home too. Our father was part of this clan."

"I'm torn between awe and anger," Shay said. "I wish they'd told me before, but I understand why they didn't. For the same reason I didn't tell Cody about the baby after I came back. I guess we always try to protect those we love. Have you talked to your mother yet?"

"No. I'm still too mad at her." Bree leaned forward. "I just can't grasp it. I was so much like my father— Robert. We did everything together. I had this incredible connection with him. Orla, ha, that's more understandable. We never had anything in common. I loved her, but we were totally different."

"Can you remember anything about your real mother, Layla?"

"No, I was young when she died."

Bree was only a few months older than Shay. She longed to know how her father managed to have children by two different women in such a short span of time. It didn't sound very noble, but she had to believe there was more to the story.

"Do you think your grandmother knew you weren't Robert's child?"

"I don't know. She went to see him just before he died. She seemed different when she came back. I wonder if he confided in her then. When I get home, I'm going to see if I can find Layla's things. Grandma never threw anything away. Layla may have kept a journal. Most of the women in our family do." Bree touched the tiny pearl bracelet on her wrist. "I think this was hers. My mother, Orla—I don't even know what to call her anymore—she gave me this before the wedding. She said I needed something that belonged to my mother. I'd never seen Orla wear it before."

"I know you're angry, Bree, but Orla loves you. She was really hurt when she left. If I had confronted my feelings back then, I would have realized Cody never got the letters. We wasted a lot of time. Talk to your mom. Listen to her side of things. Don't waste time being angry." The irony didn't escape Shay, that she was defending someone who had perpetrated a lifetime of lies.

"I know. I just need some time."

"Don't take too long. You can't get any of it back."

"You're right," Bree said, idly rubbing Edward's cross.

Shay felt the talisman, warm against her skin, and wondered how Edward had felt having little girls so close in age, but from different mothers. Did the women know about each other? "You're welcome to share this talisman."

Bree smiled. "Keep it. That way we each have a piece of him." She patted Edward's necklace. "Later, maybe we'll trade."

"You said your grandmother gave you the necklace?"

"She did. The night my father died."

More often than not, Bree still referred to Robert as her father. He raised her from the time she was small, like Nina had raised Shay. Wasn't that what a father, or an aunt, did?

"I got locked in Faelan's crypt," Bree continued. "I'd always been scared of that crypt. I think Grandma thought the necklace would comfort me after the ordeal and help keep the nightmares away. I had terrible dreams growing up, about death and destruction and monsters."

"You must have been terrified," Shay said.

"At first. I screamed and clawed the door, and then I heard a voice. It was my shiny man. He used to come to me in dreams, I think to counter the nightmares. He told me I had something important to find. Then, in the crypt, he told me my father was dead, but he had sent me another protector, and he showed me a man's eyes. Faelan's eyes. I saw them just as plain as I can see yours now. I wasn't afraid anymore. I was so sure the necklace had kept the nightmares away and that some-one would take it from me, that I hid it under a loose floorboard, where Faelan found it. It was only after I saw some sketches I'd drawn as a kid that the memories started to come back. I think Michael blocked them until it was time."

"Michael?"

Bree's eyes narrowed. "You don't know?"

"Know what?"

"Who's behind all this, the warriors, the battles, the book. Think *warrior angel*."

"You mean Michael the Archangel? He's your shiny man—" Shay gasped.

"What is it?" Bree asked.

"I think I've seen him too."

Chapter 15

Tristol stepped deeper into the woods. He could feel her drawing closer to him, but it wasn't working quickly enough. If she didn't come to him soon, he would have to go inside and take her. If he was spotted, he'd have to kill everyone there, and he wasn't ready to kill the warriors yet. He needed them to get rid of Malek first. He certainly didn't want Shay killed. If she was Edward's daughter, she was too valuable. Tristol waited until the moon shone full, and then he faded into a mist as black as his hair and vanished into the night.

Cody tried to work the stiffness out of his shoulders as he climbed the stairs. He needed a shower, and his head felt like a grenade had gone off behind his eyes. The guards were in place, Sam was still trying to locate Ellis's boss, and the warriors were using every contact and weapon they had, trying to find some trace of Malek. Sean was contacting other clans to see if anyone had spotted the demon. Bree was looking into Edward Rodgers's past to see what the demon might be after Shay, the book, or both.

He started to his room to shower first, changed his mind, and decided to see if she wanted to conserve water. As soon as he touched the doorknob, the hairs on his arm rose. His body went from tired to alert in an instant. He could feel the danger like a thick layer of fog. He didn't bother knocking. Her bed was empty and the doors to the balcony were open. Shay stood at the ledge, staring into the night.

"Shay? What are you doing out here?" The night air was chilly, but she wore only a thin nightgown.

She didn't answer. Usually her hearing was almost as keen as his.

Cody stepped through the doors, but she didn't turn. "Are you okay? Shay?" He grabbed her arm. "Shay!"

She turned, her face blank, eyes vacant, and then she blinked. "Cody?" She looked at him, puzzled, then saw where she was and hugged her arms to her chest.

"What are you doing out here?" he asked.

She opened her mouth, her expression blank again. "I don't know."

"Have you ever sleepwalked?"

"No, not until tonight."

He would have to watch her closer. Couldn't have her wandering about the castle at night. "Come on, you're freezing." He felt chilled himself, but it wasn't from the Scottish night air.

They walked into the room together.

"I was dreaming… but I can't remember what it was about." She ran her hand over the silver candlestick on the bedside table. "Thank you for bringing it," she said.

"You're welcome." He didn't know how long she'd had the picture taped to the bottom of the candlestick, but it gnawed at his stomach knowing the clan had stolen her history and her name. He couldn't imagine finding out his life was a lie. Was he soothing his own guilt by bringing her parents' picture to Scotland and letting her keep her father's talisman, which he could see outlined under her gown? He could see more than the talisman through the thin material. "Would you like something to drink? A cup of tea?"

"No, thank you." She tilted her head. "But I would like to have you, sir."

His body warmed. "Aye, my lady. At your service." He grinned and dropped his kilt.

~~~

Shay touched the imprint on Cody's pillow. Still warm. Her head was clear of nightmares for once. If she had them, she didn't remember. After a quick shower—they'd showered once last night, but sweated profusely afterwards—she dressed and went downstairs. The smell of food drew her toward the kitchen. A white-haired man met her in the corridor. His eyes crinkled at the sight of her.

"Ah, there you are," he said, sticking out his hand. "I'm Sean Connor, Faelan's great-great-nephew. Coira's in the kitchen. She's been dying to meet you. Another body to fatten up. But don't tell her I said so. Come along, now." He took Shay's arm, as if he had known her all her life. "She's been cooking for two hours, but she won't hear of hiring a cook—Look who I've found," he said to the red-haired woman bustling around the kitchen.

"She's awake," the woman said, beaming. "We've been worried about you, sleeping so much, and you haven't eaten a bite. We'll fix that. You have to keep up your strength with the way things move around here. Sit, I'll fix you a plate." She scurried over and came back with a heaping plate, silverware, and a napkin.

"What'd I tell you?" Sean whispered.

"Thank you," Shay said, charmed by the couple. "I've heard your names, but there have been so many faces to keep track of." And she had slept a lot since she arrived. "You're a nurse, aren't you, Coira?"

"And a bloody good one," Sean said.

"Thank you for the compliment, but watch your tongue," she said to Sean. "There's no excuse for rough language."

"She's got a thing about cursing too," Sean whispered. "Cursing and food. Woman's obsessed with mouths. Always making us shove food in or walloping us if a rude word slips out."

"I hear you, dear."

"And she's got ears like a warrior," he said in an exaggerated whisper. "So be warned. Eat in here, if you'd like. The others have eaten and gone or haven't come down yet."

"Have you seen Cody?" she asked as Coira filled two more plates. "We have to talk to the police, and then he's going to take me by my house to get some things." If there was enough time, she wanted to visit the place where her parents had lived. She had gone to Scotland searching for her roots, never suspecting that she settled so close by.

"Saw Cody earlier," Sean said. "He's a good man. I think he was helping Ronan with something. Here's Marcas. Have you seen your brother, Marcas?"

Marcas kissed Shay on the head and stole a bite of her sausage. "He was headed to his room, I think. I've got to run. I'm trying to track down Anna."

Shay sat at an old wooden table, explaining her story

as she ate. Sean and Coira asked questions and sympathized like grandparents. Shay had never had grandparents. Nina tried to cover all the bases; mother, father, grandmother, and aunt, but while she did a good job, Shay secretly longed for grandparents like her friends had, to make cookies for her and take her to the park or the zoo.

Coira refused to let Shay help clean up the dishes, so she explored the castle while waiting for Cody. She roamed halls wider than some of the rooms in her house. Massive rooms and staircases, with stone everywhere, on both floors and walls. It was an antique lover's dream. Old rugs, ancient tapestries, leather, and antiques everywhere she looked. She rounded a corner and ran into Faelan.

"Whoa, there," he said, steadying her with one hand. In the other, he held a tray. "How are you feeling?"

"Better. I just ate breakfast. Too much, I think."

"Coira got hold of you, aye? I just heard the same thing from Bree. No worry of going hungry around here," he said, smiling.

Cody wasn't the only one who looked good in a kilt. "Where is Bree?"

"In the library with her nose stuck in a book. Can't get her out of there." His eyes lit as he talked. He obviously adored Bree. Would she and Cody be like that?

"Where is the library? I'll pop in and see her."

Faelan pointed out a room in the opposite direction and touched Shay's shoulder. "See if you can get her to rest. She didn't get much sleep last night. She's upset over all this. Not about you, lass. She's glad to have you as a sister, but she feels betrayed. I'm sure you know all about that."

"She just needs time to sort it out."

"Aye. Between us, maybe we can help her. I think I'll like having a sister again, even if by marriage." His smile was genuine, but she saw the shadow underneath. He lost his real sister when the demon locked him in the time vault.

"I can always use a brother-in-law," she said, returning his smile.

"And if you need help keeping Cody in line, just let me know, aye?" He patted her head, as he usually did. "Tell Bree I'll be there in a few minutes with her tea."

Shay stepped through the archway, and her mouth fell open. "Jiminy Christmas!" The room was huge, two stories tall, with floor-to-ceiling shelves lining the walls and a ledge that ran around the top for access to the upper level.

"Isn't it grand?" a voice called from somewhere above her head. Bree had one foot and hand on the ladder, stretching out to reach a book.

"Are you trying to give your husband an ulcer?"

"There's a book, just there."

"Won't the ladder move closer?"

"It's stuck."

"Come down, and I'll get it."

"I've almost got it." She stretched farther, perilously unbalanced.

"Faelan will kill you if he sees you up there."

"Why do you think I'm trying to hurry?" Bree turned to grin at Shay, and her foot slipped.

"Damnation!" Faelan stood frozen in the doorway. The color drained from his face. He ran for the ladder, curses blazing from his lips.

"Don't curse at me in Gaelic," Bree said, regaining her footing but still reaching for the book.

"What are ye trying to do? Kill yerself?"

"You can judge his temper by his accent," Bree said calmly, finally grasping the book. Gripping it to her chest, she started down the ladder. Faelan plucked her off, ranting at her. When she was safely on the ground, he pulled her into his arms and crushed her in a hug.

"Did you bring my tea?" she asked, voice muffled against his shoulder.

"You daft woman, what am I going to do with you?"

Shay left them hugging and went to see what was taking Cody so long. She tapped on the door.

It opened, revealing a woman dressed in a no-nonsense dark suit and crisp white shirt, but her face and body looked like a model's. Short blond hair accented her striking face.

"Sam," Cody called from the bathroom. "Did I hear the door?"

Shay gaped at the woman. "You're Sam?" she said, backing away.

"Yes." She turned as Cody called again.

"Sam—" He stepped into view, a towel wrapped low on lean hips. His eyes met Shay's. He started to say something, but Shay turned and hurried to her room. She bolted the door and sagged against it, feeling her breakfast climbing up her throat.

"Shay?" Cody banged on the door. When she didn't answer, he tried the knob. "Open the door, Shay."

After a few moments, she picked herself up and cracked the door. He stared at her. "Can I come in?"

She didn't answer, but turned and walked toward the balcony, trying to calm her thoughts.

He followed her, still wrapped in a towel. "That was Sam."

"I figured it was when you called her *Sam*." She hadn't realized Sam was a woman, a drop-dead gorgeous woman.

"She got here last night."

Shay still didn't say anything.

"Shay, look at me." Cody turned her so she faced him, while he gripped the towel with the other hand. "You don't think there's anything going on between Sam and me, do you?"

"She's in your bedroom while you're wearing a towel. What should I think?"

"She came to get some papers. I was in the shower."

"If you say so. What business is it of mine, anyway?"

"What business… what the hell does that mean? How can you say that after what we've done? After what you told me. And this." He thumped the tattoo on his neck. "I swear you're the most stubborn, infuriating woman I know. That's why cavemen dragged women around by their hair." He followed by digging a hand in her hair and kissing her, hard, demanding, and possessive. She struggled for a minute before her lips betrayed her. The kiss softened, and he lifted his head until they were separated by an inch. "Do you think I could kiss you like that if I wanted Sam?"

"You've seen her! How could you not want her?"

"Women!" Cody growled and kissed her again. "Listen to your heart; your head's obviously screwed up. There's nothing between Sam and me."

"Never?"

He groaned. "How do women always know the one wrong question to ask? Once. A couple of years ago." He leaned back, forcing Shay to look at him. "You have my word. Come on. I'll introduce you, and then we'll go to the police station and get some things from your house."

Sam was nice, but Shay was still stewing over the matter, even after they left the police station. There was no evidence against Shay, so they couldn't hold her, but they did ask her not to leave Scotland for the time being.

"You've known Sam how long?" Shay asked as they drove to her house.

"A few years."

Great. "She's married?"

"No."

"Boyfriend?"

"No."

"Lesbian?"

"No." His responses were dry.

"She's beautiful."

"She is that." Cody gave Shay an exasperated look. "Don't make something out of it. We have other things to focus on, like a nearly thousand-year-old demon."

"So it's fine if you and Jamie go at each other like rabid wolves," Shay said, although they were being civil now. "But I'm not allowed to say anything when some gorgeous woman shows up who you've slept with?"

"That's different. You almost married the guy. I slept with Sam once. Once. How many times did you sleep with Jamie—" Cody growled. "Don't answer that." He rubbed the bridge of his nose. "I'm sorry. I know

I've been an ass, but it was hell watching him near you, knowing you were mine. I probably didn't react well when I found out he'd been keeping a lot more than his eyes on you—" He sighed. "Can we not talk about this?"

"Fine with me."

Cody grew quiet for the rest of the drive. He turned toward her house without having to ask for directions.

"How many times did you come by my house?"

His jaw twitched. "Several."

All those years she hated him, he kept watch over her, making sure she was safe, knowing she was his mate and that he couldn't do anything about it. A spark of anger toward Renee flared in Shay's chest, but she remembered Renee's dead, staring eyes and ached with sadness instead, for Renee, the victims, Cody, and herself. Renee had seen how upset Shay was after it happened. She probably believed she was protecting Shay. Everyone seemed to want to protect Shay, but she had paid the cost.

"Will you show me where my parents lived before we go back?"

"Sure." They rounded the corner, and Cody screeched to a halt in front of Shay's house. Black smoke rolled from the upper windows. Cody jumped out of the vehicle. "Call for help. Stay here." He raced up the steps and put his hand against the door, testing for heat before he opened it. A puff of smoke seeped out. He covered his mouth and nose with his shirt and disappeared.

Shay jumped out of the car and ran.

Chapter 16

SMOKE FILLED THE HOUSE. THE KITCHEN WAS IN flames, the striped curtains she and Lucy had made three months before, ablaze. The oriental rug and sofa it had taken Shay months to find was smoking. Her stuff. Her life. Gone. She ran to her bedroom and met Cody, loaded down with a laundry basket, the phone at his ear. "Get outside! I got clothes and your laptop. Go. Now! And cover your mouth."

She covered her mouth and nose. Cody let his drop and took her arm, pulling her out of the bedroom, tugging at her when she stopped to grab a picture Renee had given her. The living room and kitchen were fully engulfed with flames. Heat blasted Shay's skin. She and Cody were both coughing as they hurried for the door. Shay turned back for one last look at her sanctuary, in flames.

On the porch, she gulped in fresh air. Cody led her onto the lawn. Tears streamed down his face from the smoke. He set down the laundry basket, and the distant wail of fire engines sounded.

"Damn!"

"What?" Cody yelled over the screaming fire engines.

"My jewelry box—no! Cody, don't!" She clutched at his arm. "It's not worth it!"

He pulled free and rushed toward the house. Fire glowed red at the windows. Red eyes. Death. Shay had a vision of Cody fighting the vampires. "Cody!" she cried as he covered the lower half of his face again and ducked inside the monster's mouth.

She ran toward the house, feet sluggish, heart thumping out each second like a ticking bomb. Between beats she heard shouts as the fire truck rolled to a stop. An explosion rocked the house. "Cody!" she screamed.

A big arm caught her around the waist, holding her back. "You can't go in there," a firefighter said.

"Cody's in there," Shay shrieked.

"Someone's inside," the firefighter yelled over his shoulder.

Shay struggled with him, trying to pull away. She had to find Cody, but each time she was blocked. Tears streamed down her cheeks. She sank to her knees, the grass cool beneath her as waves of heat rolled off the fire. She stared at the flames, unblinking, as the firefighters moved toward the house. A smoky form materialized in the doorway, and Cody burst out, coughing, his face and arms streaked with black, her jewelry box cradled under one arm. He uncovered his mouth, gasping for fresh air, as the firefighters hurried him off the porch. Shay searched his face, sooty, but not burned. With a soft cry, she flung her arms around him.

"It's okay," he said, squeezing her tightly.

Someone eased her back and checked Cody for injuries. He refused oxygen, and after a minute, he pulled her close, his arms sheltering her as they watched her house burn.

The firefighters gave it a good effort, spraying her house and the others nearby, but hers was too far gone. Neighbors gathered and watched, the horror of the flames reflected in their eyes. Shay surveyed the somber faces and realized one was missing.

"Lucy isn't here."

"Your neighbor? She's probably running errands."

"She never goes anywhere," Shay said. "I do her shopping. There's a woman from her church who sometimes helps out."

"She's probably with her, then."

"Can we check on her?"

They started around the corner to Lucy's house, when Shay heard tires screeching and a bang. Voices yelled, "Shay! Oh my God, Shay!"

Shay turned back and saw Nina climbing out of a black BMW parked with one wheel on the curb, the rear sticking out in the road and the front doors open. Nina and Matilda trotted across the grass toward the blazing front porch. A firefighter tried to stop Matilda. While they struggled, Nina darted past. A second firefighter caught her. They were yelling so loudly they couldn't hear Shay calling them. When Shay reached them, the two women grabbed her in a hug, tears rolling down their cheeks. Matilda's looked like a raccoon, with her mascara running.

The neighbors slowly drifted back to their unscathed homes, as the last of the fire was extinguished. Nina held Shay's hand through it all, while Cody stood on the other side, his arm around her. Shay stared at the blackened shell of her house, dazed. Her stuff. Her life. Everything she owned, gone.

Someone mentioned an accelerant, and Shay could see the firefighters poking through the soaked and charred rubble, some spots still smoldering here and there. A flurry of activity caught Shay's attention. Three men squatted and examined something.

"Come on. We've got to go," Cody said. Something in his face sent a chill up her spine in spite of the heat from the ashes. Scanning the area, he escorted her, Nina, and Matilda into his vehicle. "I'll be right back."

Shay watched through the side mirror as he walked close to Nina's rental, looked around, and quickly drove his dagger into her front tire. It happened so fast, Shay wasn't sure she saw it.

Cody approached the grim-faced men near the burned house, spoke to them for a moment, and then jogged back, eyes scanning the area. "Let's go." He got in and started the engine. "They have your phone number, and mine, if they have any questions."

"What about my car?" Nina asked.

"It has a flat. I'll have the rental agency pick it up."

"What's wrong?" Shay whispered.

"They found bones in the fire."

"Bones?" She kept her voice low, although it probably wasn't necessary, with Nina's and Matilda's poor hearing. "Whose?"

"I hope the arsonist's."

"They're sure the fire was set on purpose?"

"They don't know for sure, but it looks that way. We've got to get back to the castle." His face was strained.

"Why would someone set the fire? As a warning?"

"More likely to draw you out into the open."

"Are we there yet?" Matilda asked from the backseat. "I need to use the little girl's room."

"A few more minutes," Cody told her.

"What a shame about the rental car. I can't believe the tire went flat," Nina said.

Shay distracted them with conversation while Cody took a long, awkward route to the castle to make sure they weren't followed. They had no choice but to bring Nina and Matilda there. Too many people surrounding Shay had already died.

Nina reached over the seat and patted Shay's shoulder. "I'm sorry about your house, honey, but you know you always have a home in Virginia."

"I know, Nina. Thank you." Shay was too brain-dead to contemplate what she would do when she left the castle. In addition to demons and vampires, now she had police, insurance agents, and fire investigators to deal with. Would they think she set the fire? Who did the bones belong to? "Lucy!" Shay blurted out. "Oh my God, Lucy."

Cody took his eyes off the rearview mirror. "What?"

"Lucy wasn't watching the fire… the bones…" She pulled out her phone and tried with trembling fingers to reach Lucy, but she didn't answer. "We have to go back and check on her."

"We can't. I'll call when we get to the castle and have someone go by her house. She's probably somewhere else."

Matilda leaned forward, peering over Cody's shoulder. "Does this castle have a dungeon?"

"God help us," he muttered under his breath as he turned into the castle gate. "If there's a dungeon, I'm sure the owner doesn't want anyone down there."

"Humph. Oh, look, Nina. He's a hunk," she said, waving at Conall, who was guarding the gate.

Nina pursed her lips. "You'd better be on your best behavior, Matilda, or they'll ask us to leave. We've never stayed in a real castle for more than one night."

"What about towers? I just love tall towers like Rapunzel lived in. Remember that tower in Ireland, Nina, where the tour guide fell down the stairs? The one that had the nose turned up like a pig's?"

"He didn't fall; you knocked him down when you tripped in your high-heeled boots. Nobody tours a castle in high heels. Poor man rolled all the way to the bottom. Cracked his tailbone and five ribs."

"His mother shouldn't have named him Porky, with a nose like that."

"His name wasn't Porky, it was Parker," Nina said.

"They didn't even give me my money back."

"You're lucky they didn't sue you."

"Here we are," Shay said, as the castle came into view. It wasn't a massive castle, but it was impressive nonetheless. Two towers rose on either side of the three-story structure. The grounds gently rolled with stands of trees, natural, not overly manicured.

"Nina and Matilda pressed their faces to the window. "It's so… exciting," Matilda said. She threw open the door and climbed out of the Range Rover. "I can't wait to explore." She trotted toward the door, stiff red hair bobbing up and down.

"I think there's something wrong with her," Nina said, and took off after her cousin.

"She's just now figuring that out?" Cody muttered.

"Sean and Coira are prepared?" Shay asked.

"Is anyone ever prepared for Matilda? They've been warned. There they are now."

Sean and Coira appeared at the doorway. They glanced at Shay and Cody and then welcomed their visitors, while Cody pulled the luggage from the trunk.

"Woo hoo… we'll see you in a little while," Matilda called. "Coira's giving us a tour. She's got red hair too. I bet she's a doll."

"She doesn't know what she's in for," Cody muttered.

"Did you warn Coira about Matilda and dungeons?" Shay asked.

"Check."

"And towers?"

"Done."

"Secret passages?"

"Damn!"

—⁓—

Malek waited until after dark to approach the castle. He had followed Tristol's lieutenant from Shay's house, where he intended to look for the book, since Ellis hadn't searched there yet. They assumed Renee hid the book in one of the pieces of furniture she shipped out. He would go back and search Shay's house later. First he wanted to get close enough to see how well protected the castle was. The first warrior Malek encountered was no problem. He was young, easily distracted by Malek's halfling. With the path clear, Malek left his halfling to guard his back and crept through the dark woods, cautiously placing each footstep against the floor of leaves, angry that he couldn't just storm in and take her. He, who had lived nearly a thousand years, was forced to play foolish games. He couldn't kill her until he knew where she'd hidden the book. She could already be pregnant. She and Cody had been together for days. Once Malek found the book, he would kill them both, rectifying his earlier mistake. There could be no offspring without a father or mother.

This time he would do the job himself, not entrust it to a frail human. Malek was so caught up in his thoughts that he didn't see the man until he was fifty feet away. The man tensed and turned. Malek slipped behind a large tree and tried to control the shift that had started, brought on by alarm. He knew the man was a warrior by his stance and the sword he was removing from its scabbard. Malek put his head against the rough bark and pushed hard, feeling it dig into his human skin, pressing against bones that were trying to lengthen. If he shifted, he knew the warrior would smell him. Malek knew a lot of things no one would suspect. He had spent centuries researching his enemies' secrets.

A large bird took flight from the branches above Malek. He jumped, and his tight hold on his shift shattered. His bones broke free of their restraints, skin thickened and stretched.

The warrior frowned, sniffed, and lifted the sword he had withdrawn. Malek waited until the warrior drew close and then lunged at him, slashing with his claws. The warrior jumped aside and swung to confront him. Malek moved in and hit hard. The warrior was strong, not inexperienced like the one he killed near the wall. Another lunge, and Malek caught the warrior's side with his claws. Blood seeped through the warrior's shirt, but he turned and came at Malek again, gripping his sword. He was quick. The sword sliced Malek's shoulder before he could move clear. He seethed with rage. He hadn't been injured in battle in two centuries. How dare this child raise a sword to him?

Malek raised his claws and rushed at the warrior. He caught him in the stomach, and the warrior went down, and then he realized it was the man Shay almost married. If he lived, he might bring a wedge between Shay and Cody until Malek had a chance to kill them. Malek heard a voice beyond the woods, and he backed away from the fallen warrior. He wasn't prepared for a full scale battle yet. He needed to get in without being seen. He had lived in castles for hundreds of years. There was always a bolt hole. He just had to find it.

"I'd bet my hair on it," Matilda said, whispering so loud in Nina's ear that her voice carried all the way up the ladder. "Look at them." The two old women stared at Niall and Duncan working on the balcony. "And that Ronan... Lordy, what else can they be?"

"Think they have any idea we can hear them?" Duncan asked.

"Doubt it. Cody says their hearing's shot. That's why they talk so loud," Niall replied, handing Duncan a trowel. "What is it they think this place is?"

"Beats me."

"You're insane," Nina said. "If you keep this up, I'm going to stick you in that retirement village Frieda Simms is in."

"You wouldn't dare."

"Try me." Nina huffed off, and Matilda turned to the men.

"Hello," she said, waving.

"Hello," Niall called, and then whispered from the corner of his mouth. "She scares me more than that two-headed demon I had to destroy last year."

"I don't know how the MacBains do it. Guess they're used to her," Duncan said.

"Oh yeah," Niall said. "How many times have you seen Lachlan since Matilda got here? He's been staying in a cottage near the back perimeter. I don't blame him. You know what really jolts me?"

"Besides her hair?"

"Forget the hair. Everywhere you turn, she's there. It's like there are ten of her. Did you hear she got locked in the tower this morning? It took them an hour to find her."

"What scares me is I saw her talking to Brodie earlier," Duncan said. "They looked like they were scheming."

Niall took a swig of water. "Brodie and Matilda. I think I'll see if I can stay with Lachlan."

"I'll fight you for it."

"My sword arm's so stiff, you'd probably take me."

"Mine too, but we can't practice until they leave," Duncan said.

Matilda headed back inside, almost running into Conall in the doorway. "Oh, hello there, Conrad?"

"Conall, ma'am."

"Hm. Nice outfit." She tilted her head, eyeing him up and down. "Don't see many men in kilts. Hmmm. What is it you do here, again, Conrad?"

"I… security. I'm with security, ma'am."

"Security, huh?" she said, eyes lingering on his legs. "And them?" she whispered loudly, nodding toward Duncan and Niall.

"They're security too… ma'am. It's a big place."

"Security?" Matilda said, drawing the word out like taffy. "Hmm. Oh, there's Shane. Shane, wait up." Through the window, they saw Shane take off like a bullet.

Duncan grinned. "The only exercise we get around here lately is running from Matilda."

"I swear. Can't we put 'em in a hotel or something?" Conall asked.

Niall chuckled. "What's the matter, Conrad? You don't like her looking at your legs?"

"She's looking at everybody's legs," Conall said. "You'd think she'd never seen a kilt."

———~~~———

Shay dressed and slipped quietly down the hall. Cody had come to bed well after midnight, another meeting about demons and vampires. Sam's image flashed through Shay's head, but she squashed it. Cody couldn't possibly use as much energy as he did loving her and still have leftovers for someone else. Nina and Matilda's door was closed. They were sharing a room so Nina could keep an eye on Matilda. Each had taken one of Matilda's sleeping pills, so they should still be sleeping. In spite of their sense of adventure, the two were getting on in years. Shay had no appetite that morning, so she went in search of the secret passage. She knew there was an entrance in the library. A table was piled with books that Bree had been studying. A thump came from near the fireplace. A dislodged book? Nothing was on the floor. She heard it again, a knocking sound. Was someone already inside the passage? *Don't let it be Matilda.* Shay had brought the warriors enough trouble without Matilda's antics.

"Hello," she called to the wall. No answer. She found the catch, and a section of wall beside the fireplace swung inward. She stuck her head inside, wrinkling her nose at the mustiness. She found a flashlight on a table and set off to explore. Some of the passages were wide enough to accommodate several people, others much narrower. The passage she was in came to a dead end. She turned and went back the other way. She heard a whisper, a tiny sound. She aimed the light at her feet to be sure it wasn't a mouse. The whisper came again, reminding her of the sound she heard at the lake. Cody? Was he in here, or was she hearing something from the other side of the wall? "Cody?"

There was no answer. She followed the passage to where it forked. A shadow moved, and her heart leapt into her throat. "Hello? Anyone here?" Just her echo, then a hiss. Her hair stood on end. She ran the opposite way, bumping into walls, stumbling. Rounding a corner, she hit a dead end. She ran her hands over the wall, searching for a catch. A section of the wall moved. She yelped and aimed her flashlight.

"Damn, that's bright."

"Ronan. Oh, thank God. I got lost in there." It must have been him she heard.

"You're found now." He smiled. "But I'm not Ronan. I'm Declan."

"You could be Hitler right now, for all I care. Just get me out of here."

"Where do you want to go? The library, the dungeon? Outside?"

"Outside." Sunshine seemed like a good thing.

"Outside it is. This way."

She stepped into a tunnel, dank and musty. "Do warriors have a thing for tunnels?" She had always liked them herself, but she'd had enough of this one.

"Aye. Got to have a way to escape."

"How long have you been in here? I heard something earlier."

"A while. I was checking the tunnel for loose stones. The part closest to the entrance is old. It's getting dangerous."

"Where does it lead?"

"Outside the castle grounds."

"A bolt hole."

"Aye."

She aimed the beam and saw that the tunnel widened ahead, but Declan opened a door in the wall, and they stepped into the sunlight. "That's better." She wasn't usually afraid of dark places. She explored plenty of caves with the MacBains, but this time she welcomed the sunshine. In the bright light, she could see Declan's hair was shorter than Ronan's, but the brothers were startlingly alike, and equally handsome. "Where are you headed?" Declan asked, surveying the place.

"Just wanted some fresh air."

"Don't wander off."

"I won't."

"I'll be close by if you need anything," he said, pointing to a balcony on the second floor where Duncan and Niall were working.

The weather was mild for Scotland, but she was glad she wore a sweater. There were several fenced areas with horses in the back field. She saw Clydesdales in one area and smaller horses in another. There was a large garage and a number of outbuildings. She saw a bare spot near one of the buildings. A giant buzzard circled overhead, landed, and tucked its huge wings away, probably searching for dinner. Shay followed a cobblestone path lined with boxwoods toward the trees where she saw the warriors stationed last night. She'd always been drawn to the woods, the smell of trees and pine needles and leaves. Some of her best memories were tied to earthy aromas. When she wasn't off playing with the boys, she often curled up with a book beneath her favorite canopied tree, resting on a bed of pine needles, sometimes just listening to the birds talk. Her solitude would last until Cody found her, usually waiting until he thought she was asleep so he could leap through the low-hanging boughs and scare the crap out of her. He then lay there with her, talking or napping, whatever notion struck. Shay stood at the tree line, closed her eyes, and breathed deeply through her nose. Something pulled at her, a feeling she couldn't place, a smell that wasn't right. She turned back, disturbed, because she liked it.

The buzzard was still there, his wings hunched around his shoulders, waiting. He moved, and Shay could see past him, where something dark lay behind the small building. A deer? She squinted and saw it move. It was alive! The damned bird was waiting for its meal to die. Shay moved closer, planning to scare it away. She saw boots, not hooves, and then legs, hips. She yelled as she ran, startling the great bird into flight.

When recognition dawned, she opened her mouth and screamed.

Chapter 17

CODY KNOCKED ON SHAY'S DOOR. IT SWUNG OPEN. "Shay?" He checked the balcony, but she wasn't there. Maybe the shower. No. The room was empty. She could be with Bree or Nina and Matilda. As much as he loved them, the two old women were going to complicate things.

The small silver jewelry box he rescued from the fire sat on Shay's dresser. He gave it to her on her sixteenth birthday. He bought it and the white-gold heart inside with the money he made from helping the farmer down the road make hay. He had known he would be leaving for training soon and worried they would grow apart with him gone so much and having to keep his secrets. Then his father had told him Shay's secret. They probably would have been better off if they just told her. He headed down to the kitchen, where Coira was banging around. The clan had offered to hire cooks, but Coira guarded her kitchen like a pirate guarded his treasure. "Have you seen Shay?" Cody asked.

"Not this morning. She didn't come to breakfast. Such a sweet girl, but she doesn't eat enough."

"I'm sure you'll take care of that, Coira." Cody grabbed a biscuit. "I'll check the library."

When he entered the room, he saw the secret-passage entrance standing open. His pulse quickened as he stepped inside. "Shay," he called. His voice echoed back to him, hollow. He smelled her and another scent too faded to identify. He followed her trail through several passages. The scent stopped where the tunnel door led outside. He stepped into daylight as Declan came around the corner, carrying a ladder.

"Have you seen Shay?" Cody asked.

"She went to get some fresh air."

A scream pierced Cody's ears.

"That was Shay!" Cody bolted toward the sound.

"Help!" Shay screamed. She knelt on the ground beside Jamie. His bloody shirt hung in tatters. Deep wounds covered his stomach and side. "Help him." Shay's eyes were wide, her face pinched. "Please, help him."

Cody and Declan knelt beside Shay. Jamie was unconscious but breathing. His knees and hands were covered in dirt. "Looks like he crawled here," Declan said.

"Run ahead of us and get Coira. She's in the kitchen," Cody told Shay. "We'll carry him." Together he and Declan carried Jamie to the house. Coira met them in the infirmary. They laid Jamie down and stood back as Coira cut away his filthy shirt, revealing long, gaping wounds.

"Claw marks," Declan said.

"They're deep," Coira said, "but the bleeding has stopped."

Shay hovered over Jamie, holding his hand, as Coira checked Jamie's vital signs. "Will he be okay?"

Cody could see the tears staining her cheeks.

"Unless it gets infected. He was lying out there for God knows how long." Coira's hands moved deftly as she cleaned the injuries.

Infection and sickness were rare among warriors. Strong genes were part of their weaponry. The biggest danger was dying in battle. "I'm going to sound the alarm," Cody told them.

When he came back to check on Shay, she was removing Jamie's jeans. She laid them on a chair and straightened his boxers, her movements smooth and sure, as if in familiar territory. Of course she was. She almost married him.

She picked up a washcloth and began to wash dirt from Jamie's arm. He muttered something and reached for her hand.

Cody eased the door shut and walked away.

The warriors assembled a group and searched the woods. It didn't take long to find signs of a fight where Jamie had been posted last night.

"You think it was a vampire?" Brodie asked Cody, who had bent down to sniff the tracks.

"There's no scent. It's too old."

"Looked like demon claws to me," Niall said.

Cody sat back on his haunches, staring at the tracks. Problem was, a vampire had a footprint just like a human... or a demon in disguise. Had one of Malek's demons tracked Shay to the castle? "We'll need guards, twenty-four seven. Shane, can you organize it? Someone tell Sean to alert the Council that we've been attacked."

Shay pulled back the sheet and lifted Jamie's bandage. She could already see a difference in the wound after just a few hours. Coira said the warriors healed quickly. The cut from Cody's sword was proof. It was just a thin line already. Other scars dotted Jamie's body. She asked him about them once. He laughed and said he was a reckless kid.

His eyes flew open, and his hand clamped on her arm, surprisingly strong. He focused on her face and relaxed his grip. "Shay." He looked down at his bandage and winced.

"How do you feel?"

"Cold."

"Let me get Coira."

"No. Stay with me."

This was the first time he'd spoken to her since the attack. Coira said he'd woken a few times, but hadn't said what happened.

"You were hurt. Something attacked you."

He frowned hard and rubbed his forehead. "A demon, I think… can't remember…" his voice trailed off, and he shivered.

"I'll get another blanket," she said, starting to pull away.

He held onto her hand. "Lie down with me, just for a few minutes. Please."

She hesitated, knowing she shouldn't, but she felt bad for Jamie. Not just for his physical pain, but for the emotional pain she'd caused him, although it hadn't been intentional. He'd offered her his heart and his home. The least she could do was comfort him for five minutes. Maybe he would fall asleep quickly and she could put another blanket on him and leave. After all, Sam had been in Cody's bedroom while he wore nothing but a towel, and he expected Shay to believe it was innocent. Was this any worse? Against Shay's better judgment, she slipped off her shoes and lay on top of the covers, stiffly, trying not to let their bodies touch. The pillow

was soft. She hadn't realized how tired she was, and
her arm burned like the dickens. Maybe she was the one
who should worry about infection. Shay closed her eyes,
to rest for just a moment. As soon as Jamie fell asleep,
she would leave.

Cody returned to the castle at eight o'clock. He missed
dinner, but he didn't care. All he wanted was to crawl
into bed with Shay and hold her. Seeing her caring for
Jamie left him with an uneasy feeling. He yawned. He'd
spent most of the day talking to the fire investigators
and looking for some sign of who might have attacked
Jamie. He found a young warrior dead, probably killed
before Jamie was attacked. The warrior had recently
arrived from Ireland after finishing his training. His
mentor hadn't come; they thought it was a safe enough
task. He shouldn't have been guarding such an isolated
section of the wall, but he talked another warrior into
switching places. Sean was taking Patrick's body home
to his parents.

Cody headed to the room where they'd moved Jamie.
If he was awake, Cody needed to ask him some questions about the attack. Perhaps they could clear the air
as well. They weren't at each other's throats anymore,
but Cody owed the man an apology. At one time Jamie
had been a friend, and now he was sacrificing his life to
protect Shay. He'd broken the rules and gotten involved
with her, but Cody had too.

Jamie's door was cracked. He lay on his back. Shay
lay beside him, holding his hand. Cody's heart felt like
a block of wood. Had seeing Jamie injured made her

realize that she still loved him? She'd cared enough to almost marry him. She had spent far more time in Jamie's bed than his, and Jamie hadn't gotten her pregnant and left her to carry and bury a baby alone. Cody turned and headed to his room, weary to the bone.

Shay was headed for the shower when she heard a knock. She threw on a robe and opened the door.

Cody stood outside. She hadn't seen him since Jamie was hurt. It was pathetic how badly she wanted to run into his arms and feel his heart beating safe and sound against hers, but the warriors were swamped, trying to keep the place surrounded and trying to find Malek and the vampires. She noticed his face, pale and tight.

"Cody, what's wrong? Is it Jamie?" She had just left him minutes earlier.

His jaw clenched. "Jamie's fine," he said, his voice rough. "I heard you come in and wanted to see if you were okay."

"I'm good. I was just going to take a shower."

"Okay, then." He looked her over once, cold as a stranger, and turned to leave.

"Wait. What on earth's wrong with you? One minute you're telling me I'm your mate, the next you're acting like a robot."

He stepped inside and closed the door. "I don't share my women."

"What are you talking about?"

It was like she flipped a switch. The ice in his face melted and bitterness gushed out. "I saw you with him."

"Who?"

"Jamie."

Oh no. "If you mean—"

"I saw you in bed with him." He looked almost as angry as he had when he and Jamie fought at Cody's house.

"I wasn't—"

"Are you denying it?"

"No, but… it wasn't like that."

"What was it like, then? Tell me that. What do you call it when a man and a woman are snuggled together in bed? Friends? Not in my book."

"We weren't snuggling, and he was freezing. Don't look at me like that. He needed body heat and a little comfort from a friend. I was fully clothed on top of the covers. I shouldn't have done it, but I felt sorry for him. He is my friend, Cody. He'll always be my friend, but I'm not in love with him."

Cody's jaw worked. "Damn. I don't know what to think. You say you don't love him, but seems every time I turn around, you have your hands on him."

"It was no more than being a nurse."

"I don't know any nurses who crawl into bed with their patients to warm them up."

"You know what I mean." Shay moved closer and touched Cody's arm. "I'm sorry. It was a stupid decision, but nothing happened. I swear it. I love Jamie, but not like that. Not like I love you."

His expression and body went completely still. "You love me?"

In all their lovemaking, she'd never said the words. Maybe because she was afraid. Those words carried commitment, expectation. Shay untied her robe, letting it fall. "Come here, and I'll show you how much."

After they were finally sated with love, they slept. The darkness crept in, shadows twisting and writhing in her head, dark and light, evil and good. She felt *him* beckoning her as she dreamed. Her skin was hot, the scratch on her arm throbbed.

"Come to me." He waited in the trees. She couldn't see him, yet she knew his face. Pale, long hair, black as midnight. He smiled and she gasped at his beauty.

———

Cody brushed a strand of hair from Shay's face and kissed her neck, but she didn't wake. Her brow wrinkled and she muttered something under her breath. Her face was pale, drawn, as if she fought troubled dreams. Or had he just worn her out? His stomach rumbled. He needed food after all the energy he expended. His legs and hips felt heavy as lead, but his heart soared. Shay loved him. He had no doubts now. If he didn't stop thinking about it, he'd have to put on a sporran just to get to the kitchen. He and Shay had gone from the bed to the shower and back to the bed again, from desperate to languid, both trying to make up for nine lost years. He felt a stab of sadness again, thinking about the baby he and Shay lost, the pain she suffered alone, but focusing too much on grief or pleasure could affect his ability to keep Shay safe. He should probably sleep in his own room tonight. He climbed out of bed and put on his kilt. He started to pull up her covers and saw the mark on her arm. It looked red. He'd get Coira to check it.

He headed to the kitchen and met Duncan. "Anybody seen Matilda? She's missing again."

Coira stopped wiping the kitchen table. "Bloody

hell." She slapped her hand over her mouth and then frantically crossed herself.

"It's all right, Coira. Matilda could make a saint curse." Cody sighed. "Nina hasn't seen her?"

"She's the one who alerted us."

"She's probably out terrorizing the guards," Ronan said. "She asked one of them if this was some kind of gigolo operation."

Cody grimaced. "We've got to get her out of here before she destroys thousands of years of secrecy."

"I saw her headed toward the library earlier," Coira said. "Her and that giant cat."

"The library? Damn it. The secret passages." Cody hurried down the hall with Duncan and Ronan behind him. The hidden door stood open.

"Blimey," Duncan said. "Might as well start offering tours."

Cody stuck his head inside. "Matilda? I hear something," he said to the others. "Anybody got a flashlight?"

"Here." Ronan pulled one from his sporran and turned it on. The three men entered the stone passage, following the narrow beam of light.

"That way," Cody said. "Matilda?"

They heard running, and a second later, Matilda flew into Cody's arms. "Oh, thank heaven." Her hair stood on end, covered by cobwebs. Red lipstick was smeared across her cheek. "I got lost. I couldn't figure out which way I came in. I don't know what to do. I think I killed a man."

"You killed a man down here?" Ronan asked, glancing at the others.

"Over there, around that corner. But I don't think he

was a man. I saw this shadow and thought it was one of you. I called out, and he leapt at me. He hissed. I've never heard a man hiss."

"You sure it wasn't the cat?" Duncan asked.

"No, I was holding the cat, only because it was dark, and my flashlight was dying," she said, defensively.

Cody moved toward the corner where Matilda pointed. "Nothing here."

"How did you kill him?" Ronan asked, eyeing Matilda doubtfully.

"Holy water."

"Where the hell did you get holy water?" Duncan asked.

"Well, I was clutching my bottle of water to my chest. I carry one with me so I don't get dehydrated. The doctor said I need to stay hydrated. And I got lost, like I told you, and I started praying somebody would find me, and since I was holding the water, I guess the praying must have blessed it. Or it might have been the cat."

"The cat blessed the water?" Duncan asked, scratching his head.

"No. Killed the man. When he hissed at me, the cat hissed back and jumped at him."

Cody caught Ronan and Duncan's worried gazes.

"Then I threw my water bottle at him." Matilda held her heart. "I think I might faint."

"Come on, Matilda," Duncan said. "I'll take you up. Ronan and Cody will check it out. I'm sure it was just a shadow."

"I've never seen a shadow with red eyes."

"It couldn't be," Ronan said, his voice somber, as Duncan led Matilda away. "Maybe she's insane."

"She's not normal, but she's as sharp as your sword."

"What the hell did she see, then?"

Cody aimed his light along the walls. "Damn."

"What is it?" Ronan joined him, his gaze on the beam of light on the floor. A bottle of water lay in a pile of dust.

Cody felt the blood rush from his head. A vampire. "They got inside. They know she's here."

Ronan looked as if he'd turned to stone. "Alert the guards. I'll look down here."

Cody whirled and ran back to the castle. He opened the hidden door and burst into the library, where half the house had gathered around Matilda.

"...and it hissed with these big red eyes, and the cat flew out of my hands... where's the cat?" she asked, looking around.

"Did you actually see this... man?" Duncan asked.

"Well, no. It was shadowed, but when the cat leaped at the man, I heard this terrible screeching sound. I figured it was the holy water melting him."

Nina entered the library. "What have you done now, Matilda?" she asked, staring at her cousin's cobwebbed hair.

"I killed a man," Matilda said.

"You just saw a shadow," Cody said, motioning for the warriors to join him.

"Of course it was a shadow," Nina said, "just like the one you saw back at the house. We'll make an appointment and have your eyes checked as soon as we get home."

"She saw shadows at home?" Lachlan asked, making a rare appearance. Since Matilda's arrival, he usually slept in one of the cottages and guarded the woods.

"Out behind the house. Let's get you to bed, Matilda."

Nina took her cousin's arm and led her from the room. "You've got to stop exploring, or they're going to throw us out. Oh, has anyone seen Shay?"

"She's asleep," Cody said.

"I just stopped by her room," Nina said. "She's not there, and her room is cold. Someone left the window open."

Cody broke into a run, feet pounding down the corridor. He heard the others behind him, but he didn't stop. He burst through Shay's door. The room was empty, balcony curtains swaying in the wind. He hurried outside. She wasn't there, but a ladder rested against the ledge of the balcony. His heart lurched. He scanned the grounds and saw something white moving toward the woods. A dark shadow stood just inside the tree line.

"No!" Cody leapt from the balcony, springing into a run when his feet touched the ground. He sprinted across the castle grounds. "Stop!" he yelled as Shay moved closer to the trees. "Shay! Stop!"

He saw a blur of white dart between Shay and the shadow, and the shadow jumped back. Cody ran faster. When he reached her, Shay stood staring into the woods, her body stiff, face unresponsive, like the night on the balcony. The shadow was gone. "Shay?" Cody touched her, but she didn't move. She looked as if she'd been drugged. Half a dozen warriors ran up behind Cody. "Where the hell are the guards?" Cody asked.

"There's one," Ronan said, running to kneel by the prone form several feet away. "He's unconscious."

"Same here," Shane called, on the other side.

"I see another one farther down," Niall said.

"This one's coming 'round," Ronan said.

The young warrior jumped to his feet and drew his

sword. Ronan fell back, narrowly avoiding losing an ear. The warrior's gaze darted wildly. "What happened?" He blinked at Shay. "Where'd she come from?"

"It's okay," Ronan told the guard. "Something knocked you out." Ronan looked at Cody. "I'm going after it."

"You can't go alone," Cody said, but Ronan was already gone. "Niall, go after him before he gets himself killed."

Niall took off after Ronan, lithe as a panther, for all his bulky size.

Cody kept a hand on Shay, who looked like she might collapse. "Lachlan, get every warrior we have out here. Barricade this place. Someone check the secret passages and the tunnel."

Shay shook her head, looking around as wild-eyed as the guard. "Cody? What are you doing? Where are we?" She looked confused. "Where is... he?"

"Who?" Cody asked.

She looked toward the woods. "I don't know," she said, and her body slumped into a faint. Cody caught her, swinging her up into his arms. He ran with her toward the castle, shouting out to the warriors swarming the place.

Coira was waiting in the infirmary, readying her medical supplies. "Put her here," Coira said.

Cody placed Shay on the bed and stood back as Coira checked Shay's pulse. "She seemed fine an hour ago." What the hell was happening?

"Pulse is slow. What's this?" Coira asked, looking at the red scratch on Shay's pale skin. It looked even angrier.

"She said she scratched it. I was going to get you to look at it." He leaned down and sniffed. It didn't smell sulfurous, like a demon scratch, but it probably wouldn't, since it was several days old. "Is it infected?"

"I don't think so, just inflamed. Her pupils are normal," she said, shining a light into Shay's eyes. "That's good." The blood pressure cuff beeped. "Blood pressure is low."

"Maybe we should take her to the hospital," Cody said. They tried to avoid hospitals if possible. It opened the door to too many questions they didn't want to answer.

"I think she'll be okay. Let's let her rest for a bit. What was that out there, Cody?"

"All I saw was a shadow with black hair."

"You think it was the same thing that attacked Jamie?"

"I don't know." Jamie hadn't been able to remember much about the attack. "Why didn't he hurt Shay? He just stood there, like he was waiting for her."

"This is unnerving. Those things getting inside the castle wall, even inside the secret passages. I'm starting to wonder if Angus was right about the traitor."

She wasn't the only one wondering it. The castle had two lines of guards around the perimeter. How had this— whatever it was—found the place and gotten through?

"Go find it, Cody," Coira said fiercely. "Before this thing finds Shay."

Cody bent and pressed a lingering kiss to Shay's forehead, and stood, his face set tight, prepared for the hunt. He knew what had to be done. He would destroy Malek, at least weaken him, even if it meant his own death. But there was one place he needed to stop first.

"Malek? Hell, are you sure?" Cody asked.

"My memory was cloudy before, but now I'm positive," Jamie said, his face gray. "How did he find her?"

"He must have followed us from the airport or from Shay's house. I suspect the fire was a trap to draw Shay into the open, but if someone followed us, he was invisible. We had another breach earlier. Someone tried to lure Shay outside, but it wasn't Malek. This guy had black hair."

Jamie threw back his covers. "Is she okay? What happened?"

"Coira's taking care of her. She'll be fine." He couldn't consider anything else. "The three guards closest to where we found her were unconscious. All they remember is hearing the wind. Next thing they knew they were waking up. The other guards farther away were unaffected, but they didn't see what was happening. Ronan and Niall are tracking it. I'm headed out now."

Jamie swung his feet to the floor and went pale with the effort. "I'll come with you."

"You still need rest."

"I'm sick of rest."

"You need to heal," Cody said, putting his hand on Jamie's shoulder. "You're lucky to be alive. Not many can say they've battled one of the old demons hand-to-hand and lived to tell about it."

"You said another warrior was killed before I was attacked. It must have weakened Malek. That's probably the only reason I'm alive."

"Maybe, but you are alive, and you're a good warrior, and we'll need you when you've recovered." He hoped Jamie took the words for the apology it was. It wouldn't make up for his jackass jealous behavior, but it was a start. "We have other warriors coming to help."

"I feel like a bloody invalid, lying here while the castle is attacked. Are you sure Shay's okay?" he asked stiffly. It was still awkward for the two of them to mention her.

"She's okay, thanks to that damned cat. It darted between Shay and whoever was in the woods. It might've saved her life. Matilda's too. You don't know about Matilda. She said she killed a man in the secret passage. We found a pile of dust."

"Vampires? Inside the castle!"

"Must have entered through the tunnel. Matilda thinks the cat attacked whatever she saw. Hell. That cat probably saved all our lives. If the vampire had waited until we were asleep, he could have killed us one by one."

"Maybe it's a vampire-killer cat. So a castle that's remained a secret for centuries has been breached three times in a matter of days, by a demon and a vampire and who knows what else?"

"I don't know what that was outside, but he must be powerful, to knock out three warriors without even touching them. I'm beginning to think the whole underworld has joined forces against us."

"What's next?" Jamie asked. "Werewolves?"

Cody's mentor had told him about a creature he saw when he was a kid, a human that changed into an animal. Daniel swore it wasn't a demon. He spoke of it only once, when he had too much whisky following a hard battle.

Jamie shifted, wincing. "Is someone guarding the tunnel?"

"Shane and Tomas checked it earlier, and we've posted two guards there."

"Maybe we should move Shay to New York," Jamie said.

"If we move her, we'll risk having her out in the open until we can get her inside the castle walls there. Even though we've been breached here, more warriors are on the way. France has a dozen on the way, and Ireland's sending twenty." He hadn't asked the clan in Ireland, not after sending one of their own back in a casket, but they had volunteered. "We can line them up shoulder to shoulder, if we have to." Cody looked around the room, trying to decide how to ask Jamie what he wanted to ask. "I need a favor."

Jamie looked surprised. "I'm listening."

Cody held Jamie's gaze and remembered staring at him across the body in the woods, thinking Shay was dead. "If something happens to me… I want you to take care of Shay." His throat tightened at the words, but he had to make sure she would be okay. Jamie loved her. He would protect her. Give her a good life.

Jamie watched him for a minute and then he nodded. "You have my word."

"Thank you."

Duncan stuck his head in the door, his scowl even more pronounced than usual. "Has anyone seen Sorcha? Bloody woman's never where she's supposed to be."

"She's guarding the gate," Cody said. He hadn't seen Sorcha and Duncan together since Duncan kissed her during the Council meeting.

"I'm going to check on her," Duncan said, passing Coira on the way out.

"Have you been to the bathroom tonight?" she asked Jamie.

He rolled his eyes. "Not yet."

"Better do it while you have a man to help you, or I'll have to stick a bedpan under you. I'm going to sleep in the infirmary so I can watch Shay. Don't forget your pain pills. Won't do anyone any good if you don't rest so your body can heal."

"Damn," Jamie said, after she left.

"Uh… you need to go?" Cody asked.

Jamie nodded and slowly sat up. It took him a minute to stand. Cody put his arm around Jamie, supporting him, and helped him into the bathroom, wondering if this was some kind of karma or penance for acting like an asshole.

———

Ronan frowned as Bree stood over Shay's bed. He and Niall had spent the night hunting that thing in the woods. Cody left minutes after they had. He hoped Cody had better luck. It was as if it had vanished into thin air with not even a track.

"What's wrong?" Faelan asked Bree.

She leaned closer and touched the bandage on Shay's arm. "Vampire," she said, and blinked several times. "She's been marked by a vampire."

Chapter 18

RONAN FELT AS IF HE HAD SWALLOWED A FROG. "ARE you sure?" he choked.

"I think so," Bree said.

Faelan moved closer. "Marked by an ancient demon and a vampire? Damnation. Poor wee lass."

Bree pressed her hand to her forehead. "I think I need to sit down."

"You don't need to sit down, you need to lie down," Ronan scolded. To Faelan he said, "She's been hanging off those ladders in the library like a monkey when you're not watching."

Bree gave Ronan the evil eye.

"I don't need you to take care of my wife," Faelan said to Ronan. He turned to Bree. "Are ye trying to drive me mad?" He swung her up in his arms and carried her sputtering from the room.

The whole clan couldn't keep Bree out of trouble. Ronan wished he could just tell Faelan about the baby, so he didn't have to worry about letting Bree's secret slip.

"You think it's a bite?" Coira asked, unwinding the bandage to check Shay's scratch.

"Scratch, bite, it doesn't matter," Ronan said. "If her blood's been tainted by a vampire, she needs a transfusion."

"A transfusion? I don't have enough blood. She'll

have to go to the hospital, and Cody will kill us if we take her outside these walls. You know how he feels about her."

"There's no time for the hospital. She's his mate. What do you think he'll do if we let a vampire lure her away? I think she's been marked."

"Cody said she got the scratch days ago. Why isn't she dead? I thought vampire bites were supposed to kill, drain the blood, you know," Coira said.

"I think marking a victim is different, like injecting a poison or drug. It makes you weak at first, and then if it doesn't kill you, it makes you stronger."

"And how do you know so much about it?"

Ronan looked away. "I've been researching."

Shay opened her eyes. "Where am I?"

"You're in the infirmary. You... passed out. Can you tell us what you were doing outside?" Coira asked.

She blinked slowly. "Him. I was going to him."

"Who?" Ronan asked.

She looked puzzled. "I don't know."

"The vampire is trying to lure her to him," Ronan said.

"What on God's green earth do they want with her?" Coira asked.

"I don't know, but we're not going to let them have her. We'll have to do it here," Ronan said. "And it will have to be my blood."

"Your blood?" Shay asked, her voice groggy. "What are you doing to me? I want Cody."

"We're going to give you blood," Coira said.

"I'm O-pos—"

"O-positive, I know," Ronan said. "All warriors are."

"I'm no warrior," Shay whispered.

"Aye, you are," Ronan said. "Well, you most likely are."

She slumped against the bed. "Cody lied to me again." She passed out.

"Do it fast," Ronan said, watching Shay's breathing grow more shallow. "I'll take responsibility."

"You say she had red hair?" Cody asked. He'd run into Nick's friend at the police station when the guy came to see if there were any new leads in his friend's murder.

"That she did," Nick's roommate said, "but I couldn't say what she wanted with him. Seemed all secretive like."

"Was the woman young?" Sorcha immediately came to mind, but Sorcha wasn't the only red-haired woman in the world. Maybe for Duncan…

"That's what was so noticeable. She wasn't young at all. She was old, and her hair…" the guy held his hands out over his head, "like the color of… you ever see a baboon's nose?"

It couldn't be. Cody tilted his head. "Nick didn't mention her name?"

"No. Just said he was playing Cupid. He was a good bloke. We roomed together for a year. Treated me like a brother."

"I'm sorry. Can you tell me what the woman was wearing?"

"Now that was bloody odd. Purple, and another thing…" he leaned closer, as if imparting national secrets. "She had cleavage."

Matilda.

"They found what?" Cody had just returned to the castle when Sam caught up to him in the corridor.

"The neighbor, Lucy Bell, the bones belonged to her, but the fire didn't kill her. She was already dead. Just wanted to give you a heads up that they'll probably have some questions for Shay. Honestly, I think they suspect Ellis killed her, but you'd better use that super mojo you got and solve this thing fast. There's some weird stuff going on."

If Sam only knew.

"If anyone owes you favors, now's the time to call them in. The cops are getting nervous about talking to me. If my superiors find out what I've done for you, I'm toast."

Why kill an old woman, unless she interrupted something she shouldn't have, like someone searching for a stolen book? A neighbor who lived behind Shay claimed she saw a man near Shay's house the night before the fire. Maybe the fire wasn't to lure Shay into a trap, but to hide a dead body.

Sam left to make some phone calls, and Cody went toward the infirmary to check on Shay. He'd spent the whole day tracking and following leads. He was fairly sure Nina and Matilda had something to do with Nick and those phone calls.

Coira met him at the door. "Cody, you're back." She darted a glance inside.

"What's wrong? Is it Shay?" He hurried inside. She was in bed, attached to a tube. An iron fist closed around his heart. "Why are you giving her blood?"

Ronan lay on a table near her. He looked pale. "Bree had one of her visions. The mark on Shay's arm is from a vampire. Her blood is tainted."

"A vampire? Bloody hell! Why didn't you call me?"

"We had to work fast," Coira said.

"Is she okay?" If something happened to her, he didn't know if he could live, but she actually looked healthier than she had in days.

"She's doing much better," Coira said. "Her color is improving by the minute."

Ronan watched Shay, his expression growing soft in a way Cody didn't like, and then Cody saw the gauze on Ronan's arm.

"Whose blood?" Cody asked.

"Mine," Ronan said.

"She has your blood?" A warrior's blood was powerful. He'd seen transfusions create bonds between warriors, give them a stronger sense of brotherhood than they already had. What would it do between male and female?

Faelan walked into the room, catching the last of the conversation. "Bree said Shay had been marked. It might be why she was sleepwalking outside. Who knows what the vampires can do? Track her. Summon her."

Ronan started to say something, but stopped. He looked so pale Cody wondered if Coira had taken too much blood.

Cody touched Shay's forehead. She didn't have a fever, and she looked much better. "It should've been my blood," he said, stroking Shay's hair as Coira removed the tube.

"I know," Ronan said quietly. "But in this case it had to be mine."

"Why?" Would he have to fight Ronan for her now?

"I have immunities you don't have." His jaw clenched. "I was bitten by a vampire."

"During the battle?" Cody asked.

"Not at the castle. Two years ago, and I suspect a vampire killed my brother, Cam."

"Oh my," Coira said, putting gauze on Shay's arm.

A harsh breath sounded at the door. Declan stood frozen, staring at his twin. "A vampire? You think a vampire killed Cam? And you didn't say anything?"

"You knew there were vampires two years ago? Why didn't you warn the clan?" Faelan asked.

"I didn't know it was a vampire, then. Nobody believed vampires existed in this day and age. When we saw the vampires at Druan's castle, I knew I'd made a mistake."

"Mistake? How could you not know you've been bitten by a vampire?" Faelan asked.

"Cam and I were hunting. We destroyed four demons. Something attacked our camp that night. I'd gone to take a piss when I heard Cam scream. The night was so black I couldn't see what it was, but it was fast and strong. I attacked it, and I don't know what happened. When I woke up, Cam was gone. I saw the blood where it dragged him off, but the trail disappeared."

"You never found the body?" Cody asked, slipping his hand over Shay's. He felt her pulse throbbing softly under his finger. It must be his imagination, but he thought it sped up.

"No. We looked, Declan and I, and a lot of others, but there was no trace of him. At first I didn't notice the marks on my neck. They were small. When they started burning, I thought they must be scratches from a demon."

"Damn it! Why didn't you tell me at Druan's castle?" Declan asked, face tight with anger.

"I wanted more information first. I think that blond is important. He can give us answers."

"Why would being bitten by a vampire make you better suited for Shay's transfusion?" Cody asked. "Isn't getting bitten a bad thing?"

"I think if you don't die, you develop immunities to their poison," Ronan said. "I don't understand it, but there's more to it than just draining a victim's blood. I think I got stronger afterward. My eyesight and my hearing seem sharper."

"You're my bloody twin, and you're just now telling me?" Declan slammed his fist against the wall and stalked out, passing Jamie on the way in. He wasn't moving fast, but he looked a lot better than he had before.

"What's wrong with Shay?"

"Jamie Waters, what are you doing out of bed?" Coira hurried over to him and checked his bandage.

"Sorry, Coira, I remembered something I needed to tell Cody." Jamie walked to Shay's bed. "Is she okay?" When he saw Cody holding Shay's hand, his jaw tightened, and he looked away.

"She had what we thought was a scratch on her arm," Cody said, pulling his hand from Shay's. He didn't want to make things harder on Jamie than it already was. "Bree said a vampire marked her. Ronan gave her some blood."

"A vampire? She's marked by a demon and a vampire? Is she okay?" Jamie asked, worry shadowing his eyes.

Coira nodded. "Much better."

"What did you want to tell me?" Cody asked.

"I remember where I heard the name Anson Masters. He was Renee's client."

"Are you sure?" Cody asked. "The police didn't mention it."

"Yeah. I called Renee a few days ago, to see how Shay was doing. She sounded uneasy. I asked if she was okay. She said she had to deliver a chair to a client, Anson Masters. She didn't say anything else. I figured she was just in a rush."

"What do you want to bet he's the client she didn't like? Shay thought Renee said something about 'faster,' but she could have been trying to warn Shay about Masters."

"I think so. I checked the invoice for the table. It was in my wallet. His name was scribbled on the corner. I think she was trying to give us a clue," Jamie said. "She probably sent the table to me because she knew I had a top-secret job. She thought I was military. She probably figured the table would be safe with me." Jamie gave a humorless laugh.

"She didn't know you'd be guarding it from vampires," Ronan said.

Sam stepped into the room. "Did someone say vampires—" She broke off, staring at Jamie. Her eyes flared and she looked away, her cheeks growing pink.

"Uh, we were just talking nonsense," Cody said. "Sam, Jamie Waters. Jamie, Samantha Skye. You met the others already."

"You're Sam?" Jamie asked, eyebrows cocked. He and Sam nodded in greeting but didn't attempt to shake hands.

"Jamie says Ellis's boss, Anson Masters, was a client of Renee's," Cody said, watching Sam's blush fade. He couldn't remember ever seeing her blush.

"Now that's interesting," Sam said, pulling her gaze from Jamie. "He left out that little detail. I haven't been able to find him and wondered if you had anyone you could spare. This guy's harder to track down than Osama bin Laden."

He could *be* Osama bin Laden, for all they knew. Cody was pretty sure Osama was a demon. Some of the wickedest rulers in human history were either demons or minions. "Jamie, think you're up to helping Sam?" He looked much stronger than he had before.

Coira planted her hands on her hips. "Cody MacBain, what kind of foolishness are you putting in this boy's head? He needs to rest a couple more days."

Jamie patted Coira's shoulder. "I'll be fine, Coira. You know I'm a fast healer."

"I know you're hardheaded; that's what I know."

He glanced from Shay to the mark on Cody's neck. "You'll take care of her?" he asked Cody, and something passed between them, like a final changing of the guards.

"I will," Cody said. "You have my word."

Jamie nodded.

"I'll take it easy on Jamie," Sam told Coira, and this time Jamie blushed.

"I'm holding you and Cody responsible for him," Coira said.

He gave one final look over his shoulder at Shay, his expression torn. "Lead the way," he said, following Sam.

"When we're in the car," Sam said, "you can explain why you were really talking about vampires. It wouldn't surprise me to find out Cody's a creature of the night." After they left, Shay coughed. Coira and Cody rushed to her side. She struggled to rise.

"Relax now," Coira said.

Cody grabbed Shay's hand. "How do you feel?"

"Betrayed."

"What have I done now?" Cody asked.

"You lied to me," Shay said, after the others fled the room.

"How did I lie?"

"I'm a warrior? Ronan had to tell me."

Damn.

"You said you'd stop."

"We weren't sure you were a warrior."

"But I might be?"

"It's possible." He sighed. "I think you probably are. The Watchers thought so at one time, and they're usually right. I wasn't hiding it from you; there's just been so much going on."

"So I've found out I'm a warrior a year before I have to retire?" She sat down on the bed.

"You can always choose to remain active. That's what Anna plans to do. So does Ronan." That distressing thought had him so troubled he almost missed what she said next.

"What you said about the demons using the book to kill warriors when they're born, do you think that's what happened to me? I was left for dead as a baby, and someone is obviously worried enough about whether I'm alive to dig up my fake grave. And Bree thinks it's an ancient demon."

Cody sat down next to her. "God forbid. It's possible that Malek believed your father had the book and left it to you. It's all speculation. We don't know anything for sure except that someone is after you, and someone stole our *Book of Battles*." He reached for her hand. "Are you mad at me again?"

"A little."

"I should have told you. I would have, but there's been so much happening. And subconsciously, I probably didn't want to put another burden on you. I love you. I want you safe."

"I know. I kept secrets too, but we have to stop," she said, leaning her head on shoulder.

"Shay, I have some bad news. There's no good way to say it. Lucy is dead."

Shay's mouth tightened, and her eyes teared up. "The bones?"

"Aye. I'm sorry."

"How?"

"She didn't die in the fire. She was already dead."

"Was it Ellis?"

"The police suspect him, but they may need to ask you some more questions."

"Everyone around me is dying. If we don't stop this thing, everyone I care about will be gone." She gripped his hand and linked their fingers.

"I'll fix it," he said. "I promise."

~~~

"Coira wants to know how Jamie's doing," Cody said into the phone. Sam and Jamie had been gone only for a few hours, but Coira was like a mother hen with the warriors.

"He's good," Sam said. She sounded breathless, making Cody wonder exactly what kind of good Sam meant.

"She said to make sure he changes the bandage and gets plenty of rest."

"I will. We're going to check out another lead I have on Anson Masters. Shouldn't be so hard to find him with that streak of silver in his hair, but he seems to have vanished from the face of the earth."

"Silver streak?"

"Yes. It's quite startling, according to the guy at the police station. Why?"

Cody cursed and smacked his fist against the wall. Anson Masters was Malek. "Don't try to find him. Do you hear me? Don't. He's too dangerous."

"How do you know?"

"I know. Tell Jamie. Tell him that Anson is Malek."

"Who's Malek?"

"Jamie will know. Don't touch Anson. Swear to me." After she promised, Cody hung up, pissed that he hadn't thought to get a description of Ellis's boss. He thought his appearance with the letter providing evidence against Ellis had been a little too good to be true. Malek had posed as Renee's client while his minion, Ellis, had posed as Shay's, probably trying to discover her identity. Malek must have gotten the book from Bree's ex-boyfriend, and Renee probably stumbled onto Malek's plot and hid the book. Malek must have assumed Renee put the book in one of the tables and shipped it to Shay. How the vampires found out was a mystery, but it put Shay in the middle of a war between vampires and demons.

Why hadn't Michael assigned Malek to a warrior? Was he going to let the demon slaughter them all?

"Ronan, are you all right?" Coira asked. "You hardly

touched your dinner." They were having an early meal so the warriors could start hunting. "You need your strength after giving so much blood."

"Yeah, you look rotten," Bree agreed.

He looked like a man tormented, Cody thought. Declan was pissed at Ronan for not telling him about Cam, and Ronan was eaten up with guilt for not warning the clan about the vampires two years ago, even though he hadn't believed it himself until recently.

"I'm fine." Ronan glanced at Shay—he'd been doing a lot of that since the transfusion— frowned, and pushed his chair from the table.

"Vampires, demons, both wanting our book. What a mess," Sean said. He'd just returned from taking the warrior's body home.

"At least Shay is looking stronger. You're the picture of health," Coira said, patting Shay's cheek as she put down a plate for her. Shay had surprised them all by joining them.

"I actually feel wonderful," Shay said, sipping her iced tea, "but I had the weirdest dream while I was unconscious."

"Tell us about it," Bree said. "We could use some make-believe after this real nightmare we've been living in."

Shay looked almost nervous, first glancing at Bree, then at the others around the table, and finally Cody. "I've had similar dreams before. There was a man. He was tall, really tall, and beautiful. He was so bright, it hurt to look at him." Everyone froze, staring at Shay. "He told me to destroy the demon."

A loud ding sounded as Cody's fork chipped his

plate. He saw Ronan's knuckles go white on the door casing, his face pale. "What demon?" Cody whispered.

Shay swallowed. "Malek."

Chapter 19

"SHE CAN'T," CODY RAGED. "SHE'S HAD NO FORMAL training." They were in the library, where he insisted on talking to the warriors in private after Shay's announcement, which created pandemonium. As if they didn't have enough to worry about.

"How can she fight an ancient demon?" Duncan asked.

"For once, I agree, Duncan," Sorcha said, looking a bit wan herself. Cody didn't know if it was because of the prospect of battling an ancient demon or that she hadn't recovered from Duncan's kiss. "A woman who just learned she's a warrior, going up against an ancient demon?"

"Out of all of us experienced warriors, only two have been assigned an ancient demon," Brodie said. "What's Michael thinking?"

"Watch it," Duncan warned.

The warriors didn't always understand their orders, but they never questioned them. This was different. Shay would die. Was Michael going to sacrifice Shay to get rid of Malek? It made sense now why Malek had tried to kill Shay twenty-five years ago, but how had Malek known she was the one who was supposed to kill him?

"While I agree with you all," Faelan said, "if Michael assigned Malek to Shay, then it's for a reason."

"What if it was Bree?" Cody asked. "Would you sit back and say 'Michael knows best' then? You told me when Bree was locked in a time vault, you considered having yourself locked in one so you could wake up when Bree did, and then you used your talisman to free her."

Faelan blew out a hard sigh. "I don't know what I'd do."

Sean pursed his lips. "It's a dilemma. Sometimes these things don't make sense on the surface."

"There's only one thing to do," Cody said. "I'll kill him."

"You can't," Duncan said. "You'll die too."

"What choice do I have? I won't let Shay go up against him." How could the archangel expect Shay to do it?

"Even if you somehow manage to kill Malek, you'll die. Where does that leave Shay?" Sorcha asked.

"You can't do it, Bro," Lach added.

"I'll do it," Marcas said, quietly.

"No," Cody said. "It has to be me."

"No one's killing him today," Sean said. "Let's think it through."

"Excuse me," Coira said from the doorway. Her face was flushed as if she'd been running. "Ronan just called. He's tracked a bunch of vampires to Beauly Priory, and they have the *Book of Battles*."

———⁂———

Someone knocked on Shay's door, interrupting her turmoil. The whole castle was in an uproar over her dream. She opened the door. Cody stood there, hands in his pockets.

"How'd your meeting go?" she asked, her voice grating. She hadn't been invited.

"I'm sorry, Shay, but I needed to discuss some things with the warriors in private."

"Warriors? Michael seems to think I'm one. Stop protecting me, Cody. I'm a big girl, big enough to be assigned a demon of old." The words swelled in her throat, choking her. Seeing the way he paled didn't help, but she quickly got her emotions under control. "You've tried to protect me all my life. It's time to let me go."

"Let you go?"

"Let me live."

He pulled her close. "If you go up against Malek alone, you might not live. I can't lose you. I lost you once before, and I won't do it again. Do you hear me? I *won't* lose you again." His face was inches from hers, the flecks of gold in his eyes nearly covering the hazel. His mouth was tight, with frustration, not anger; she had known him long enough to know the difference.

She touched his face, soothed the bunched muscle beside his full mouth, and stroked his jaw line, feeling the new growth of beard. "If you try to do what I think you're planning, I'll lose you."

Some emotion worked behind his eyes. "We haven't made any decisions yet. We'll come up with something."

"We? You're still doing it. I'm the one assigned to destroy Malek, but you're trying to solve the problem without me."

He ran his hands through his hair. "You don't know how to destroy him." His chest rose and fell in a hard sigh. "Let's not argue about it. I wanted to see you before I go."

"You're leaving?"

"Ronan tracked the vampires to Beauly Priory. He thinks they have our book with them. He's waiting for us there."

"Do you have to go? Who's guarding the castle?"

"I have to help. Only a few of us are going. Most will stay here, and the warriors from Ireland have arrived to help. Still, I don't want you to leave the castle. I'd prefer if you didn't leave this room." His eyes showed worry.

She smoothed down his hair and ran her hands over his neck and shoulders, feeling the solid strength of muscle and bone. He was a warrior, but he was also human; he could bleed. And he could die. Her hand moved down his arm, and his hand turned over, linking with hers. Cody lowered his head.

"Promise me you'll be careful," he said, his breath a whisper against her mouth.

She buried her face in his neck, the side that had the mate mark, *her* mark, feeling his pulse beating there. "You're the one going after vampires." He held her tight. Too tight. "What's wrong?"

He leaned back, studying her face as if trying to memorize it. He kissed her, tender at first, then desperate.

Faelan appeared in the hallway behind Cody. "Ready?"

Cody pressed his lips to her hair for a long moment. "I have to go. I love you. I've loved you forever. Always know that." With a look that made her knees weak, he turned and strode away.

The warriors parked behind Beauly Priory, near the river, where they had less chance of being seen. The priory had been built in the thirteenth century by monks. There wasn't much left of it, other than a few walls and the north transept, which had been restored and used as a mausoleum for the Mackenzies. If the vampire legends were accurate, and the vampires needed to avoid daylight, that was where they would be, since the roof of the priory had long since been gone. It was almost dusk; they wouldn't sleep much longer. Only ten warriors were here. They agreed not to pull more from guarding the castle. It should be enough to catch the vampires off guard and get the book. The warriors entered the priory grounds, moving stealthily, weapons hidden. So far, they hadn't met any other visitors.

Cody slipped the dagger from his boot. Marcas and Lach were at his back, which gave some comfort, as did the others, whom he considered brothers.

"P-s-s-s-t." Ronan stood behind one of the old walls motioning to them. "They're in the mausoleum," he said, when they reached him.

"How many?" Lach asked.

"Nine, maybe more. They must be using the mausoleum to rest during the day. They're stronger at night. I don't know why they're staying so close to the castle, but it can't be good."

"Well, we'd better hurry before they wake up," Brodie said, looking at the lengthening shadows. "We're losing daylight."

"You sure they're vampires?" Shane asked.

Ronan nodded. "I saw that blond vampire. Nobody touches him. He's mine."

Duncan pulled out his dagger, which made a soft ring when he extended it into a sword. "Guess we take their heads, like we did in Druan's castle."

"Works every time," Sorcha said, pulling her dagger from her boot.

"If the legends are right and they're sleeping, we can

grab the book and lop off their heads before they wake," Niall said.

"Keep one," Cody said. "We need to find out why they still want Shay." Just speaking her name made him ache all the way to his bones.

"I'll keep the blond," Ronan said. "He should have more knowledge. Quiet now. We don't know how sharp their hearing is, and we don't want the neighbors getting nosy."

"No battle cries, Brodie," Sorcha said.

"One friggin' mistake," Brodie said.

"But outside the Sistine Chapel?" Sorcha said. "I thought that tourist would have a heart attack when you stabbed that old woman."

"She wasn't an old woman any more than I am."

"Shut up, you two," Ronan said. "Keep to the walls and stay out of sight. We don't want an audience. Let's go." Ronan and Cody reached the door to the mausoleum first. Ronan put his ear to the door and shook his head, to show that he heard no sound. The warriors lined up, swords ready, and Ronan eased the door open. "Damn!"

A hiss came from inside. Ronan rushed in with Cody right behind him. Several vampires had been lounging on the floor and the crypts, not a one of them asleep. They leapt up and rushed toward the door.

Ronan took the head of the one closest, and the vampire fell to dust. Another rushed at him, slamming him against a wall. Cody picked off two trying to get out the door, clearing the path for the others to move inside. A short vampire leapt at him, teeth dangerously close to his neck. Niall batted the thing down, and Cody drove his sword through its heart. "Thanks."

"Don't mention it," Niall said, and turned to meet another one.

The space was small, making for dangerous fighting. Cody attacked every vampire in his path, taking his anger and frustration out on them so he didn't have to think about what he had to do.

"Leave some for us," Lach said, behind him.

The vampires were strong, and quick, but not as fast as they were in the woods. They were, however, escaping.

"The blond just got away," Shane said. "He has the book." He turned and cut off a female vampire's head so fast Cody didn't even see the blade swing.

Ronan took off after the blond vampire, picking up the bow he had left by the door. Declan headed out after him. The vampires that were left spread out among the priory ruins. Dusk had settled, giving the warriors some cover but not enough if anyone was nearby. "Get them," Cody said.

"Keep the one who has the book alive," Faelan called.

Ronan had the blond vampire pinned to a tree with an arrow on either side of the heart. The vampire hissed, bearing broken fangs, his eyes burning with hatred. He tried to pull free, but the arrows were stuck deep.

"I got it," Ronan said, dodging the creature's short fangs as he removed the satchel. "Here, I think the Mighty Faelan should hold the book until we can get it to Sean."

The vampire's eyes widened. He stared at Faelan, and the blue in his eyes turned red.

"He seems wary of you," Ronan said.

Faelan took the satchel, opened it, and looked inside. He closed the satchel again.

"Aren't you even going to look at it?" Brodie asked.

"That's for Sean to do," Faelan said.

"They're all dead," Marcas said. "What are we going to do with him?" He nodded toward the vampire.

"Take him to the castle," Ronan said.

"Sure we want to do that?" Duncan asked.

Cody tucked his dagger back inside his boot. "This is our chance to find out what these things are and what they want." He had to save Shay.

"Whatever we do, we need to do it fast, before someone sees him," Marcas said. They bound the vampire with so much rope, his clothing couldn't be seen.

"He looks like a damn mummy," Brodie said.

"No one in sight except a few kids over by those houses," Lach said. "They're not paying attention."

They loaded the vampire into one of the Range Rovers. "I'll meet you back at the castle," Cody told them.

"Where are you going?" Marcas asked, his eyes narrowed.

"I've got something to do first."

Shay stood at the French doors, looking over the driveway. The night was beautiful. It should have been like a thousand others, but it wasn't. Both vampires and an ancient demon were after her for God knew what reason, the same demon who killed her parents and tried to kill her as a baby. Michael the Archangel had told her she was assigned to destroy the demon. Twenty-six-year-old Shay, versus a nine-hundred-year-old demon, and vampires, one who marked her for God knows what. Not a normal night.

From what she overheard of the meeting, Cody wanted to take on Malek, but the others were trying to talk him out of it. Shay wouldn't let him do it. A warrior couldn't destroy a demon as powerful as Malek, unless the warrior was assigned; otherwise, he would die. She wouldn't let Cody die. The whole thing seemed ridiculous. Cody, a seasoned warrior, revered by his clan, killer of an ancient demon, couldn't touch Malek, but Shay, with no experience whatsoever, who never killed anything except Ellis and one vampire, was expected to take down a demon who was nearly a thousand years old. What was it about God working in mysterious ways? Maybe he was bored and wanted to stir things up.

On the other hand, she wasn't a complete weakling. She killed that vampire at the cabin, and Cody claimed she'd moved just as fast as the vampire had. Maybe she should have gone to Beauly Prior with the warriors. They were powerful, but their talismans didn't work against vampires.

She watched the dark shadows of the guards, pacing first one way, then another, bodies alert, watching. She glanced at her watch. Cody and the others had been gone for two hours. The warriors suddenly halted, and Shay heard vehicles coming down the driveway. She watched as two Range Rovers parked. The doors opened, and the warriors piled out. She searched for Cody, but he wasn't there. Had he been injured?

She ran downstairs and met Bree in the hallway. "They're back," Bree said. "And they've brought a vampire."

"Where's Cody?" Shay asked.

Bree frowned. "I don't know. He didn't come back with them."

"He's okay?"

"No one was hurt."

"Bree," Faelan called, and Bree moved away.

Shay held on to the wall for support, breath wheezing through her lungs as she remembered the look on Cody's face, the desperation in his kiss, urging her to remember that he loved her.

He was going after Malek alone.

"Shay, darling, how are you?"

Shay stepped inside the adjoining rooms that her aunt and Matilda shared. "Good. How's Matilda?"

"The most somber I've seen her. The vampire thing really shocked her."

"She believes it was a vampire?"

"We tried to convince her otherwise, but I think she knows."

"I have something to say to you, Nina. I should've said it years ago, but I was so focused on my pain, I didn't stop to think about how much it hurt you when I left. I'm sorry. I know you were trying to protect me. You always wanted what was best for me." Although attempting to kidnap Jamie was a little extreme. "You gave up your way of life to help me, and I never considered that. Please forgive me." Shay wrapped her arms around her aunt. "I've been so selfish."

"No, you haven't." Nina stroked Shay's hair. "We took your life from you. We just didn't have a choice. Or maybe we did. I've wondered so many times over the years whether I should've told you." Nina's eyes moistened. "When you came into my life, I thought my world had collapsed. My husband had died a few months before, and I had nothing to live for. Until you. You became my life." Nina hugged Shay and kissed her cheek. "I'm sorry about everything. Not telling you, trying to kidnap Jamie so you could be with Cody."

"Nina," Matilda called.

"She just found out about Nick's death. I feel so terrible."

"About Nick?"

"It's our fault he's dead."

"How is it your fault?" Shay asked with a sinking feeling in her stomach.

"We hired him to stalk you."

As it turned out, it had been Nick's idea. On Nina and Matilda's last visit, Nick had overheard them at the pub discussing the dilemma of Cody and Shay. Nina was certain they belonged together. Being a romantic at heart, Nick hatched the scheme to frighten Shay into coming home. He said that was the only way Cody and Shay would know they belonged together, and he offered to do the job. Of course they insisted on paying him for his stalking time.

After consoling Nina, Shay took a long look at her aunt's face, committing the soft brown eyes, the short gray hair, and kind face to memory. She wished she could tell her about the past, all about it. If she survived, she would, but there wasn't time now for the questions it would bring. She said good-bye and made her way to Cody's room. She lay on his bed and closed her eyes, letting his scent roll over her as a lifetime of memories flashed by, from toddlers to teens, laughing and bandaging each other's wounds. From making love in the hayloft to the time spent at the cabin, and here, when she told him she loved him. All the moments that comprised their lives. Cody was her world. He always had been. She wouldn't let him make this sacrifice.

Shay rose from Cody's bed and went to her room. She tugged on a dark coat and put a flashlight, a bottle of water, and her cell phone in the pockets. Shay tucked a butcher knife into her boot. She hoped Coira wouldn't miss it.

In the sitting room attached to Shay's bedroom, she pushed the catch that opened the door to the secret passage. The air was musty inside. She moved as quietly as she could, knowing that some hidden doors opened to rooms throughout the castle, and the warriors had hearing like bats. It was like a tomb, save for the soft scuffing of her shoes. The light flickered with her movements, throwing shadows on the wall. Shay shivered, hoping she remembered the way. She came to the winding steps that led to the first floor. A din of voices sounded close by. She recognized the entrance to the library. The warriors must be gathered there. She couldn't believe they brought a vampire to the castle.

She stopped at the section of stones where she had met Declan. She pushed the catch, and it opened to the tunnel. He said the far end was old and dangerous, but the vampire had used it, as well as Angus, the warrior who was killed. Shay hoped it held up for her, although what she planned was probably far more dangerous than a decrepit tunnel.

The passage narrowed after she passed the door

where she and Declan had gone outside. She could feel the dampness and hear water trickling. She stumbled several times over fallen stones, but she concentrated on Cody, his face, the determination she saw there. If she didn't stop him, he would die. Malek must be watching the castle, so Cody would be nearby too. Shay had caused him untold pain by severing a friendship because he tried to protect her, by hating him for something he hadn't done. She wouldn't let him die for her too. If Michael said it was her duty to destroy Malek, then by God, she would destroy Malek.

The darkness lightened, and she knew she was close to the end, finally. She stumbled outside and grabbed a breath of fresh air. She saw two warriors lying on the ground. Her heart sank as something sharp scraped her chest. "Nearly a thousand years in this dimension, and I thought humans incapable of surprising me. I guess I'm wrong."

Chapter 20

THE MAN WAS TALL, THE SILVER STREAK IN HIS HAIR glinting in the moonlight. He traced a fingernail along the whitish lines of Shay's scar. "I don't know how you did it. You were as good as dead when I left you, just like your mother." He raised his gaze to her face, showing a touch of awe. "You look like her, not your father. He was dark, like your sister. They couldn't protect you. No one can protect you." He moved closer, his eyes growing angry. "I won't allow you to spawn my enemy."

"I don't know what you mean." This must be Malek. He had the silver streak in his hair.

He smiled an almost serene smile. "You don't know, do you? How sad. This god you serve doesn't even bother to give you the basic information. A child born to you and Cody was destined to destroy me." Malek's smile faded into a sneer. "Alexander MacBain. But he won't succeed. He won't exist, not from a dead mother. I failed to destroy you the first time. I won't fail the second."

Shay fell back as if she had been hit. *Alexander*. It couldn't be. What about her dream of Michael?

"Here I am, nearly a thousand years old… duped by humans. Now, tell me where you've hidden my book, and I'll consider killing only you, not your entire clan."

Shay looked at his immaculate disguise and wanted to rip his face off. He'd killed her mother and father and stolen her life. He would not get Cody or the clan. "If

I give you the book, you will kill the whole clan," she spat out.

He looked surprised, then spun at the screeching sounds coming from the woods. Men burst from the trees, moving so fast she couldn't see their feet. Vampires. Shay backed away while Malek and his demons were distracted, and she bumped into something hard.

"The party's just starting," the vampire hissed behind her. Shay turned and drove her butcher knife into his heart before he could close his mouth.

He fell to dust, and another vampire cried out, "Rod!"

Bree hurried along the passage where she had seen Shay in the vision. She had to stop her. Damn these visions. This one had come too late. Faelan and several of the others had gone to the dungeon to question the vampire. There hadn't been time to warn them. She had to stop Shay before she got outside the walls. *He* was waiting. She opened the door for the tunnel and heard a sound behind her. She turned, and her flash-light illuminated two garish figures. Bree yelped, and the figures screamed.

"Oh my God." Matilda clutched her chest. She wore a lime green jogging suit that almost glowed in the dark. Her red hair stuck up like porcupine quills. Nina had on gray, her hair in pink foam curlers.

"What are you doing here?" Bree asked frantically. She had to hurry.

"We followed Shay," Nina said. "She came to my room. I think she was saying good-bye. I don't know what she's up to, but I'm scared. We heard the door to the secret passage shut when we got to her room. Matilda couldn't remember how to open it. By the time we got inside, Shay was already gone."

"I know where she's going," Bree said, "but you need to go back, get the men. I'll go after her."

"I'm not going back until I have Shay," Nina said, puffing out her chest.

"And I'm not going back alone," Matilda said, stepping closer to her cousin, waving her flashlight at the floors and walls, her eyes wide.

"Well, come on then. We have to catch her before she gets outside."

They hurried through the narrow tunnel and finally reached the end. "She's already out." Bree's head pounded with fear.

Matilda poked her head outside. "I think I see something."

"Wait." Bree grabbed Matilda's arm. "You can't go out there. It's too dangerous."

Matilda went anyway. "There are two men here. I think they're dead," she said.

Bree and Nina hurried over to Matilda. Bree didn't recognize the warriors. They must be new ones who arrived from Ireland or France. "Does anyone have a phone? We have to call Faelan." They needed help, but she couldn't risk calling out to the guards.

"I do," Matilda said.

They heard a scream, and Bree shot ahead, not waiting to see if Nina and Matilda followed.

Faelan's cell phone rang. The number was unknown. He

stepped back from the warriors surrounding the vampire's cell. He was chained to the wall by hands, neck, and feet. Only his eyes moved, red, angry, flashing fire, and occasionally when they fell on Faelan, confusion. He'd refused to answer any questions.

"Hello?"

"Faelan, this is Matilda. Come quick. We're on the demon's trail."

"What demon?"

"What's his name, Bree?" Matilda asked, and Faelan could hear his bride's frantic reply. "Malek."

"Holy—quiet," he bellowed at the warriors, and everyone, even the vampire, gaped at him. Faelan clutched the phone against his ear. "Where are you, Matilda?"

"Outside the secret tunnel. Malek has Shay. There are vampires and demons, too, and they're all fighting. I have to go now. We're going to try to rescue Shay."

"Oh God," he said, locking eyes with Ronan. "Malek has Shay. Bree, Nina, and Matilda are trying to rescue her. If that's not bad enough, a bunch of vampires and demons are fighting."

If Coira had been in the dungeon, she would have washed all their mouths out with soap. The warriors left two guards to watch the vampire, and the rest hurried upstairs. They grabbed weapons and yelled out instructions, deciding that ten warriors would follow the tunnel and ten would go through the woods. "Be careful. You can't use your talisman, or we're all likely to die," Faelan said. His heart was in his throat. All he had lost, and now this. How could he live if he lost Bree?

Shay looked at the vampires circling her. At least twenty, fangs extended, eyes red. They were angry. The others were fighting with the demons in a nightmare of howls and screams.

"She just killed Rod," the one with spiked hair said. "I say we drain her and tell the master we couldn't find her."

A brown-haired vampire shook his head. "You want to be the one to tell him she's dead?"

What could she do against twenty vampires? She killed one at the cabin and one here, but she was only human. She had to do it. If she died, Cody would face Malek alone. She gripped her butcher knife and focused, allowing her senses to sharpen, calm to descend, and then she leaped, catching the spike-haired vampire off guard. From the corner of her eye she saw Bree rushing at them, moving as fast as the vampires. Nina and Matilda stopped, staring in shock at the scene.

"Kill her," one of the vampires said, charging Bree.

No! Not her sister. Shay ran at the closest vampire and drove her knife into its heart. It crumbled into dust. Several feet away, Bree was doing the same. The sisters shared a glance, turned, and continued to fight. The vampires were at a disadvantage. They couldn't kill her, for fear of their master, but they needed to keep her from killing them.

"Capture her," the brown-haired one said.

Shay and Bree stood back to back as the vampires circled.

"Wait until they get closer," Shay told Bree. "Then attack."

After leaving Beauly Priory, Cody drove back to the castle and parked in the trees where the cameras wouldn't see him. He slipped through the woods to the fence. He sent four young warriors guarding the most secluded boundary of the fence deeper in the woods to stand guard. They didn't question him. Cody's sword and gun were hidden in his boot, making him look weaponless. He knew Malek would come. Cody sat down to wait. He had to do it for Shay.

Cody's talisman warmed against his chest. The mark on his neck tingled as the sounds of fighting drifted to him. He jumped up and ran toward the hisses and yells. His nose registered the odors a second before he saw the chaos. Vampires and demons fighting, gnashing with their claws and teeth. In the middle of the fray, Shay and Bree stood back to back. A group of vampires circled Shay and Bree. Cold tentacles moved like fingers along Cody's spine. Bree held a dagger that Cody recognized as one of Faelan's, and Shay gripped a butcher knife. Cody raised his sword and crept forward. If he could take out the ones on the fringes and work inward, he would have a better chance of saving Shay and Bree.

"Now," Shay said. She and Bree launched themselves at the vampires, moving in high speed the way Shay had done at the cabin. Several times he wondered if he imagined it. He hadn't. The women plowed through the vampires, plunging dagger and knife into their hearts. He supposed they aimed for the heart. He couldn't see the vampires' bodies, they moved so fast, but it appeared Shay and Bree could.

Cody ran for the closest vampire, swung at it as it streaked past, and saw the form turn solid for a second. He hit it, but the blow wasn't lethal. Damn it! How were Shay and Bree doing it? He struck again, slightly higher, and caught the creature's neck. It dissolved into dust, and he turned to the next enemy, this one a demon. It disappeared the minute he took its head.

Amid the hissing and screeching that battered his ears, Cody heard a human cry. Whirling, he saw Malek at the edge of the fight, holding Shay. Cody's blood chilled at the sight of the ancient demon looming over the other combatants. His skin was thick, the bones in his face prominent, and his hair coarse but streaked with silver. His sharp claws were poised at Shay's throat.

"Let her go," Cody said, trying to slow his heartbeat, "and I'll take you to the book."

"No," Shay said, standing tall. "He doesn't know where I've hidden it. Let him go, and I'll give it to you." Fury blazed alongside the fear in her eyes. She was up to something.

"Ah, sweet, human love. How thoroughly sickening." Malek threw back his head and laughed, his voice harsh. Catching him off guard, Shay whirled and drove her butcher knife into Malek's side, extracted it, and plowed through the demons surrounding him. Malek grabbed for her and screamed, rubbing his hand. Edward's talisman fell to the ground. A demon tackled Shay, hauling her roughly to her feet, but not before she slipped her knife into her boot. "Don't hurt her," Malek bellowed. "She's mine to kill."

Cody knew he was powerless. If he tried to use his

talisman, he would kill them all, including Shay and Bree. The vampires were gone, dead or retreated.

"Kill them," Malek roared and ran off, dragging Shay with him.

Cody looked from Shay to Bree, who was bending to pick up Edward's talisman. He couldn't save them both. Shay was his mate. Bree was Faelan's, and she was pregnant.

"Go," Bree screamed, aiming Edward's talisman.

"No!" Cody shouted. "You can't!"

"I can," Bree yelled over her shoulder. "Go after her! Nina, Matilda, close your eyes!"

The demons screeched and rushed toward Bree. Cody felt the air shift and the ground tremble. It was too late. It couldn't be stopped. What would be, would be. Cody sprinted after Malek and Shay.

———◦◦◦———

"This way," Faelan called to Ronan. "Hurry." They moved through the thickest part of the woods, slapping branches out of their way, taking the hit when they missed. His pulse thudded in his ears. Ronan, Declan, and Duncan were on his heels. Niall and Shane were a few yards away. He heard the collective gasp behind him, as others saw what he did. Bree stood facing a wall of demons. Nina and Matilda were turned away, hands shielding their eyes. The air shuddered and the ground shook.

"What the hell?" Ronan said, as the white flash blazed out from Bree's hand. He and the others threw their arms over their faces, but Faelan kept running, as screams split the air. He opened his eyes and saw Bree on the ground. A roar sounded in his ears as he sped toward her. He didn't know if it came from him or Ronan.

"Bree!" Faelan dropped down beside her.

"Oh my God. Did you see that?" Bree said, sitting up, eyes wide.

Faelan pulled her to her feet and wrapped his arms around her. "What are you?" he muttered, pulling her into his arms. The other warriors skidded to a stop behind him, faces slack with shock.

"We just killed a bunch of vampires," Bree said. "It was incredible. I've never moved like that, but we've got to go after Shay. Malek took off with her."

"I'm going after her," Nina yelled.

"Get her, Ronan," Faelan said. "We'll go after Shay."

Ronan started after Nina, as hisses sounded behind them.

Ronan threw Nina over his shoulder and dumped her behind a bush beside Matilda, as a dozen vampires rushed at them from the trees.

—⁓—

After the talisman light disappeared, Cody glanced back and saw Faelan and the other warriors with Bree. She was alive. There was no time to question how she used a talisman or survived, but thanks to her, he had only Malek to face. He saw a group of vampires rush at the warriors from the trees. Cody kept going. He hurtled a fallen log and shoved a tree limb out of his path so hard the tree cracked. Shay and Malek were fifty feet ahead. He poured on a burst of speed, lungs burning, legs aching. He had to catch them, but Malek was fast for a demon. Cody needed to slow him down. He stopped, pulled a knife from his boot, drew back his arm and threw. The knife sank between Malek's shoulders. He stumbled, and Shay yanked free.

Cody lifted his sword and ran toward them. "Run!" he yelled to Shay. He swung the sword, but Malek jumped back, and it struck his arm. He bellowed and attacked Cody, slashing his side with sharp claws. A god-awful scream echoed through the clearing, and Shay leapt on Malek's back, both legs cinched around his thick waist, as she hacked at his neck.

What the hell was she doing, trying to cut off his head with a butcher knife? "Get back, Shay!"

She let go and dropped to the ground. She didn't seem to have the same speed and strength as she had with the vampires. Malek turned on her as Shay scrambled away. Cody leapt in, driving his sword into Malek's chest. It wasn't a fatal blow, and Cody felt himself weakening from his attempts. Malek whirled, catching Cody's arm. He needed to act fast, while he had strength left to use the talisman. He didn't know how long he would last against an ancient demon. The one he killed before had been assigned, matched to him, but he couldn't use the talisman with Shay there.

"Please, Shay. Run!"

She stood her ground, holding her knife, the glint of fury still burning in her eye, as she watched Malek. Did she want revenge? His only chance was to continue to weaken the demon by sword so one of the other warriors could finish him off, assuming they defeated the vampires. Cody waited until Malek rushed at him. He stepped aside and gave a mighty swing with his sword, but Malek ducked and the blade caught him in the arm.

Malek turned, teeth and claws bared. Cody sidestepped and swung again, his hands slick with his own blood, and caught Malek in the ribs. The demon roared in pain and knocked Cody's sword from his hand. "I'll make her die slowly for that and force you to watch."

Malek lurched toward Cody, claws extended, but turned with a roar. Cody's sword was lodged in Malek's lower back, as Shay darted clear. Malek ripped it out and pointed it at Shay as he advanced on her. "You dare use a knife and sword against me? When I'm finished, you'll wish I'd been successful twenty-six years ago."

Cody would have to use his talisman and trust that Shay would run. There was no other choice. Cody gave her a quick glance, knowing it would likely be his last. She was scared, but she stood straight and fierce. God, he loved her. He always had. How could he leave her? They had wasted so much time, lost so much, but this tactic was the only way to ensure that she lived.

While Malek was distracted with Shay, Cody readied his talisman. "When I give the signal, Shay, close your eyes," he yelled. "I beg you. When it's over, run!"

Her eyes widened. She shook her head. "No."

Cody aimed his talisman. "Close your eyes, Shay. I love you." He chanted. The air grew heavy. From the corner of his eye, Cody saw the demon lunge for Shay and pull her in front of him, a human shield.

"No!" Cody roared, but it was too late to stop the talisman. "Close your eyes!"

Shay lifted her leg and retrieved her knife from her boot. Her eyes locked with Cody's. He could see it in his head, just as they had so many times before. It all happened at once. She spun out of Malek's grasp. With

Chapter 21

CODY HEARD BUZZING IN HIS EARS. HE SLOWLY OPENED his eyes. Everything was blurred. He blinked several times and saw lights twinkling above him. Stars. Night. A metallic taste lingered in his mouth. Reality slammed back into focus. *Shay!* He rolled to his knees. His side burned, and his head felt like a thousand pins stabbing his skull. Where was Shay? He blinked again, trying to clear his vision, and saw her. She lay on her side several feet away, unmoving. Struggling to his feet, he lurched toward her as the blackness clawed at him like fingers of hell, broken only by the brilliant flashes in his head. He felt burnt, inside and out. He dropped beside her. "Shay! Wake up." She didn't move. He felt for her pulse. It was still. "No. No." He pulled her into his arms. "God, no."

Voices called behind him, feet pounding, cries of alarm.

"Cody, give her to me." Marcas tried to lift Shay, but Cody wouldn't let go.

Lachlan dropped beside him, and together he and Marcas pried Shay from his arms, as the world spun.

Someone grabbed his arm. "You're injured, Cody. Let them help her." Faelan pulled off his shirt and pressed it to Cody's side. When he took it away, Cody saw blood. A lot of blood.

Shay lay on the ground with Bree bending over her, pressing on her chest. Ronan was near her head—Cody blinked—kissing her. Blackness threatened to overtake him again, and when it cleared, he dimly recognized that Bree and Ronan were trying to resuscitate Shay. The other warriors gathered in a circle around them.

Cody pulled away from Faelan and crawled to Shay's side. "Let me," Cody said.

Bree pushed against Shay's heart. Cody breathed into her mouth, begging her to live. Cody felt air stir on his lips, so faint he thought it was his own. He felt it again. His heart surged, sending a wave of pain through his body. "She's breathing. She's breathing. I love you," he whispered as the black abyss swallowed him.

—⁓—

Shay saw a flash of light and heard voices.

"What are you doing out of bed again?" The voice was familiar. "You're a fine warrior, but a lousy patient, Cody MacBain. I told you to stay in bed. What have you done with your IV?"

Cody. Shay opened her eyes and saw Cody lifting his head from her stomach. His eyes were sleep-blurred, his face lined from resting against her bunched covers. "Sorry, Coira, it was getting in the way."

Coira gave him a stern look and at the same time patted his cheek. "Sleeping in that chair next to her bed isn't going to make her—well, look at that. She's awake."

"Shay." Cody leaned closer, his eyes devouring her face. "Are you okay?"

"Move back a bit, Cody, and let me check her over. Shay, dear, how to do you feel?"

"Like I've been hit by a train."

"That's to be expected. You gave us a right good scare. Both of you nearly dead when they brought you in. How about your head? Does it feel all right? You both had nosebleeds something terrible."

Shay touched her temples. "Okay, I think," she said, staring at Cody, who stood off to the side, not taking his eyes off her. He wore sleeping pants and a T-shirt, his jaw shadowed with a beard. Shay wanted to cry, seeing him alive and whole. She reached for his hand. "I thought you were dead. Malek?"

"Destroyed."

"How?"

Coira shook her head. "Let me finish up with her, and I'll leave you two alone. The others are in the library." She bent close and peered at Shay. "I'll let them know you're awake. They'll be thrilled to see you. I've had to post guards at the door to keep them out of here." Coira checked them both thoroughly. "Now climb back in bed, both of you. You've a ways to go before you can go tramping out of here."

Cody leaned over Shay's bed, pressing his face to her hair. "I thought I'd lost you, Shay."

She gripped his shoulders and buried her nose in his T-shirt, breathing in his scent, feeling the muscle and warmth of his skin under the cotton. "How did Malek die?"

"The only thing I can figure is that we killed him together. You stabbed him through the heart at the same time I hit him with the light from my talisman. The timing must have been perfect."

"I remember the flash of light. And then you calling to me, kissing me."

"You were dead, Shay." His voice was rough. "You weren't breathing. We resuscitated you."

Shay reached for Cody's hand. "Hold me."

He gave a wry smile. "Coira didn't say which bed I was supposed to get in." He eased in next to Shay. It was a tight fit, but she snuggled against his chest, listening to his heartbeat. She'd almost lost him. She ducked her head so he wouldn't see her tears.

"Hey, now," he said, tilting her chin. "No crying. We did it. We destroyed Malek." Cody's hand tightened on hers. "Everyone's fine. Coira's been letting them in here two at a time. I think the battle with Jamie probably weakened Malek, and Bree helped. She used Edward's talisman to destroy Malek's demons."

"I didn't think anyone could use another warrior's talisman unless it had been reassigned."

"They aren't supposed to. At least that's what we've been taught."

"She can kill vampires too," Shay said.

"I saw you both. I don't understand it, but I saw it."

Shay lay her head against Cody's battle marks. She heard the faint whispers again, almost like music, soothing. "Malek said something strange. He said our child was destined to destroy him."

Cody frowned. "Our child? So he was trying to kill you to stop you from having a child?"

"He even told me his name. Alexander. That's what I named our baby."

A look of sadness crossed Cody's face. "Then he was assigned to kill Malek."

"But Michael said it was me."

"Malek must have been reassigned to you."

Shay traced the battle marks with her finger. "How did Malek know who was assigned to kill him? That's alarming."

"It is, but the *Book of Battles* was missing for a long time. He must have seen it," Cody said. "Let's hope no one else did."

"I think Alexander would have been a great warrior," Shay said, her throat tight. "Like his father."

Cody brushed a kiss over her hair. "And strong, like his mother."

Shay blinked back tears and snuggled closer to Cody.

"I'd say they're feeling better. What do you think?" Lachlan said from the doorway. Ronan stood behind him.

"I'd feel better if we had some privacy," Cody joked as the warriors approached the bed. "Seriously, thank you. You saved our lives."

Ronan looked at Shay and grinned. "Anytime she needs resuscitation, just let me know."

"Jackass," Cody said, lightly punching Ronan on the arm.

Voices sounded in the hallway. "The troupe descends," Lachlan said. "Coira said everyone could come in for ten minutes."

The room filled with people and the air swarmed with smiles and laughter and gratitude and a few jokes about Cody and Shay in the same hospital bed. When Shay grew tired, she closed her eyes, listening to the voices of her family and friends. She slid her hand into Cody's and knew she had come home.

"Darling." Nina hugged her as soon as Shay and Cody entered the library. Coira had made them rest for another day before releasing them, and a celebration had been planned. "He hasn't left your side," she whispered, glancing at Cody.

"I know." Shay reached behind her, and Cody took her hand.

"I knew it would work out," Matilda said. "I never doubted it once. When you're feeling better, I'll let you read my vampire book."

"Don't worry," Cody whispered. "No one will believe it."

They ate and talked, recounting the nightmare, Malek and vampires. They considered what to do with the blond vampire in the dungeon who wasn't talking, and what it meant to the clan and the castle now that the demons and vampires knew of its location. There was hope that all who knew about the castle had been killed, but everyone was left with an uneasy feeling. They puzzled over how Cody and Shay managed to kill an ancient demon without being killed themselves, how Shay and Bree killed those vampires, and how Bree used Edward's talisman. They all agreed that Shay and Bree must have acquired some kind of vampire-hunting skills from their father, although no one knew why he had them. Bree was going to look closer into Edward's past, hoping to unravel the mystery. There was also supposition that Bree was both a warrior and a Watcher, something the clan had never seen before.

Faelan shook his head and frowned. "She can't be a Watcher or a warrior. I won't let her."

"Yes, dear," Bree had said, patting his cheek.

Plied with food and conversation, several of the warriors were throwing darts with some friendly gambling on the side. Duncan and Sorcha had disappeared, and

Brodie was taking bets as to whether they would come back fighting or kissing. They arrived minutes later, and from their heated faces, it could have been either.

"You realize you took on a demon of old, unassigned, and lived to tell about it?" Ronan said as Cody took his place before the target. "I'd say you've used up your luck, my friend."

"I don't need luck to beat you," Cody said, laughing. "It's all skill."

"He's good," Lachlan said, petting the cat. "I've been trying to beat him for years."

Shay studied the cat. As if it knew it was being watched, it turned its head and stared at her with intelligent green eyes, just like the owl that had helped her kill Ellis. She hadn't told anyone about that. She hadn't seen the owl's eyes at the lake, when the vampire marked her, but she suspected they were green, and she suspected that owl was the reason the vampire hadn't done more than mark her. That was a puzzle for another day. She had enough to deal with for now.

After Cody won, he happily took Ronan's money. Ronan searched out a new opponent. "Ah, Orla, there you are. Feel like throwing a few darts?"

"Goodness, no," Orla said, shuddering. She had been upstairs sleeping after arriving in the middle of the night. Bree had confided that although things weren't perfect, at least they were talking.

"I'll take you on," Bree said.

Ronan frowned. "No, you won't. You need to rest."

"Why are you so bloody worried about my wife?" Faelan asked Ronan. "Don't you think I can take care of her?"

Ronan gave Bree a loaded look, and Sorcha gasped. "She's pregnant."

Faelan's jaw dropped, and Orla let out a squeal. "Pregnant? Pregnant! I'm going to be a grandmother?"

"A bairn?" Faelan asked, dazed. "We're having a bairn?" He stared dumbly at Bree, who was scowling at Sorcha.

"I'm going to have a grandchild," Orla wailed and clutched for something to hold on to, which happened to be Ronan. She wobbled, and two perfect tears trickled down her face. Ronan steadied her and pressed a handkerchief into her hand.

"A bairn," Faelan said in wonder, followed by a frown. "Damnation! You used the talis..." he glanced at Orla and stopped, his face ashen. Everyone looked at Bree, horror dawning on every face as they contemplated her battling vampires and demons, using another warrior's talisman, while she was pregnant. "You need a doctor."

"She needs an obstetrician," Orla said. "Your gynecologist can recommend someone."

Faelan pressed Bree's hand, as if to convince himself she still had a pulse. "Who's this gynecologist?" he asked.

"He's the guy who gets to see as much of her as you—" Lachlan broke off when Marcas elbowed him.

Ronan scowled at Sorcha. "You just couldn't keep your mouth shut, could you? Bree wanted to tell him herself."

"You knew?" Faelan said to Ronan. He turned on Bree. "Ye told *him* before ye told me? Why would ye do such a thing?"

"I wanted you to be the first to know, but you rushed off from the reception," she said.

"You knew about it at the reception?" Orla asked, her face crumpling.

"It's my fault for pulling him away," Cody said, his voice cutting through the others.

"I wanted to tell you," Bree said to Faelan, "but I didn't want you distracted."

"Do we know the sex?" Orla asked.

"No, Mom. I'm not that far along." Bree gave Shay a sympathetic glance.

"We'll need a pediatrician and a nursery," Orla said, having regained her composure. "Green, I think. It's a neutral color."

"I always liked green," Brodie said. "Blue's good too."

"Not blue," Lachlan said. "It might be a girl."

"Who cares?" Sorcha said. "Who made the rule that blue is for boys?"

Cody slipped his hand in Shay's, gently squeezing, as the group settled into a lively discussion of everything from names to breast versus bottle. "Are you okay?"

His face had the same bittersweet look she probably wore. Happiness for their friends. Sadness for their own loss. Shay leaned her head against his shoulder, so solid and strong, and thanked God she had found Cody again. With him at her side, she could withstand anything. "I'm fine."

A short while later, after Orla retired for a long soak in the tub, Sean brought out the *Book of Battles*. A whisper of awe spread around the room, and everyone leaned forward to look. Most warriors had never seen the *Book of Battles*, since the Keeper locked it away in a place known only to himself, but the book had been missing for longer than anyone in the room had been alive, except for Faelan, and Sean said after all the trouble, they at least deserved to see the thing they had been willing to sacrifice their lives to protect. Shay scooted closer, wishing she could touch it. After Sean disappeared with the book, the warriors discussed the vampires and demons, what they might have learned from the book, and what they planned to do with it. Shay leaned against Cody, content but tired.

"Ready for bed?" he asked.

"Ready for home. Take me to Virginia."

Tristol moved closer to his sleeping prisoner, studying the man's height, the size of his muscles. The capture had gone surprisingly well for such a powerful warrior. If this part of the plan worked, Tristol would bring his beloved race back to the glory they had once known, before their maker had abandoned them. He closed his eyes, remembering the soft, golden voice close to his ear, the stories of grandeur that could all be his. He would focus on strengthening his army now and find Edward's emerald later. With Malek dead, Shay and Bree would be safe, giving Tristol time to figure out what secrets the sisters held. It was possible that neither of Edward's daughters knew about the emerald. Edward may have hidden it. When Tristol opened his eyes, he saw the prisoner's eyes were open, his dark gaze violent before it became shuttered. If this one proved worthy, the first prisoner could be destroyed. He had grown dangerously strong, killing several of his vampires.

"Bring him food," he called to the guard. "I have to leave. The Dark One has summoned me." Yet again. It was growing tedious. "Keep the prisoner a secret. No one can know he's here. Increase the experiments."

———*w*———

"Why are we here?" Shay asked, following Cody up the ladder into the hayloft. It was the first time she'd seen him since they arrived this morning. She had slept a great deal, trying to adjust to the time difference.

They sat cross-legged in the hay, like they used to do as kids.

"I found something I want you to have." He handed her a picture. It was a birthday party. Shay's hands trembled as her eyes swept quickly across the scene. A woman holding a little girl, about a year old, while a man stood beside them, laughing as the woman wiped icing off the little girl's face. Shay could see Nina in the background, much younger, smiling, and Matilda, her hair a different shade of red than she wore now. Shay's heart tightened, and she looked away from the man and woman, avoiding the rush of emotion choking her. She absorbed the other details, the cake with pink and green icing reading *Happy Birthday Dana*, and the single flickering candle. The pile of presents, tied with ribbons and bows.

She felt Cody's hand touch her shoulder. Taking a breath, she let her gaze return to the couple and the child. Shay's eyes stung as she searched her mother's face, the hair color, the nose and smile, so similar to her own. Her cherished black-and-white obituary photo hadn't given those details.

Shay's green eyes—and Bree's—had come from the man. Edward was tall, handsome, his hair dark. Shay wondered if her interest in dark-haired men had started long before she met Cody. A tear rolled down Shay's cheek, dropping onto her mother's face. She blotted her mother's face and imagined a light, flowery perfume, and the sound of a man's deep laugh.

"Where did you find it?" she asked, drying her eyes.

"It was in an old book locked up in the basement. I think my dad had it with him the night they left Scotland with you. We think there may be some more things hidden in a safe deposit box. Marcas is checking. I'm sorry, Shay. I wish I could change things. I didn't know what to do. We couldn't be together until I was finished with my duty. There was too much danger, and it wasn't my place to tell you something the clan had decreed must be kept secret."

"You tried to protect me, I know that now, so did the clan. I'm sorry I didn't know my real parents, but you did what was best. And look what I gained."

"Nina, surrounding me with love, giving me a home. Your family, uprooting their lives to protect mine, taking care of me." Shay put the photo aside and touched Cody's chest, where his heart was beating strong. "And you. What would I have done without you?"

"But I wasn't there for you, Shay. I should have made you understand how I felt about you. If I could do it over, I think I'd tell you the truth and let the chips fall, but I can't honestly say for sure." He shrugged one broad, beautiful shoulder. "Forgive me?"

"If you'll forgive me for believing the worst of you when I should have known better. If I hadn't been so stressed, believing something that wasn't true, maybe the baby would have lived."

Cody brushed a kiss on Shay's forehead. "The baby will always be part of us. We won't forget him."

Shay nodded rubbed the small sword branded on Cody's wrist.

"Before we can move to the next step, I need to know for sure that there's nothing between you and Jamie."

"Just friendship. I didn't intend to, but I used him as a substitute for you. Every man I've gone out with has been a substitute for you. I've hurt Jamie."

Cody smiled. "I think Jamie's found something to ease the pain." Cody cupped Shay's chin. "I love you, Shay. I always have. I always will. I want to spend the rest of my life with you, grow old with you." He pressed a finger to her lips, stopping her from speaking. "And that's a serious consideration, because warriors live a long time." He grinned and dropped his finger. "So if you're going to get tired of me by the time I'm ninety, I need to know now."

"Are you proposing to me?"

"I am."

"Don't I get a mate mark?"

"Sometimes women don't get one, but I think this is yours," he said, and her neck tingled where he touched her birthmark. "It's darker than it was when you were a kid."

"You think that's my mate mark?" Her fingers brushed his as she tried to feel the mark.

"I do. Will you marry me, Shay? Will you be mine... forever?" A hint of shadow darkened his eyes. "Will you trust me?"

She took his gorgeous face in her hands, kissing his

strong jaw, the scar over his eyebrow, his straight nose, and finally his lips. "I will, I always have been, and I do. You're my life, Cody MacBain. You were my life when I was a kid swimming in the lake, and you'll be my life when we're teaching our great-grandchildren to sword fight."

He wrapped both arms around her neck and rested his head against hers. "God, I love you, but we may need to set some boundaries for this dangerous stuff."

"Are you being overprotective again?"

"I can't help it. You can argue with me, even bite me again, but don't expect me not to try to keep you safe."

"As long as that goes both ways. But how can we marry if I'm a warrior? I won't be twenty-eight for another year."

"We don't know for sure that you're a warrior. But I'm not taking any chances on losing you again. The clan will have to live with more broken rules."

"If I am a warrior, will you be the one to train me?"

"Unless the clan assigns you a mentor."

"Would it be a female?"

"Not necessarily. I don't mind if it's a male... as long as it's not Ronan."

Shay squeezed Cody's hand. "Can we get back to that marriage proposal?"

"In the clan, when a warrior finds his mate, they pledge their intentions. We consider it a marriage, of sorts, until it can be done properly. Kind of like hand-fasting. It's binding until the union can be blessed in a church. Will you bind yourself to me now, Shay?"

She slipped both hands in his. "I already am, but you can say the words."

Cody's hands were warm on hers. "I, Cody MacBain of the Connor Clan, pledge to you, Shay Logan, my heart, my life, my body, and the protection of my sword, as long as we live and beyond. Will you have me as your mate?"

Shay nodded. "I will, if you'll accept my heart, my body, my life, and the protection of my…"

Cody's lips twitched. "Candlestick?"

"…my candlestick."

"I accept. You're mine," he said, and the intensity in his eyes and his voice made her shiver. He wound his hand in her hair. "Never run away from me again."

"Never. But shouldn't we have witnesses?"

"We have God and that bloody cat." Cody looked at the big white cat perched on a nearby hay bale. Shay had asked Ronan if she could keep the cat until he was ready to go home to Montana. "You know in the olden days, a marriage wasn't binding until it was consummated."

"I thought we covered that part already."

"Well, I think we had things a bit backward before. We'll start over in the proper order. You have any objections to hay, again?"

"None." She smiled as he settled her in the hay. "I love you."

"And I love you," Cody said, his head lowering to hers. The cat meowed, gave them a green stare, ran to the ladder, and disappeared.

"Guess he knows we don't need a witness for what I'm about to do next," Cody said, his hazel eyes darkening.

"What would that be?"

He reached for her shirt with a wicked grin. "How about I show you?"

Acknowledgments

As always, I'm so grateful to my critique partner, Dana Rodgers, for her marvelous help and encouragement, and for last-minute work sessions. I want to thank my family. They mean more to me than all the books in the world: My mother, who embodies the grace and generosity I wish I had. I'm still learning from her. My father, who is the gentlest soul I know and partially inspired the character of Old Elmer. My brother, sister-in-heart, and nephew, some of the greatest people on earth. My husband, for his devotion and creative contributions to the really cool stuff in the books. My children, who are imaginative and wonderful beyond words. My agent, Christine Witthohn of Book Cents Literary Agency, for being the best agent in the world, and to my editor, Deb Werksman for believing in this series.

About the Author

Anita Clenney writes paranormal romance and romantic suspense. Before giving herself over to the writing bug, she worked in a pickle factory and a preschool, booked shows for Aztec Fire Dancers, and was a secretary, an executive assistant, and a Realtor. She lives with her husband and two children in suburban Virginia not far from Washington, D.C.